THE
BINGE-WATCHING
CURE

EDITED BY BILL ADLER JR.
AND SARAH DOEBEREINER

Published by Claren Books, www.clarenbooks.com

Dedication from Bill Adler
To my parents, who knew I was reading late at night under my blanket with a flashlight, but let me anyway.

Dedication from Sarah Doebereiner
To my mother, who always encouraged my excessive love of words.

ACKNOWLEDGEMENTS

Chris O'Brien and Laura Griffioen at Jet Launch, www.jet-launch.net, added many magic touches to The Binge Watching Cure, including additional proofing (oh, do I ever need that), production, and putting the book in sync with Amazon.

Fiona Jayde of Fiona Jayde Media, http://fionajaydemedia.com, designed The Binge-Watching Cure's wonderful cover.

TABLE OF CONTENTS

INTRODUCTION

We like gulping television programs as much as anyone else. Put the phone on silent, fire up a tub or two of popcorn, get comfy on the couch and let the hours of binge-watching take us over, like aliens temporarily inhabiting our minds.

It's great. It's luxurious. Binge-Watching feels like soaking in a lavender scented bath, with, well, a giant screen so you can binge-watch.

There's great stuff on television, too. While the days of television drivel aren't over, television programming has become a realm where both quantity and quality are magnified with each new season. Television is no longer "what is there to watch?" It's become, "How am I going to find the time to watch everything?"

We'll confess here with your editors' favorites. Bill Adler can't get enough of *Outlander* and *The Americans*. Sarah Doebereiner's eyes glaze over with *American Horror Story* and *Fairy Tale* on.

Although quality television programs no longer rot your mind like *South Beach*, *Painkiller Jane* and *Modern Men* (don't know these shows — consider yourself lucky, or look them up) did once upon a time, there comes a time when ever television addict needs to move onto something better, more productive and satisfying. While the television won't kill you, the Oreo cookies and pizza might. And you know deep in your heart that there's something better for your brain and soul that staring at a screen until the end of time or your cable service stops, whichever comes first.

The natural alternative to binge-watching is reading. Of course. Reading is a good for your brain and good for your body because at the very least you have to turn pages while reading, in contrast to binge-watching, for which the only required physical activity is the occasional blink. Reading is fun—and trust us about this—as entertaining and enjoyable as watching the greatest of television shows. It's just that you haven't gone near a book in a such a long time that you wonder if you can even read one again.

How do you cure your Netflix (or Amazon, Google movie, Hulu, or other service) addiction and return to your first love, reading books? You know you want to read more. You know you enjoy reading. You know you look forward to finishing a book because then you can start a new adventure.

But how? How do you get into reading when the siren call of streaming movies becomes more powerful every year? A three-hundred page novel is daunting in the face of Netflix and friends' wonders. It's too easy to put on pajamas, pour a glass of wine, and offer your eyes to a TV, tablet, or computer screen until sleep summons you.

Enter *The Binge-Watching Cure: Fabulous Stories that Start Small and Grow Longer. The Binge-Watching Cure* is an anthology of short stories of increasing size. The first story is mere Twitter sized, short enough for anyone with even the greatest phobia about reading fiction again to read. The next story is 100 words. Then 500, then longer, all the way to novella length. By the time you've finished reading *The Binge-Watching Cure*, you'll be able to tackle Joyce and Pynchon. Or at a minimum, you'll enjoy novels you hear about from friends and family. *The Binge-Watching Cure* will reignite your love for reading; it will better your life.

And you know what? These are great stories, spanning a diversity of genres including romance, science fiction, crime, spiritual, horror, literary and more. We spent a year looking for exciting, beautifully written, enthralling stories. We know you're going to enjoy them.

A husband and wife face a cancer diagnosis with mixed reactions; a catastrophic train wreck gives a circus troupe (and their tiger) baffling powers; a death-obsessed couple are willed the cremated remains of a complete stranger and must discover why. In this eclectic collection, you'll witness: a First Sergeant come face to face with the horrors of war, a couple's role-playing night-on-the-town, a post-apocalyptic thriller, a philosophy on cat ownership, and a young woman with seven days to live out a lifetime of love.

Just as you enter a cold swimming pool one body part at a time, get used to drinking beer sip by foamy sip, or learn to enjoy spicy food in little, fiery nibbles, *The Binge-Watching Cure* gradually acclimates you to reading longer and longer stories, until a novel-length book goes down smoothly, tasting sweet, and making you want more.

We hope you enjoy your rediscovered love for reading.

Bill Adler Jr.
Sarah Doebereiner

HALFWAY

by Sarah Doebereiner, Twitter Size

The distance between two people can only be bridged with compassion.

Sarah Doebereiner is an author, editor, and excessive reader from central Ohio. For more information visit: sarahadoebereiner.com.

Her hand fans out on a cotton tablecloth. Mine hovers above the unforgiving white, until the tip of her finger lifts and crosses over mine.

THE POWER OF PATIENCE

by Bill Adler Jr., 100 words

In this micro science fiction story, James discovers that the most powerful force in the universe is patience.

Bill Adler Jr. is the publisher of Claren Books. His most recent work of fiction is No Time to Say Goodbye, *a time travel, love story novella. Adler's tweets at @billadler, and his personal web page is www.adlerbooks.com. A version of* The Power of Patience *was originally published in Paragraph Planet.*

No longer unnerved by the skyscrapers surrounding his wooden house, James settled into his couch for a beer, as he did every night. Years ago, when he refused to sell the house in which his family had lived for generations, James resigned himself to a deathbed view of steel, glass and shadows. He didn't understand why, but a century later James knew that all he needed was patience, and the towering buildings would eventually fade into dust.

THE GUN

by Hákon Gunnarsson, 200 words

In this short, literary fiction, a man recollects a time when his friend almost shot himself.

Hákon Gunnarsson is an Icelandic writer who lives close to Reykjavík. He has written nonfiction, and fiction, but so far only part time. His dogs will tell you his only real job is to feed and take them for walks.

There was a gun on the table. I know what you are thinking, but no, that's not what happened. You see, even though the bullets were there, the firing pin wasn't. My friend sat at the table—his brow sweaty—staring at the gun. When he'd pulled the trigger, he'd thought it would work, but it didn't.

"I can't even do that right," he said.

How do you reply to something like that? Do you nod? Do you say: "No, you can't." What? Tell me. It's been months since I stood there, and I still don't know what the right reply would have been.

For a few moments, I couldn't move. I wanted to scream at him, but instead I walked to him, and put one hand on his shoulder. It made him jump a little, but he didn't turn to look at me. He saw nothing but the gun.

I'm not sure how long I stood there. A long time? It probably wasn't. Eventually, I walked out of the room, and rang for help. I'm told he's doing a lot better now, but I'm not. In my head, I'm still standing there, waiting for the gun to go off.

CATEGORICAL THINKING

by Nat Gertler, 500 words

A narrator describes her philosophy of cats, and how the more cats you own, the more they own you. She then encounters a retired man with a cat philosophy all his own.

Nat Gertler is a comic book writer, an award-winning author, and a professional Peanuts nerd. He is also publisher of the eclectic About Comics line (www.AboutComics.com), offering everything from the adventures of Licensable Bear™ to reprints of the classic Negro Motorist Green Book. He lives in Camarillo, California in a house filled with people with the same last name, which seems to him a striking coincidence.

I t's cat number five where the line is drawn.

If you have one cat, you have a cat. Two cats means you have a couple of cats. Three cats equals some cats. Four cats is a bunch of cats. With cat number five, the cats have you.

You can keep four cats off of your chair; you can't keep five. You can find times of the day when four cats are quiet, calm, sleeping even, and not in need of food, but not five cats. When there are four cats, they share timidity; with five, one always has to show herself to be brave enough to bounce onto your bed and curl up on your soft, comfy face.

The five cat rule plateaus. You can sneak in a sixth, seventh, or even eighth without an uptick in the chaos. However, when you cross the nine cat line, they break up into teams, and then you find yourself negotiating between sets of cats, trying to settle territorial disputes. At twelve cats, your house exudes catness, which draws neighborhood strays to try to sneak in your doors or slam against your windows to investigate.

I tried explaining that to the man, as he stood in front of me with his cardboard box full of mewing sounds, trying to tempt me. I tried explaining that I did not want to discover what the next limit was, that I was already beyond twelve and thus dangerously close to whatever the next stratum would prove to be.

"I understand that, ma'am," he said, with a charming half-smile brightening up his lined face. "But . . . well, let me introduce myself. My name is George Oddleby. You ever hear of Oddleby And Sons Investments? Probably not, it's a small place as such things go. But I was one of the 'and Sons.' Dealt mainly in commodities, in futures. You know what that is? I bought and sold things like wheat, but not wheat that existed yet, I bought and sold farmers promising the wheat that would be harvested in June. Now, the people I sold these futures to didn't actually want wheat in June. They wanted to gamble, to place a bet. They wanted the weather to be bad in May, so they could sell their futures at a high price to someone who was going to need wheat in June despite the shortage. I made sure that, profit or loss, they always sold their futures off before they got stuck actually owning wheat that they had no use for.

"Now, I am not offering you cats. I am offering you kittens. Kittens are a very different thing. They are *cat futures*. They do not count as cats until they become older. You can safely add them to your inventory without crossing any numeric rubicon. Just be sure to unload the kittens before they make their transition. And you can always unload a kitten. People love kittens. Well, most people. Not me. I love cats."

So, it was clear that he not only had cats, he had a philosophy of cats. It may or may not contain any great truths, but he had a way of viewing the cat situation such that it made sense to him. I found that charming.

And so, you look around my place, and you must think that I have (or, really, I am had by) an awful lot of cats, even for an old lady, but please realize I do not have as many as you think.

Only seventeen of these cats are mine.

The rest are my new step-cats.

THE NEWS

by Kelsey Dean, 800 words

A husband and wife face a cancer diagnosis with mixed reactions. He struggles to make the best of the situation; she battles insecurities and fears about how she will be changed by the treatments.

Kelsey Dean lives in Seoul, where she spends most of her spare time writing, painting, and trying adventurous ice cream flavors. Her work has appeared or is forthcoming in numerous literary journals and anthologies, including Ember: A Journal of Luminous Things, Persistent Visions, and Cicada. Her YA story, Starfishing, is available on audible.com, and her poetry has been nominated for a Pushcart Prize. You can see more of her work at: http:// kelseypaints.tumblr.com/.

The silence in the car was neither hostile nor peaceful. It was the kind of silence that hangs heavily when no one can think of the right words, because no words are adequate. Ibrahim glanced at Kate as he pulled up to the stop sign at the exit of the hospital and saw that tears were hovering at the edges of her eyelids. He swallowed, keeping the panic contained as a hard knot in his stomach.

"They're going to cut it all out, and you'll be fine," he said, reaching over to squeeze her hand. She closed her eyes and leaned her forehead against the window.

"You'll even get a brand new pair of boobs," he said with an exaggerated eyebrow waggle. She looked back at him with a mixture of irritation and sadness; the ridiculous motion of his dark, wide eyebrows didn't make the corner of her mouth twitch like it usually did.

"Although, I don't really understand the whole nipple grafting thing," he continued. "Do they have trays of spare nipples waiting around in the fridge or something?"

At that, she burst into tears. The corners of his mouth tightened as he snapped it shut, and he rested his hand on her leg and kept it there. She held her breasts in her hands the whole way home as Ibrahim racked his brain for the right joke to take the hurt away.

* * *

The scent of well-spiced fajitas drifted up the stairs that night, but it wasn't until Ibrahim walked into their bedroom with a plate of Kate's favorite food that she noticed. She had been curled up in the recliner, staring out the window. Not speaking, not moving, not crying. Her shoulders slumped, and her hair was sticking up as if she had been running her hands through it in distress. He set the plate on the bedside table and knelt at her feet. He gathered her hands up in his own, and rested his chin on her knee.

"Listen to me," he said gently. "Despite my enthusiasm for them, your breasts have never been a contributing factor in my love for you."

Kate's eyes met his. She didn't speak, but waited for him to continue, as he always did when she was silent. He knew how to coax her voice back into place, no matter what was choking her.

"Sure, they're nice, but they aren't *you*. You won't be anything less without them."

She shifted her gaze. He followed it to the framed photograph of the two of them with their three children, now grown and living on their own. In the picture, Amina was still a baby, securely cradled against Kate's chest, with Ibrahim and the twins arranged on either side and grinning widely.

Ibrahim reached up and placed his palms on Kate's cheeks. His heat brought some of her usual rosiness back.

"Kate. Alby, hayati; my heart, my life. You'll still be a mother. You'll still nurture our children, and their children. You'll still be my wife. And you'll still be a woman, the best woman. The only woman I ever wanted."

Kate's watery blue eyes filled again, and she let out a harsh sound that was both a laugh and a sob. She shook her head. Then, she bent down and kissed him suddenly on the mouth—a deep, lingering kiss like the ones of twenty-plus years ago, when they were young and hot-blooded and desperate for each other. She sank onto the floor with him, not pulling her lips away from his until the two of them were tangled and uncomfortable against the spindly legs of the bedside table. Their aging knees and hips protested as they pressed into the thinly-carpeted ground.

Ibrahim gave her breasts a little squeeze as she finally pulled away.

"Well, it was nice knowing you," he said to them, bending to kiss first one, then the other. His attempt at humor was tentative, his voice soft. He smiled earnestly up at her, his face still hovering around her heart. Kate responded by letting out more of a laugh than a sob—a significant improvement from five minutes before. She sniffed and straightened her back.

"They were getting saggy anyway," she said ruefully, giving them each a light pat. Her voice cracked a little, but she cleared her throat. Then, she settled into the curve of Ibrahim's arm and pulled the fajitas on her lap.

"That's my girl," said Ibrahim as he scooped the first bite of onions and peppers into her smiling mouth. One missed its mark and fell onto her chest, threatening to slide along the crack of her cleavage. He quickly bent to slurp it up and spoke into Kate's bosom, punctuating his words with loud kisses that made her laugh.

"Tonight, my friends, we feast in your honor."

THE BLIND MAN

by Kurt Bachard, 1,000 words

A blind man thinks that all of his problems are over when his wife tells him about a cure for his blindness, but his sudden ambition reveals the ugly, bitter truth about their relationship.

Kurt Bachard lives in South London, UK. A Pushcart Prize Nominee, his fiction and nonfiction have appeared in numerous publications, including Alfred Hitchcock Mystery Magazine, the Black Quill Nominated Shroud Magazine, and Ryga: A Journal of Provocations, among others. He can be reached at bachard.wordpress.com

As usual after breakfast Terenti Dmitritch, a young blind man, remained at the table to hear his wife, Sveta, read the newspaper. Although his two children had left for school more than an hour ago, he could still feel the cold lingering brush of their flippant kisses on his cheek and still smell the acerbic mint of their toothpaste.

"Listen to this," Sveta twittered. "Thanks to pioneering techniques developed in a California laboratory, scientists have discovered a cure for blindness."

Terenti gripped the armrests of his chair as Sveta read the article to him in full.

"God listens to the prayers of honest men," he said when she'd finished. "At last, I'd be able to see your face . . . and my children's faces. All the faces I've longed to see. And the places I've longed to travel to see."

"Travel? Where would you go?" Sveta demanded.

"I'd travel the world of course . . . I'd see the entire world," he said.

"You would leave your family at the drop of a hat?"

"You call the cure for blindness a drop of a hat?"

"You know what I mean. Yesterday, you were saying how important family is to you. Now, you talk glibly of leaving your children fatherless."

"I said no such thing, Sveta. God, how you dramatise. Of course, we would take the children with us. Travel would broaden their minds."

"But their lives are here, their school, their friends. You can't uproot them on a whim."

"Again, Sveta, you put words in my mouth."

"What about me? I don't want to travel. I'm happy here."

"Happy? So, you're happy in this dead suburb? It stifles me, crushes me." He clenched his fist, as if squeezing the air. "You call me blind, but can you not see how blindness has cramped my ambition? Seeing again would set me free from this rat trap to be the man I should have been."

He heard Sveta gasp. "You call our marriage a trap? Shame on you . . ." Her tone turned to one of bitterness. "Tell me Terenti, what could you be? What ambition are you talking of? You have no trade, no skill. In fact, without us you have nothing. I've given the best years of my life to look after you."

Terenti lowered his fist; his head tilted, eyes closed, as if listening to some distant sound. He thought: *how she now reveals her resentment towards me. All these years harbouring it secretly. I've been a liability, and now she admits it.* He squirmed, feeling as if the possibilities this new cure promised might drive him mad in an instant. Warm filtered sunlight pressed against his eyelids. He felt touched by that light. *Where I could go, and what I could do? There is no end to it. Contentment here? No, no, that's for the pigs wallowing in the mud—they know no better. To grow content and pot bellied, pah! This life disgusts me now, disappoints me.*

He recalled a disappointing intimacy with Sveta just the night before. *Her aged corrupted body,* he thought . . . *and I soak up her pathetic gratitude in desperation. God, how it sickens me. My blindness all these years, my awful dependency. Dependency yes . . . yet, I retain my youth, my strength. No need to be so dependent with eyes, no need. Did I ever truly love her? Perhaps, it was just a convenience. But why do I even think this? I could change my life, away, away with this stifling darkness— blindness has suppressed me for too long.*

"Terenti?" Sveta's voice, tinged with impatience.

As if emerging from underwater, he broke from his reverie.

"I never knew how much you resented me," he vexed. "But now, I can hear it clearly in the timbre of your voice. So, I have always been a liability to you? If that is how you feel, then I would be happy to go on alone"

Again that sharp intake of breath from Sveta, a faint whistle through the gap in her teeth only he could hear. "What in God's name has come over you?" she cried. "You're talking crazy. What would you do without us after all these years?"

"I would live, Sveta, live." He made the word live sound as if it meant the Universe. "Do you know how I've longed to live as I should? You call this living? Domestic prison. Blindness prison." He slammed his fists on the table, making the cups and plates clatter. "Yes, yes, I have been a liability to you. But God give me back the power to be the man I was destined to be, the power to stand alone, and I'll show you—"

He stopped as he became aware that Sveta sobbed.

"Sveta, why do you cry?" He touched her fingertips with his.

"I'm not crying," she wheezed, "I'm laughing you fool."

He could hear fear trapped in her voice. Was she pretending to laugh? Perhaps tears fell that he couldn't see.

"The article was an April Fools' joke, Terenti," she lied. "I'm sorry."

Trembling, he sank back in the chair and clutched at his chest, his heart pinching. Blood rushed to his head as the warmth of light that pressed at his blind eyes mocked his sightlessness. Darkness hemmed him in once more, and he realised that he hated her passionately for wanting to keep him blinded, and hated likewise this life and everything about it, and that this is how it had been all along. A cruel disaffection had lurked beneath the surface of false suburban contentment, an ugly violent truth.

Gritting his teeth with resolution, he began to stand up.

"Where are you going?" Sveta asked.

"To hang myself."

"Do you think you can do that without my help?" she asked tartly.

Feeling exhausted by his anger and confusion, he sank back into his chair, moaning. A conflagration burned in his soul.

BYPRODUCTS

by Hanna Alkaf, 1,500 words

For Rashal, home is where her family is, and where the food is comfortingly warm, spicy, and familiar. So what happens when she is forced to build a new life and a new home without either of the things she holds most dear? **Byproducts** *is an exploration of food, memory, and what it means to be a child of conflict starting anew in an alien world.*

Hanna Alkaf is a freelance writer of both fiction and nonfiction; at least, when she isn't busy with naptime, mealtime, bath time, Mickey Mouse Clubhouse time, or any time her 3-year-old decides to wrestle the baby.

It seemed to Rashal that everything in this strange country was but a shadow of home. The faces around her were pale and doughy, the language strange and soft, the weather damp and gray. Sometimes, she stuck out her tongue for no reason other than to lap the moisture out of the air and let it settle on her tongue, soft as a kiss. Even the sun, when it shone, shone weakly and tentatively. It was never warm.

The white ghosts told her their names were Susan and Pat, and that this was her new home. Susan had hair that glinted

16

gold in the afternoon sunlight; Pat's stomach bulged over the waistband of his khaki pants.

They spoke to her kindly and offered her new things; she took them and smiled her thanks. She didn't mind the new clothes—dresses patterned with bright flowers and trimmed with lace, blue jeans stiff with newness, t-shirts that still held their perfect store-fold creases, fluorescent underwear decorated with images of manically grinning cartoon characters she didn't recognise. Nor did she mind the new shoes, crisp white trainers with black stripes on the side. Everything in her ragged blue backpack—well, everything that hadn't been swept away or fallen apart—had already been worn multiple times before being passed on to her, by Nadya and even by Hassan, and would be worn by little Saffiyah after her. Well—would have been worn. ("Stop complaining. If it isn't falling apart, it's still good," Mama would say, busily sewing up yet another rent, patching up yet another tear).

To wear something for the first time it had ever been worn by anyone; truly, this was luxury.

What she did mind was the food.

Rashal dreamed of food often, as she had ever since she left home.

On the long, dusty journey to the boat, she dreamed of the little bakery just down the street from her home that sold her favourite *helawat al jibn*; if she was very, very good, Baba would come home bearing a bag of this just for her, soaked in sweet, sticky orange syrup and oozing cheese with every bite ("You'll spoil her," Mama would grumble, but with a twinkle in her eye as she wiped smears of syrup from Rashal's mouth).

On the boat, with the wind and the water whipping up a chill that worked its way down to the bone, as one by one, each of the passengers packed tightly against each other fell silent, listening to the howling wind and the creaking of the boat's wooden slats, she leaned against her mother and dreamed of *kibbeh* fresh from the kitchen, of filling her mouth with the soft pastry and biting down onto that heady mixture of meat and spices and walnuts.

Floating along in an almost-black sea, surrounded by driftwood and wreckage and still bodies—the frayed ends of Hassan's red scarf trailing in the water beside her, Nadya's hand with its bitten nails ("A filthy habit," Mama would scold) still clinging to a piece of wood as though it might save her—Rashal dreamed of her aunt's meatballs soaked in the rich sauce made from wild cherries; she dreamed of freshly grilled *shawarma* from her favourite stand, chunks of boldly flavoured meat wrapped in warm flatbread.

And even when the strange men shook her and shouted at her to wake her up, soaked to the very core and lying on the pale sandy shore of a new world, she didn't answer; instead she dreamed of steaming cups of *kammun* and piping hot bowls of *keshkeh* and anything, anything at all to keep her warm.

* * *

Here, the food was tasteless and dry; it choked her with every bite, though she tried not to look as though she minded ("Do as you are told and mind your elders," Mama had always told them). Pat and Susan plied her with an endless array of it: hot toast with strange, impossibly red jam from a jar, greasy fish and chips and bright green mushy peas from the chip shop down the road, roast chicken smothered in brown gravy. Rashal ate everything that was placed before her, moving her jaws mechanically, up, down, up, down, until it was all gone and Susan smiled and called her "good girl," and all the while she ached for just one bite of something, anything, that tasted like home.

At night, she crept to the top of the stairs when she was supposed to be asleep and listened to Susan and Pat and their murmured conversations over the clink of the glasses they filled with expensive wine at the end of each day.

"Do you think we did right, taking her in?"

"We talked about this, Sue. We have a lot to offer a child."

"But she's so quiet, so strange. Do you think she's happy here?"

"Anything's got to be better than where she was, love."

* * *

At school, when she finally went to school, the other children stared at her.

The teachers kept calling her Rachel. "My name is Rashal," she said again and again, but they could not make their tongues bend the right way. Instead, she was given special lessons to make her tongue soft and pliable and submissive, so that she could speak the way they spoke.

A little girl with blond pigtails sidled up to her during recess; a smile began to make its way tentatively onto Rashal's face. "Are you an immigrant?" the little girl asked.

Rashal felt her face grow hot. "What is an immigrant?" she asked.

The little girl shrugged. "You steal our jobs and plant feckin' bombs; you're going to kill us allllllllll," she sang out, with an air of one reciting favourite nursery rhymes. Then, she ran off to the swings, her blond hair swinging jauntily from side to side with each step.

At recess, Rashal poked at lumps of fried meat they called chicken nuggets, with pale strings of fried potatoes, and dreamed of grape leaves stuffed to bursting with chunks of spiced lamb and rice (but she still ate it up, every single bite—Mama hated it when food went to waste).

* * *

The day she came home from school and saw a jar of olives on the kitchen counter – fat, juicy olives swimming in amber oil—she couldn't help herself.

She flung her backpack down and sat down at the table. Then, she reached for the jar and slowly turned it over and over in her hands. The fancy curling script proclaimed the name of an upmarket gourmet food store in town; a line in smaller text proclaimed them to be a PRODUCT OF SYRIA.

Just like Rashal.

Before she even understood what she was doing, she had unscrewed the golden lid. Then, one by one, she began digging olives out of the jar. She stuffed in as many as she could at once; she chewed and swallowed until her jaw ached and oil dripped down her chin and onto the table's worn wooden surface, where it turned dings and scratches in to pools and rivers.

Rashal ate and ate and ate, and as she ate she thought about all the things she hadn't thought about while she was thinking about food: She thought about where Mama kept her jars of olives, lined along the steel shelves at home and always at the ready at mealtimes; she thought about strolling through her grandfather's olive grove with Babah as he explained how they grew. "Syria is the birthplace of the olive tree," he told her, as she nodded her little head seriously; of course it was.

She thought about Mama twirling about the kitchen, stirring that pot, tasting from that pan, expertly kneading dough, doing five things at once; of Babah making his way home from his little tailor's shop, head bowed, tired, yet always with the biggest smile for his children; of Hassan and Nadya and Saffiyah shouting and laughing, flying kites on windy days; of the whistle of missiles flying through the air; of covering Saffiyah's little ears to protect them from the sounds of explosions and the angry yells and the cries of pain.

She thought about home.

* * *

"Rashal?"

The jar was empty. Rashal looked up at Susan's confused expression, her face slick with oil and tears. "I'm sorry," she said, gesturing towards the empty jar, the mess on the table.

"I'm sorry. I will clean." Her shoulders slumped. "I will do better."

Susan's face softened. "I will too," she said, touching Rashal on the shoulder.

And without saying anything more, Rashal understood that this was a promise. Perhaps, just perhaps, this could become a home after all.

LITTLE PIG

by Anna Taborska, 2,000 words

Fleeing from a hungry wolf pack, a young mother has to make a horrific choice.

Anna Taborska is a British filmmaker and horror writer. She has written and directed two short films, two documentaries and an award-winning TV drama. She has also worked on over twenty other film and television productions, including the BBC TV series 'Auschwitz: The Nazis and the Final Solution' and 'World War Two: Behind Closed Doors—Stalin, the Nazis and the West'. Anna's short stories have appeared in a number of 'Year's Best' anthologies, and her debut short story collection, 'For Those who Dream Monsters', published by Mortbury Press in 2013, won the Dracula Society's Children of the Night Award and was nominated for a British Fantasy Award. A new collection of novelettes and short stories (working title: 'Bloody Britain') is planned for release soon. You can watch clips from Anna's films and view her full résumé here: http://annataborska.wix.com/ horror.

Little Pig by Anna Taborska was originally published in The Eighth Black Book of Horror (2011).

Adam waited nervously in the International Arrivals hall of Heathrow Airport's Terminal 1. Born and bred in London, Adam had never thought of himself as the type of guy who would import a wife from Poland. His parents had made sure that he'd learnt Polish from an early age; while his English friends had played football or watched 'Swap Shop' on Saturday mornings, Adam had been dragged kicking and screaming to Polish classes in Ealing. But it had all paid off in the end when he went to Poland one summer and met Krystyna. Since that time, the smart, pretty brunette had relocated to London and moved in with Adam. They were engaged to be married, and it seemed to Adam that all the members of his fiancé's family had already visited London and stayed with them—all, that is, except Krystyna's grandmother, and that was who Adam was now waiting for. Krystyna had not been able to get the day off work, and Adam was anxiously eyeing every elderly woman who came through the arrival gate, in the hope that one of them would match the tattered photograph that Krystyna had given him.

Eventually, a little old lady came out alone. Adam recognised her immediately and started to walk towards her, stopping abruptly as he saw the woman slip, drop her glasses and, in a desperate effort to right herself, step on them, crushing them completely. Upset for the woman, Adam began to rush forward, only to halt as she started to laugh hysterically. She muttered something under her breath and, had he not known any better, Adam could have sworn that what she said was "little pig!"

* * *

The sleigh sped through the dark forest, the scant moonlight reflected by the snow lighting up the whites of the horse's eyes as it galloped along the narrow path, nostrils flaring and velvet mouth spitting foam and blood into the night. The woman cried out as the reins cut into her hands, and screamed to her children to hang on.

The three little girls clung to each other and to the sides of the sleigh, their tears freezing onto their faces as soon as they formed. The corner of the large blanket in which their mother had wrapped them for the perilous journey to their grand-parents' house had come loose and was flapping violently in the icy air.

"Hold on to Vitek!" the woman screamed over her shoulder at her eldest child, her voice barely audible over the howling wind. But the girl did not need to be told; only two days away from her seventh birthday, she clung onto her baby brother, fear for her tiny sibling stronger than her own terror. The other two girls, aged two and four, huddled together, lost in an incomprehensible world of snow and fear and darkness.

The woman whipped the reins against the horse's heaving flanks, but the animal was already running on a primal fear stronger than pain. The excited yelps audible over the snow-storm left little doubt in the woman's mind: the pack was gaining on the sleigh—the hungry wolves were getting closer.

That winter had been particularly hard on the wolf pack. The invading Russian army had taken the peasants' livestock and, with no farm animals to snatch, the wolves had been limited to seeking out those rabbits and wild fowl that the desperate peasants and fleeing refugees had not killed and eaten. Driven half-mad with starvation, the wolves had already invested an irrevocable amount of energy in chasing the horse, and instinct informed them that it was too late to give up now—they had to feed or had to die.

The horse was wheezing, blood freezing in its nostrils as it strained through the snow. Its chestnut coat was matted with sweat whipped up into a dirty foam. Steam rose off its back like smoke, giving the bizarre impression that the animal was on fire.

The woman shouted at the horse, willing it on, and brought the reins down against its flanks. She had only been fending for herself for three days—since the soldiers had tied her husband to a tree, cut off his genitals and sawn him in half with a blunt saw—but she knew instinctively that without the horse she and her children would die. If the starving wolves did not kill them, the cold would. They still had many miles to travel—and they would never make it on foot. The time had come to resort to the last hope her children had left.

The woman pulled on the reins, slowing the horse to a more controlled pace. She tied the reins to the sleigh, the horse running steadily along the forest path. She tried not to look at her shaking, crying children, clinging onto each other as they were thrown around the sleigh—the pitiful sight would break her, and she must not break. She must not lose the battle to keep her children alive.

"Good girls," she muttered, without looking back, "hold on to your brother."

She stood up carefully in the speeding sleigh and reached over the side, unfastening the buckles on the wicker basket attached there. She opened the lid as slowly and as carefully as the shaking sleigh would allow. The sight that greeted her made her stomach turn, as fear for her children gave way to shock and panic. She howled in despair. A sudden jerky movement sent her sprawling back into the sleigh. She pulled herself up and clawed at the basket again, tearing the whole thing off in an effort to change the unchangeable.

"Little pig!" screamed the woman, her eyes wild and unseeing. The children screamed too, the madness in their mother's voice destroying the last remnant of safety and order in their world. "Little pig." she screamed. "They took the little pig."

The woman fell back onto her seat. The horse was slowing. An expectant howl pierced the darkness behind the sleigh. The woman grabbed the reins and struck at the horse's flanks again. The animal snorted and strained onwards, but even in her panic the woman knew that if she tried to force any more speed out of it, she would kill it, and all her children with it.

The howling and snarling grew closer, forcing the horse's fear onto a new level. It reared and tried to bolt, almost over-turning the sleigh, but its exhaustion and the snow prevented its escape from the hungry pack.

The wolves were beginning to fan out on either side of the sleigh, still behind it, but not far off. One of the beasts—a battle-scarred individual with protruding ribs and cold yellow eyes—broke away from the others and made a dash for the horse, nipping at its heels. The horse screamed and kicked out, catching the wolf across the snout and sending it tumbling into the trees. It pulled itself up in seconds and started back after its companions.

The reins almost slipped from the woman's bleeding, freez-ing hands. She tightened her grip, wrapping the reins around her wrists. If only they were closer to her parents' village, she could let the wolves have the horse—it was the horse that they were after. But without the horse they would all freeze in the snow long before they reached safety.

The pack was catching up with the sleigh now; the wolves spilled forward, biting at the horse. The woman shouted at the wolves, whipped at them and at the horse with the reins, but there was nothing she could do. She cast a glance at her daughters: the two little ones pale as sheets, Irena holding onto Vitek as if he were life itself. And Vitek—her perfect little boy.

The woman remembered her husband's face when she first told him he had a son. His face had lit up; he had taken the little boy from her and held him in his big, strong arms . . . her husband . . . then an image of the last time she had seen him—seen his mutilated corpse tied to the old walnut tree in the orchard.

She was back in the present, fighting to save her chil-dren—losing the fight to save her children. The little pig was gone—she had put it in the wicker basket at the side of the sleigh and fastened the straps when the soldiers were getting drunk inside her house. She had gone back to the barn to get the children, to flee with them under cover of darkness to what she hoped would be the relative safety of her parents' village. Someone must have seen her put the little pig in the basket, someone cruel enough to take the time to do up the straps after sentencing her children to death in the wolf-infested forest.

The little pig was gone and another sacrifice was needed in its place to protect the horse. The woman prepared to jump out of the sleigh. She turned to Irena and shouted, "Give Vitek to Kasia!" Irena stared at her mother blankly. "Give your brother to Kasia!" The woman's voice rose to a hysterical pitch. Four-year-old Kasia clung onto her two-year-old sister, and Irena began to cry, clutching her brother even tighter. "Give him to her!" screamed the woman, "I need you to hold the reins." But even as she said it, she knew that the six-year-old would never be able to control the terrified horse. Her own hands were a bloody ruin and she wondered how she was able to hang on as the frantic animal fought its way forward.

"Irena! Give Vitek to Kasia—now!" But Irena saw something in her mother's eyes that scared her more than the dark and the shaking sleigh and even the wolves. She clutched her brother to her chest and shook her head, fresh tears rolling down her face and freezing to her cheeks.

A large silver wolf clamped its jaws onto the horse's left hind leg. The horse stumbled, but managed to right itself and the wolf let go, unable to keep up with the horse in the deep snow—but not for long. As the chestnut reeled, the sleigh lurched and the woman panicked. She had to act now or lose all her children. She could not give her life for them because they would never make it to safety without her. But a sacrifice had to be made. If she could not die to save her children, then one of them would have to die to save the others. She would not lose them all. One of them would have to die, and she would have to choose. The delicate fabric of the woman's sanity was finally stretched to its limits and gave way. She threw back her head and howled her anguish into the night. All around her the night howled back.

The woman turned and looked into the faces of her children. A sharp intake of breath—like that taken by one about to drown. She took the reins in one hand, and with the other she reached out for her beloved son—her husband's greatest joy; the frailest of her children, half-frozen despite his sister's efforts to keep him warm, too exhausted even to cry, and the least likely to survive the journey.

"Give him to me!" she screamed at Irena. The girl struggled with her mother. The woman wrenched her baby out of her daughter's grasp and held him to her, gazing for a moment into his eyes. The woman smiled through her tears at her son. Snow was falling on the baby's upturned face, the frost had tinged his lips a pale blue, but in the woman's fevered mind, her baby smiled back at her.

Two of the wolves had closed in on the horse and were trying to bring it down. The woman screamed and threw Vitek as far from the sleigh as she could. There was a moment's silence, then a triumphant yelping as the wolves turned their attention away from the horse, and rushed away into the night. Irena cried out, and her little sisters stared uncomprehendingly at their mother, who screamed and screamed as she grabbed the reins in both hands and whipped the horse on into the dark.

As the first light of dawn broke across the horizon, an eerie sight greeted the sleepy village. The sleigh rolled in slowly, as the exhausted horse made it within sight of the first farmhouse. It stood for a moment, head drooping, blood seeping from its nostrils, its mouth, from open wounds along its flanks. Then, it dropped silently to the ground and lay still.

In the sleigh sat a wild-eyed woman, staring but unseeing, her black hair streaked with white, reins clenched tightly in her bloody hands. Behind her were three little girls. Two were slumped together, asleep. The third girl, the eldest of the three, was awake—she sat very still, eyes wide, silent as her mother.

* * *

"Irena?" Adam reached the old lady and touched her arm. "I'm Adam." He bent down and picked up what was left of Irena's glasses. "I'm sorry about your glasses," he told her, handing the crushed frames back to her.

"No need to be sorry," said Irena. "It's just a little pig."

Adam was taken aback. It was bad enough taking care of Krystyna's relatives, but she had never said that her grandmother was senile.

Irena read Adam like an open book.

"A little pig," she explained, "a small sacrifice to make sure nothing really terrible happens . . . during my visit."

"I understand," said Adam. He did not understand, but at least there was some method in the old lady's madness, and that was good enough for him. He paid the parking fee at the ticket machine, and they left the building: a tall young man pushing a trolley and a little old lady clutching a pair of broken glasses.

SPY NIGHT

by Scott Merrow, 2,500 words

Spy Night *is a light-hearted story about Ed and Margie Lobaski, a middle-aged couple who hope to spice up their marriage with a monthly role-playing night-on-the-town. This month, they're playing spies, and everything seems to be going well . . . until they cross paths with the mysterious, red-bearded man.*

Scott Merrow has been writing short fiction as a hobby since retiring from the Air Force ten years ago. He recently had a story, The Good Mother, *published online at Short Fiction Break. He has six other stories forthcoming in various online and in-print publications. He and his wife Paula also co-write short screenplays. To date, ten of them have been produced. The films and scripts have won several awards on the film festival circuit. Scott and Paula live in Colorado with their two crazy dogs.*

Margie Lobaski leaned deep into the closet, shuffling hangers on the bar until she found what she was looking for. She emerged holding up a slinky, black dress. *Yikes, it's tiny!* she thought, somewhat discouraged.

She pulled and stretched it a little, this way and that, trying to judge how much of a struggle it would be to squeeze herself into it. She sighed, pulled it over her head, and shimmied in. Poking her head out, she adjusted the spaghetti straps, and had a look in the mirror. A little bulge here and there—*not exactly the look I was hoping for, but it'll have to do.*

Downstairs in the den, her sister Jeannie was reading a magazine when Margie walked in. "Thanks again for watching the litter tonight, Jeannie." She hooked her thumb toward the kitchen and the raucous sounds of three kids arguing. "We have a hard time keeping babysitters."

"No problem, sis, I wasn't . . . whoa! Look at you. You look hot! What's the occasion?"

"You really think I look okay? I could barely squeeze into this thing."

"You look fabulous. Really. I wish I looked that good in something like that. So what *is* the occasion?"

Margie hesitated. "Don't laugh. You're not gonna believe this. And you gotta promise you won't tell Mom, okay?"

Jeannie crossed her heart. "Promise."

"Tonight's our monthly one-night stand."

"Your what?"

"Well, I read about this idea in *The Big 4-0 Magazine*." She hesitated, deciding where to start. "Our marriage has sorta hit the doldrums—that's the part you can't tell Mom."

"Okay, okay."

"So, anyway, I figured we needed some kind of spark. And this magazine article suggested a one-night stand, once a month or so. Complete with role playing. That way, every month, we each get a night on the town with a more exciting version of each other. Just to jazz things up a little. Tonight's our spy night."

"Spy night?"

"Yeah. Ed's playing a spy, and I'm his femme fatale, like Mata Hari." She looked herself over, bulges and all. "Or whatever."

Jeannie chuckled. "So where is Mr. Double-Oh-Seven, anyway?"

"He's at the hotel, getting everything ready."

* * *

Twenty minutes later, Margie strode across the lobby of the Starlight Hotel, her stiletto heels click-clacking as she walked along. She stopped at the front desk to check out the room arrangements, then she proceeded to the bar. She paused at the door for just a moment to adjust her fishnet stockings, then she glided in.

The atmosphere was perfect—dim lighting, jazzy music not too loud, the vague sounds of intimate conversations at a couple dozen tables around the room. Very film noir.

She scanned the room for Ed, but seeing no sign of him she took a seat at the bar. The bartender sauntered over.

"Vodka martini," Margie ordered. *What the hell*, she thought, and then added, "shaken, not stirred." The bartender rolled his eyes.

I was sure he'd be here before me. Then, something caught Margie's eye. A scruffy-looking man sat at a dark corner table. He had a bushy red mustache and beard, and he wore sunglasses and a gray fedora. He was glancing furtively around the room. As Margie watched, he took a pen from his jacket . . . and began talking to it!

The bartender brought her martini. "Here ya go. Shaken and unstirred."

Margie chuckled and took a quick sip. "See that man over there in the corner? With the beard?"

"Yeah."

"Has he been here long?"

The bartender thought about it. "Maybe an hour or so."

They both watched him for a moment, then Margie asked, "What's he's doing, anyway?"

The bartender shrugged. "I don't know," he said, walking away. "It looks like he's talking to a pen."

Margie sipped her drink as she studied the man. The beard looked fake, and with the sunglasses and hat his face was pretty well hidden. *That's got to be him.* She gulped her drink and headed for his table.

She approached quietly behind him. He was still talking to his pen. "North, 38, 52, 15 point 54; West, 77, 03, 21 point 43 . . ." His voice was deep and gruff. *Nice touch,* Margie thought.

Over his shoulder she whispered in her sexiest voice, "What's the frequency, Kenneth?"

He jumped, startled. "What?" He quickly put the pen down.

"What's a sexy man like you doing all alone in a place like this?" she purred.

He cleared his throat. "Are you Olga?"

Ah, the game is afoot. "Da, dahlink," she said in her best faux-Russian.

He spoke into the pen again. "She's here." Then, he held it up to his ear. He looked closely at her face. "Yeah. Five-three, dark hair, slinky dress." He looked her over again. "Kinda chunky . . ."

"Hey!" she protested, punching him in the shoulder.

"She's a feisty one," he said into the pen, then set it down. He pulled an envelope from his jacket pocket and handed it to her. "Here. Take care of this until Milo comes."

"Marlow?"

"No . . . Milo. Don't give it to nobody but Milo. And don't open it. Get it?"

"Of course, dahlink, I get it," she said, smiling seductively. "And thees ees for you." She slid her room key card across the table and walked away, swaying coquettishly to the jazzy music.

He stared after her, then examined the card. "Hey," he called out. "There's no room number."

"Three-fourteen, beeg boy," she answered as she sashayed out the door, hips undulating in rhythm with the sound of her high heels click-clacking on the tile floor.

Upstairs in the room, she quickly changed into a skimpy nightie, poofed up her hair a bit, and spritzed on some of Ed's favorite perfume, "Night of Oriental Delights." Then, with the envelope in hand, she sat herself alluringly on the bed, propped up against a couple pillows. And she waited.

She wondered about the envelope. *He warned me not to open it*, she remembered, *but . . . was that just a tease? Did he really mean . . . open it? A real spy would*, she thought. She held it up to the light, but the envelope was too thick. No way to steam it open here in the hotel room, so she tried to pry it open carefully, but without much success. Finally, she just tore it open. There was a small white note card inside. Embossed at the top, in bold letters, it said, "Be Like Bond." Beneath that there were three hand-scribbled lines:

You must retrieve the plans by midnight.
Remember—trust no one!!! Especially "you-know-who."
The codeword is Octopussy.

Just then, she heard a noise at the door, the sound of a key card sliding in the slot and the electronic lock opening. She tucked the envelope under the pillow. The door swung open, and there stood Ed, her Ed, wearing a white dinner jacket, black bowtie, and carrying a briefcase and a bottle of champagne. The red beard and sunglasses were gone—*must be part of the game. He looks pretty good in the tuxedo, though.*

He leered at her in the flimsy nightie, and his eyes widened slightly. "Hello, my dear," he said in his most debonair tone of voice. "And who are you?"

"I'm Olga, beeg boy" she replied. "And you . . . you are Milo?"

He hesitated. "Uh, yeah. I'm Milo."

"You're a real queek change arteest, dahlink."

Ed looked at himself in a mirror and chuckled. "Yeah, I guess so. And, man, it's hard to find these monkey suits in my size. Short and wide." Then, he caught himself and snapped back into character. He crossed the room, set down the briefcase and the bottle, sat on the bed next to Margie, and took her in his arms. "You look ravishing, my dear," he said as he kissed her.

"Why thank you, dahlink," she answered, kissing him back. *Hmmm*, she thought, *this spy game is alright.*

They kissed passionately for a few more minutes, then Ed got up and took off his dinner jacket. Margie remembered the envelope. "Dahlink, do you have the plans in the briefcase?"

"Oh, I have plans in the briefcase, alright. Yessiree."

"Might I have a look at them?"

"Not just yet, my dear. All in due t . . ."

There was a knock at the door, followed by the sound of a key card sliding in its slot.

They both froze.

Then the door opened, slowly, and in walked the red-bearded man. Ed and Margie stared at him, eyes wide. He gaped at them, too, eyes even wider.

Margie, laying on the bed in her nightie, sat up straight and covered up a little. The bearded man turned to Ed. "Who are you?"

"Um," Ed stammered, "I'm Milo."

The man drew a pistol from his jacket and pointed it at Ed. "You're not Milo."

Ed and Margie shot surprised glances at each other. Then, Margie got it—*all part of the game.*

The man closed the door behind him and cautiously circled the room. He gestured with the pistol toward Ed. "Sit in that chair and put your hands behind your head." Ed hesitated. "Do it! Now!" he shouted. Ed and Margie both jumped.

Geez, this guy's good, Margie thought.

Ed sat in the chair, hands behind his head.

"Alright, then," the man said more calmly, "Who are you really?"

Ed glanced at Margie, who was looking back and forth between the two men. He raised one eyebrow and sneered. "They call me 'The Viper.'"

Margie fought hard to stifle a laugh.

"The Viper?" The bearded man looked puzzled. "And just who do you work for, Viper?"

"Hah." Ed was getting in to it. "That's for me to know and you to find out."

Geez, Ed, great line, Margie thought.

The bearded man cocked the pistol. "Enough of this nonsense, Viper. I know you have something I want or you wouldn't be here. What's in that briefcase?"

"My homework," Ed said sarcastically. "I go to night school."

"Oh, a wise guy. Open the briefcase, or I'll kill you right now."

"You can't kill me, Mr. Red Beard. You need me." Ed leaned back in the chair, hands behind his head. "The briefcase is wired with explosives. If you try to open it with the wrong combination, KA-BLOOEY! We're all dead and everything in the briefcase is up in smoke."

"Alright then, I'll kill the girl." He pointed the pistol at Margie. "You two seemed to be getting real cozy when I walked in."

Margie assumed this was her cue. "No, no, I vas just trying to get ze plans. Ve veren't getting cozy. There's nothing between us, dahlink."

The bearded man circled the bed, the gun trained on Margie. "How did you even know about the plans?"

"It was in the envelope."

"I told you not to open the envelope," he shouted. Keeping the gun pointed at Margie, he said to Ed, "Enough of this. You two are obviously in cahoots. You've got to the count of three to open the briefcase, or the girl gets it." He took a couple menacing steps closer to Margie. "One . . . two . . ."

"Okay, okay," Ed cried out. "I'll open it. Don't shoot her." He set the briefcase on his lap and dialed in the combination.

Margie could hardly contain her excitement as Ed slowly opened the briefcase. Then, suddenly, everything snapped into fast motion.

Ed pulled something out of the briefcase and held it up. It was a can of Silly String. He mashed the button and let a barrage of purple string fly across the bed toward the bearded man. The bearded man, startled by the incoming string, stumbled backward, and the gun went off.

BAM!!!

Yikes, that was loud, Margie thought.

Ed tossed the briefcase aside and launched himself toward the bed. Margie ducked as Ed's foot landed on the corner of the bed and he catapulted through the air toward the dumbfounded bearded man, blasting him with Silly String all the while.

When Ed landed on the man, the gun went off again— BAM!!!—and they both tumbled to the ground.

Margie couldn't believe her eyes. "WOO HOO!" she shouted. "Nice move, Viper!"

The two men rolled and scuffled on the floor, first one on top, then the other, arms and legs flailing. Margie was amazed. *These guys are good. Ed, you devil!*

Then, the bearded man got the advantage. He rolled on top of Ed and pinned his arms behind him. He pointed the pistol at the back of Ed's head. "All right, Viper. Your time's up. Looks like I'll get the plans *and* the girl."

Then, he pulled the trigger.

BAM!!!

Ed lurched, then stopped struggling. The room was quiet.

Margie's heart pounded as she waited for the next move.

She looked at Ed, lying motionless. She watched the bearded man climb off him.

Then, Ed slowly reached up and rubbed his ears. "Cripes, that thing is loud." He rolled over and grabbed the bearded man's leg and pulled him back on the ground. But before Ed could start tussling again, the bearded man shouted, "Octopussy! Octopussy!"

"What?"

"That's the codeword. Octopussy. I shot you, so you should be dead. You can't keep fighting. Those are the rules. So, I called Octopussy."

"What are you talking about? What rules?"

Then, the door burst open. A large, very stern-looking man rushed in. He was all business.

"Who are you?" asked Margie, now totally confused.

"Jameson, Hotel Security. Someone reported shots coming from this room." Then, he saw the pistol lying on the floor. In a flash, he pounced on it and rolled into a sitting position with the gun level. "Everybody freeze!"

The bearded man raised his hands. "But officer, it's a fake gun."

Jameson examined the gun in his hand. "Oh, yeah." He turned it over again. "Sure looks real, though."

"Sounds real, too", said Ed, rubbing both ears.

"Would someone please explain what's going on here?"

The bearded man answered. "We're playing 'Be Like Bond'."

"What?!?" exclaimed Margie, Ed, and Jameson simultaneously.

"'Be Like Bond'," repeated the bearded man. "The game." He saw the puzzled looks on their faces. "Uh, you *were* playing, weren't you?" He looked back and forth between Margie and Ed, both staring blankly. "'Be Like Bond'? The role playing game?"

Ed looked at Margie. "Honey, do you know this man?"

"No. I thought you did."

Jameson said, "Well, if he was in a role playing game, and you don't know him, what were you two doing?"

"We were having a one-night stand," Margie answered. "Our own role playing game. It was in a magazine. It's supposed to spice up your marriage. This month we're spies. Last month, King Arthur and Guinevere. The month before . . ."

"Alright, alright, I get it. You accidentally stumbled into each others' games." Jameson shook his head incredulously. "Geez, what are the odds?"

Just then, a man and woman walked into the room.

Jameson looked them over. "And just who are you?"

In a conspiratorial tone of voice, the man said, "I'm Milo."

"And I'm Olga, dahlink," the woman added. "The bartender said room three-fourteen."

The bearded man slapped his forehead. Jameson shook his head and laughed. Ed looked at Margie. Margie looked at Ed.

"Sheesh," she said.

* * *

Later, after the room had cleared out and the dust had settled, Margie and Ed finished the champagne and collapsed into bed. They snuggled together in the dark for a while, Margie feeling a little frisky, but Ed was just too worn out from all the excitement. She could hear him drifting off to sleep. She shook him.

"Honey?"

No answer. She shook him again.

"Ed? Honey?"

"Mmmmm?"

"Next month, can we do Zorro?"

"Mmmm. Okay."

A few seconds of silence.

"Ed?"

"Mmmmm?"

"Can I be Zorro?"

THE FINAL CHAPTER OF MARATHON MANDY

by Zach Shephard, 3500 words

In a future where humanity has spread beyond the confines of Earth, otherwise-inhospitable moons and planets are terraformed to serve as suitable colony worlds. To this end, NASA employs the services of specialists known as campers: survivalists who pitch their tents within these freshly modified environments, looking to gauge their viability as new homes for the human race. Unfortunately for Mandy, not all moons take kindly to being terraformed—and when things go south, she reacts in the only way she can.

Zach Shephard's fiction has appeared in places like Fantasy & Science Fiction, Galaxy's Edge and the Unidentified Funny Objects anthology series. He spends a lot of time taking and teaching kickboxing classes at his local gym, mostly because he spends even more time eating foods he probably shouldn't. For a full list of his published stories, check out zachshephard.com.

He told me if I stopped running, I would die.

So I ran.

I stayed close to the river. The land there was flat and easy to navigate. I might have been able to find a shorter path on the hillside to my right, but that place was full of trees and boulders and nasty things I didn't want to think about just then, so I stuck with my current course.

My boot sunk into a puddle and smashed a mirror that reflected gray skies. I stumbled and lost a step, and wondered if that would be the one that cost me.

No time to think about it. I shook the idea from my head and sprinted to make up for the difference.

"You're going too fast, Mandy—at that pace you'll tire out before you get here."

I didn't respond. Reaching for the call button on my communicator seemed like too much work just then, and I couldn't afford to lose my stride.

So I ran.

As everything crumbled around me, I couldn't help but wonder where things had gone wrong. Life was supposed to be better here. I'd been promised a world without distractions—a place where I could read in quiet solitude, and embrace nature's beauty without feeling like an outsider. It wasn't supposed to be like this.

A tremor boiled the river and sent me sprawling. I hit the carpet of rounded stones and shot back to my feet before I had a chance to think about the new cut on my chin or the pain in my hip. Somewhere behind me, I heard an explosion that could have been a volcano erupting or more of our equipment malfunctioning—or possibly both, because one often led to another.

I didn't look back. There could have been a wave of lava or ash coming my way, but seeing it wouldn't change things. Craig had calculated my pace, and we both knew there was no way I'd get to base in time if I stopped to do any sightseeing.

So I ran.

Craig's voice called out over the cataclysmic rumbling and gave me a progress update that wasn't very uplifting. I gritted my teeth and cursed myself. For the first time in my history as a NASA camper, I wished I hadn't pitched my tent so far from base. You spend your whole life trying to get away from people, then just when you get what you want . . .

There was a loud crack like a branch snapping off a tree. I ignored it at first, figuring it was just another symptom of the world we'd killed. But when I heard it again and saw a puff of dirt explode on the ground in front of me, I knew I had a whole new problem on my hands.

I looked across the river. There, Gerrickson was sprinting just as hard as I was. Except he was doing it with a pistol in hand.

He fired two more shots, and I ducked and hunched my shoulders. My pace slackened, and Craig noticed.

"Mandy! What's wrong? Why are you slowing down?"

This time, I felt like responding.

"Why the hell is Gerrickson shooting at me?"

I didn't hear another shot. Gerrickson must have been content with slowing me down. Now that he had a strong lead, he focused on racing toward base. I picked up my pace again, hoping Gerrickson wouldn't have time to cast a glance over his shoulder.

Craig's voice returned: "Listen—I need to level with you, Mandy. There's a reason the captain sent all the campers so far away from base on the last mission."

"You said we needed to cast a wider net; that we needed to gather more data to figure out why this moon was rejecting the terraform."

"I said what I was told to say. But that was then. Now, I don't care what the captain thinks. I'm telling you the truth."

He said something more, but I missed it when a rockslide rushed down the hill to my right. The billowing dust-wall came straight at me, and I felt like an ant scrambling under the shadow of a boot.

I tore my gaze from the oncoming disaster and kicked hard. My legs felt like they were going to rip right off my body. My heart was about to explode.

Somewhere behind me, the wave smothered my tracks and hissed into the river. I didn't bother looking back, because I didn't want to know how close it was.

I slowed from my sprint but kept moving at a strong pace. Gasping for breath, I reached for my communicator.

"Sorry," I said over the groans and growls of the dying moon, "but if you want to tell me the truth, you'll have to speak up."

Craig gave me another disappointing status update, then started his story over.

"You were right," he said. "It's true that we needed more data. But that information was being collected for the benefit of future expeditions. This moon was lost to us the moment it started rejecting the terraform so violently."

"Are you telling me—"

"We never intended to fix things here."

I felt my inner world collapse, just like the one around me.

"You sent me out here to die?"

"It's more complicated than that, Mandy."

"How does it get more complicated than—"

Gunshots. Apparently, I'd caught up to Gerrickson. He was firing across the river again. I ducked behind a boulder.

"Mandy, you're slowing dow—"

"I don't need a progress report! Just tell me why Gerrickson is shooting at me!"

Craig sighed into the communicator. "There are a lot of supplies to be brought along when terraforming a moon. We're restricted by expenses and engineering. If we could bring everything we wanted, we would, but things never seem to work out that—"

"Get to the point!"

He swallowed. "It's the escape shuttle, Mandy. It's not big enough for all of us."

I didn't say anything. I couldn't. Rage had fused my teeth together.

"There's enough room for the main crew," Craig said, "but mission control decided that in the event of a disaster, the campers were expendable."

Of course we were. After all, we weren't the chemists or biologists or engineers. We were the guinea pigs who pitched their tents in the wilderness to see if the land was habitable; we were the survivalists who collected samples we didn't even understand, so the big brains back at base could have something to study.

A bullet ricocheted off the boulder, and I sunk farther behind my cover. The river thrashed like a diamond-jeweled snake in the throes of death. Everything in the world sounded like a roaring jet engine. I didn't have to check my watch to know I was running out of time.

"You still haven't told me why Gerrickson is shooting at me," I said. "If you're leaving the campers to die, shouldn't he be saving those bullets for you?"

"He's just trying to increase his chances."

"What?"

"The engineering team tried to fix the problem, Mandy. We didn't want to abandon you. So, when we saw that this place was rejecting us, we got to work modifying the escape craft. We tried to make room for everyone, but this thing was built with minimalism in mind to begin with—there's not much that can be removed if we want it to continue functioning. But we did make some progress, and . . ."

"And?"

"There's one seat left."

At that point I think something may have erupted nearby, but I was too angry to really notice.

"I'm sorry," Craig said. "It was supposed to be a secret— the campers weren't supposed to know. It should've been first come, first serve. But someone must like Gerrickson enough to have filled him in, because he realizes what's going on."

I pulled my pistol from its holster. I'd always liked Gerrickson, but he'd left me with no other choice.

Time was running out. Everything was falling apart. If I stayed behind that boulder any longer, the world was going to open up and swallow me.

So I ran.

Gerrickson was too far ahead for me to hit, but I shot anyway to slow him down. It worked, for a time—he panicked and flattened out on the ground, but popped back up and started running again as soon as he realized that waiting wasn't really an option.

"You lost a lot of time when you stopped back there," Craig said, "but you're faster than Gerrickson. You can push the pace longer than he can."

"Sounds like you're playing favorites."

"Maybe I am."

I didn't say anything, because I was hoping it would end at that. Craig had different ideas.

"Listen, Mandy, what happened at the landing party—"

"—is not important right now. I'm sort of busy at the moment."

"Fine. But before you shut me out again, at least let me tell you this: it might not matter that you're faster than Gerrickson. You lost too much time when you stopped for a breather."

"A *breather?* I wasn't resting, I was being shot at!"

"Whatever the reason, the result is the same—I've calculated your movement rate, and I'm not sure you'll get here before we launch."

"How close are the other campers?"

"We've lost contact with Janeway and Rosario. Their side of the moon was the first to go."

"So, it's just Gerrickson I have to worry about."

"Just him and the clock."

Right on cue, a bullet skipped off the ground nearby. I fired a few shots on the run and Gerrickson went down.

He held his leg low, around the ankle. I saw red oozing between his fingers. For a brief moment, my instincts overpowered my brain and told me to go help him. I took a step toward the river, but stopped when Gerrickson started firing at me again. I turned away and continued toward base. He had no chance of catching me at that point, but I fired a few blind shots behind me anyway to scare him off. It must have worked, because he quit firing back.

My gun was empty, and I didn't have another clip on me, so I tossed it aside. One less thing to carry.

Then I saw the bear.

It wasn't the type of Earth-bear you're thinking of, but that's the closest comparison I can make. The thing was like a grizzly with a line of stegosaurus plates down its back, wrapped in a coat of green-and-brown tiger fur. It descended the rumbling hill at full speed, on a path that was looking to cross my own.

Most animals you'd come across in that type of situation would be primarily concerned with escaping the chaos, but those bears were extremely territorial, and I had a feeling this one was trying to chase me off rather than save its own skin. I guess its motivation didn't matter either way, because I was in its path and there wasn't room for the both of us. My only options were to get ahead of it or hang behind and let it pass, and if I slowed even a little, I was a dead woman anyway.

So I ran.

The ball of muscle and fur barreled down the hill. When it hit flat land, it only got faster. At that point, there was no longer any question in my mind: the bear wasn't fleeing. It was coming after me.

It kicked across the riverbank stones and opened a mouth full of dripping teeth. The growl that came from its throat was somehow louder than the death of a moon.

The bear made its final lunge, and I dove to the side. I rolled to a stop near the edge of the river, belly-down with my arms covering my head. I waited to feel the teeth and claws sink into my back, and wondered if my body would even notice the pain over all the fatigue and desperation.

When I looked up, I saw the bear sprawled out next to me. Its mouth was open and its tongue was lolling out. There was a hole in its head where Gerrickson had shot it.

Maybe he'd been aiming for me, but I prefer to think he realized he was out of the race and wanted at least one of us to survive. I once again found myself with the urge to go back and check on his ankle wound, but I was already behind schedule and didn't want his gesture to go to waste.

I got to my feet, ran three steps and fell over from exhaustion.

Getting up again was the hardest thing I'd ever done.

As I stumbled alongside the river, I clicked on my communicator.

"Craig," I said, "if you get a chance to patch through to Gerrickson, tell him—"

"He says you're welcome. And good luck."

I wish I could have looked back and waved. Especially now that I know how things ended up.

I got my second wind and sprinted toward camp. I passed a ravine that hadn't been there before and a bear that wasn't interested in me. My feet were bloody inside my boots, or at least they felt that way. My legs didn't feel like anything at all.

I saw a canoe up ahead near the bank of the river. Rosario had left it there about a month ago. I wasn't sure I'd be able to navigate the rapids when the river was trying to digest itself, but I also wasn't sure how long I'd be able to keep running. I hit the communicator and asked Craig to figure out my best option. No response. The canoe was getting closer, closer, closer . . . and then it was gone, receding into the Ragnarok that chased me. Even if Craig were to answer at that point, it was too late to backtrack and paddle my way home.

So I ran.

And then, just when I was getting close, I saw something rise above the trees and shoot into the ashen sky.

I tried to contact Craig. I tried to contact anyone else on the team. No one responded.

In hindsight, I shouldn't have been surprised.

I limped into base anyway, hoping that maybe there was a second ride waiting to depart. There wasn't. I was alone among a bunch of tents and panicked footprints.

I sat on a crate and watched the shuttle disappear, while somewhere in the distance a volcano ripped apart the sky.

I let my head hang and caught my breath, and thought about all the things I could have done differently.

It had seemed like the best deal anyone could ask for: I was given the opportunity to see the stars, to settle a new world where the touch of mankind was still faint and nature was something you didn't need a museum ticket to see. Ever since I was a little girl, I'd wanted to run away—from technology, from pollution, from the corrupting hand of man and from the people who raised me.

I shook my head and couldn't help but laugh at the situation. All my life, all I'd ever wanted was to be left alone. And now that I finally got my wish—now that I finally had a world all to myself—it was going to swallow me whole. Or maybe it would asphyxiate me, or just burn me to death. I guess I don't really know what the procedure is when a moon decides it isn't going to be terraformed. I hadn't exactly planned on that happening.

For the first time in my life, I didn't like being alone. Then, I remembered that Gerrickson was still out there, stranded by the river.

So I ran.

My body hated me, but I didn't care. I probably wasn't going to be using it much longer anyway.

I ran through a world of ash and smoke. I stumbled across spider-web cracks in the ground that would probably be canyons if I passed that way again. I entered the calmest, narrowest bit of river I could find, and halfway to the other side, I nearly gave up and just sank to the bottom.

But I continued on, and after an eternity of pounding my heavy feet against the shaking ground, I found Gerrickson. He was right where I'd left him.

He was dead.

The wound on his ankle didn't look bad. The one on the side of his neck was much worse. And to think, firing those last blind shots as I escaped had seemed like such a good idea at the time.

I wanted to just sit there next to Gerrickson's body and wait it out. I wanted the end to come and take me, because I was too tired to continue on. But then, I remembered one of the gadgets back at base, and knew I had one last journey to make before the world devoured me.

So I ran.

* * *

So here I am, hunched over this modern-day equivalent of a message in a bottle while a moon takes its last breaths around me. I'll launch the comm-capsule as soon as I've finished recording everything, and maybe some passing spacecraft will scoop it up and learn from our mistakes. Of course, you won't be getting any useful scientific analyses out of me—all you're getting is my story, because that's all I've got left.

I came to this moon to explore. I came here to lose myself in the woods, to spend time reading and writing and observing a new, wonderful world. And now, thanks to the budgetary concerns of some faceless politicians at mission control, I'm going to die.

But I guess that's just the way things go.

It's sort of funny. Even as my time dwindles away, the thing I regret most is leaving my book back at camp. When I got the call to return to base in a hurry, I didn't even think to take it with me. And now it's sitting there, alone, with my bookmark stuffed into its final chapter.

I can smell the forest fires in the air. The sky is dark with ash and it's getting harder to breathe. The world is ripping itself to pieces around me, and yet, all I can think about is that unfinished book.

My camp is miles away. Probably even farther now, since most of the old routes have likely been obliterated or buried. But even if that book were on the other side of this moon, I wouldn't care—I've got to get back to it. I've got to find out how the story ends. And as far as I can tell, there's only one way to make that happen.

So I'll run.

THE SAINT OF BRIGHT RED THINGS

by Charity Tahmaseb, 4,000 words

In Nazi-occupied France, Marigold Jenkins, the daughter of ex-patriot Americans, must keep her identities—all three of them—a secret. She navigates the streets of Paris armed with a bright red handbag, scarlet lipstick, and a compact tailor-made for her role as a courier in the resistance. But when a train accident leaves her concussed and stranded in a provincial hospital, Mari must navigate a new reality, one that leaves her at the mercy of a German officer. She must decide whether she can trust this man—and what she must sacrifice in order to do so.

Charity Tahmaseb has slung corn on the cob for Green Giant and jumped out of airplanes (but not at the same time). She's worn both Girl Scout and Army green. These days, she writes fiction and works as a technical writer.

The sharpness that stabbed her lungs each time she pulled a breath did not scare Mari. The spike of pain in her temple was of little consequence. No, it was the clean sheets against her skin, the pillow that cradled her head, and the soft prayers of the Sisters that frightened her the most.

The last thing she remembered was the screech of the train. The last thing she saw was a spider web of cracked window glass splattered with brilliant red. After that, blue sky, crushed grass beneath her, stones stabbing her spine. Her purse, the straps looped through one arm. The tug when she refused to give it up. The last thing she heard were those orders barked in German.

The last thing she said?

Oh, God, not in English. Please, not in English. The panic sliced through the fog clouding her mind, but the clarity didn't last. A new bank rolled in, doubt married to fear—and pain. The spike of it radiated across her skull, down her neck.

Even so, sounds penetrated. A rattling cart. Consoling murmurs. The gentle whisk of fabric against the floor.

With deep reluctance, Mari cracked open her eyes. The light assaulted her, the stab of it like something solid, something she could swallow, something that would choke her. She took quick, shallow breaths, and spread her arms until her fingertips reached each side of the bed, searching, searching. Her forearm felt naked without the purse's straps. She came away with nothing but the clean edge of the sheets. Under, then? Or on a side table? Check everywhere. Oh, but that meant moving.

"You're awake." The nun wasn't much older than she was, with hazel eyes and freckles far too frivolous for the somber wimple. "Would you like some water?"

The sister helped her sit. It was all Mari could do not to cry out when the water flooded her mouth, soothed her throat. Had she screamed when the train jumped the tracks? Her throat was raw enough for it.

"Better?" the nun asked.

Again, she nodded.

"Where am I?" The words came rough as if she hadn't spoken for days.

"You're in hospital." The nun murmured the name of the town—somewhere between Paris and Blois.

"What happened?"

"You should ask . . ." The nun glanced toward the entrance to the ward. She didn't elaborate. She didn't need to.

There, in shadows, stood a man. Even from this distance he was obviously German, and from his bearing, obviously an officer. Mari licked her lips, swallowed back the bile in her throat, and reached once again for the water.

The man's footfalls echoed against the floor. A hush fell over the space, as if they all held their breaths for the length of his stroll down the center of the ward. The sister turned and busied herself with the cart of medication, the wings of her wimple hiding her face.

He halted at the foot of the bed with a single click of his heels and an almost gracious bow. "Fraulein."

She nodded, and squinted against the light, his form blurry.

"I am Major Messner," he said.

She blinked. Was he the local commander, then? That would account for the hush, that collective intake of breath. Still, was he better or worse than the Gestapo? Better, certainly, although much depended upon what sort of man Major Messner was.

"I was hoping you could assist us."

One who spoke passable French, at least.

"You were in a train wreck. The tracks were sabotaged," he continued. "We are hoping those passengers riding on the west side might be able to . . . provide us with information."

Images came flooding back. That spider web in red. Her purse clutched tight, even when the jolt threw her into the window. Had she been traveling north or south? This, she couldn't remember. The uncertainty of that simmered in her belly like slow-acting poison.

"Do you remember anything, Fraulein?" the Major

prompted. "Anything at all? Perhaps you were glancing out the window and saw something . . . someone?"

"I remember very little," she said. This, blessedly, was true. Her words, however, betrayed the state of her throat. She reached a hand for the water glass only to find him plucking it from the side table and bringing it to her lips.

"*Merci*," she managed.

"Let's start with something easier, shall we? Where were you headed?"

The uncertainty returned, panic gripping her mind, rendering her mute. North or South? Which was it? Sweat bloomed along her limbs, the thin blanket and cool sheets suddenly stifling. Where she was headed depended so much on who she was. The name on her papers would tell her, and those would be in her purse.

She was . . . who then? Marguerite, the dancer? (Bless her mother's insistence on ballet lessons.) No. Too flashy. Marguerite would never leave Paris for . . . she eyed the small ward . . . wherever here was. Too provincial. Françoise, the shop girl? Yes! She was little Françoise, almost certainly.

Mari hadn't been herself, hadn't been Marigold Jenkins since her mother planted a perfumed kiss on her cheek and fled Paris for the endless blue skies and palm trees of Hollywood, her father in tow. And then, of course, the Nazis came.

"I was returning to Paris after visiting my mother in the countryside," she said, as if her mother would ever live in the countryside in any nation. "She's . . . not well."

"Returning?" The major cocked an eyebrow. A single word filled with doubt. A single gesture a death sentence.

But she was Françoise, a silly bit of fluff. Despite the ache, Mari tilted her head, trained her eyes on him, and in all innocence asked, "Was I going, Major?"

His jaw twitched. It was enough of a lifeline for her to continue.

"Truthfully, Major, I think only my throat remembers what happened." She let her fingertips light on her neck.

"Understandable."

Was it? And would this German officer understand when she provided no information, real or fabricated?

"I will return when you're able to talk."

Before he turned to leave, Mari called out, "Major Messner?"

He inclined his head, unfailingly polite. He was, she realized, not as young as she first assumed, his hair shined silver rather than gold, and the lines around his eyes and mouth spoke of a man who had seen a certain share of life before the war.

"My purse. I don't suppose." She glanced away, down at her hands folded demurely on the blanket. "It's a . . . never mind."

To her surprise, he took a knee at her bedside. "Go on."

"It's only." And here, she peered up from beneath her lashes. "My lipstick, and compact." Mari touched her cheek. "I only wanted . . . but it's not important."

Major Messner laughed, the sound indulgent. "You shall have your purse, Fraulein. I shall see to it personally."

"*Merci.*" *And thank you, Françoise, you silly, vain cow.*

His footsteps echoed again on his walk up the ward. When he cleared the door, it was if everyone took their first breath in fifteen minutes. Mari's heart thudded. Was her request bold or merely reckless? How closely would they inspect her purse before turning it over to her?

The nun returned with a pitcher of water. Under the cover of refilling Mari's glass, she spoke.

"I should tell you, Mademoiselle, that Major Messner likes to . . . cultivate pretty brunettes."

Mari raised her chin. Her hair, although tangled, looked nearly black against the white of her pillow.

"Despite this." The nun's fingers lighted on Mari's temple. "And this." They moved to her cheek. "You are very pretty indeed."

"Is that a warning, Sister?"

"No," the woman turned from her, "but it may be your salvation."

* * *

Major Messner was a man who kept his promises, or at least ones made to pretty brunettes. The next morning, the purse was resting on the side table, its red crocodile skin far too brash for the hushed atmosphere of the ward.

Henri hated the purse, always said it called too much attention to her. What he meant was Nazi attention, in particular the sort of Nazi officer who cultivated pretty girls.

"We must fade into the background, one of a thousand Parisians made drab by the war. We do not want their attention." Henri said this with the authority of a father figure, and then continued with the persuasiveness of a lover. "*You* do not want their attention. You do not want to be thought a collaborator."

"But I am frivolous," Mari had argued, "either as Marguerite or Françoise. It marks me as a fool, not a collaborator."

The purse was like a broadcast signal. It told the world, or at least, those here in France, that she was not a threat. She was silly and thoughtless and spent money she didn't have for things she didn't need. After last month's successful run, even Henri had agreed. Mari was their best courier.

Now, she reached a hand for her purse, her salvation. Inside, she encountered her papers. The air pent up in her lungs seeped out. No whoosh of breath. No obvious relief. But yes, she was Françoise.

She rummaged until her fingers encountered her compact and lipstick tube. The little brush was missing. No matter. She could dab some on, lightly, with her ring finger. To have him fetch her makeup and then not use it would invite folly, indeed. What she didn't use on her lips, she could smear on her cheeks, give herself a schoolgirl blush.

Something told her that Major Messner would like that.

Mari ran her fingertips around the compact. Aside from her mother, only she knew of the false bottom. Not even Henri knew. She eased it open just enough to slip her pinky inside, to check to see if the contents were there.

They were. The slip of paper. With codes. Always a dangerous thing. Possibly the most dangerous thing of all. But necessary. And in this case, small. She could chew up the evidence and wash it down with the half glass of water that sat on the table.

Mari felt herself sink into the bed, her pillow soft beneath her head. She was safe. They all were safe. All she needed to do was slip the paper from the compact and send it down her throat. Her fingers inched toward the paper when a single thought froze her.

A trap.

What if the Major had found the list? What if her purse, delivered so promptly, was bait? What if they were waiting to see what she would do, whether she was working for the resistance or was merely an empty-headed shop girl?

Leave the list in place or slip it out?

She eased the false bottom closed—for now—and opened the compact. A tiny yelp emerged from her throat. Oh, she wouldn't need any additional color from the lipstick—she had far too much of it already, in ugly purples blooming across her cheek. Both eyes looked bruised. Her lips were uncommonly red, and she couldn't account for it. Applying makeup to a face in such condition seemed nearly as foolish as keeping that slip of paper hidden.

She closed the compact without making a sound. Then she clutched it and the lipstick against her chest. It was like keeping a vigil.

Hold very still. Be very quiet. Act the part of the shop girl, so happy to have her things back. Stay alert. Do not sleep. Above all, do not sleep.

Only when the footsteps taken with military precision stopped at the end of her bed did she realize that she had succumbed to sleep, lipstick and compact loose in her grip.

* * *

Her hand clenched around the compact. It was an instinctive move that Mari hoped the Major didn't see. His gaze darted to her clenched hand and then met her eyes. This man missed very little.

"I didn't mean to startle you, Fraulein."

"No, I . . . I merely dozed off."

"The sisters said your head injury might make you sleepy."

Did they? She supposed they had. Certainly, that wasn't a lie. And yet. The information, or perhaps the way it was phrased felt . . . dishonest. How many patients escaped interrogation due to sleepiness? Perhaps the sisters added something to the soup served earlier. Had it tasted odd? Mari blinked, trying to bring Major Messner into focus.

"I also made the mistake of looking into the mirror," she said, for it sounded like something Françoise might confess.

"The bruises will heal." He turned then, nodded at the nun attending the ward.

She rushed over with a straight-back chair and placed it next to Mari's bed.

"Thank you, Sister." He gave the perfunctory bow. So polite. So civilized. So deceptive. How could a nation of so unerringly correct individuals be so brutal as well?

The Major sat, arms resting on his thighs, hands clasped. He leaned forward. "The bruises will heal," he said again, this time his voice softer, as if the words he used might heal her face. "There won't be any lasting damage, except, perhaps to your memory."

"My memory, Major?"

"Of the accident. The doctor mentioned that head trauma can cause memory lapses, especially of the event itself."

"I remember blood—I think it was blood. It was red." Mari fingered the lipstick. "But then, so is my lipstick. And I remember hearing German, but that must have been after."

Yes, after," he echoed. "Those are . . . good details, good things to remember."

Were they? What was this man about, and what did he want from her, other than—to quote the sister—cultivate her?

"Your compact is quite intricate," he said.

"It was my mother's." A truth among all the lies. Also, something a shop girl like Françoise might not own. Or she might. With the war, one never knew, did they?

"I'm afraid my lipstick won't last, at least not until . . ."

Until what, Mari, you fool? The end of the war? Yes, the perfect topic of conversation when speaking to a German officer.

"May I?" He held out his hand.

Mari unclenched her fingers, a slow unfurling that she hoped looked more like pain than reluctance. She passed him the tube—a precious commodity, that. He inspected it with clinical detachment.

"It should last," he said. "If you're frugal."

"How frugal will I have to be, Major?"

"That depends," he said. "I am not the only official inter-ested in the train accident." His gaze flickered toward the door and the presence that shadowed the entrance. Plain clothes, not military. Gestapo then?

"You might want to use your compact, freshen up before they speak with you." He stood and turned his back as if to give her privacy for the task.

A trap or her salvation? And if she took that salvation, what was the cost? The shadows at the threshold stirred. She slipped the list from the false bottom, tore it once, twice, then shoved the pieces into her mouth. The paper was thin, like onionskin, but stuck everywhere—her molars, the roof of her mouth, against her tongue.

The sound that emerged from her throat was muted, barely a cough, but the Major handed her a glass of water. She washed away the list of codes, and he took the glass from her hand with one last bit of advice.

"Remember those good details, Fraulein."

* * *

It wasn't the first time silly Françoise had attracted the attention of the Gestapo. It was, however, the first time they asked her about one of their own.

"How well do you know Major Messner, Fraulein?"

"How . . . well?" Mari scrunched up her forehead, as if terminally confused by the man's question. His gaunt face reminded her of a cadaver. The war had not been kind to him. She guessed that peace, when it arrived, would be less kind.

Her whole body trembled. But then, she reasoned, little Françoise would also tremble if confronted by the Gestapo.

"He . . . asked me about the train accident, what I remembered. Then, he brought me my purse." She displayed the compact and the lipstick in outstretched hands almost like making an offering.

"Yes," the man said. He cast the items a disdainful look, but—opinion aside—swept them up and passed them to his partner. "We need them for our own investigation. This as well." He caught up her purse and passed that along as well.

"So, you've never met the Major before?"

"I don't meet many Germans, only those that come into the shop, and then only Monsieur Reime deals with them because . . ." She glanced away, eyes downcast.

"Because why, Fraulein?"

She shook her head. "I'm not supposed to know."

The man leaned forward. "Indeed. And why is that?"

Mari bit her lip. She cast a look at the nun who stood several feet away. In a flash of inspiration, she crossed herself. She pushed forward, and if on cue, the Gestapo agent leaned ever closer.

"*Préservatifs.*" She hid her face in her hands, peering at the men through a v in her fingers. Yes, silly Françoise barely knew what a condom was, never mind having cause to use one. "They . . . trade in *Préservatifs.*"

The man's lips twitched, ever so slightly. His partner looked away, and she had the distinct impression he was laughing.

"Of course, Fraulein," the man said. "You . . . shouldn't know of such things."

She regurgitated her good details. *I remember seeing red— like my lipstick. It's red, too. And hearing German. But that was after. You must have brought everyone here, to the hospital. That was kind of you.*

"Yes, Fraulein, we brought everyone here," the man said. He stood. "I will still need to take your things."

She nodded.

"But you have been most helpful."

She saw the look he gave his partner, a barely contained roll of the eyes for the silly French cow who had nothing on her mind but her bright red purse and lipstick.

Only when they cleared the door did she dare exhale and shut her eyes. And only when the lights were dimmed for the night did she allow herself to cry.

* * *

He was waiting for her when she left the hospital.

Mari walked the cobblestone path with care, oddly out of balance without her purse. Yes, the Gestapo had kept that, and her mother's compact, and the bright red lipstick. They were no doubt in the hands of some other silly French cow or perhaps a German one. What a prize all three items would make.

The spoils of war.

Major Messner clicked his heels and gave her that slight bow. "You look well, Fraulein. Your bruises are healing."

She touched her cheek. "Yes. They are."

"I have something for you."

What could that be? When he didn't move, she knew it was her job, as the civilian, the lesser in this relationship, to step closer. So, she did. Honestly, hadn't she taken that step already, back in the hospital?

"Your hand," he said.

She held it out. A moment later, the tube of bright red lipstick fell into her palm.

"I couldn't retrieve your purse or the compact. Beautiful item. Lovely craftsmanship. Was it really your mother's?"

"It was," she admitted.

"For that, I am sorry."

She let her fingers curl around the lipstick tube.

"I made the convincing case that I wanted to embark on my own little affair." He spoke these words not to her, but just past her shoulder, as if absorbed in the sight of the road behind her. Mari nearly turned to see what had captured his attention, but knew she'd discern nothing.

"You might say my . . . proclivities are well known." Now he looked at her. "Returning your lipstick would *clinch the deal*, as you Americans might say."

Her heart lurched. Her vision tunneled to a single bright point. She stumbled, an ankle twisting beneath her weight. He caught her arm, steadied her.

"It's all right," he whispered.

Was it? How could it be? Her mouth dry, she stared up at him, his eyes shaded by the brim of his uniform hat.

"What gave me away?" she whispered.

"Nothing you need worry about."

She exhaled a jagged rasp.

"Well, truthfully, your accent."

She'd spoken French as a toddler. Henri always said she had a charming way with words. As Marguerite, she could croon, smoky and seductive.

"You sound like her, a distinct American twang."

Had that one summer at her grandmother's—roasting beneath the relentless Savannah sun—betrayed her?

"As I said," he continued, "nothing you should worry about. I might be the only man in the Reich who would recognize such a thing."

"Her?" she ventured.

He pressed his lips together, something like a sigh escaping him. "Her name was Rachel. Her father was an American, from Texas, I believe."

That would account for the twang.

"Her mother was French." He paused, considered the road behind Mari again. "And a Jew. And Rachel?" He shut his eyes for an instant. "She was stubborn. Even so, I could have saved her."

Mari nodded, the love affair playing out before her eyes. A young German officer and a Jewess? Yes, that was destined to end badly.

"I chose not to."

"Would she see it that way?"

His laugh was short and bitter. "I suspect that, if she could, she would ask me that very same thing."

"What do you want from me?"

It was a bold question, here under the linden trees. Their leaves rattled as if they disapproved of that boldness, of the thought that had entered her head. Would she let this man, this German, this Nazi cultivate her?

Yes. Yes, she would.

"Do you pray, Fraulein?"

"Pray?"

He nodded toward the church at the end of the street. Her mother had worshiped at the altar of Diaghilev and the Ballet Russe, and then later, vodka. Her father paid homage to simile and metaphor, not that Hollywood appreciated either. Mari herself had no faith, unless it was the belief her lipstick would last until the end of the war.

"Do you want me to pray for you, Major Messner?"

"I want you to pray for a quick end to this war."

"What will you do then?"

He stared past her again, his eyes ever alert. Slight movement caught her attention. His hand. His sidearm.

"Then, I will pray for your soul," she said

"Don't waste your prayers on things that don't exist."

The rumble of an automobile caught her up short. The momentary flicker of panic in his eyes shot fear through her. A Citroën rumbled past, sleek and black, its pace slowing to a crawl, the sun glinting off the double chevrons of its grill. The Major leaned in, clutched her chin with a finger and thumb.

"You are so very much like her that I am nearly tempted," he said a moment before he kissed her.

The car sped up.

In the quiet, he released her. He nodded once, bowed, and Mari took uncertain steps down the lane and toward the church. Her heels clicked, the leaves rattled, and the far off sound of a car backfiring—or of a gunshot—echoed.

The church was cool and dark. Mari covered her head, crossed herself, and collapsed into a pew. She stayed for hours. She thought he might come for her.

He didn't.

The weight of something, his soul perhaps, drove her to her knees. She knelt, forehead on clasped hands, and prayed to the saint of bright red things—of lipstick and handbags and filigrees of blood in cracked windows. It was far easier than praying for those things that didn't exist—a French shop girl named Françoise, a Jewess named Rachel, a German officer named Major Messner.

And a lone American named Marigold Jenkins.

FIRST DAY AT AN KHE

by Monty Joynes, 5000 words

First Day at An Khe *won the national military writing award when it was first published in Proud to Be: Writing by American Warriors (Vol. 1) — Southeast Missouri State University (Nov. 2012). According to judge William Trent Pancoast, it is "an odyssey of a medic's first days in Viet Nam: Phil Warren, working to exhaustion in triage in the biggest fire fight the base hospital has had to deal with thus far in the war. He was put on duty by the First Sergeant, and never logged in, never relieved in triage for over two and a half days because no one even knew he was there. The story builds tremendous momentum, and in the course of the odyssey, the author compacts the elements of a tour of duty into Phil's triage experience—battle, religion, life, death, comradeship, service, courage, compassion, anger, duty, humor, and the loss of self. This is a fine story and I thank the author for the experience of reading it."*

Monty Joynes is the author of 22 published books that include his five novels in the Booker Series, two making-of-the-movie books, and two biographies including For Love and Treasure: The Life and Times of the World's Most Successful Treasure Hunting Family (July, 2015). He is a national award-winning author for his military combat fiction, and he is the librettist for an oratorio that premiered in France in 2015. Monty and his editor wife Pat live in the Blue Ridge Mountains of North Carolina in the USA.

T he 270-mile flight to An Khe in the rolling coastal plains was hot on the crowded Air Force C-130. Phil and the other replacements assigned to the flight found seats around the cargo that was lashed down in the huge plane's bay. There was no way to see the country below, so Phil leaned against his duffel bag and tried not to think of what he might do if the aircraft took hits from ground fire. In the thirty hours that Phil had waited for his hop to the 1st Cav base, he had seen the lightning of shellfire around the Saigon airbase.

When the ramp opened, Phil and the others filed off into a hot, dusty afternoon. The heat and humidity were exceeded only by the dust clouds kicked up by the helicopters. Phil had never seen so much helicopter activity. The sound of them was everywhere. He was used to the Hueys used for medivacs, but the Cav had huge Chinooks, and Cranes, and gun ships of every description.

A sergeant was yelling at him. "Get your gear on that truck, goddamn it! Let's clear this area."

The truck made two stops in a tent city that seemed to cover acres of the landscape before Phil's turn came. Two other replacements got off at Phil's stop; one was a medical records specialist, and the other was a cook. The pyramidal orderly tent had a dirt floor and a makeshift arrangement of field desks, typewriter tables, filing cabinets, and chairs. The lights were bare bulbs strung from the roof poles. The only reassuring color in the room was the red glow of the light on a coffee urn sitting atop an artillery shell crate.

"I guess you're the replacements," a clerk said to them. "You've arrived at a hell of a moment. I don't have time to process you in right now. Find a seat and stay out of the way."

"What's going on?"

"The Division is in a hell of a firefight up country. We're taking mass cals, and the hospital is pure chaos."

The new men, out of place in their class-A uniforms, looked at each other and then found seats in the hot orderly room tent.

Suddenly, a large man rushed into the tent. Phil recognized the abundance of stripes on his sleeve and guessed that he was the First Sergeant of the Hospital Company.

"Who are these people?" he demanded from his clerks.

"They're replacements, First Sergeant. Just got in. I haven't even had time to look at their orders."

"Any medics? Is either one of you a medic? I need a medic."

"I'm a corpsman, Sergeant," Phil admitted.

"Good. You're coming with me."

Then, he turned to the clerks. "We need medics, and we need blood. Get me some volunteers. You can start with these two. March them down to the hospital as soon as you can."

Phil could smell the carnage before he could see it. The First Sergeant trotted ahead of him, leading them through a maze of tents. Phil recognized medivac choppers landing above the tents just ahead, and then they rounded a large hospital tent, and Phil saw the triage. Doctors and medics worked among the wounded on the ground while litter carriers shuffled the bodies in and out of the confusion. Everyone except the wounded seemed to be yelling. The closer Phil got, the more horrible details came into focus. The First Sergeant gripped him roughly by the arm when he stopped in awe of the scene.

"This is what you're here for, goddamn it. Now, shake it off. You've got to go to work."

Phil was handed over to a master sergeant who was too busy to do anything but push him toward a doctor who had just risen from a litter.

"Here's some more help, sir."

There were no introductions. Someone passed Phil and pushed a canvas bag of supplies into his chest. He knelt beside the doctor and, for the first time, got the full view of a traumatic casualty. The soldier on the litter was missing his right leg below the knee. Fragments of white bone could be seen protruding from the pulpy mass of bloody flesh at the stump.

"Give him 75 milligrams of Demerol. I need a fresh pressure bandage and something to elevate the leg. Get me an IV started."

Phil found the Demerol in the supply bag. Fortunately, as he looked up from preparing the injection, he saw an IV team, and he, too, became part of the clamor.

"IV! IV! Over here."

Phil cut the sleeve off the private's uniform and hesitated before plunging the needle into the arm. The doctor had found the pressure bandage and was tying it off around the wound. Phil was surprised at how little blood was actually oozing from the stump. He used the soldier's pistol belt with its two canteens still attached as a wedge to raise the limb.

"Get him to surgery," the doctor said as he moved to the next litter.

Phil rose to one knee and searched for a litter team.

"Litter! Litter!" he shouted to no one specifically.

A bloody hand gripped his shirt. Phil jerked away in fright. Then, his eyes followed the arm until he saw the patient's face for the first time. The face was filthy with dust and streaks of blood that had been transferred from the bloody hands. His eyes were dazed in shock and from the morphine he had received in the field.

"I know it's gone. They couldn't even find my boot. It was a mortar. They got a lot of us, didn't they? Those goddamn Charlies."

Phil tried to remember what he had been taught to say to a patient in shock. What were some of the reassuring phrases they learned at Fort Sam?

"Litter! Litter!" was all that came to his lips.

"Did PJ make it?" the bloody hand asked.

"PJ?" Phil said absently.

"My buddy. PJ. He got hit, too. I'm going to make it. I sure hope PJ makes it. I'm going to make it, ain't I?"

"Sure you're going to make it. I'm going to get you a ride here in a minute. Litter! Litter! And you're going to be fine."

A litter team finally responded to Phil's frantic waving and carried the infantry private to the surgery.

Phil lost track of his doctor but saw another calling for a corpsman. He picked up his supply bag and stepped between the bodies to reach the doctor's side.

"Get me a cut down set and some fluids."

Phil saw the doctor holding the remains of a hand. The fingers were gnarled and charred a dry, lamp black. Twisted bones and flesh, torn by some cataclysmic event, communicated a sudden queasiness to his stomach. He was glad to run for the nearest IV team to collect the needed supplies.

While the doctor worked to start the IV, he told Phil to look for other wounds. There were tears in the pants, and as he cut away the cloth, he revealed many small, but nasty wounds. The pieces of shrapnel were still visible in punctures and lacerations. Phil found others above the waist.

"That's debridement room stuff. Don't worry about that now. Mark him for surgery, first on the hand."

Phil noted four fat black bulges on the exposed leg and brought them to the doctor's attention.

"Are these hematomas, sir?"

"Hematomas? For Christ sake, how long have you been around here? Those are goddamn leeches."

The stench of the wounded made Phil nauseated, as if the sights he had already seen inches away from his face were not enough to induce vomiting. An odor he came to identify as the smell of burned flesh was a new, piercing sensation. It was mixed with the more familiar emanations of human sweat, urine, and feces.

Phil did not know where to focus his vision when he was not giving a shot, holding up an IV bottle, or updating a medivac tag. The only thing he dreaded more than facing the wounds was looking into the faces of the wounded. He was afraid of what they might see on his face. He was initially so sick to his stomach that he could hardly walk. Then, an ambulatory trooper with a bullet wound in the shoulder vomited on him as he helped the doctor make an examination. Phil turned as if he had been shot, fell to his knees, and retched until his stomach had nothing else to offer up. No one other than the wounded trooper seemed to notice.

"I'm sorry," he said to Phil as the medic regained his composure.

"I'm sorry, too," Phil said, still shaking involuntarily from his protesting abdominal muscles. "This is my first day."

"I wondered why you were in your class-A's."

"Yeah. Well, I think I'll burn these tomorrow. Can I have some of your water?"

The trooper used his good arm to offer Phil his canteen. The water was hot, but Phil welcomed it to rinse his mouth of the foul bile taste. He looked up to see the young staff sergeant nodding at him.

"Go ahead, drink your fill. I'll get some more. The doc said you would show me to the debriding room, or something. I guess they've got to probe for whatever hit me. I hope that morphine I got in the field lasts until they finish."

For a second, standing amid the dying and the maimed, they exchanged a smile and soon parted, never knowing each other's name.

Phil continued to be intimidated by each new patient although he was giving shots without hesitation, directing cases from the triage to other areas of the hospital, and putting his hands on the supplies the doctors called for. As soon as he had carried out the doctor's orders on a patient, and had seen him dispatched to surgery or another service, he would respond to the nearest doctor and help with a new case. The doctors did not wait for Phil to finish before they moved to another body. Phil knew that *they* had the harder job. They had to make the decisions about who went to surgery first. The assignment in triage was to save lives by rapid diagnosis and by-the-book screening. Wounded who could be saved by immediate surgery went first. Cases that required surgery, but were not life threatened by waiting, were given a lower priority. Pain was not a factor.

Phil's uniform lost all identity when viewed from the front. It could have been any color or hidden any rank. There was no part of it left unstained by blood or worse. Phil's hands were dark and sticky with clotted blood. He still put his dirty hands over raw wounds to stop the outpouring of blood that sometimes happened when the doctor probed a wound or removed a pressure dressing.

There was no way that his training at Fort Sam, or his ward experiences at Fort Dix, could have prepared him for mass casualties and the horror of the triage. Phil wanted to scream. His head was splitting in a sharp blade of pain that dominated the space above his eyes. His mouth tasted like a field shithouse. He was sure that he had already had the runs in his pants. He still fought off waves of nausea. Just when he thought that his nose had had its olfactory senses blocked out by the constant assault of stench, a new threshold would be established with another piercing, ugly aroma.

If he had been able to scrape the crystal on his watch, he would have been aware that he had worked over fifteen hours, throughout the night, and still the helicopters landed and disgorged the dead, the dying, and the disfigured. Already, he hated the sound of them. The *wop-wop-wopping* of their blades, and the dust and sand whirlwinds associated with their landing.

He was weak from hunger and thirst, but he felt he could never eat again until he was clean of the gore on his body. His hair and brows were matted with it. His three-day beard captured it and bound it to his face.

He found a moment to rest, and someone handed him a paper cup full of steaming coffee. It was late morning. Already 90 degrees. There were flies everywhere. He sat in the dirt and leaned against a tent pole. In spite of his tense stomach, he began to drink the coffee. Ants and unnamed insect creatures crawled across his outstretched legs and paused to feast off the products of war. Phil did not even attempt to brush them away. He wondered if he himself was going into shock. Sometime last night, he shot 50 milligrams of Thorazine into the arm of a hysterical young rifleman. Phil considered giving himself a similar shot.

The next hours were more of the same organized chaos. Phil saw many of the same types of wounds over and over. He began to anticipate what the doctors needed, and they worked better as a team.

Phil saw many sucking chest wounds where a shell had penetrated a man's chest cavity, causing the lung to collapse. The entry and exit wounds had to be sealed with a Vaseline gauze dressing. The sound of the air being sucked through the wound made a whistling sound. Frothy blood sputtered from the ragged holes. Phil assisted in the placing of a Kelly clamp on several cases. The fact that most of the patients were conscious—and even talkative—during the procedure made him wince every time the probe ripped through the chest-cavity membrane with a pop, and blood shot out its top. The Kelly clamp provided chest drainage so that the patient would not drown in his own fluids. It was held in place with a few quick sutures, and a drainage tube was attached.

Phil learned rapidly the significance of fixed dilated pupils. He saw the remains of boys who looked more like a bundle of rags than mortals. He got angry when he saw them being brought into the triage on the canvas litters.

"Don't put that down there," he finally shouted at a litter team just about to lower the stump of a body. It had no arms or legs visible.

"Fuck you," said the young private who was obviously a Cav rifleman. "Everybody that comes off those choppers is going to see a doctor. We ain't taking no wounded straight to Graves. Do you understand me? I'll get my fucking M-16 if I have to."

"Hey, easy, man. We're not fucking over anybody. We're on your side," Phil reassured him.

"You a doctor?"

"No. I'm a corpsman."

"Well, do something then. At least see if he's alive, for God's sake." the nervous soldier said, his voice trembling.

Phil did not want to face the pitiful remains of the man at his feet, but he realized that he could not run from the confrontation with the litter bearer. As he started to his knees, he caught sight of a metallic cross hanging around the belligerent soldier's neck. The man had been constantly fingering it since he had put the body down.

Phil searched for the remnants of the victim's head and placed his hand on what had been the neck. There was no pulsation. The medivac tag said KIA, initials scrawled on the form by a medic far away in the elephant grass of the highlands. Phil paused, head down, still on his knees, wondering how he was going to console them. He straightened his back and made the sign of the cross. He was not a Catholic, and he hoped that he had gotten the directions of the sign in the right order. Then, he looked up into the faces of the infantrymen.

"I'm sorry, he's gone."

The one with the neck chain crossed himself devoutly.

"Shit," he said in dejection, "I knew he was dead. But it just ain't right to rush him over to Graves without somebody doing something. He was a man. Maybe he was a Catholic, like us. A priest, somebody, ought to say something. Anything."

"I can't stay here, guys. I've got to help the doctors. Why don't you say a "Hail Mary" while you're taking him over to Graves. I'll say one as soon as I can."

The two litter carriers picked up their load and began the "Hail Mary" as they walked away. Phil saw a doctor beckon to him, and as he moved, he tried to remember the Catholic prayer without success. Maybe it was the wrong prayer anyway. Wasn't there a prayer, a special prayer, that Catholics say at the time of their death? Phil was raised a Baptist; how should he know? But he felt no pride in having deceived the litter bearers. For one of the few times in the last mad hours, he had actually given comfort to another human being. Comfort that was not dispensed from the tip of a syringe. He wished he could give himself the comfort of religion. A religion that could explain the waste and slaughter of humanity.

Sometime during that night, Phil fainted from extreme fatigue. He was not the first to falter because of the long hours without rest or relief. Some 20 hours before Phil collapsed, the hospital Sergeant Major had established 15-hour shifts for enlisted hospital personnel. But since Phil's name was not on the Sergeant Major's duty roster, he was never relieved. A few doctors and medics knew Phil's face from the two and a half days he had been in the triage, but no one knew his name or claimed responsibility for him.

The First Sergeant had forgotten about Phil, and as far as the orderly room was concerned, he was AWOL.

Phil woke on a canvas litter suspended by its wooden poles between two crates of medical supplies. He had been put out of harm's way in a supply tent and forgotten again. As his sensibilities recovered from their somnambulistic flight, he became acutely aware of the outrageous stench of his own body and uniform. A close second to this indignity was the parched ugliness inside his mouth. His entire frame ached, and it was with balancing difficulty that he managed to free himself from the litter without falling face down on the dirt floor.

Phil did not recognize his whereabouts nor did he remember how he came to be there. His last recollection was calling for an IV team. He was dazed as if drunk. He stumbled toward the tent flap and the sound of a driving rain making pools beyond the door.

Outside, he found himself behind the main hospital. Whoever stacked him in the supply tent had had a long carry. The rain was refreshing. Phil suddenly had the urge to rid his body of its filth. He could not find his shirt buttons under the hardened globs of blood and muck so in desperation he ripped the garment away from his chest and flung it away from his body. He walked a few yards away from the shirt and plopped down in the mud like a drunk. His shoelaces were caked in dried blood so he kicked at the heels until they were forced off his feet. Next came the socks and the khaki pants. He flung them away. He used mud by the handfuls as an abrasive to wash away the clotted black blood from his hands and arms. The process was a slow one, but finally he saw his own flesh appearing from under its ghoulish covering. He mud scrubbed his face and neck and then lay back on the ground to let the rainwater fill his gaping mouth. He lay soaking, rinsing in the heavy monsoon rain until he was no longer thirsty.

His formerly white-boxer, army-issue shorts were blood stained around the waistband. The seat contained the results of Phil's diarrhea. Two days' worth. He peeled the repugnant garment away from his backside—and was going to cast it away—but reconsidered. He turned them inside out and washed them in the nearest mud hole. By the time he finished scrubbing the cloth against itself and the gritty mud, the stains of blood and diarrhea looked alike. Malevolent brown. He held the pants in front of him to rinse in the rain and then put them on to cover his nakedness.

If anyone observed Phil during his antics in the rain, they never reported it or mentioned it to him.

Phil searched for the nearest army authority. He was disoriented but heard voices from a tent and found an NCO.

"I'm reporting back to duty," he said to the astounded sergeant as he walked into the tent out of the rain.

The sergeant paused, seeking a reference in his mind, and then said in carefully measured, almost melodic tones, "That's fine, son. I think I know where you belong. Wait a minute, and I'll take you over there myself."

Phil nodded. The sergeant found his poncho and turned the ward tent over to a medic who had been smiling unnaturally at Phil since his arrival.

Phil followed the sergeant through a maze of large, dark tents until the NCO opened the door flap of one and ushered him inside.

"Somebody's ass is going to be in a sling," the sergeant said to the Psychiatric Ward attendant who greeted them. "I just found one of your patients wandering around the area."

It took little explaining and a bed check of the Psych patients to convince two sergeants that Phil was newly assigned to the hospital company.

"All my gear is still at the orderly room. I haven't even signed in yet," Phil reminded them.

"Your ass is in a world of shit, trooper," said one sergeant.

"I told you, I've been in the triage ever since I got here. The First Shirt put me to work over there and then never came back. I was never relieved. Is the battle still going on?"

The rain had stopped the major combat assaults by the First Cav. Helicopters don't fly well in heavy rains. So things were caught up in triage, and the hospital was in a state of exhaustion. Those still on duty prayed for continuing rain so they could get their turns at sleep.

They gave Phil directions to the orderly room; and before he departed the Psych Ward, one of the sergeants said with a leer, "The First Shirt is going to love this."

On his way to the orderly room, Phil wanted to avoid being seen out of uniform. Staying off the main streets of the hospital area, which had become soupy mud flats, Phil picked his way over tent ropes and around tent pegs toward his destination. Behind one of the tents he discovered a pile of cast-off field gear. From the damaged condition of the webbing, pistol belts, canteens, ammo pouches, and packs, he guessed that the equipment had accumulated from the battle casualties.

Seeing no on-lookers, Phil began to pick among the packs in search of food. There were many cans of C-rations undamaged. Phil may not have known the location of the mess tent, but he was not going to be hungry any longer. The tiny metal can opener with its collapsible blade opened first a can of peaches and then a can of soda crackers. Phil found peaches in three different packs. The First Cav must sure like peaches, he thought, as he found a comfortable backrest amid the discarded equipment.

Phil did not feel ridiculous sitting in his underwear, eating three cans of peaches in the rain. The peaches were sweet, with just a hint of pucker. He drank the heavy syrup, and it changed the vile taste in his mouth to nectar. He forgot with the pleasure in his mouth that the men who had carried the peaches were probably dead.

When Phil appeared in the orderly room tent, the First Sergeant was startled enough by the sight to spill his coffee.

"Who the hell are you?" he demanded, after inspecting Phil at close range.

"I'm Warren, the new replacement."

"Well, Warren, the new replacement, you sure as hell need a shave, and you are definitely out of uniform."

"He's AWOL, too, Sarge," one of the clerks said.

"I am not AWOL, either," Phil shot back. "Don't you remember me? The day I arrived, you dragged me over to triage."

"Don't point your finger at me, boy," the Sergeant replied. "Is this your gear over here?"

Phil saw his duffel bag and service cap in a corner of the tent. "It looks like it."

"Well, where the hell have you been, Warren? And where is your goddamn uniform?"

Phil erupted.

"It's so fucking covered with blood, and brains, and shit, real human shit from gut wounds, and vomit, and sweat . . . it's so fucking foul that I couldn't stand to wear it! You left me in that Godforsaken triage until I dropped, Sergeant. I don't even know what day of the week it is! I'm no fucking trainee. I'm a goddamn medic, and I've been proving it over, and over, and over again on your mass casualties. Where in the fuck were you when I was up to my ass in other people's blood and guts? Your uniform looks too fucking clean to me. You want to see my uniform? You want to smell it? I'll get the goddamn thing for you if you're so concerned about my uniform." Phil turned and started walking for the door.

"Wait a minute. Calm down. Wait a minute, goddamn it!"

Phil stopped and turned at the doorway. The First Sergeant's voice softened.

"I remember something now. I guess I did put you into the triage." The Sergeant paused. "I guess I forgot about you, too. Come over here and sit down—please."

Phil went limp again after the injection of anger that had caused him to stiffen. He limped across the tent floor and dropped into a metal folding chair that the sergeant offered.

"Have you had any chow?" the NCO asked.

"I don't even know where the mess tent is," Phil answered without looking up.

"Look, Warren," the Sergeant said quietly bending over him, "we just fought the biggest battle of the war, and we took a lot of casualties. No one was prepared for it. Things got a little crazy around here. You got the shaft. I'm sorry."

Phil continued to slump in his chair and remained silent. He seemed to have no more energy to move or to speak.

The Sergeant ordered his clerks to assign Phil a bed in one of the enlisted hooches and to find him some food. Then he poured the near-naked Private First Class a cup of coffee.

"The hospital CO wants to put all the men who worked the triage up for the Army Commendation Medal," the top kick said as he handed Phil the coffee mug. "You might get yourself a decoration on your first day here."

"Can't do it, Top," the remaining clerk in the tent said. "According to the Morning Report, Warren was not a member of the unit during the Plei Me action. We've been carrying him AWOL for the last three days."

"Shut up Dozier, will you?" the First Sergeant snarled over his shoulder.

"We'll pick him up on the Morning Report tomorrow, Sarge. But until then, he's not officially here, so he can't qualify for any . . ."

The Sergeant interrupted his studious company clerk who was cleaning his government-issued, brown-framed glasses over the keys of his typewriter. "Didn't I tell you to cut it off?"

Then to Phil he said, "Warren, I want you to take the rest of the day off. Take your time getting settled and report back here tomorrow after midday chow. Why don't you get into your gear there and find yourself a pair of fatigues. The company commander might wander in here, and we'd have a lot of explaining to do. Aren't you a little chilly? Being wet, and all. Wouldn't you feel better in your uniform?"

One of the clerks returned out of the rain with a small box in his hands.

"The cooks wouldn't give me any A-rations until chow call, Top, but I got a box of C's."

The Sergeant opened the box, examined the labels on the cans, and selected one to open.

"You're in luck, Warren," he said as he opened the can. "Here's the best thing they ever put into a C-ration carton. One of these in the field will get you three or four of anything else. I know this is going to taste real good to you about now."

He handed the open can to Phil. "They're peaches, son. Sliced peaches. Go ahead. You can drink them right out of the can."

ZUMP

by Beth Patterson, 6,000 words

Fiona recounts her adventures in helping to raise her best friend's unruly, young, gifted child, who has a strong sense of social justice but not social mores. The six-year-old Hannah creates havoc on the playground with a fabricated obscenity, and in the process, uncovers a man's plans to illegally dump oil.

Beth W. Patterson was a full-time musician for over two decades before diving into the world of writing, a process she describes as "fleeing the circus to join the zoo." She is the author of the books Mongrels and Misfits and The Wild Harmonic, and she is a contributing writer to seventeen anthologies. Patterson has performed in seventeen countries across the Americas, Europe, Oceania, and Asia. Her playing appears on over a hundred and forty albums, soundtracks, videos, commercials, and voice-overs (including seven solo albums of her own). More than a hundred of her compositions and co-writes have been released. She studied ethnomusicology at University College, Cork in Ireland and holds a Bachelor's degree in Music Therapy from Loyola University, New Orleans. Beth has occasionally worn other hats as a body paint model, film extra, minor role actor, recording studio partner, record label owner, producer, and visual artist. She is a lover of exquisitely stupid movies and a shameless fangirl of the band Rush. You can find her at www.bethpattersonmusic.com.

The jarring burst of funky slap bass on my nightstand is a tiny apocalyptic herald of doom. I should never have set my ringtones to songs I love. Now, I associate the Brothers Johnson's masterpiece "Funkadelala" with a state of emergency. I'm just glad I had the foresight to make mental notes of this, or else Stanley Clarke and Bootsy Collins would likewise make me grit my teeth. I don't have to be at the theater until five p.m., and I was hoping to have a good nap for once.

Tonya's voice has that pinched, over pleasant tone she usually assumes when she's secretly panicking.

"Good afternoon, Fiona. This is just so wonderfully tragic. It's a beautiful Monday, and I've been summoned to the office of Crack This Guy Drainage Solutions. There's also a special agent from the Environmental Protection Agency's Criminal Investigation Division here. Everyone's having conniptions because of something my six-year-old child did at school. You need to tell them everything you can remember about picking Hannah up at the playground on Friday. *Now.*"

Tonya is my best friend. She is also a ruthless lawyer and almost never gets rattled.

"Wha—?" I begin.

"They're listening to me tell you this. Just get over here. Can you bring some aspirin—*no!*" Slightly off the receiver, Tonya snaps, "With all due respect, that is *not* some sort of code word for whatever you people think a theatrical scenic designer might be in possession of." The line goes dead.

I roll out of bed, rummage for some decent clothes, and tell my husband, "Looks like there won't be any scenery painting today for me. Our scapegrace niece is at it again."

* * *

Driving to my best friend's house, I desperately try to guess what little Hannah is up to. I've been so accustomed to having a gifted child in my life that absurd is the new norm. She's not my biological niece, but Tonya is as close to a sister as I'll ever have.

Last week's trip to the zoo should have clued me in that a little girl on any extreme side of the bell curve is going to be extremely high maintenance. Now that I think about it, I'm sure it was bizarre for the average bystander to see a six-year-old point at a zebra in its pen and exclaim, "Look! It's made in China!" Even stranger still was that I had to explain she had a plush zebra at home named Made in China. Hannah thought what was printed on the attached tag was the name assigned to it by the toy factory. And yeah, that she was so young and read everything she saw.

We looked like an odd trio anyway: a white woman, a Hispanic man, and a black child. My husband Javier and I never cared much about what people thought of us—we wouldn't have chosen our line of work if we had. Still, when it came to the feelings of the girl we called our niece, we were a bit more sensitive. People's gazes lingered on us a bit too long, and when we caught them staring—as we always did—they would pretend to be admiring young Hannah's beauty.

Normally, she wore her hair parted down the middle and split into two pom-poms, but for a trip to the zoo, she wanted to sport a proud Afro because she said it made her resemble a lion. That particular day, she looked like a '70s retro angel complete with a bellbottom jumpsuit, compliments of our costume designer, Artie, who was another avuncular figure to her at the theater—albeit a bit more fabulous.

Thankfully, she was oblivious to her own cuteness, but she had the hearing of a bat and didn't miss a thing. And the more surreptitious the comments were, the more keenly she homed in on them.

That fateful day some clueless person rattled off the query I hate the most. "Is she adopted?" is one of those sticky-sweet questions that can mean anything from "aren't you a do-gooder?" to "did you kidnap this child, you perv?"

The inquisitor, with matching rouge and lipstick the color of silk roses left on a sun-bleached grave for far too long, batted her tarantula eyelashes. The supercilious smile plastered on her face was what I found the most offensive of all.

Luckily, we didn't have to say a word. Hannah had this covered. She seemed to have picked up quite a few tricks in recreational theatrics by hanging around so many people in the theater business—especially Javier and me. Which is why she never, ever missed an opportunity to create a scene, and we loved her all the more for it.

She tilted her little head, enormous liquid black eyes wide as if processing some new information. Assiduously studying the backs of her hands, she held them up to my own for comparison before suddenly shrieking, "Mommy, you didn't tell me you were *white!*" The poor hapless busybody backed away slowly like one would from a snarling dog, trying to melt back into the crowd. "You've probably passed on bad genes. I won't be able to dance."

"Sir?" someone asked my husband. "Don't you think you and your wife should have discussed this sooner?"

Javier tried to intervene, but he was laughing too hard.

* * *

Three days ago, my special ringtone for Mrs. Babineaux, the school principal, ambushed me. I was smack in the middle of painting a giant sewer grate for the theater's next show, and Alice Cooper's "School's Out" jingling on my phone sent my pulse racing. Splashed with hues of gray, green and brown, I groaned. Hannah stirring up mayhem meant that I had to drop everything.

As a single mom and a top-notch attorney, Tonya had to work so hard that I was designated as the secondary guardian who had to pick Hannah up from school whenever she got in trouble—which was about once a week. It wasn't Hannah's fault, really. At age six and already placed with the second graders, she was still bored in class, but the school felt that higher placement might cause social maladjustment. I'm pretty certain that they were talking about Hannah's sake, but it was her poor little classmates who were having quite a shock.

Hannah once told me in confidence that she did not want to be placed any higher than the second grade because she did not want to risk the temptation of dating boys too far out of her age group. I didn't know how to respond to that, but it worried me. Say what you will about the delinquent courtship displays in adults, but nothing is quite so warped as male competition to impress females by outdoing each other on how many crayons they can insert into their noses.

"What did she do this time?" I asked by way of greeting. Last week, she and her teacher, Mr. Landry, verbally duked it out in front of the class because the poor bastard was trying to refresh the children's minds in basic geometry: triangle, circle, square, and rectangle. And that's when my little, gifted niece decided to set him straight by pointing out that all squares are rectangles. When this hapless didact made the grave error of attempting to correct her, she gave him the definition of a rectangle: a quadrilateral in which the angles are equal. I'm sure he wouldn't have called for backup if her tone had been a little less condescending when she said, "All squares are rectangles, but not all rectangles are *squares*."

The week before would have been uneventful if no one had investigated her free-drawing project. She had, at least, been quietly seated, bothering no one. Yet, I really think she could have at least drawn a cute little duck or something, and waited until she got home to her private stash of crayons and paper to depict Perseus carrying the severed head of Santa Claus. I would be a hypocrite to advocate curbing artistic inspiration whenever it strikes. Still, some of the other children were deeply disturbed.

Mrs. Babineaux's beleaguered voice brought me back to the present. "She was caught swearing on the playground."

"*What?*" I was incredulous. For all that, this micro village consisting of Tonya, Javier, and me was doing its darnedest to raise a gifted child. One thing that we have tried to instill in Hannah is to hold a civil tongue.

The principal's ensuing sigh was so sustained that I decided to just find out when I got there.

"I'll be right over," I told her and hung up.

* * *

It was still recess when I arrived on the school grounds. The L-shaped territory of the playground flanked half the building like a ragtag moat. It was separated into two sections with appropriate equipment for each age group: swings and monkey bars for the older kids in one half, and plastic blobs of modern art for the younger children to climb on. Smack at the crossroads, where diabolical bargains tend to be struck, was the drainage ditch, where a jar-headed boy was looking triumphantly bewildered at a retreating man in dirty coveralls.

I knew this punk-ass kid. Little Stevie Capello was a notorious bully. Someone caught him trying to throw a puppy off a bridge the previous month, and whether it was taunting the smaller kids or putting boogers on the backs of girls, his antics had won him a number of ruffian followers.

The children were shouting something I couldn't quite discern. When one individual cherub broke loose from the pack and drew near, I made out that the word was "zump." Some of the kids were screaming it in each other's faces, while others were chanting it like a protest.

"The kids are out of control with what they believe is an obscenity," Miss Verzwyvelt, the teacher on duty, said in a stern voice. "They were even taunting a contractor who seemed to have failed to repair the drainage ditch before recess. He said he was there to pour some sewage treatment in the pipes. He was just leaving the premises when all hell broke loose, but got sidetracked when he had to answer his phone. So, he grabbed his empty barrel, threw it on a dolly, and stormed off in the direction of his truck. Poor guy. His livelihood interrupted by a bunch of little *monsters*. Now, they're all yelling *zump*. Is this some ancient curse from your Irish heritage or something?"

"It isn't a real word!" I snapped back, hoping I was right.

"Well, it doesn't even matter that it isn't a real word." Miss Verzwyvelt spluttered. "All that matters is that they all think it's inappropriate, and they are defying protocol. And guess who the little ringleader is?" She pointed her finger like a sword at my niece, who was looking especially innocent today in a pretty yellow dress. "She told little Stevie Capello that it was the absolute worst word you could say."

"So, have the principal call *his* mom. *He's* the one with the notorious potty mouth!" I'd heard that kid's recreational rantings when I'd picked up Hannah after school, and he always sounded like munchkin-sized Yosemite Sam with Tourette's Syndrome.

"Hannah knew exactly what she was doing. I was keeping my eyes on a game of tag, but I heard the whole exchange. She said, 'Have you heard about the *new curse word* everyone has been saying? It's *so bad*, you can't even spell it! You can't even know the first letter.' I have to hand it to her though, that's probably the first time little Stevie has ever said 'please' in his whole life. So, she drew it out for several minutes, giving him one letter of this taboo neologism at a time. And she put on such a good act that the other kids are convinced of a scandal. Mrs. Babineaux wants her removed, if for no other reason than she is an instigator, and her mere presence is an aggravation."

The silence was awkward, yet altogether too familiar, as we walked together through the parking lot.

"Get that thumb out of your mouth," I ordered her.

"Would you prefer that I took up smoking instead?" was her rhetorical parry.

"Okay, fine," I acquiesced. "But don't let your mom see you doing that. She's already feeling guilty because she works so much, and she's afraid that you aren't getting enough affection."

"I already have all the affection that I could *ever* want, Aunt Fiona."

"Nice try, kid. What do you want?"

"A jellybean."

"No way. There's too much sugar."

"Some peanut butter crackers then."

I sighed, fishing around in my purse. Two people with whom you should never negotiate are a terrorist and a six-year-old.

"Why does everyone think I'm adopted?" she asked at last. "Is it because I'm black and you're white?"

"No. It's because I'm blonde and you're so damned smart."

"Dammed? Like stymied?"

Damn indeed. Here I was trying to raise her not to use strong words, and I just let one fly myself, even if it was pretty innocuous compared to what most kids say these days.

"Okay, look, I guess if you're going to swear, you might as well do it right. Here's the difference between the two words . . ."

Hannah took some notice of my careful lesson.

"Now," I said, finally having won her undivided attention. "What's going on with this *zump* bit?"

"I made it up. This morning Stevie pushed a kindergarten girl into the dirt when the teachers weren't looking, and I wanted to see him get taken down for good. As soon as he realizes that not only doesn't he know all the bad words, but that a younger girl tricked him, he's going to be plenty mad. And all the other kids are gonna know it."

So, I had on my hands a gifted *enfant terrible* with a heart of gold. *At least her mother is going to know what to do with this child.*

* * *

"What are we going to *do* with this child?" Tonya asked, sprawled out on her living room couch. After this harrowing day—me with Hannah, and Tonya with a murder trial that had gone on for far too long—we'd decided to splurge and split a bottle of red. Argentinian Malbecs are her favorite. I'd been saving a special blend of Malbec, Syrah, Pinot Noir, and Grenache for an emergency such as this.

"I'm just tired," my best friend sighed, burying her face in her hands. "People make assumptions about me because I'm a black, single mom—"

I cut her off, lowering my voice to a murmur. "Anyone whose opinions are worth a shit knows that Gary—your lawfully wedded late *husband*—was a brilliant physicist. And he spoke six languages to boot."

Her laugh was mirthless. "His genius mind didn't do him a damned bit of good when he got hit by that bus because he forgot to look both ways."

"I'm fairly certain he just looked the wrong way first," I said. "He'd just gotten back from Japan, and people drive on the left side of the road there."

"We'll never know. Ah, my genius absent-minded late hubby. His absence still hurts so much. I see his subversive wit in my little girl every day." Her eyes were so wistful; I felt a lump thickening in my throat, as it often did when she spoke of Gary. I missed him too.

"He would have been so proud of her."

"He would have been scared to *death*," she corrected me. "Do you think he would have known what to do with a little carbon copy of himself, wrapped up in an adorable little package of sugar and spice and everything nice? *Damn.*"

"Mommy, you said a bad word." Hannah piped from the next room.

"How did she learn that?" Tonya asked me.

I took a guilty sip of my wine.

Saved by the almighty God of Subject Changers, the headlights of Javier's car illuminated the living room window like a very slow *aha!* moment. At the slam of the car door, Hannah came running out to greet him.

"Uncle Javier," she shrieked. For our niece's benefit, he usually remains in whatever costume his role requires when he drops in after rehearsal.

She studied his getup with a critical eye. "You look like George Washington."

"You're about a century off, baby."

"Battle of New Orleans?"

"Ooh, so very close. Wrong country, though. I don't think you're familiar with this musical. It's called *Les Misérables*."

"Aunt Fiona played some of the soundtrack for me." She launched into a song that sounded like the chorus of "Red and Black," lyrically superseded by "Doe, a Deer." Javier took advantage of the precious moment of freedom to stride over, hug Tonya, and plant a kiss on top of my head.

"Uncle Javier, are you and Aunt Fiona going to have an anchor baby?" Hannah chimed back in.

"A *what*?" We three adults gasped in unison at our tiny ringleader's cue.

"I overheard these ladies at the zoo talking. You know how grownups always stare at us when we all go out together? Well, this one lady was looking back and forth between Uncle Javier and Aunt Fiona, and she said, 'He probably just wants to have an anchor baby so he can stay in the country.' I think it would be so *awesome* to have a baby that breaks the news on TV!"

At the sight of my husband and my best friend with their mouths flopped open like fish that have just been forced to read the tabloids, I made a herculean effort to close my own jaw with a mighty click.

"Of course, a baby wouldn't be able to talk. Its brain would still be growing. But it would have enough *cognitive function*"—she clumsily tried on these oversized words like her mother's high heeled shoes—"to hold up pictures and use basic sign language—"

"I don't think you ever lacked the ability to talk," Tonya chuckled.

"Mommy, it isn't nice to interrupt people. Anyway, I used to want to be a reporter when I grow up. But actually, I want to be one right now. And an anchor baby and I could be a team. Everyone would pay attention to a baby delivering news about stuff like war and climate change. People would say, 'What kind of world are we leaving for that little baby?'"

"Hannah," I hazarded, "an anchor baby isn't . . ." Tonya stopped me with a look.

"I already have a story. I used mom's phone to call *The Daily Astonisher*, but they just laughed at me."

"You *what?*" We three grownups seemed to be in perfect sync as of late.

"They said they weren't interested. I never got around to discussing my pay, which I think would have been fair. I told them I was a freelance journalist, but they didn't want to see a sample of my work."

"Honey, they might not employ six-year-olds," Tonya tried to mollify.

"I lied. I said I was ten. Anyway, are you going to hear my story or not?"

"Do we have a choice?" Javier asked quietly.

"I heard that! Look, there's a man who wants to dam the Vermilion River."

"Sweetie, what makes you so sure of this?" asked my saintly friend.

"I heard him on the playground. He was there to look at the drainage grate, which he said needed some chemicals. And his cell phone rang, and while the other kids were yelling *zump*, I followed him. He said, 'Damn the Vermilion River! Cleaning it up will be someone else's problem.'"

"Honey, he probably didn't mean—"

"Mom, I *know* the difference between dam like "to stop the flow" and damn like the bad word. Aunt Fiona told me."

The look Tonya gave me never would have spared Perseus, severed head of Santa or no.

"Look, I had to set her straight, okay?" I said defensively. "This might have prevented more trouble."

"At least you didn't say *zump*," my niece pointed out.

"Hannah!" I chided.

"See? A word is only bad if you believe it is. *Zump* wasn't even a real word until today, and you're already mad. Anyway, this man wants to pour oil into the river. That would mess up our environment, like . . ." She struggled for a word. "*Big time.*"

"Hannah," my patient husband intervened. "Your Aunt Fiona is very, very tired, and I'm sure your mom needs to get some rest as well."

"Goodnight, Uncle Javier and Aunt Fiona," she chirped, giving us a hug that encircled all four of our knees. "Mommy, will you tell me a bedtime story? I *know* I can read," —this part she announced for the benefit of us all—"but I like the way you tell them off the top of your head. Especially, the one about Prometheus and the eagle who tore out his liver every day."

Javier smirked. "See? We're not responsible for everything."

"But I prefer the one Aunt Fiona told me. It's Irish. It's about a hero named Lugh who destroyed the evil eye of Balor with his *slingshot.* I have a slingshot too!"

If anyone can convey an obscene gesture with a look, it's Tonya. I resolved to buy an even better bottle of wine for the next time.

* * *

At Angelle Hall the following day, organizing dress rehearsal was like trying to run kittens through a hamster maze designed by Escher. Not only that, but it was a Saturday, and Hannah wanted to come along. Tonya had signed her up for Daisy Scouts, but her girl-child had already raised loud objections to the homemade bird feeders in the first meeting, proclaiming that fruit-flavored cereal loops were toxic to wildlife, as was the yarn on which it was strung. I knew that my best friend needed a day to chill, so it was the theater for my niece.

To keep herself amused, Hannah had brought along several books she loves: a couple of Shel Silverstein tomes and a Harry Potter paperback. She stayed by my side, flipping through her literature, as I scrutinized two-dimensional inns, gates, and wedding arches.

Her main preoccupation was her slingshot, though, and she soon became wriggly. Behind the stage was some discarded scenery left over from last season's production of *Annie Get Your Gun.* I told her that if she stayed with Mister Artie, the costume designer, she could use my former magnum opuses as target practice, with old wood chips as ammo.

Javier was unflappable during his flawless execution of "Bring Him Home," even with the intermittent *Thwack! Thwack! Thwack!* emitting from backstage. My husband was nothing if not patient.

Then, the cast needed to iron out a few bugs at the barricade. I marveled at how much effort I had to put into creating what appeared to be a haphazard trash heap—even if it was designed to support the weight of a dozen men.

Something was definitely awry with the battle scene. In the melee of mutinous schoolboys and the waving of a giant red flag was a tiny girl in shorts wearing a makeshift headscarf wielding a pocket-sized, ballistic toy. Some of the soldiers were falling to the floor, holding their legs, and a few of them weren't even acting.

"*Hannah*," Javier roared, pushed to his limit at last. "You have to audition for a part, just like everyone else."

"This is real-life practice," Hannah shot back. "There is a bad man working for Crack This Guy trying to damage our ecosystem, and we have to put a stop to it. You have inspired me to *revolt*."

I was at her side in a flash. "I'll tell you what," I said. "I have an old tablet that I just cleared of data. I was going to have it recycled, but if you can sit quietly for the rest of the dress rehearsal, you may keep it."

"Like, forever and ever?" my niece brightened, wide-eyed at my attempt at negotiation.

"Forever and ever," I promised.

"Can I take pictures and videos with it?"

"Sure," I agreed hastily. "Just please sit quietly, and don't try to help the revolution. Some good guys have to die in this scene, and although it's very sad, it's what the guy who wrote the story wanted."

"You mean Victor Hugo? Okay, fine. You have a bargain, Aunt Fiona."

Something in my gut told me never to trust an acquiescent child, but I had too much work to do then and there.

* * *

Now, I'm in the office of Douglas Diamond, CEO of Crack This Guy. The big man is very, very concerned. The EPA officer, who introduces herself as Agent Winship, stands in the background, watching everything like a drone. We are six: Hannah, Tonya, Javier, Mrs. Babineaux, Miss Verzwyvelt, and me.

The little twerp had produced an entire amateur video on the tablet I gave her yesterday; a video which is now on Diamond's computer. The agent makes me watch it over and over again; a montage of stills with magnetic letters, spelling out my niece's conspiracy theory:

CRACK THIS GUY DRAINAGE SOLUTIONS AND PLUMBING EMPLOYEE DUMPING OIL IN LOCAL WATERWAY. ECOSYSTEM IN DANGER!!!

The montage becomes a snippet of video footage from next to the drainage ditch. It quickly cuts to Mrs. Babineaux's bemused face—slightly askew, as if covertly taped from someone's bookbag—and the principal saying, "Drainage problems? We didn't have a problem with the drain on the playground." And then, a final clip of the pad pointed at my young niece's face, triumphantly announcing, "This is Hannah Zeno on location at Orangewood Elementary."

The fact that she added Gustav Holst's "Mars" as an audio background is a nice touch, but I would never say that out loud—especially to Hannah—because this act of defiance has definitely gone too far.

The company owner's smile at my niece gives me the chills. "I see you've taken it upon yourself to catch a bad man in my company," he booms.

"Don't patronize me," Hannah growls.

"How old did you say she was again?" Winship asks.

"Six," Tonya groans.

"You know, don't you, that false allegations are illegal?" I chide Hannah. "Your mom could have a lawsuit on her hands, and this could affect her entire career as a reputable attorney."

Hannah says nothing for once. The Big Bird shirt she has chosen to wear belies her diabolical mind.

Diamond's smile is strained. "I take great pride in the ethics of my hiring. None of my men are criminals."

"Why would somebody *do* something like that anyway?" asks Hannah, and for once, I can tell she isn't acting.

"Money," Winship replies. She addresses all of us, "Ships must have functioning oil pollution systems. They also have an oily water separator. It's expensive, but it's the law. Those who don't wish to make such an investment turn to illegal dumping. Dirty oil usually gets discarded into the sea, but

I would imagine that some cheapskate mariner is bribing a handful of guys to throw it into assorted places that are less obvious. Dumping a few barrels down drainage ditches and waterways would be less noticeable than one huge spill." She nods at Diamond. "It may be that one of your underlings is trying to make a little extra cash, maybe if he's part-time. This is not going to bode well for your company, let alone your more honest men."

"Well, my full-time employees get benefits, and their schedules are too full to allow them time for anything else," Diamond declares. Then, he sees the look in the little girl's eyes. "I mean, they still get to go on vacations and things," he backpedals. Smart man. If Hannah already thinks that a homework overload is unjust, then the wheels are already spinning about what grownups must go through.

"But Mrs. Zeno, there is no way that a six-year-old could possibly have made this video," Winship says to Tonya, combing a hand through her short-cropped red hair.

Uh-oh.

"Miz Winship," Hannah pipes. "People have underestimated me for the entire six years of my life. Making this video was easy. People say that even a child can do it, which is *very* condescending. That's why the newspaper hung up on me, which was unnecessary."

"Why didn't you call the police?" the agent asks gently.

"Well, you're here now, aren't you? You're even *better* than the police . . ." I can see that her charm is working on the hawkish woman. "How else was I going to get your undivided attention?"

* * *

One by one, all the workers of Crack This Guy Drainage Solutions file in the company's giant meeting room, and every single one of them is seething. We three guardians instinctively press around the little girl, who grumbles about

96

the invasion of her personal space. We are grossly outnumbered by thirty-something workers in their boots and overalls. Diamond is poker-faced.

"We have a little kid sleuth gonna put one of us in the slammer?" a worker asks, and the others snicker.

"Excuse me, but I'm in the room." Hannah protests with even more asperity. "I can't vote, and I can't drink, but I have a curfew, and I have to eat broccoli. You have *no idea* what it's like to be a second-class citizen. I can even write my name in cursive, but my teacher wants my work to look like everyone else's. He's stamping out individuality. Second grade is a *cult.* So the least you all can do is treat me like a human being."

Diamond hunkers down on one knee to meet Hannah eye to eye. "Why don't you tell my men everything you saw, and then we can all go to lunch and forget this ever happened?" he cajoles in an obsequious display for his lackeys. "I'll even spring for Chuck E. Cheese."

"Chuck E. Cheese *brainwashes* children," Hannah snarls. "And their mascot is a giant *rat!* How clean can their food possibly be?"

Diamond looks like a man who's just been bitten on the nose by a chipmunk.

"Hannah," Tonya warns in her calm before the storm mom voice. "I don't doubt that Mr. Diamond is just trying to be nice. He doesn't know of your convictions."

"I have plenty of evidence, even if there's no DNA." She turns to Diamond. "Do you know what DNA is? It's in every cell of our bodies. Do you ever watch *NOVA* on TV?"

"Young lady, would you *please* just start at the beginning?"

"Mr. Diamond, we second graders know all about the drainage grill that lies between the back entrance to the lower grade classrooms and the monkey bars," Hannah begins in an assertive tone that she could only have picked up from observing her mother in court. "There's a rumor that a little boy fell down there years ago, trapped by the grill before he could get out—"

"Gee, I wonder who started *that* legend?" Miss Verzwyvelt mutters.

"Actually, Miss Verzwyvelt, according to sources, that rumor has been circulating for years. And anyway, I can tell the difference between a spooky story and something I actually saw. I'll give you evidence right here." She produces from her pocket a toy Millennium Falcon.

"Honey, our workers don't care about *Star Wars*."

"Actually, I saw every movie in the cinema on the day each one came out," a male voice from the back of the throng mutters.

"This is more than a toy," Hannah announces triumphantly. "It can record up to fifteen seconds of speech. Observe . . ."

She presses a button, and a tinny voice says, "*Damn the Vermilion River! Cleaning it up will be someone else's problem. This is a perfect spot for that oil and you know it. You got the barrels?*"

"How did you get that recording?" another employee asks.

"I followed the man," Hannah replies with a shrug. "I couldn't see his face, but I listened."

"*Hannah*," Tonya barks. "Not only is that unethical, but it is *dangerous*. You can't just follow a stranger!"

"Hey, we ain't dangerous," a worker pouts.

"Anyone who does that is gonna make the rest of us look bad," another says, his tone carrying a hint of warning to his peers.

"Sweetheart, you got us all wrong," a third wheedles. "We just want to do our jobs and go home like everyone else."

"Excuse me, sir, but what is your name?" Hannah asks with a deceptive sweetness that chills my blood ever so slightly.

"CJ Romero," the man replies, fidgeting a little.

"This is a *clandestine* operation, which means done in secret because you can get in trouble. Somebody thinks there's oil to be dumped in the river and wants to stop the flow, or even worse—is using a bad word to say that he doesn't care."

"Baby, you probably just heard someone talking about a little spill on the surface from somebody's motorboat," Romero croons cloyingly. "There ain't no dumping in the Vermilion."

"How would you find that out?" Hannah asks wide-eyed. Her naïve tone even fools me for the barest of an instant.

"Well, honey, dumping oil is illegal. There would have to be people doing it on the sly for bribes."

"You know a lot about dumping oil. And your voice sounds familiar. I'm pretty sure it was *you*," my little social justice warrior asserts.

"I've never even been near your school."

Without another word, Hannah reaches into her pocket and procures her tiny slingshot and a marble. Before anyone realizes what she's doing, she takes careful aim and thwacks Romero squarely in the kneecap.

"*Aaaargh!* You little . . . *zump!*" he screams. Miss Verzwyvelt gasps. Diamond looks like a deer in headlights. "Okay, fine, I did it!" Romero roars, clutching his knee.

Hannah turns to the authorities with a smug expression. "Any further questions, Your Honor?"

* * *

Opening night is a huge success. Tonya and Hannah have brought a huge bouquet of flowers for both of us, and Hannah wants to ride back to her house in our car. After all, not every kid gets to be chauffeured by Jean Valjean.

I reach for the bag of Bertie Bott's Every Flavour Beans I keep in my purse. These sweets range in flavors from blueberry to sausage. The one I've been saving for Hannah is wrapped in a tiny shred of tissue. Freeing it from its identifying cocoon, I innocently hand it behind me to her car seat in the back. "Here, have a jellybean."

She pops it in her mouth, and her shoebutton eyes go wild. "*Eee-yew,* you gave me a *soap* flavored one."

"See, now I've washed your mouth out, kid. That'll teach you to say the z-word."

She giggles, and cradling her slingshot, begins humming the melody of "Little People" to herself.

"Okay, I won't *say* it anymore. Can I have another jelly-bean?" she wheedles after a moment.

"Not until you get them to stop logging in the Amazon," my husband half jokes.

She says nothing else, only whips out her tablet and begins tapping on the screen, no doubt looking for clues as to how to go about this. The electronic pad illuminates her face in a drowsy grin, and before long, her little head begins to nod.

Before she drops off to sleep, she aims the screen of her device at the back of my head. Even in the rearview mirror I can see that the unspoken word she's typed is *zump.*

THE HOURGLASS AT SEA

by Frances Park, 7,000 words

The Hourglass at Sea takes place in 1969 when Margaret Ahn, nicknamed Monkey, falls in love on a cruise ship sailing across the Pacific, only to realize she has seven days to live out a lifetime of love.

Frances Park is the author of ten books including the novels When My Sister Was Cleopatra Moon *(Hyperion),* To Swim Across the World *(Hyperion) and the children's book* My Freedom Trip: A Child's Escape from North Korea *(Boyds Mills Press). She's currently at work on a literary novel about a former prostitute in South Korea following the Korean War, as well as a collection of personal essays.*

The Dining Room aboard the S.S. President Roosevelt was pure MGM: Amidst a velvety glamour of dripping chandeliers, a classical quartet, silver baskets of bread and flowers everywhere you looked, tuxedoed waiters escorted two hundred gowned and groomed people to their assigned tables. A dress code meant coats and ties for both men and boys, and if I didn't know better, chiffon for women. Perhaps because our family was larger than most, we were assigned to

101

sit at the Captain's table; center stage and visible to all. Our waiter was Head Waiter Max Blossom, a tall, charcoal-haired gentleman of irrelevant age and of such comical pomp and valiance his mere presence set the entire Dining Room in motion.

Sam Ahn introduced first his wife and then his children to the towering waiter the way proud patriarchs do—as if we were all deserving of a Nobel Prize. Max Blossom bowed to us in turn, lavishly praising Mr. Ahn for having the loveliest muumuu-ed wife on board, a well-mannered napkin-in-his-lap son named Peter and *two charming flowers at the table*, my big sister Holly and me.

"Hello, Holly-Blossom! Hello, Monkey-Blossom! Stop the ship—I'm in heaven now!"

Holly glanced around coquettishly. The Dining Room was her Paris.

"Excuse me," I said boldly.

"Yes, Monkey-Blossom?"

"Will the Captain be sitting with us?"

"No, the Captain and his crew always eat late, at the second shift," Max Blossom explained. Then, he flared a nostril, raised a brow and pretended to whisper, "They get the leftovers."

The Ahns barely had time to break out in laughter.

"*However . . .*"

We put our water glasses down, silenced.

"You do have a very important job to do for the Captain while you're here."

"What?" we wondered.

"Why, warm up the seats!"

Max presided over us during much of our meal, explaining to us kids what consomme was and how it was *supposed* to be served cold; placing rolls on our bread plates with long silver tongs; refilling our glasses with opulent flair; picking up Peter's napkin two if not three times from the floor and chatting about everything under our suns. We loved it. His gift: treating people like royalty while crowning himself part of the family. And in the time it took to snap his fingers, he understood who we were.

"Holly," Mommy said, "you wear too much green on your eyes. You look like Catwoman."

Peter stifled a laugh with a cough.

1969 was Holly's moment of bloom. Overnight, she was Holly-esque: her hair was long and luxurious, her ears pierced, her minnow-eyes sequin-like with the help of Jade Pearl eye shadow. Holly-a-go-go.

"I'll tone it down," Holly promised, particularly compliant. She paused and licked her lips. "Dad."

Impishly, as Max refilled his wine glass to the brim: "Yah, Holly-Blossom?"

A round of Ahn family chuckling turned heads

"Can we go to the Coketail party tonight in the Moonlight Room?" Holly asked.

Mommy scoffed. "Cocktail party? No."

"*Coke*tail party, Mommy."

"I said, No!"

"*Yobo, kanchana . . .*" our father spoke to his wife tenderly in Korean, explaining how the ship scheduled teen activities from noon to midnight for the week-long voyage across the Pacific before our family would disembark in Honolulu, and then fly onto Seoul to visit relatives. Movies, games, parties, but no drinking. My siblings and I couldn't speak Korean, but we could understand some of it. Max, too, it seemed—our new friend was winking confidently.

To the party we would go.

* * *

So, there I was on the first night of our cruise name-tagged Miss Margaret Ahn at a Coke-topped table, one of a dozen or so, in the Moonlight Room. Holly stationed on my left, Peter on my right. Headcount, about eighty, several shy of puberty.

Pimples a-plenty. In a predominantly white sea, a foreign buzz rose like smoke above 'Midnight Confessions' on the record player. The accents were unmistakably continental, from Asia, Africa, Europe. I wished I could stare, but didn't dare. My sister was bolder; her eyes were searchlights. Unblinking.

"There's this one boy . . ."

Surely, Miss Holly Ahn was never going to sleep again.

I drank my Coke. A shiver shot through me.

The Teen Program Director bent over to lift the needle off the record player. Her flowery mini-skirt hiked up, exposing thick thighs and a hint of pink panty above clunky white sandals. I could see my poor brother blush from here to Honolulu. Before the night was over, that scene would replay—how many times—until no one took note anymore, not even the boys. She was probably in her mid-twenties, and antsy like a little girl who has to pee badly. At first glance: powder blue eye shadow and white lip gloss against blonde bobbed hair and a lifeguard tan. At second glance: horsy teeth and desperation.

She blew into a microphone:

"Welcome aboard, kids! Most of us have already met but for those of us who haven't, I'm Pamela Gleason. I go by Pam, and I'm here to make sure this is one of the *most memorable weeks of your life!*"

I must have moaned and Holly must have heard. An ever-so-slight alarm in her face went off: don't spoil this once-in-a-lifetime evening. *Please?*

"First, let's get acquainted! I'm going to pick three boys and three girls." Pam began pointing at heads, showing no mercy; one, two, three, one, two, three— "Come on, ladies and gents, *scoot, scoot*, on the dance floor!"

Holly gazed at the chosen lot. Her face was love-stricken. Positively hypnotic. If I burst into flames, she wouldn't have blinked.

Now, I knew why.

He was Asian in look, yet not in dress or manner. Airs came off him like cultured mist; off his posture, his tailored black jacket, his John Lennon specs, the dreamy way he ran his hand through his hair and sighed—not American, either. A mythical boy not from any land I lived in where the royal sculptor went to work to chisel the perfect—

Creature.

Specimen.

Dream.

"His name is Adam Kang," Holly whispered. "Isn't he the most darlingest thing you've ever set your eyes on?"

Adam Kang.

More Coke. Another shiver shot through me.

"Is he—"

"Korean? Yes, but bred in London. His father is some diplomat. I met him earlier, on Deck—Adam, that is. Then, I looked him up in the cruise directory. Mr. Adam, sixteen. So sweet you want to bite him. Or, you know . . ."

At sweet sixteen, she'd never been kissed—yet.

"I think he could be the one," she nearly squealed.

Pam instructed her little dancing crew to "Pair up! When you hear the music, start dancing. When the music stops, that's your cue to go out there and pick a new dancing partner—pronto. Not necessarily the boy or girl of your dreams, *just the first person you see*. Now, the music will start, and then it will stop again. Does everyone follow the pattern here? The night's not over until everyone is up here rocking and rolling and we're one big happy family!"

The lights dipped low and on came 'Midnight Confessions'. The Moonlight Room became a discotheque of lights, music, moving shadows.

I drank my Coke and burped up desperation.

"Peter?"

"Uh-huh?"

"If you get asked to dance before me, pick me on the next round, okay?"

He looked at me, seasick. Peter would do anything in the world for me except: "Dance with my *sister?*"

"Peter, *please . . .*" I pleaded.

"Man alive, Monkey," he groaned.

"*Please!*"

"Okay, okay," he said.

Holly sat queenly in her chair. Expectant. Her eyes closed, revealing a fresh dramatic sweep of Jade Pearl. She was waiting for the music to stop, waiting to be asked to dance by a certain someone. And there he was, wading through a sea of commotion. Coming towards our table! The sight was nothing short of electrifying. My head turned to Holly's; on cue, her eyes opened like a doll's. She was ready, so ready. And yet.

He was looking at me, not Holly.

My heart went high-voltage.

"*Dahnce?*" he said.

My lips parted stupidly. Possibly drooled. Did he say *dahnce?* His too-lovely too-pale face twisted with nothing short of romantic despair.

"Please? You *cahn't* break my heart."

Holly and everyone partying on the SS President Roosevelt may as well have jumped overboard. Like some lovesick mermaid, I got up and the vision led me to the dance floor. I would have sunk to the bottom of the sea with him.

When we reached our destination: "I'm Adam," he said, so Britishly. "And you are?"

"Margaret." Did I snort?

He smiled, causing the near-collapse of my knees.

"Hello, Margaret."

'Midnight Confessions' resumed. Like most girls my age, I was an expert go-go dancer in the privacy of my bedroom, as Holly was in hers—I watched Hullaballoo, too. But never, not in my wildest dreams, would I have imagined that the first time I would step on a real dance floor, it would be with a boy even remotely resembling the likes of Adam Kang.

The next moments were a spellbound, youth-drunken blur. Yet, that diminished nothing—I would seal this memory forever! When our time was up—too soon, too soon!—He gave me a look too British for an American girl like me to interpret. *Good-bye? Must we part? No, no, no . . .*

"*Go, go, go!*" Pam was yelling like she had to pee to high heaven.

Everyone mad-dashed for new partners for the third round. I grabbed the first boy I saw and repeated this silly and wonderful game four times, at least. Yes, I danced like I owned the ship—after all, I had the title of being Adam Kang's first choice!

The Moonlight Room evolved into an hour of nonstop dancing, thinning out when a few people made a dash for the door or got Coke refills. Pam applauded our efforts, and the Coketail party officially broke up. Some, like me, lingered. I was hoping for a glimpse of you-know-who, even the back of his head on its way out. Not to speak to, just to draw out the dream I would take to my pillow tonight and eventually back home and to all the pillows I would ever lay my sleepy head upon—even my last.

Just a glimpse to last me the rest of my life.

No such luck.

And what about Holly? I remembered her sitting at the table alone—her wishful glitter gone—until at least my third dance. Then, she vanished. I hoped someone, anyone, had asked her to dance, but there was no way to tell. Peter, who was picked early on, got gobbled up in the crowd, and I hadn't seen him since.

* * *

"Why did he ask *you* to dance?"

"For the hundredth time, Holly, I don't know!"

My sister was drilling me from the top bunk of our cabin. Lights off, her swollen red face was masked in the darkness— she'd been crying.

"Well, it's like Pam said," she snapped, "no one had to pick the boy or girl of their dreams, just the first ones they saw."

Holly didn't mean to hurt my feelings. She just didn't want to feel unpopular. At your moment of bloom, you're supposed to be picked, not publicly rot on the vine. So, I couldn't and didn't blame her for revising history: Adam Kang went blindly in the crowd and took the first girl he saw who just happened to be me.

Yet, I knew the truth.

Adam Kang sought me out.

And he said, *You cahn't break my heart.*

I would treasure those words forever!

* * *

Though she was Holly-at-breakfast as usual, Holly hated me for the rest of the trip. I felt bad, but I had my ship-life to live, and so, half-hidden behind a pair of banana yellow sunglasses, I spent the next morning searching for Adam. Just to see him, watch him move, not to speak to him, no way. I was too lovesick, too stupid. Surely, whatever he saw in me last night was as gone as mist around the moon today.

* * *

If you ventured down to the Dining Room at noon, you could indeed dine there, but the moment you were greeted by a lone waiter craving light, you knew you were in the wrong place. Instead, most passengers were hovering over a spectacular buffet in the Starlight Room on Deck. Tables were set out, although everybody preferred to stand and connect with the sky and the ocean and others on board. Max was orchestrating the entire show. The ship was his castle on the sea.

"Something about the sea air turns ordinary people into famished warthogs," he uttered to me while flashing a million-dollar smile for the public. "Look at that son-of-a-gun, piling on those devilled eggs like he's the only one in line. Tell everyone in your family to take two plates before all the food's gone . . . Oh, Monkey-Blossom," he tooted, "I think you have admirer . . ."

Looking back, how bold of me, the way I walked over to where he was standing, not inside the Starlight Room but on Deck peering in at me; and how bold of him, the way his hand went for my sunglasses as if they were ours, not mine, to take off. Somehow, we and the universe understood that it would take these brash moves to bring us together. For, there was not time to linger on modesty or coyness lest our passion be swept away on the tides. So, yes, what a terribly seductive boy Adam Kang was, even though his fingers were tapered and his touch was tender as he removed my sunglasses and accidentally-on-purpose brushed my face. I never felt so naked, so beautiful.

Volcanic!

"I *thought* that was you," he said.

Within the hour, we were inseparable.

* * *

Within twenty-four hours Adam and I would go through a whole courtship as if ship years were measured in hours. If we didn't seize the moment we'd miss the boat and a sinking, rocking regret would haunt us all our lives from the minute we stepped off the SS President Roosevelt to some lonely day in the future when we were old and weary on moth-eaten couches on separate continents watching merry bicyclists from our windows. Regret, haunting afterthought, our elderly silhouettes—you grow up fast when you know you only have a week to do it, so we did.

Years later, I was convinced something divine was at play, that somehow our adult souls had lurched back in time to knock some sense into Margaret Ahn at fourteen and Adam Kang at sixteen so that we could see things in a mature light once he took off my sunglasses in a move so erotically charged losing my virginity years later would be nothing. Yes, something desperate and divine grabbed our bony young shoulders and shook off all the blushing bullshit with a hiss-whisper: *This is it, you little fools, most of life will be a long, drab drive to nowhere so make this happen—now!* Divine, like a magical compass pointing to Adam and me as we stood with our adolescent giddiness beneath an orange sun while the rest of the ship blurred, like darting tropical fish, our coordinates miraculous yet morbid; in the end, we met so we could carry this to our graves.

Our enchantment was instant, rushed, soul-stripping, no questions asked. We kissed within the hour, and said *I love you* countless times before the sun went down over a Hollywood horizon that was ours, all ours. *I love you*, on the tips of our eyelashes while we watched 'Follow Me Boys' at four o'clock movie hour; *I love you*, on the secret quiver of our lips as we pined for each across the Dining Room at dinner, *I love you*, our young chests in rhythm with the rise and fall of the Pacific waves while '*My One and Only Love*' gushed in the background. Everything was a sigh, a murmur, a gasp, like love in the movies only it's not pukey when it's you. A lifetime of love, after all, had to be squeezed into the remaining days of this journey.

How could I cram a life's worth of Adam Kang into one week?

* * *

On deck, beneath an opulent white moon, I zeroed in on his flashing wire-rimmed eyes and hung onto every word uttered from his lips as we exchanged biographical information like we were racing against the hourglass, our time runneth up.

"My real mum died when I was very small, Margaret; two, actually. I do remember her clearly, though. She was a *yangban*—"

"A what-ban?"

Adam looked wholly disappointed in me. True, I spoke little Korean, but I was no dope and defended myself.

"What?"

Of course he, of a certain genteel class, forgave me with a kiss on the hand which I didn't need but would take. "You're adorable, Margaret. A *what*-ban." He forced a smile that clashed with his charisma. "A *yangban* is a person of wealth or aristocratic birth; in my mum's case, both. She was a descendent of King Sejong with a powdery complexion and very tall—"

"How tall?"

"Five foot five," he said. "Average for an English woman I suppose but not for Korean women of that generation. Most stood four foot ten in their *comoshins*." Teasing me: "You do know what *comoshins* are, don't you, Margaret?"

"Of course I do," I replied. *Comoshins* were canoe-shaped rubber shoes; in gray-hues for poor feet, peacock-colored for the well-to-do. "I'm five foot five in my Dr. Scholl's." I pointed to my feet just in case Dr. Scholl's weren't sold in England.

"And probably still growing! But you were nursed on American milk, I presume. I mean, you were born in America, were you not?" To my nod: "Where, exactly?"

"Cambridge, Massachusetts. Do you know where that is?"

"New England," he said in his worldly way. "There's a Cambridge in *old* England, too."

"I knew that," I said sassily.

Adam winked at me. He was beautiful to begin with. I was cute, but no beauty according to Holly. Yet, I must have fed off his rays because for the duration of the trip I would feel bewitchingly ripened by the humid air. My hair fell in Polynesian princess waves and my lips got glossy like the girls in the Slickeringo ads.

I winked back.

"My mum towered over everyone, even most men, and she had this proud mare of a walk." His statuesque imitation of her saddened me. "Wherever she went people would yell out, *Oma!*"

"Even in England?"

He laughed sadly—for who in England said *oma*?—and planted an old-geezer kiss on my forehead. "She never lived in England, Margaret. We moved there when I was four."

"And when did your dad remarry?"

"He didn't."

"He didn't?"

"He had two wives."

"Oh . . ." My father's friends in Korea were the same way, with second wives or mistresses. The exception was his closest friend, Mr. Oh, whose wife was a professor at Ewha University. They were what few Korean couples were—equals. "You would never have two wives, would you?"

"No." Oceanic laughter erupted from below—the Promenade Deck—and Adam blurted: "I can't believe I met you, Margaret. I didn't even want to leave England, you know. I mean, I have my mates and my cricket. And Korea is such a depressing place, the bombed countryside and downtown Seoul which is even worse than the London slums because the children, well . . . they look like us. And it makes me sick to my stomach, the way they stare at you like you have something to give them when you don't. Don't get me wrong, I feel sorry for them, most of all the small children with their hands all bandaged and bloodied, begging under those godless skies—many are lepers, you know—but I can't do a thing about that except feel guilty that I'm a diplomat's son who's served crust-less sandwiches by Miss Emma at tea time made with jam that has a Golliwog face on the jar, no less, and Miss Emma, as you can guess, is a Negro."

"What's a Golliwog face?" I asked him.

"It's like your little Black Sambo," he said. "It originated from the Golliwog rag doll, caricature at its worst. But as vapid as this may sound to you, Margaret, I just want to be a regular fellow who doesn't have to see or think about Golliwogs and little beggars. And I really wanted to skip the trip this summer now that I'm sixteen—I can take care of myself. My father had said if I did well on my exams, he would consider it. And I did, but he didn't."

"You can give them money," I said.

"Give who money?"

"The little lepers you feel so sorry for. You don't just walk by them like some snoot, do you, Adam?"

"I do walk by them but not like some snoot." Vacant sigh, crowned by stars. "Please don't judge me right now, Margaret. I do enough of that myself, and it's not a pretty picture."

"So, why don't you give them money if you feel so sorry for them? I always do. My dad gives all us kids money before we go out, a wad of *wons*." *Wons* were paper money that made you feel rich in your pocket despite their nickel and dime worth.

"Well, my father won't allow it. He's rather . . . elitist."

"A snoot, you mean."

"No, a shit!" he cried. "I'm sorry; I didn't mean to say that. Must we talk about him, Margaret? This was all leading up to something else: that I didn't want to be here but here I was. Then, I saw you and I was glad, grateful even, that my father made me come."

We backed up, ducked in the shadows and kissed for a long time.

Fluttery-eyed: "When did you first see me, Adam? At the Coketail party?"

"Earlier, at dinner. I saw your sister first—what's her name—and saw you sitting next to her."

"Holly," I said, embarrassed for her. "Her name is Holly."

"Yea, Holly. She's quite nice, your big sis."

"Yes," I said, "she's . . . your age."

"And you're a whole year younger."

"No . . ."

"No?"

"I'm two years younger."

The earth tilted, ever so slightly.

"The directory said you're fifteen," he insisted. "Miss Margaret, fifteen."

"That was a misprint," I squeaked.

"Are you telling me, Margaret," his fingers slipped from mine, "that you're only fourteen years old?"

For the first, but certainly not the last time in my life, I sensed that sickening disorienting fear of losing a dream, of it slipping away from me. *No, no, no . . .* Yes, I was young, just going into high school. What difference did it make? Did the ocean out there care? The more-opulent-than-ever moon? In any realm, we would die at approximately the same time. The dream, slipping away. I should've known this was too good to be true. Maybe, I was still sleeping in my bunk or even back home. *No, no, no . . .* this was real. I was in the South Pacific. I was with Adam who wasn't the kind of person to take back his already-declared love. Our romance of ten hours was a decade in ship years.

"I'll be fifteen in October," I said without apology.

"Oh? October what?"

"Ninth."

His silence was divorcing. The hour was late, nearly ten. Suddenly, I missed my whole family—Dad, Mommy, Holly and Peter—scattered on the boat, coordinates unknown. A pinched guilt. Ouch. You meet someone and then lose track of the ones you love. Was that how life worked?

Finally, my young hero took my chin and spoke with such sensuality he spoiled me for life: "I am in this world and you are in this world. That's all that matters."

* * *

The last hour of that first evening covered another year of courtship. Adam and I touched on many topics, watchful of the hourglass. Growing up Asian in England/America (fine/fine— *we'd show scars later*). The schools we attended (Eton College, called a college but not a college at all/Falls Church High). The music we listened to (Mozart and Cream/The Beatles). Our happiness scale (6/8). Our belief in God (not sure/think so). Sexual experience (little/very little). College choices (The Sorbonne/University of Virginia). Second college choices (Oxford/William and Mary). Our dreams (none/write books). In days to come, revisionist histories would emerge followed by probing and minor confessions, but that first night, all was splendid on this side of the earth.

Adam's fever peaked as if from two opposing forces—the moonlight out there and his own dark cast here. "Margaret, remember earlier today when we spotted that dot of an island way off in the ocean?"

"Yes." We were trying to figure how far away it was—I guessed three hours but three hours later it hadn't budged. When I had joked that Gilligan was stranded there, he said Gilligan who.

"Our waiter, Anthony, told us it will actually take two days for us to get close enough to it to see that it's no more than a clump of rocks, three or four trees and a family of birds. But it's there, that's what's important. Like your dream to write books. You can see it, can't you, Margaret? The island—the dream. I can't wait for the day you conquer the world, and I can say I knew you."

I squinted. I couldn't see the island, cloaked in night, but maybe it was there.

* * *

Minus cameo appearances at breakfast and dinner where five tables separated us like the ocean, I was always with Adam. From sunrise to sunset he was my sweetheart and angel, til

Saturday do we part. My loyalties lied with Adam as if we'd been married fifty years. Holly, the dreaming-turned-suffering sister who, with one pursed-lipped look or snort might make me believe otherwise, was relegated to the background of cruise noises and squawking skies. I had Holly for the rest of my life. I had Adam for one week.

And our time was ticking!

By Day Three our love was out in the open. Even the sweetly dippin' seagulls knew about Margaret Ahn and Adam Kang. We were the young darlings of the SS President Roosevelt, holding hands even as we swam. We might never see each other's homes or bedrooms, we might never walk down a school hallway together, we might never know love on land, but we knew each other the way people do when their love has a death sentence.

With no-nonsense urgency.

"Don't cry, Margaret."

On the third night, I cried anyway, into his shoulder. "Nearly half our time is up! And we just met!"

The ocean was portrait-still. The night sky, too. Both would still be here, unchanged, in a million years. But not us, not Adam and me. In four days, we would go our separate ways. In decades we'd be dead.

Clocked romance meant a doomed horizon.

"I know," he said with true lament. "But must we talk about it? Now?"

"You don't even care!"

"I do!" He cupped my head with his hand and squeezed it all over like a luscious grapefruit. "Margaret, if I live to be a hundred, I shan't ever forget you."

In a swift move, he locked himself behind me and we faced the Pacific Ocean together.

"Adam?"

"Margaret."

"Why do you like me?"

"Why wouldn't I, silly?"

"Holly is prettier."

"I only noticed you," he replied diplomatically.

"You don't find her pretty?"

"I don't find her anything. I mean, yea, she's pretty, I suppose. Like a pom-pom girl. But you have something else. Like you smoke long cigarettes or have deep dark thoughts."

"I don't smoke."

"But you do have deep dark thoughts, don't you?"

"I guess."

We cranked our heads—mine right, his left—and smooched a little.

"Adam, what will you remember most about me?"

"That you wore yellow sunglasses."

"That's *it*?"

His voice, lit and comical: "I'm teasing you."

"Oh."

He gushed abruptly—"I'll remember everything!"

Right then, I wondered who we would have been had we been raised not in the United States and the United Kingdom but in Korea. We would bow but not kiss. We would be other people speaking in hushed, formal tones. *Panpaken manasoyo.* Stripped of Western influence, our walks and talks and gestures, the way we chewed our food, would be Oriental. Our heartbeats, too. Neither a Gilligan nor a Golliwog would mean to a thing to us.

"And I'll remember the way your hair smells and moves and our first kiss, which was your first-ever kiss," he spoke ever-so-sentimentally.

Punishing him: "But not yours."

"No . . ."

"Tell me about your first kiss."

Adam wisely steered course. "And I'll remember that you were a lucky girl who had a dream to write books and parents who loved you." He propped his chin on the top of my head.

"What's your dream, Adam? You must have one."

A biting laugh. His heart, his essence, was mine lock and key, but his life in England was under wraps, belonging to a sad soul all his own. In the past two days, I got fleeting glimpses of it; and it was like seeing the one you want run from you through rain and fog and you want to stop him, capture him, and tell him all is well, but you can't because you'd be lying. His father sounded cruel and his mother had no mind of her own. Older sister Isabelle was too beautiful for her own good and used it to hurt every young man who had hurt her when she was a school girl with a bowl haircut. Now, she led them on, then broke their hearts.

"My father tells me my dream is to enter the world of high finance."

"What's that?"

He sighed brokenly. "A stupid way to spend a life."

"Then, don't do it!" I cried. To his *tsk*: "Please."

We fell silent as the ship cruised slowly under a midnight blue tent of punched-out stars.

"And you, Margaret? What will you remember about me?"

I turned around and saw his face in a halo of light; his wire-rimmed lenses opalescent as moons. He was tall for a Korean male of his generation, standing a full head above me. Perfect.

"Everything," I said.

* * *

My parents approved of Adam but prohibited us from kissing. I amended the law—never out in the open, in broad daylight. Little lovebirds that we were, we dove into countless dark corners. You can't imagine how many nooks and crannies existed on a ship of that size! We found them all.

One would assume that the only two Korean families aboard the SS President Roosevelt would gravitate toward each other. But Mr. and Mrs. Kang, stern and reserved, would have nothing to do with us. In their eyes, the Ahns from America were the opposite of *yangbans*—mere *sangnums*. Adam never came out and said so, but sparing introductions was telling. As far as I was concerned, Adam's parents were on another voyage, on another sea. If his father so much as looked my way I would shoot him a look he would never forget.

How dare a man with two wives judge us?

* * *

Neither Adam nor I participated in the farewell Aloha Show, a show put on by Teen Director Pam. It would only take time we didn't have away from us, our hourglass. We had no grains of sand to offer. Now that the small but symbolic island had come and gone it would, like us, only exist from now on in our minds' eye, lest someday we cruise once again on these mythical seas and spot it and each other—not likely. Maybe in the back of our minds—behind the curtains and clutter and bullshit—we could envision our futures as lonely still-life figures on park benches in different hemispheres, barely breathing, barely seeing, mistaking trash on the ground for pigeons; and cringed at the prospect of recalling the other as merely *Oh, yes, yes, that girl/boy, in that ship show*. Better to remember, however faint, the electric hitch in our slim hips as we walked to the dance floor, the sunglasses coming off, the innocent glitter of our faces at night, and feel a shiver of something. Anything.

One afternoon, from two to four, we spied like a friendly two-headed monster; we peered into the Moonlight Room where rehearsals for the Aloha Show were taking place on the so-called stage, a dance floor sectioned off by masking tape. By now, Adam and I were Siamese in soul—his Asian, Shakespearian, brain-blowing beauty meant very little by now. He was just Adam, my Adam, part of me, cheek-to-cheek— and it felt like it would always be this way, despite the ugly reality that crept up every so often like a deformity best hidden under the blanket.

"You're just going to forget me!" I wailed.

"No!" He vehemently denied it. "No! Margaret!"

"You don't care about me!"

Adam was stunned by the first in a series of love-spats over our remaining days, spats that quelled quickly because it all boiled down to one scary reality: I had to live the rest of my life without him.

"Why on earth would you say that, Margaret?"

"Because," I began, no doubt pouting, "you act like we're never going to see each other again."

To which he stuttered, and I got weepy. We fell into the shadows; that is, the shade of a big umbrella. *Don't cry, don't cry*, I pleaded with myself, *not now*. Soon, too soon, I would leave the ship, leave Adam who would sail on to Yokohama. Who would he talk to, ask to dance, swim with? Our spell-binding underwater-like dream was coming to an end.

"We never will, will we, Adam? We'll never see each other again."

He winced. "I hope to, really and truly . . ."

"We *must*, even if it's years from now . . ."

"The thing is, you won't love me when you're all grown up, Margaret. Right now, you think you will, but you won't. You'll see me for who I am. Or am not."

"Stop it! When you say such ridiculous things they'll start sounding true to you, and you'll start believing them."

"I'm not like you, Margaret. I have no real character to speak of. No hobbies or passions all my own. Maybe a thought or two, that's it. That's all I am."

"I said, stop it. Please."

"But I'll write you," he humbly offered as someone who would, were he as regal as he looked, give up his crown but never his self-loathing. "Will you write me, Margaret? Will you write me back?"

"What a dumb question. Yes!"

"But for how long?"

I wanted to say *forever*, wanted to say it so badly if pangs could kill I'd be long dead. "How long do you *want* me to write you, Adam?"

Blindly, frantically, he fished for my hands. Once found, he exclaimed—"Forever!"

* * *

Day Five brought rain which meant hiding for cover and catching the four o'clock movie, 'Cat Ballou'. We snuck out early and scrambled down to the gift shop which sold little wooden ships, brown Hawaiian dolls (*"Good—no Golliwogs!"*), shell-strung leis, candy bars, gum and toiletries. Then and there, Adam bought me a bottle of Ambush cologne. Upon purchase, we vowed we would love each other forever. Even if we married others and had children and grandchildren, nothing, no one, could compare to you, replace you. Never, ever! The cashier, a dull biddy, frowned as if we were too young for such declarations, and then went back to dusting a copper globe.

* * *

Meeting Adam proved to be a magical interlude to an other-wise uneventful adolescence for me. Without the Polynesian breeze, my hair flattened, my lips parched—not a single boy noticed me for years. But in this loveless state, I did do what Adam had begged me to do: write. Courage is a crazy thing; it came word by word; first in long scribbled blue airmail letters to Adam, then in type on onionskin paper to Adam; until I went beyond letters and beyond Adam and, like the words, writing became who I was, however painful; the flip side of that heart carved into my heart. Deep.

At least I had the memory of him and the cinema of our final moments together.

* * *

We had met at the break of dawn to fulfill an impossible promise: to figure out the rest of our lives. Adam was waiting for me on the Promenade Deck. Cool air shot up my sundress.

"Adam!"

"Margaret!"

FLASH!

Everything—the sky, the ocean, the horizon, the Deck, the shadows—took on a turquoise cast. Not like God threw a bucket of paint or sprinkled blue and green glitter on our sphere. It was more transparent. Ethereal.

Blinking, Adam and I stood side-by-side, so close our souls locked one last time.

"I feel like I'm in a surreal dream or painting, Margaret. Or underwater. Yes, that's it—underwater! Do you feel it, too? Do you see it?"

"Yes," I murmured.

"This can't be happening."

"Adam?"

My sweetheart closed his suffering eyes. "Don't, Margaret. I asked you that first night not to break my heart but you are, Margaret, you are . . ."

"Why can't we meet in Seoul?"

Our time in Seoul would overlap by nearly two weeks.

"We've been through this before, Margaret. I can't. This isn't London where I can just board a bus by myself and meet you; I'd have to have permission from my father and make arrangements for a driver and . . . it's just not going to happen. He's not going to let it happen. Please don't ask again . . . not unless you want to kill me."

My voice trailed. "Maybe we'll pass each other on the streets of Seoul . . ."

With an artificial nod: "Maybe . . ."

"Or we could make a *secret* plan, Adam," I said with a sudden, stupid girl-chirp. "I could plan to be in front of the Bando Hotel on a certain day and if you could somehow make

122

it there, then, well . . ." His fallen face told me otherwise, and I whispered uselessly. "And if you couldn't, well, then, you couldn't." My eyes shut with tears. "I'd understand. I would."

"Please don't cry over me, I'm not worth it. I'm nothing," he said so very tenderly, proof that kindness can kill you. Only then did I note his rugged appearance at this serene hour on Day Seven: he was unshaven, uncombed, beautifully wrecked.

"Don't say that, Adam. Promise me you'll never say that again as long as you live."

He laughed and shook his head fuzzily. Then, reluctantly: "I promise."

However precious and ticking, the next few seconds were necessarily silent.

"Speaking of promises, don't you dare break your promise to me, Margaret. Go home and write. Conquer the world, don't conquer the world; the important thing is to write your heart out like you're writing your Last Will and Testament. What I guess I'm very poorly trying to say is, make your dream mean something. Will you do that for me? For you?"

I couldn't imagine harboring any dream that didn't include Adam Kang. I liked it up here, with him.

"I promise."

"Good," he said, his work done. "In the meantime, I'll be expecting little previews in the mail from Miss Margaret, fourteen, soon to be fifteen."

In the turquoise glow we split a stray cocktail napkin and took turns scribbling down our addresses—one pen, his. His instructions were precise.

"Write to me here at Eton once school starts. But until then, write to me at my friend's flat. If you send letters to my house, I can't predict their fate. You know what always seems to happen in the movies."

I only knew what was happening here. We were about to swim our separate ways. I got jitters. Death jitters.

"Here's my address," I said. "Don't forget the zip code; in America the zip code's *very* important . . ."

"Let's say good-bye now, Margaret," he said, all heat and regret. "Not in public, not in front of my family. Promise me we shan't look at each other at breakfast."

"Adam?"

"Yea?"

My teeth began chattering, and I could feel the skull of me, Margaret Ahn without the long hair and Pacific dreaminess in her face. A morbid thought hit me like a guillotine: one day we would be nothing but bones in far-apart forgotten graveyards.

Oh my God! I cried, so scared.

"I don't want to say good-bye."

"I don't want to say good-bye, either."

Our old souls lurched back in time to save us from breaking down in tears like the children we actually were. We clasped hands, we sturdied ourselves. Life was a bitch; learn it now.

"I love you, Margaret. I won't ever forget you."

"I love you, too, Adam. I won't forget you, either."

"Maybe someday," his eyes fluttered with shame, "you'll write about me, and I'll have some small place in the universe."

I couldn't address his statement then; it was too big, too tragic. But I would, in letters to come.

"Adam?"

"Yea?"

"We never figured out the rest of our lives."

"No," he lamented, "I suppose our lives will figure it out for us."

"Do you hope we see each other again?"

"God! More than anything!"

And then in the cool dawn, so moody and aqua-blue my memory cannot possibly do it justice, we kissed for the last time.

Our hourglass was up.

THROUGH FIRE AND FLOOD

by Kristy Baxter, 8,000 words

In 1889, Cora McAllister, a schoolteacher in a bustling coal town, falls in love with her dearest friend, Felix Bayer. The would-be lovers face prejudice and hardheaded family members head-on, but the chaos and destruction of nature's wrath may prove to be more than they can handle.

Kristy Baxter writes short stories and novels. She holds an MFA in genre fiction from Western State Colorado University and teaches at the University of Pittsburgh at Johnstown. When not writing or teaching, she spends time with her husband, two cats, and four ducks. She tweets at @kbaxwriter.

Adjusting her hat one last time, Cora McCallister set out from the boardinghouse. The May sun shone at last, although a chill and the scent of rain lingered in the damp air. A half mile away, the southwestern Pennsylvania hills rose, full and green. After several days spent wearing grim smiles and hauling water from basements, the people of Johnstown filled the streets, all talk of the annual spring flooding forgotten. The sharp, burnt scent of mills and foundries hung over the valley, lingering despite the closure of most businesses for Decoration Day. Bright banners and American flags hung from poles, windows, and trees.

In honor of the holiday, Cora wore her best afternoon dress, pale green with an impressive bustle, and her favorite hat. She waved at neighbors and strangers, tentative happiness taking wing in her chest. Colorful flowers sprouted everywhere, an atmosphere of cheerfulness and anticipation lifted the town, and her dearest friend finally returned from medical college—this day promised nothing but joy and laughter. Excitement trembled through her knees and stomach. Today marked her first reunion with Felix since Christmas. *He's Dr. Bayer now*, she reminded herself. His lifelong dream, realized at last.

Three of her students chased each other down the street, shouting a greeting as they passed. One of her fellow board-inghouse residents, a young miner who wore a perpetual layer of coal dust even on a holiday, tipped his hat.

"Afternoon, Cora. Fine weather we're having."

"Yes, Jacob, and just in time for the holiday."

"You'll be out planting if this weather holds, I imagine?"

She grinned. "Are you offering to help?"

"My thumb's as black as coal." Jacob laughed. "But I'll help you take care of the harvest."

Shaking her head and smiling, Cora went on her way. Snatches of different languages and dialects floated through the air, mingling with laughter and the occasional raucous shout. The streets overflowed with people, the crowd thickening as she drew closer to Main Street.

She scanned the crowd for Felix. They'd watched the parade together for thirteen years, ever since they first met. Felix, eight years old and teetering on the edge of ungainly, had acted the part of a true gentleman, helping a six-year-old with rips in her dress and scuffed boots climb onto the sturdy branch of a tree in the public square. That perfect vantage point served them every year until they grew too old to climb trees—in public, anyway.

Every year since, they'd met at the corner of Main and Market Streets, right next to the square. Reaching the meeting point, she stood on tiptoes and craned her neck. Every blond head, every set of broad shoulders in the crowd sent her heart stumbling through her breast. And every time she looked closer and found a stranger instead of Felix, disappointment settled on her shoulders.

Distant music drifted through the air, launching a thrill of excitement through the crowd. A heavy hand fell on her arm, and she whirled, startled.

"Cora." Mrs. Bayer's thick German accent turned the name into a guttural grunt. Her tight-lipped expression seemed more appropriate for a disliked acquaintance than her son's lifelong friend.

Her green gingham dress, overstarched, hung too stiff on her wide frame. Mrs. Bayer herself appeared overstarched, her posture so rigid it was a wonder her back didn't snap in two. Her hat perched atop an immaculate bun—if a wisp of graying hair escaped, Cora was certain, it was only with Mrs. Bayer's express dispensation.

Next to her, Felix's nine-year-old sister, Luisa, beamed up at Cora.

Cora smiled. "Good afternoon, Mrs. Bayer. Lulu, it's lovely to see you."

Mrs. Bayer frowned at her use of Felix's pet name for his sister. Cora shifted, uncertain of the reason for such a chilly reception. She turned her gaze back to Luisa.

"Are you enjoying your holiday?"

Luisa bobbed her head, blond curls bouncing with the movement. "Yes, Miss McCallister."

Clearing her throat, Mrs. Bayer nudged Luisa aside. Her steely blue eyes—so similar to Felix's, but missing his frank cheerfulness—narrowed at Cora.

"My son, you are looking for him?"

"Oh, yes, Mrs. Bayer. Did he come with you?"

"Yes, he is here." She puffed out her chest and lifted her chin, then turned toward the square.

Cora followed Mrs. Bayer's gaze. Pots of flowers dotted the green expanse. Felix sat on a bench in the nearest corner. He glanced around the crowd, searching each face. Cora cocked her head. Her old friend had transformed into an appealing stranger, his strong jaw and broad shoulders lending him an air of strength and confidence. Something new and different attended him, changing the set of his mouth, straightening his back.

And then, Bette Heinrich settled next to him, snaking her hand through the crook of his elbow before he even offered his arm. Her lips moved as she murmured something. Felix dipped his head closer to hear.

Cora's stomach dropped. Bette, the "good German girl" whose praises Mrs. Bayer sang like a church hymn. Felix's complaints about his mother's fixation on the girl always brought a sympathetic smile to Cora's face. They'd laughed many times at the reliability of Mrs. Bayer's compliments.

Last Christmas, he'd shaken his head and sighed. "'Bette's such a good German girl, Felix. Bette will give you so many children, Felix. Bette will cook all your favorite meals, Felix.' The sun rises in the east and sets in the west, and Mama fills every moment between with 'Bette this, Bette that.'"

Mrs. Bayer's smile turned triumphant. "They look perfect, yes?" Two shining blond heads bent toward each other.

The gay chatter and laughter, the bright colors, the scent of sweaty bodies swirled around Cora. Her heart generated all the heat of a lifeless chunk of coal, although it sat heavier than steel in her chest.

"Yes. Perfect." Her voice emerged in a shaky whisper.

"Mama says Felix and Bette are going to have a wedding," Luisa piped up.

The coal cracked in two, but its weight doubled.

Mrs. Bayer's sharp gaze heralded a warning. Cora shrank back.

"All is well, Cora. Mr. Bayer and I, we want what is best for Felix. You can see he is happy, yes? Leave him to her." She grasped Luisa's hand and marched away, her shoulders straight and her gait cheerful.

Across the street, Felix's attention shifted from Bette to the crowd again. *He's looking for me*, Cora thought, *but it doesn't matter.*

Then, his gaze caught hers, trapping it. His smile crinkled the corners of his blue eyes. The distance between them vanished, Bette faded to a pale specter, and the world around them turned into a quiet, insignificant blur. The coal in Cora's breast lit, then smoldered, and she worked to keep her expression neutral as she gave Felix a polite nod. Habit pushed her hand up, and she waved, fingers trembling. Her feet itched to run, to escape, to carry her to peace and quiet. She needed to mull over these changes in her heart, examine them, understand them—and make them stop.

Instead, she pasted a tight smile onto her face as the parade approached, drum corps and carriages and veterans. A cheer rose from the crowd. The procession passed between Cora and Felix. Free of his gaze, she melted into the crowd and hurried home.

* * *

Felix's heart throbbed, threatening to smash his ribcage to splinters. There stood Cora, her flame-red curls peeking out from under her lavender hat.

He hated that hat. He'd hated it since she first showed up at his house with it perched on her head. An impractical hat, far too big, and it hid her bright green eyes unless she lifted her chin and looked at him dead on. He never told her, because she loved it so, and he loved her. And besides, her love of enormous hats kept her pale skin creamy despite the hours she spent digging, planting, harvesting. Cora, his Irish rose, who made every other flower wither away in shame when she flashed that wide, infectious smile. When introspection turned her face away, the delicate line of her profile made Felix, the most unartistic boy in existence, wish he knew how to draw.

At seventeen, watching her turn dreamy and distant as she worked her father's fields, he'd wanted to brush the pale skin of her cheek with his thumb, learn its silkiness. At nineteen, he'd wanted nothing more than to kiss her, discover the softness of her lips like a voyager finding new lands.

Finish your education, he'd told himself during those long years. *Become a man who's worthy of her. No point in asking her until you deserve her.* And now, at twenty-one, a newly minted doctor after three grueling years, he wanted nothing and no one else for the rest of his life. His hands trembled, his breath came short, and anticipation tingled in his stomach, but he'd know his future soon enough.

Next to him, Bette chattered away. Mama's insistence on accompanying him to the parade and subsequent order to stay on the bench had raised a few questions. Bette's appearance a few minutes later answered all of them.

Bette, a girl who stayed at home with her parents throughout their youths, who cooked a fine *schweinshaxe,* whose accent thickened and rearranged her words because she spoke the mother tongue more often than English.

Bette, a dull spark next to Cora's fire and wit.

The parade made its way up the street, obscuring his view of her. She'd looked so distant, pale and lifeless, not like herself at all. Of course, they usually watched the parade together, but Mama's scheming ruined that. After three years of avoiding the Bette issue, it now sat next to him, placid but determined. Mama's dreams loomed large, threatening to stamp out his own.

I suppose I've run away from the good German girl for long enough.

"Bette," he said, turning to her and sliding his arm away from her grip, "it seems our parents want us to marry. Well, my mother does, at least."

The light dawning in her eyes made his words tumble out faster.

"And, while I think you're a nice girl who will make some lucky man a fine wife, that man is not me. I'm very sorry."

Her face fell. "But your mama, she said we are to marry."

"I apologize that she led you to believe that was possible. It's simply not."

A storm approached, creasing her forehead and narrowing her eyes. "Cora McCallister."

"Again, I'm sorry." Felix sighed. "Sometimes, my mother doesn't quite realize that this isn't the fatherland."

"Your mama, she will not like this."

"I know. I've known that for a long time. In fact, I've had years to prepare for it."

"*I* do not like this. We are to marry. This has always been, since we were *kinder* together. You know this."

"That is my mother's opinion. I've tried to discourage her, but as you may have noticed, she's a stubborn woman. Fortunately for me, that's a family trait. I wish nothing but the best for you, Bette, but I'm going to marry Cora . . . if she'll have me."

"This is a mistake you are making." Bette stood, smoothing her dress. "Felix, I say goodbye now."

"Goodbye, Bette."

She swept away, not looking back once, and not looking jilted in the least.

Looking to the sky, Felix let relief wash over him. At least he'd handled *that*. The biggest challenges lay ahead, though. In the distance, the sky darkened, clouds turning the color of ash as if to confirm his thoughts.

He watched the parade for a few more minutes, shaking his head as an old, white-haired Union veteran in a carriage brandished his wooden leg at the crowd and offered spectators sips from his bottle of whisky. The gentleman tumbled out of the carriage, then popped back up like a jack-in-the-box—an impressive display of agility for an elderly man with one leg.

Felix rose, put on his hat, and went to find Cora.

* * *

Cora knelt in the tiny garden behind the boardinghouse, her hands desperate for occupation. Dirt and seeds, new life springing up under her touch, the satisfaction of plucking out weeds—these things erased her troubles, at least for a while.

"I'm a farm girl without a farm," she'd told Felix a few months after her parents died, when she sold the farm to pay off the creditors.

Her wistful tone had hinted at what she'd lost. Growing up in the open air, laying under a sky blanketed with stars; she thrived in big, empty spaces. She'd lost her parents and her sky. Her world had dwindled to the few stars that outshone the hellish red glow of the foundries and a patch of earth no bigger than her childhood bedroom.

Judging from the darkening clouds closing in on the city, heralding yet more rain, she'd soon be trapped within the dingy walls of her room in the boardinghouse. Her evening would consist of helping Mrs. Dormer haul buckets of water out of the basement with the other tenants. The same conversation repeated itself, with a few variations, every time:

"Think the dam might break this time?" Jacob, or perhaps Mr. Charles, would ask.

"Don't be silly," Mrs. Dormer would say. "Every time it rains, someone's worrying over that dam, and every time the sun comes out, we're right as rain, pardon the pun."

"And even if it breaks," Sally, Mrs. Dormer's levelheaded daughter, would break in, "it's miles and miles from us. Let South Fork and Mineral Point wring their hands. We'll be perfectly fine."

"Say," Jacob would say, "did anyone hear what Mr. Heiser's boy Victor said to Mrs. Ness?"

And so on, every day until the rain stopped at last. Cora plunged her fingers into the heavy, wet dirt once again. Despite her frantic gardening, that broken piece of coal in her chest weighed her down. She wished for a particular kind of foolishness, the ability to deny her feelings. These ones insisted upon recognition.

I'm in love with him, she thought. *I'm in love with my most treasured friend, who's supposed to marry another girl.*

Drat.

A shadow stretched out beside her, its lines distorted but familiar—but the parade still clattered, blared, and whooped in the distance.

She turned, shielding her eyes from the sun. He stood above her, a halo of light obscuring his features.

"Oh," she said, swallowing her surprise, "hello."

He reached a hand down, and she took it after a moment's hesitation, letting him help her to her feet. His eyes twinkled, hinting at a secret.

Keeping his hand in hers, she dropped into a playful curtsy. "Dr. Bayer. Congratulations are in order, I presume."

A grin spread over his face. "Yes, and thank you. You can call me Felix, as always."

"Well, I'm quite honored. How does it feel to be a doctor?"

"It feels . . . not quite real yet. But good, just the same. It's going to be wonderful, Cora."

He'd talked for years of establishing a practice in the city, helping people, being respected. Every time, a little glint snuck into his eyes.

"I missed you at the parade," he said.

The first parade we haven't watched together in thirteen years, she thought.

"I'm sorry. Th-the noise bothered me."

He raised an eyebrow. "But you love everything about the parade. Most of all the noise."

Of course he pinpointed her fib with marksman-like accuracy. The excitement of the parade, the joy of the crowd always drew her in. She'd even come close to hollering one year.

"Well, it was a bigger crowd than usual." Cora crossed her arms. "And besides, the planting season is almost finished. I have a few more seedlings to transplant, and the rain's kept me inside."

"Cora," he said, then stopped, looking away and tightening his lips. When he returned his gaze to her, his eyes beamed bluer than a summer morning. "Cora—I don't want to marry Bette."

The coal in her chest flared back to life again. Her voice hid in her throat for a moment. "Oh? I thought you couldn't live without a good German girl who will give you many little German children and cook all of your favorite German foods."

He grinned. "I might, in fact, survive without said German girl. I sometimes wonder if it's a case of exposure, actually."

Cocking her head, Cora let a small smile dance across her lips. "Exposure? How do you mean?"

"When autumn first comes, it's a relief after the summer heat, yes? But then, it turns to winter, and soon enough you're cold all the time." He shoved his hands into his pockets, tilting his chin downward and gazing at her through the golden fringe of his lashes. "And if you're continuously exposed to the cold, like the night we got caught in that snowstorm on our way home from Meryl's Christmas party out in Ebensburg, it can seriously harm you."

Cora laughed. "We nearly died," she said, "but somehow all I remember is how funny you looked trying to dig the runabout out of that snowdrift with your bare hands."

He offered her his arm. "You tried so hard not to giggle— very admirable of you."

Delighting in his warmth, dizzy with pleasure, Cora slid her hand into the crook of his elbow. "And it's very chivalrous of you not to mention my abject failure."

"I'm always a gentleman." He led her to the little back porch, where a battered pair of chairs awaited. "But as I was saying, exposure can kill you. As, for instance, might be the case if you spend most of your life hearing that one particular girl is the only girl for you."

"I see." They settled into the chairs. "Well, that explanation makes perfect sense. You're suffering from Bette exposure."

"Exactly."

Silence fell between them—not awkward or unpleasant, but content and comfortable.

"So," she said at last, "you've dashed Bette's and your mother's hopes, all in one fell swoop?"

"We-e-ell, just one set of hopes so far."

Cora nodded. When he helped her with her arithmetic in their old school days, Felix always insisted on getting the easy problems out of the way before moving on to the hard ones.

"It's all preparation, practice for the harder parts," he'd tell her.

Of course he applied that same method here, even if this issue made the hardest arithmetic problem in the world look simple in comparison.

A few fat raindrops splattered against the wooden floor. The clouds completely obscured the sun now—it was only three-thirty but the sky held no more light than at dusk. An invitation inside hovered on her lips, but if they took their conversation to the stuffy parlor, Mrs. Dormer's gossip train would deliver the news to Mrs. Bayer by morning.

Reading her indecision, Felix stood. "I suppose I should be going. School is back in session tomorrow?"

Cora grimaced. "Yes. I'm sure the students will be wonderfully focused on a Friday, after an exciting day off."

He took her hand and covered it with one of his own "Maybe I'll come by after dismissal? Or you can come up to the farm for dinner? You haven't visited in ages."

Cora shifted her weight. Mrs. Bayer's demeanor at the parade intimated her feelings toward Cora. A tremor of fretfulness skittered through her stomach.

"Perhaps," she said. "But you'd best get home before the deluge really starts. Again."

Still holding her hand, he took a small step so they stood a few inches apart. She stared up into his eyes, lost in their blueness, their kindness. A soft, slow smile touched his lips, and for a long, warm moment, no one existed but them, and the world opened itself like a blooming flower.

A door slammed somewhere inside the boardinghouse. He stepped away, regret sliding across his expression for an instant. She wanted to reach out, pull him back. She clasped her hands behind her back.

His smile returned. "Tomorrow, then?"

Not trusting herself to speak, Cora nodded.

"Good," he said. He opened his mouth as if to add something, then grinned. "Good."

* * *

After a soaking wet drive into the woodland and farmland above the city, the scent of sauerkraut greeted Felix at the door. Luisa came running. She threw her arms around his waist.

"Oopf!" Felix staggered back with exaggerated clumsiness. "Should I get accustomed to being assaulted with affection every time I walk through the door, or will this fade in time?"

She grinned up at him, her embrace loosening a little. "I like having my brother home again."

"Ah. So you're trying to break my back to ensure I stay here forever?"

Blinking, Luisa pulled back. "But won't you? You'll marry Bette, then you'll build a house on the farm and help Papa with the planting and the harvesting and the animals. That's what Mama said you'd do."

A sigh rose in Felix's chest, but he pushed it down. "Go practice your sums so Miss McCallister doesn't give you a dunce cap, Lulu."

He meant to tell his parents about Cora at dinner, but Luisa's excitement gave him pause. Better to break the news to her in his own way. Even if he waited until she'd gone to bed, sounds carried well in the little farmhouse, and Mama's temper would quiet for nothing and no one.

Tomorrow, then, at breakfast, after Luisa left for school.

The waiting made for a long evening, and the incessant pounding of rain against the roof mixed with Mama's smug glances to fray his nerves as the family ate dinner. Papa, either sensing the storm clouds gathering under his roof or annoyed at the ones outside, kept his head down as he shoveled sauerkraut and knackwurst into his mouth.

A tinge of guilt wormed its way into Felix's heart. Defying Mama promised to be a loud, disruptive affair, but he'd survive it. Papa's quiet, level stare, though—the idea of meeting that faded blue gaze, so direct and honest, and declaring his intentions—*He just wants what's best for his family. That's all he's ever wanted. I hate to disappoint him, but I'm a grown man and I have to do what's best for me.*

After dinner, he distracted himself by quizzing Luisa on her arithmetic and vocabulary. Then, the family worked to haul important items upstairs to keep them safe from yet another small flood.

"Perhaps we should start a tradition of carrying everything upstairs before the spring thaw," Felix joked as he carried a stack of books upstairs, "and then bringing it back down sometime in July."

All through the night, he lay in his childhood bedroom, rain roaring against the roof, unable to sleep. Morning dawned gray, the clouds continuing their torrent as though punishing Johnstown for an unknown offense.

"Papa took Luisa to school," Mama said when he appeared downstairs. "She should stay home, I think, but he insists."

Felix nodded. When Papa returned, then, he'd open the bag and release the squirming, yowling cat within. Mama set him to work hauling water from the basement. After a cold half-hour of sloshing about the muddy water with a bucket, Papa's footfalls resounded through the floor above him.

A little twinge sprang up in his stomach, but Felix went upstairs, changed into dry clothes, and took his place at the battered wooden table with Mama and Papa. Even the eggs, bacon, ham, and potatoes of Mama's incomparable *bauern-fruhstuck* failed to inspire an appetite. The head of Papa's prize stag watched him, harsh accusations in its eyes. How had he lasted a decade under its baleful stare?

No more.

"I don't want to marry Bette. I'm not going to marry Bette."

Mama shoveled a forkful of egg into her wide mouth, not pausing an instant. "Bette, she will make you a happy man."

"No, she won't. I'm not going to marry her."

Papa's gaze darted between them, but he said nothing.

"A good German girl like Bette, she is the only wife for you."

Felix took a deep breath. "I'm going to marry Cora. If she'll have me."

Papa watched Mama, Mama stared at Felix, and Felix lifted his chin and refused to look away. The stalemate broke at last when Mama's fork clattered to her plate. Her face flushed. She pushed her chair back, heedless of the loud scrape of chair legs against dry wooden plank, and rose to her full height.

"You do your duty as our son and marry Bette. No more talk of Cora."

Felix stood. "You cannot force me to marry anyone. This is America, Mama, and things are different here. I will marry Cora if she'll have me, and no one else."

Outrage filled Mama's eyes. "You are a traitor to your family, your country if you do this. Your country, *Germany*, not America." Her voice rose with each word. 'You throw away your tradition, your heritage, your family. Papa, speak with your son. Make him see sense."

With that, she swept from the room.

Papa steepled his fingers. "What are you doing, Felix?" The level stare, the disappointment arrived.

Felix squared his shoulders. "I'm making a choice. I'll never be happy if I marry Bette. And there's no reason why I should. It's silly to make the birthplace of someone's parents the sole basis for a marriage."

"But Bette, she can keep German traditions alive. This is basis enough."

"I know enough of our traditions to keep them alive, Papa."

"Oh, have you learned to cook German food while we sleep? Did Cora learn our language so she can teach it to your children? Is she Lutheran now?" Papa stood. "This farm, it is yours if you use it well—providing for a *German* wife and *German* children. Children who share our heritage and religion. If not Bette, then another German girl. But no other."

"That's fine." Felix hoped his voice sounded stronger to Papa's ears than it did to his. "I don't need the farm. I'm going to start my own practice. I've told you that for years."

"Then, be a doctor. Hire workers for the farm."

"I don't want that if it means losing Cora."

"Do you want family? Because if you marry her, you lose your family." Papa switched to his native language for the final blow. *"Der Gescheitere gibt nach, der Dumme fällt in den Bach."*

He left, but his words remained, an echo from childhood. Every time Felix butted heads with Mama or Papa, they trumped him with that proverb. He usually chose to follow its guidance:

The wiser gives way, the fool falls into the creek.

He let out a long sigh, then smiled. *The storm came, and I survived it.* Grabbing his coat and mashing his hat onto his head, he hurried out the door.

It's time to fall into the creek, he thought.

* * *

Cora stood at the window of the schoolhouse, peering through the thick curtains of rain. The water in the streets stood about two feet high. The few students in attendance crowded around her, the smaller ones stretching onto tiptoes to look out the window. A few inches of water slopped about their feet.

"I believe I should take you home, children," she said.

They didn't pause, didn't panic. They gathered their things and hurried to the door. Most of them lived nearby, but a few—Luisa included—came down from the farms in the hills. She'd take those children to relatives' houses or, failing that, to her own home.

An hour later, she and Luisa made their way to the boardinghouse, soaked and shivering.

"We'll find you a blanket to wrap you in when we get there, Lulu."

Luisa trudged through the dirty water, now nearing three feet high in places, her little legs pushing against the resistance. Cora knelt and gestured for Luisa to climb on her back. Thus, they arrived at the boardinghouse, both of them buzzing with the adventure of it all despite their discomfort. Water covered the front steps and lapped against the door.

Climbing to the second floor, they encountered no one, but indistinct voices drifted from a few rooms. Cora stripped the quilt off of her bed and wrapped it around Luisa.

"Here, sit on the bed. I'll find you something else to wear so that your clothes can dry."

Nodding, teeth chattering, Luisa settled on the bed. Her blond curls glued to her face, she watched with plain curiosity as Cora searched through her clothes.

"Mama says we have to keep Felix away from you," she said.

Shaking her head, Cora dug an old flannel nightdress from the chest of drawers. "Does she, now?"

Luisa took the nightdress, and Cora turned around to give her a moment's privacy.

"Yes, Mama says Felix has to marry Bette. She said she doesn't want any of her *enkelkinder* to be Catholic."

Cora winced. "Hm. That's . . . fascinating." Trying to make her expression impassive, she turned back around. Luisa stood in the nightdress, which reached the floor and gathered around her feet.

"And Mays says that Papa says Felix has to marry Bette because he loves his family and he'll never leave us. Do you think he'll marry her? I don't want him to leave the family."

Cora pushed down the hysterical laugh threatening to strangle her. Luisa stared at her, awaiting her answer.

"Lulu . . ."

"Yes, Miss McCallister?

She forced a smile onto her face and took a long, deep breath. "I'm going to put on some dry clothes. After that, let's play checkers, shall we?"

* * *

Arriving in Johnstown, Felix raised his eyebrows. The Conemaugh River and Stony Creek, which ran along the northern and western borders of the town, swelled over their banks, where they joined the rainwater filling the streets. He gave up trying to get through town in the runabout, leaving it and the horse at a stable. The streets lay empty, but a few people called down greetings from second or third story windows.

Turning back would be prudent, and certainly more comfortable, but he'd wade through boiling lava to find Cora—and Luisa, whom he wished had stayed home—and ensure their safety. A long, taxing walk to the school found it empty. He wanted to check the boardinghouse, but the fast rising water forced him across a bridge—which threatened to wash away at any moment—to Westmont Hill at the city's edge.

He huddled under the trees for a few cold, wet hours with only the sound of rain smacking against leaves for company. Impatient, he climbed higher up the hillside to survey the city. Up, up he went, thick mud sucking at his shoes, until he reached a small clearing that offered a good vantage point. Numerous church bells struck four o'clock, their tolls echoed through the mist.

The gray city spread out in the valley, miserable under the oppressive clouds. Opposite Westmont Hill, the hills rose again, encircling the city but for a small gap at the northeastern point, through which the Conemaugh River snaked. Below him, in the lower part of the city, the river joined the creek. His gaze found the square, then tracked three blocks west to find the boardinghouse. Cora and Luisa most likely sat in the parlor or Cora's room, warm and safe. Once the rain ceased and the water levels lowered, he'd make his way back into town. He'd tell Cora he loved her, pull her into his arms, kiss her, and never let her go.

A train whistle shrilled from beyond the opposite hill. It screeched on and on, far longer than usual. He tensed. It stopped at last, and he nodded. A long silence followed.

An explosion rocked through the valley. Felix flinched. A moment later, a black cloud rose behind the opposite hills.

A bone-shattering roar followed it, like a mythical giant tearing the world in two, and then his hands flew to his mouth in horror as a colossal wave—*Dear God, it must be thirty feet high, no, forty at the least*—burst through the gap, dark, churning, and inescapable, obliterating everything in its path.

* * *

The long train whistle interrupted the game of checkers, but Luisa had nearly all of Cora's pieces, anyhow. Cora rose from the floor to glance out the window. Her room offered a view of the city and the northeast hills if she stood on her tiptoes in the corner.

The whistle stopped, but the explosion that followed sent a chill through her blood.

"Lulu, come here, quickly now."

Luisa scurried over, bunching the nightdress in clenched fists to avoid tripping. Cora pulled her close.

I must keep her safe.

Black smoke rose behind the hills, thick roiling clouds of oily darkness billowing toward the sky.

A mountain, moving somehow—*how can a mountain move, that's so silly*—thundered through the gap.

No, not a mountain.

Fear quaked through her limbs as a wall of water, impossibly huge, roared into the valley. Debris choked it, convulsed within it, turning it brown and black.

Houses, parts of houses, stores, machinery, trees, and there—*no, not a locomotive, that's impossible, but yes, it can't be anything else.* The wave tore down everything in its path, knocking over houses and buildings before subsuming them into itself.

She hoisted Luisa up, clutching her in shaking arms. Luisa's high wail overflowed with terror.

"It's going to be fine, Lulu, just fine—"

The wave hit and the house shuddered, trembled as if in fear, creaking and cracking, threatening to fall apart. She stumbled several steps but managed to keep hold of Luisa, who buried her face in Cora's shoulder.

The water slapped against the wall a few feet below her window. Within the morass churned leaves and branches, a mantel clock, a bicycle wheel, a bale of barbed wire from the wire works. Homes and roofs and tree trunks and chunks of bridges tumbled past, some slamming against the house. Another few minutes, seconds, even, and the house would crumble beneath them.

Shaking Luisa to get her attention, she pulled away to meet the girl's eyes.

"Darling, we have to climb out the window and find something that might carry us to safety. Can you come with me?"

Luisa nodded, but the stark white of her face belied her agreement.

"I'll hold you tightly the entire time. It'll be like a game, all right? Come along."

She opened the window and clambered through the window, ducking her head and pushing Luisa's down to squeeze through, so they sat astride the wide sill. Part of a roof approached, bobbing up and down, on a path to slide right next to the house. If she timed it right . . .

Sucking in a deep breath, she leaned out, and—tightening her one-armed grip on Luisa—twisted out of the window to fall onto the roof. The fall jarred her, cracking through her bones, but Luisa kept hold, little fingers digging into her shoulders.

"We have to hang onto the roof!" Cora shouted.

Luisa scrambled off of her, grabbing at the ridges of the tin sheeting for purchase. Rolling onto her stomach, Cora followed suit. Together, they pulled their way toward the peak of the roof.

Around them floated neighbors and strangers. People used roofs, train cars, logs as rafts. Others flailed in the water, trying to grab any available piece of debris. The waterborne ruins of the city tossed several below the surface and crushed others. Mrs. Fenn from the dry goods store rode a tar barrel through the flood, its contents splattered over her skin and dress, wrestling with the barrel as the current turned it this way and that. The congregation of the desperate bounded and lurched past homes still standing, where people stared out windows and ran over intact roofs. Whether in the water or above it, though, fear stretched every face into grotesque contortions as screams and sobs, prayers and curses rose above the chaos.

* * *

Felix's knees melted beneath him as the wave swept over the city, carrying the contents of neighboring towns. A second, smaller wave came to join it. It spread out over the valley, crushing houses and churches and stores to nothing, then collided with the hillside thirty feet below him with a thunderous explosion. The impact rocked him off his feet.

The wave, finding no outlet at Westmont Hill, then turned back the way it came. It unfurled over the lower half of the city.

His hands dug into the mud and his knees sunk into the ground. His heart crashed against his ribcage, it's fast but uneven rhythm roaring in his ears to mingle with the sounds of pandemonium swirling in the valley.

Water and wreckage flowed over the Stone Bridge until debris choked its arches. Then, more and more, machinery from the mills tangling with trees and girders, freight cars smashing into nearly intact houses and buildings. And there, at the rollerskating rink where he and Cora once laughed at their inability to stay upright for more than a minute—it joined the ruins of their town heaped at the bridge. Over the next half hour, the debris piled up and up, then out and out, a hopeless mass. Each heavy collision with the mountain of wreckage brought a chorus of wrenching screams from within.

Felix's horror grew every minute, spreading through his veins like black sludge. His legs refused to push him upright. Stretched out before him, soaked and tossed about, the city of his birth cried out. Somewhere down there, amidst the chaos and the death, Cora and Luisa needed him. He had to find them. Then, he could help others.

He stood. Closing his eyes to shut out the scene, he took a deep breath and prayed for the strength to help as much and as many as possible after he found his sister and Cora.

Opening his eyes, he swept one last glance over the valley before taking the first step of his long descent into hell.

* * *

Everything floated together across town, slowing to jam the tight space between two brick buildings. Cora and Luisa's roof crashed into the churning mass. Clenching her teeth, Cora fought to keep her grip. Tree trunks, freight cars, building girders shot from the water around them. The pressure built and built until, at last, the buildings crumbled. The mass burst past and over the obstructions, into open water.

They sped along on the current, bobbing up and down, hugging the tin roof. On and on, only slowing when the tempestuous waters slammed them into buildings. Ahead loomed the Stone Bridge, a viaduct built by the Pennsylvania Railroad two years before. Its seven arches stretched across the river, but now the river raced over it. Cora's stomach dropped as their roof hurtled over the bridge and then plunged down into the shallower waters filling the canal. The jolting pace of the current kept on, though, knocking them about like toy dolls. They edged closer to the bank, where a few people stood. A woman, her dress torn and bedraggled, leaned over and reached out a hand. After wrapping an arm around Luisa's waist, Cora caught the woman's hand. A barefoot man, his suspenders sagging, jumped in to help, and together the bystanders hauled Cora and Luisa to shore.

Breathless, shuddering, Cora lay on her side in the muddy earth, her skirts tangled around her legs. When Luisa crawled to her, curling into a ball and nestling into her side to heave helpless sobs, she let the tears come at last.

* * *

The desperate cries pulled at Felix as he reached the bottom of the hill. He shut them out. Cora and Luisa came first.

Mrs. Morley ran up to him, her dress soaked and torn. Wild brown eyes pleaded with him as she pulled at his hand.

"Help, please, my husband and my children, they're at the bridge—"

"I can't." He tried to withdraw his hand from hers, but she held tight.

"Please, my *children*."

Felix's gaze swept over the scene. People gathered at the bridge, trying to extricate survivors from the building piled up there.

"All right," he said at last.

Felix helped pull survivors from the wreckage, his breath catching at each flash of red hair from within. He paused to assess the severity of each victim's injuries, treating the life-threatening ones in any way possible before moving on to the next. A few blocks away, church bells tolled five o'clock. An hour ago, in a different life, in another world, he'd stood on the hillside, thinking of Cora and smiling.

With the help of two other men, he pulled a tar-splattered Mrs. Fenn from the jammed debris. She sagged against him, gaze blank, muttering about her children. A quick examination found no serious injuries, so he guided her to the group of dazed survivors they'd already found.

He found Mrs. Morley's family in the remains of their house. Only a small portion of a window allowed escape, but the rescuers managed to evacuate the father and all four children.

On and on he went, climbing over the remains of his city to pull people free, giving medical attention if possible, helping many and losing more. Numbness set in as darkness fell, and the rescuers gave in at last. They'd saved seventy or so.

He stepped away from the wreckage. Jacob, the coal miner from Cora's boardinghouse, separated from the survivors congregating on the riverbank and pumped his hand up and down. His brown eyes shone, bright and hectic. Long gashes along his arm and face testified to his ordeal—a light encounter with barbed wire from the wire works. Far worse injuries had come from the wreckage.

"Thank you, Mr. Bayer. I didn't expect to escape that mess." Haggard and drawn, he looked as though he'd aged ten years.

Not Mr. Bayer, he thought with a start. *Dr. Bayer.* The weight of the title pushed his shoulders down, when a few hours ago it had possessed all the weight of a feather.

A shout rose up from near the wreckage. "Fire!"

A flood and a fire all at once, it's too much, it's impossible. But the scent of smoke insisted on the reality of the situation. Felix turned to offer his assistance. After a few steps, he whirled, an inquiry about Cora and Luisa on his lips, but Jacob had vanished.

* * *

Cora awoke at dawn on a cot in the front parlor of someone's house. She hadn't an inkling who lived there, as several branches of a family had gathered to aid the shocked, the wounded, the wandering. Luisa curled up next to her, face slack, curls tangled, chest rising and falling in a slow rhythm.

A sharp knock at the door brought the woman of the house—or one of her relatives, perhaps—scurrying through the parlor. A moment later, Mrs. Bayer burst into the room, her face drained of color, her dark-ringed eyes telling the tale of a fearful night.

Her gaze swung to the cot. "Luisa," she whispered.

Careful not to rouse Luisa, Cora slid from the bed. The movement sent pain flaring up her back, down her arms and legs. She glanced down at her borrowed clothing, a too-large skirt and a too-small shirtwaist, and pulled a ragged shawl tighter around her shoulders. She imagined her flame-red hair gone white, her skin sagged and withered, a handful of decades stolen from her—surely, nineteen had turned to ninety while she slept. She hobbled to Mrs. Bayer, who stood frozen in place.

"My Luisa," Mrs. Bayer said, her glance darting between the cot and Cora. "How did she survive? How?"

"I took her to the boardinghouse. When the flood struck, we caught a roof floating past and rode it through the flood, nearly all the way here."

Mrs. Bayer's lips tightened. She looked away. "My girl, you saved her?"

"Of course." Cora straightened, trying to don her school-teacher demeanor. She'd survived hell and horror. Mrs. Bayer no longer unnerved her.

Nodding, Mrs. Bayer looked back at her. "And my Felix? Have you seen him?"

Dread, cold and slick, slithered up her back. "I thought he'd have been safe at home, in the hills. He . . . he was in the city?"

"Yes. I have been looking, but . . ."

They stared at each other for a moment, fear passing between them. *We both love him*, Cora thought. *She finally understands that.*

"I'm going to find him," she said.

Mrs. Bayer turned to watch Luisa again. A muscle twitched in her forehead, but she wore a determined grimace. "My Felix. You can—that is to say, I will not protest if you—"

Cora considered making Mrs. Bayer actually say the words. Instead, she let out a long breath. "Yes, Mrs. Bayer. Thank you."

Luisa twitched, moaned, then sat up, blinking and yawning. "Mama?"

Mrs. Bayer cried out and flew to her daughter.

Cora set out into a gray, ruined world. People wandered the streets, some looking for shelter, others for loved ones. She waylaid everyone she passed, asking after Felix. With each sympathetic shake of a head, her heart climbed higher into her throat.

A deep male voice called out to her. She whirled, Felix's name on her lips, only to find Jacob.

"You're alive!" he cried.

The reality hit her again, death's icy breath on her neck, their narrow escape. How many mothers, fathers, children had the flood taken? She took a deep breath and nodded.

"Oh, your friend, the one who was off at school? Bayer?"

Her breath caught. "Felix?"

"Yes, that's the one. He saved me. Pulled me from the window of a house that got caught in the jam at Stone Bridge."

Her heart raced as fast as her feet wanted to. "Is he still there?"

"He was last night."

She needed no more. She turned to toss a hurried bit of gratitude over her shoulder before breaking into a sprint.

In the distance, the fire raged toward the sky. Her scuffed boots slapped over eight ravaged blocks before she found him sitting alone on a stranger's muddy, debris-strewn lawn. His blank stare slowed her pace. She paused to take stock—he possessed all limbs, looked sound of body and handsome as ever, still able to make her heart turn cartwheels and dance jigs, even with dirty, soot-streaked clothes and face.

She forced herself to ease up to him. Kneeling beside him, she put a hand on his shoulder. He turned, staring at her for a long moment before comprehension swam into his eyes. One shaking hand rose to caress her cheek.

"Cora." He said her name as though praying, as though asking a vital question, as though no word in any language meant more. As though her touch carried him back from a fearful precipice, where he'd stared into an unimaginable abyss.

But it was perfectly imaginable to Cora—she'd stared into it, too. She pulled him close, and he wrapped strong arms around her. His lips touched hers, not the innocent kiss she'd dreamt of, but a kiss overflowing with passion and pain, a kiss for the new, ravaged world they lived in now. He pulled back to gaze at her, eyes shining.

They melted into each other, clutching at one another in the ruins, and she whispered his name over and over, a promise for the future, for a life after the wreckage and the grief, for hope.

Their world lay in pieces around them, but the clouds above parted to let a sliver of light pass through, and a new day began.

DOG ISLAND

by Melissa Yi, 9,000 words

Dr. Lou Van Leeuwen flies north of the 60th parallel, figuring he can make a quick buck after graduation by working with the Inuit, before he hurries home to his pregnant wife. Instead, he finds himself in a village shrouded in mystery—with one woman who could break his heart.

Just like Lou, Dr. Melissa Yi spent a month of her residency in the remote Inuit town of Puvirnituq. She ate raw ptarmigan, cooked caribou, and boiled goose. Melissa writes the Hope Sze medical mysteries, which was hailed by Publishers Weekly as "entertaining and insightful." In the latest, Human Remains, Hope joins an innovative Ottawa stem cell research team, only to discover a dead man in the snow. Melissa loves to connect on www.melissayuaninnes.com, Facebook (https://www.facebook.com/MelissaYiYuanInnes/), and Twitter @dr_sassy.

P uvirnituq. Lou Van Leeuwen had never heard of the place two years ago, and now he was in the aisle seat of an Air Inuit Dash 8, sucking on a caramel to stop his ears from popping as they descended on the town of Puvirnituq, a cluster of blue and red houses surrounded by snow.

Lou wouldn't have chosen to spend a month north of the 60th parallel, in the most remote regions of Canada. But truly isolated regions paid the best after graduation from family medicine residency. He could make $10,000 in a week. By pressing the flesh, getting to know the system, and sucking up, he could make more in seven days than the underpaid, underworked clinic docs made in two months.

Of course, in the meantime, the cheap-o residency program wouldn't pay for his wife Alicia's plane ticket, and they couldn't afford a $2500 plane fare plus a month's leave of absence from her substitute-teaching job in Montreal. They had a baby on the way.

While the plane tilted toward the earth, Lou glanced across the aisle at a little girl kicking her legs in the air. Lou liked kids okay. But now that Alicia was pregnant, they seemed omnipresent. Even on the long flight up, he'd been startled to catch something moving out of the corner of his eye.

A baby had crawled in the aisle toward him.

Lou must've looked surprised, because the mother had immediately scooped her son up. The baby had kicked his moccasin-clad feet, but hadn't cried out.

For the first time, Lou had felt strangely touched. He'd never seen babies do anything but cry and sleep on planes. This mother had trusted the other passengers not to step on her child.

Maybe kids wouldn't be so bad after all.

At last, after spending the day rising and descending into every Cree and Inuit village on the way, the plane landed with a thump, a bounce, and a squeal of brakes at its final destination. Lou's teeth clenched, but he smiled. Welcome to Puvirnituq.

They clambered down the plane's stairs onto the concrete tarmac. It was still winter in May. Snow mounted on either side of the runway. The wind stung his cheeks, so he paused to pull on his parka hood. Then the smell of gasoline drove him up the airport stairs.

The airport was basically one big room with a plate glass window to watch incoming planes. Kids pointed and yelled. One small girl in a pink dress stood so close that she smudged the glass with her nose.

A little boy pounded out of the airport door, down the stairs to the tarmac, and into the arms of a middle-aged man who crouched down to his level and picked him up.

Lou felt something twist inside his stomach. Alicia was pregnant. What the hell was he doing here?

But he couldn't think about that. Lou's duffel bag stuttered down a ramp of metal rollers, and he seized it. Now, all he had to do was find the guy to take him to the hospital.

Around him, teenagers grinned at each other, families hugged, and everyone called out. Inuktitut was a funny language. Guttural. Not like anything he'd heard before. He was glad they were speaking their own language. So much for globalization. They all sounded fluent and then some.

"Hi!"

Lou spun around to see a short Inuit man in a green soccer jacket. "Are you here for the Chimo Hotel?"

"Uh, hello. No. I'm here for the hospital."

"Okay." The man walked up to the next white guy and said, "Hi! Are you here for the Chimo Hotel?"

Slowly, the airport emptied. Lou saw an elderly Inuit lady, stooped but still smiling, bearing down on the little girl in front of the window.

The girl, who looked about five years old, froze in her a frilly pink dress. She clutched a windbreaker in her right hand. She stared at the old woman.

The crone smiled. She was only a foot away.

The little girl darted across the room and climbed on an empty blue chair. A young woman with chin-length black hair scooped her up.

The old lady stopped short and sucked her cheeks. She lowered the head, pretending to study the floor.

Lou had thought that the Inuit respected their elders. Shouldn't that little girl let the old lady hug her? Or, if she was a bit shy, the mother could have reassured her.

But, now that he thought about it, in the olden days, didn't the elderly climb on ice floes and float out to sea?

Why was he even thinking about this stuff? Lou shook himself. He'd just finished his licensing exams over the weekend. He was exhausted.

If he wanted to impress this hospital, he couldn't stay marooned at the airport. He had to get out of here.

He maneuvered his way over to the expressionless young guy at the front desk. "Hi. I'm the new resident doctor from Montreal. Is someone here to take me to the hospital?"

The guy's eyes flicked past Lou's shoulder. "No one is here now. Wait. Someone will take you."

Lou sat on his duffel bag by the window to watch for a vehicle. It was 2:40 p.m. Where the hell were the hospital people? He whipped out his no-service phone to check for the number before heading for the pay phone. Local calls were free, a sign informed him. Well, that was civilized.

A woman answered after the fifth ring. She said something in Inuktitut.

"Hello? Is this the hospital?"

"Yes." The word was flat, the s drawn out, sibilant but comprehensible.

Somehow, he'd expected better English. "Hello, this is Dr. Van Leeuwen, the resident doctor from Montreal."

Long pause. "Who you calling?"

"I'm calling for my driver. Someone is supposed to pick me up from the airport."

Longer pause.

He tried again. "Who is picking up the doctor from the airport?"

"Who you calling?"

"The driver! Do you have a driver? That's what I was told."

Longest pause. "Okay. We send a driver."

"Thank you!" He hung up. The guy at the front desk was staring at him. Who cared. If this was the way they ran the hospital, it was going to be a long four weeks.

He sat down to wait on his duffel bag. There were only about five passengers left in the airport. They were waiting to fly to Salluit, one of the few Quebec village north of Puvirnituq. A yellow Twin Otter plane landed, and the last people boarded.

It was 3 p.m. He called the hospital again. "Hello, this is Dr. Van Leeuwen. I'm still waiting for my driver."

The operator said, "You want Dr. Van Leeuwen?"

"No! Give me Dr. Charbonneau, please." Dr. Valérie Charbonneau had better coordinate this.

The phone rang and rang, and eventually he got, "Bonjour, vous avez rejoint le bureau de Dr. Charbonneau—"

Shit! She wasn't even there. He felt like pounding the receiver into the wall.

The desk guy was eyeballing him again. Lou said, "Excuse me, are there taxis to the hospital?"

The guy wrinkled his nose. "No taxi. You need a driver."

"They can't figure out how to send me one!"

The guy shrugged. "The driver will come."

"There is no driver! I've been waiting here almost an hour!" He took a deep breath. "Can I walk there? How far is it?"

More nose-wrinkling. "You need a driver."

"I know that. I—"

A little girl swung behind him. "A-a-aaaa-aaaaaaah . . ." she said, her voice, bouncing with each step. Lou recognized her ruffled, pink dress and was momentarily distracted.

He turned back to the counter, but the Air Inuit guy had already stepped out to talk to the girl's mother. She was wearing a violet Gore-Tex parka and now had a firm grip on her daughter's hand. The woman glanced toward Lou, showing a round face, pointed chin, and brown face less tanned than the other Inuit.

The airport guy returned. "Mina can drive you." He nodded at the woman.

"She can? Oh, that's great." He crossed the room in five strides and held out his hand. "Hi, I'm Lou Van Leeuwen."

She hesitated, then dropped her daughter's hand to shake his. "Hi." Her voice was muffled.

"Mina?" he said, imitating the airport guy's long i. It sounded like mynah, as in bird. It didn't rhyme with Tina.

She nodded, dark brown eyes flicking up to meet his own, briefly. He felt a twinge in his stomach.

The girl bounced up and down, her pink skirt poufing out with each bounce.

Mina touched her daughter's forehead and said something in Inuktitut.

Lou smiled at the little girl and squatted down beside her. "Hi. My name's Lou. What's your name?"

She buried her face in her mom's black slacks.

Mina's soft voice answered, "Her name is Elisipi."

Elisipi peeked out. Lou smiled. She hid her face again.

Lou laughed. "I get it. Well, thanks for the ride, Mina. I really appreciate it." He strapped on his backpack and hefted his purple duffel bag. "I'm ready whenever you ladies are." He smiled at Elisipi. She squealed and ducked her head between her mother's legs.

Mina called out to the counter guy as she plucked her daughter free and wrestled an indigo windbreaker on her. Lou followed them out the door.

The tundra was flat and covered in snow. An occasional rock jutted up. That was all. There was certainly no car.

Mina walked up to a black vehicle with huge wheels that looked a bit like a riding lawn mower. She climbed on the seat and lifted Elisipi behind her, then gunned the ignition. It roared like a motorcycle.

"What's this?" he yelled. He felt like an idiot.

She grinned slightly. "An ATV."

She and Elisipi basically filled up the banana seat. All that was left was a crossbar grid behind them, probably for carrying stuff. He dropped his bag on one side and parked his butt on the other. He felt very unbalanced. Plus, the thing reeked of gasoline.

She pressed the gas pedal and the ATV rolled toward the dirt road. She used her left hand to change gears. The engine sounded like it was going to strangle itself, but it couldn't be going more than 40 clicks. Probably a lot less.

Elisipi turned to look at him. He stuck out his tongue. She squealed and hid her face against her mother's jacket.

He leaned forward to yell into Mina's ear. "Why don't you have cars here?"

"No roads," she said before the wind whipped her words away.

They don't even have paved roads. The place must be a giant dust bowl in the summer.

It took them fifteen minutes to roll over the tundra to a cluster of houses. The houses all looked the same, like barns, except their roofs varied between red and blue or green.

Elisipi briefly leaned against him, then screamed and rocketed forward, hugging her mother.

He could feel every pothole in the road. Surely, this wasn't good for the testes. Alicia had persuaded him to wear boxer shorts because of a newspaper article about lower semen counts in hard core cyclists. There was no evidence that he had any trouble with his sperm, but whatever.

After a month or two, they'd decided that babies didn't make financial sense yet, and Alicia had gone back on the pill. Two months later, she'd dangled a positive pregnancy blue test stick in front of him.

Thank God accidental pregnancies on oral contraceptives didn't raise the chance of birth defects.

Alicia was four weeks pregnant now, or six weeks past her last menstrual period. When he was in a good mood, he felt awed by how early that was. It seemed so precarious, so precious. He'd delivered a handful of red-faced newborns, but too many women came to the emergency room, bleeding, cramping, and terrified that they would lose their baby.

At last, the ATV stopped at a ramp to a building that looked kind of like a giant trailer on stilts. This must be the hospital. "Thanks, Mina," he said. "Maybe I'll see you around."

Her black eyes regarded him for a moment before she nodded.

"And you, too, cupcake." He ruffled Elisipi's hair. She batted him away, giggling.

Dr. Charbonneau met him at the door. She reminded Lou of a lioness: shaggy red hair, slightly flared nostrils, and an aggressive way of jutting her chin out when she was talking, even though she was only five feet tall. "You made it! Sit down. I'll be with you in a minute."

Her office looked like any other: corner desk with a computer, big wall filing cabinets. The only interesting thing was a poster on the wall, put out by the government, celebrating "aboriginal Canadian achievements in the health industry." Lou stood up to examine it more closely. All the thumb-sized photos were of women who were nurses or nurse administrators.

Then, there was Mina. His heart skipped a beat. She was staring at the camera, unsmiling, but still, something about her face, about her black eyes, drew his gaze. Her hair was a lot longer in this picture. She had bangs. Mina Tookalook, registered nurse, it said. He smiled. What a great name. Tookalook.

"There you are!" exclaimed Dr. Charbonneau. "I forgot all about you."

Yeah. The lack of driver was a tip off. Lou faked a grin.

"Sit down, sit down. I want to tell you about working here. I've already assigned the medical student to the wards, so you're going to start on the clinic side for two weeks, and then you switch."

Lou nodded. He hated clinics, especially his own in Montreal.

The bipolar Quebec separatist who requested narcotics.

The morbidly obese woman who claimed disability for her obesity.

The psych patient who asked for a rectal exam every time he came in.

Sure, there were some normal, young patients who moved away. The debilitated and the demanding remained year after year.

Sometimes, Lou dreamed about how it was like as a kid. Trying not to sit down in front of everybody because his pants were already too short. Taking mustard sandwiches to school, while all the other kids threw their apples away.

Sometimes, the adult Lou couldn't sleep, worrying about the baby coming. Alicia had been on the pill for the last ten years. One glitch, and they'd conceived. Just when they'd been treading water forever and could finally see the S.S. Safety in the distance.

"You're such a worrywart, Lou," said Alicia, when she caught him brooding over their credit card bill. "It's all good."

Maybe she was right. He loved her, and he'd love the baby. But he couldn't help wondering, if she hadn't ovulated for ten years, why it had to happen now.

*   *   *

"Lou?" Dr. Charbonneau was staring at him.

"Yes, Dr. Charbonneau."

She gave a hearty laugh. "Valérie, please! I'm not that old! So, can you speak French?"

"Yes."

"Oh, that's good. You see, most of the older Inuit speak English, but the young people speak French as their second language. It's because the federal government used to fund the school system, but now it's the Quebec government. So, it's best if you can speak both, but we can work around it! We do have interpreters!" She winked at him.

He forced a smile.

"You'll find the medicine interesting. Lots of sexually transmitted diseases, because there's nothing to do, so that's what they do. There's only one case of HIV that we know of. So far." Her eyes widened meaningfully.

He nodded. There were advantages to isolation, but it sounded like an apocalypse waiting to happen.

"There's no cystic fibrosis, either, because the Inuit don't carry that gene. But it's coming. There's lots of intermixing going on nowadays, oh, you wouldn't believe it. I tried to do a case study last year, but it was hard to figure out the genetics because they're always adopting each other's children. I finally gave up on that study, but it's something a student could work on, if he were interested." She glanced at him out of the corner of her eyes, and Lou forced a smile. *Yes, I love doing scut work so that you can get your name on a paper. Yes, please!*

Valérie continued, grinning, "There's not much alcohol or diabetes—it's not like working with the Cree. The Inuit here are only allowed alcohol once a month. But they do drink. Almost everyone smokes, which contributes not only to respiratory infections, but also otitis media. Otitis is much more serious here than down south and can lead to mastoiditis and even deafness." She stood up. "Now, let me show you how the hospital is laid out. We've got to get you set up for your clinic tomorrow!"

As they walked, she glanced at his boots. "Let's go back to the front. You're supposed to take your boots off."

Shoot. "I don't have any shoes."

She stared at him. "Why not?"

"I wear my boots at work." This was going to be hell on respect, if he had to work in his socks. He added, "Unless you don't mind running shoes."

Relieved, she sailed onward. "Sure! Why would I care?"

So, he dropped his boots at the main entrance. The hospital was built in a circle, with three major spokes radiating outward: the clinics, the hospital wing, and the offices. They had their own cafeteria and pharmacy.

He was surprised to come upon a middle-aged Inuit woman on her knees, sweeping the floor with a single brown feather. Valérie marched right past her. "This is our cast room. And this is radiology. We have our own X ray technicians, and they do ultrasounds, too."

At Valérie's insistence, they spent some time pondering clinic charts and layout. This was a real do-it-yourself operation. There were nurses to take care of all the bread and butter complaints, like sore throats, but Lou would have to dole out his own pills and collect his own urine samples. Great.

"Oh, here's Dr. Bruce! Bruce Nelligan," she added to Lou, "but he has all his patients call him Dr. Bruce, so we do, too. It's cute."

A man with silver hair and a matching moustache crushed Lou's hand as he shook it. Lou gave as good as he got.

"Pleased to meet'cha," said Dr. Bruce. "You should have a fine time in PUV. Excuse me."

They watched him flap away in baggy, old tweed pants.

"What a dear," said Valérie fondly. "He's on sick leave right now, but he pitches in every so often. His patients miss him. Tomorrow, I'll introduce you to the rest of the group. The other permanent doctor is Dr. Gilbert, and we have two dépanneurs at the moment, Dr. Chang and Dr. Parent. And the medical student, Nick, arrived yesterday."

"Super," lied Lou.

Finally, she released him to unpack. "You can talk to Nick tomorrow and decide how you're going to take call. We'll call you if there's anything interesting. Sometimes, we have to fly to villages and stabilize patients for transport here. And sometimes, we call the Challenger, and they go directly to Montreal."

Lou nodded and smiled until his cheeks ached.

* * *

Elisipi likes dogs.

This dog is chained to a house. He has fur like butterscotch.

Elisipi is standing just out of reach. She and the dog are staring at each other. He is standing very still. His mouth is open. His breath is a cloud in the air.

Mama said no.

Mama said dogs are dangerous.

Mama's not here.

Elisipi stretches out a mittened hand.

The dog strains forward, sniffs quickly all around her hand.

His jaws open a crack.

Elisipi snatches her hand back.

The dog's jaws snap shut. He barks and prances, his fore-legs scrabbling at the air. His front paws fall to the ground.

He jerks at his chain, barking and barking, but Elisipi is already running away.

She doesn't belong here. The dog knows.

Everyone thinks she's stupid, but Mama says she's special. Mama holds her tight and says that Elisipi had better mind her, or the Qalupalik will carry her away.

Everyone knows the Qalupalik. They live in the ocean. They have long, tangled hair, green skin, and nails like claws. They wear an amautiit coat, slip babies into the hood, and take them away.

Elisipi shivers, just thinking about the Qalupalik.

Where's Mama?

* * *

Lou's apartment was bigger than he expected. There was a sitting room with a battered olive chesterfield and a dining room table. The kitchen and bathroom were at the rear, to the right, and the bedroom was on the far left. Lou threw his luggage in the bedroom and whipped out his calling card to try his luck on the land line.

Alicia sang out, "Helloo."

"Hi, babe."

"Louie, baby! How was your flight up to the koala's ear?"

Lou laughed. Alicia thought the province of Quebec was shaped like a koala. Hudson Bay and James Bay scooped out the back of the head and a body, while Ungava Bay defined the ears. "Better than trying to get away from the airport. I finally hitched a ride on an ATV."

"No. Really? What was that like?"

"Bumpy. I thought my luggage was going to fall off, not to mention me." He left out Mina and Elisipi. Alicia might not be interested in the locals.

"How's your apartment?" she asked.

"A lot nicer than 'transitional housing' made it sound. Pretty normal, except the bathroom warning lights for 'no water left' or 'septic tank is full'."

"Nice." She laughed.

He sat on the bed and dropped his voice. "How're you feeling?"

"Great!"

"Really?"

He could practically hear her smile. "Yes, really."

"Did you go to school today?"

"Of course. I have to bring in the bacon, you know."

She was teasing, but he had to say it. "Not if you're not feeling well."

"Lou-ou!" He was sure she was rolling her eyes. "How many times do I have to tell you that I'm fabulous?"

"I know. I just don't want you to hide stuff from me because I'm not there and you don't want me to worry."

"Why would I do that? It's much more fun to make you pee in your pants when you're too far away to do anything about it."

He laughed reluctantly. "Bitch."

"You knew that when you married me."

"Okay, babe. I love you."

"I love you."

"Say hi to the baby for me. And play it some Bach."

"I already did." She sighed, but all she said was, "I love you. Bye."

* * *

Lou and Nick, the medical student, lugged their groceries from the outskirts of the town. "I like the stop signs in Inuktitut," said Lou.

A dog howled.

They hesitated, but kept walking. One dog, then several, started barking. Lou and Nick rounded the corner and saw why.

A series of dogs were chained to stakes along the frozen riverbank. They looked a good part wolf, with thick fur coats and snapping jaws. Most were sandy brown, but there was one black one and one white one. All looked mean. Hooves and bones lay scattered in front of them. Their barks filled the cold air.

"Jesus," said Lou.

Nick seemed fascinated. "I like dogs."

"These aren't dogs, man. They're wild animals." Lou started up again, but Nick reached into his Co-op bag.

The dogs howled. The nearest one, the black one, lunged at him. It choked on its chain, but pranced just out of range.

"C'mon!" called Lou.

Nick hesitated. "I think they're just hungry." He grabbed his package of smoked arctic char and threw it at the black one.

The dog leapt and seized the package out of the air. He dropped it on the ice and tore the plastic open with his teeth. The rest of the pack threw themselves to the limits of their chains, straining to get at the fish. They howled.

"Shoot," said Nick. "I guess I should have given it to all of them. I don't have any other good food."

"Come on, you idiot!" Lou dragged him away. If any of those dogs wrenched itself free of its chains, he and Nick were basically walking meat with bags of even more delicious food.

Once they were mostly out of earshot of the dog riot, he took a deep breath. "Nick—"

"That was neat, wasn't it?"

"Look, Nick. I don't know anything about dogs, but those looked pretty wild to me. I wouldn't hang around giving them dog chow."

Nick looked dreamy. "Yeah, I guess I could give them dog food. That'd be cheaper than fish. I was supposed to bring that home to my parents. I've heard the arctic char is amazing."

Lou snorted. Med students fell in love with everything. Why not wild dogs? "Whatever. If they rip you to shreds, just remember that this isn't a trauma hospital. The Challenger would airlift you to Montreal."

"Hey man, chill. They're all chained up." Nick cast a glance back at the ululating dogs. "I'd love to bring one of those puppies back. Now, that's a real dog."

"Whatever, dude." Lou started walking back to his apartment.

"Wait, Lou. You see that piece of rock out there?"

Lou peered at a shelf of rock in the distance, a rift of black between the snowy tundra and white sky.

"That's Dog Island. One of the nurses was telling me."

"Yeah? They have more monstrosities over there?" Lou made a mental note never to visit.

"No. Just over the summer." Nick waved his hand. "Every summer, the Inuit take all the dogs over there by canoe. Once a week, they bring food. So the dogs fight each other, and only the strongest have puppies. At the end of the summer, the guys bring back the dogs that survive."

Lou thought about it. His grocery bags were digging ridges into his fingers. "I guess that makes sense."

"Yeah." Nick kept glancing back. "I don't think they'd mind if I took a dog. They're just going to let them kill each other."

Lou shook his head. Taking a sled dog to southern Quebec and trapping it in an apartment seemed like a bad idea to him. But he wasn't Nick's daddy. He headed home, and eventually, Nick followed.

*　*　*

Lou's clinic turned out to be a joke. His morning job was to set up patients for the afternoon.

He was supposed to flip through a file of all the people who needed to be seen that month and pick out whoever he thought was interesting and/or urgent. He sifted through the hypertension and other crap and found a cancer patient, one kid, and a guy who had abnormal liver function tests.

He wrote down three names and handed it to the secretaries. They'd call the patients in for an appointment in the afternoon. His job for the rest of the morning was to "read", always a code for "we have nothing for you to do." Lou flipped through a survey on Inuit health, surprised to see that the median age was only 23, compared to 40 for the rest of Canada. Fifty-two percent of the Inuit smoked every day, compared to only 16 percent of all Canadians. And 67 percent of children in the Western Arctic showed some degree of hearing loss. Yikes.

Two hours later, a secretary called him back. "You'll have to get two different patients." Her voice was choppy with that Inuit accent.

"Why?" he asked.

"The first one doesn't have a phone. I've been calling her on the radio, but she hasn't answered. She may be in the bush."

"Okay. What happened to the next one, the guy?"

"He's in jail."

Oh. That was a good reason. "Okay, I'll go through the file again."

She barked something that he couldn't understand and hung up. He held onto the receiver for a second, wondering if she'd sworn at him.

Valérie came by. "Did you book the obstetrics patient?"

"Ah, sure," he lied. He'd never been into obstetrics, though he found it more interesting now that Alicia was going through it.

"Good! She's a sweetheart. She worked as a translator before she became a nurse, so you should be fine speaking English."

He found a second substitute patient, a woman with abdominal pain, and leafed through the charts. At 1:15, he discovered that the secretaries had misunderstood his corrections and booked the obstetrics patient first. Of course, that was the only chart he hadn't read.

Lou had to retrieve his own patient from the waiting room. It was chaos. Some kids were literally rolling on the floor. Others pushed toy trucks or hugged stuffed animals. Their mothers and aunts chatted on the benches along the wall.

Lou looked at the chart in his hand and swallowed hard. "Uh—Mina Tookalook?"

There she was, in the corner, talking to someone, their faces partially obscured by a potted plant. Mina's round face turned to him. She wore a shy little smile.

His heart sped up. He found himself smiling back so wide that he probably looked like a clown, but he didn't care. "Hello again."

"Hi." She picked up her violet parka and said something in Inuit to her friend. She was wearing a loose navy fleece shirt and cargo pants. She boosted herself up—now that he was looking for it, he could tell that she was pregnant—and followed him to the clinic, padding along in her white cotton socks.

He sat at the desk. She headed to the examining table, but Lou waved her toward the chair beside him. She hung her jacket neatly on the door hook before settling down.

"Hi, Mina. I'm Dr. Lou Van Leeuwen."

"I know," she said simply. She had less of an accent than the secretary, but her voice was so quiet that he had to lean forward to hear her. She smelled fresh, like laundry detergent.

"Well, congratulations on your pregnancy."

She didn't answer.

He turned red. He'd always been a blusher—Alicia sometimes called him The Dutch Lobster—but usually not with patients. "Mina, if you feel uncomfortable with me as your doctor, you can come back and see someone else." Unbelievable that his first patient was the one person he'd met. Well, except for the Air Inuit guy. And the Chimo Hotel man.

"No. It's okay." She met his eyes.

And with that one look, Lou was suddenly conscious of her solemn black eyes, the wide span of her cheekbones, the mounds of her breasts under her fleece top.

This can't be happening, he thought. *It isn't. I'm married. My wife is pregnant. I am a doctor. Get back in the program.*

He cleared his throat. "What was the date of your last menstrual period? Oh, here it is. Never mind. So you're 27 weeks along. That's great. Let me see if your last doctor had any concerns—"

For the second time, he froze, but not in a good way.

25 y.o. G3P1A1, 25 weeks GA, was recently in emergency for assault. Multiple contusions on abdomen and back, cigarette burn on left upper thigh. Normal fetal heart rate, no vaginal bleeding. She refused to talk to social worker and insisted on returning home with friend. Urgent follow-up needed.

Her eyes were calm. She spoke before he did, in her shell-soft voice. "Yes, he beats me."

"Oh. Oh, Mina." He had role-played this situation before, practicing the ideal things to say to patients, but it had never happened in real life. He was so angry that he had to consciously unclench his jaw. "Do you want to leave him? Do you want help?" His head was spinning, but he kept his voice level. "I don't know all the resources, but I'm sure Dr. Charbonneau does. Why don't we—"

"I can't leave him." She levered herself up and climbed on the examination table.

"Wait. Mina." He half-laughed. It wasn't funny, but it was all just so bizarre. "I haven't even talked to you yet. Come back."

She pulled the blood pressure cuff out of the basket on the wall. She dropped it in her lap, pushed up her sleeve, and fought to wrap the cuff around her own left arm. He got the message loud and clear: just do the check-up.

He stared at her. "Mina."

She kept fiddling with the cuff. The Velcro made scratchy noises as she pulled it on and off. The sound filled the whole room.

* * *

Dr. Valérie Charbonneau listened to Lou, her reading glasses perched on the end of her nose like a supercilious librarian. Lou's voice rose. "I don't know if we have women's shelters here or what, but we'd better get her out of there."

Valérie took off her glasses and started to polish them. "Lou. At any time, did she agree to press charges?"

He sighed loudly. "No."

"Did she even tell you who it was?"

"No. But it doesn't mean we're just going to sit here and let him kill her! She's pregnant! And she has another daughter, Elisipi! She said he doesn't hurt Elisipi, but I think we might be able to get him on emotional abuse. I mean, she probably has post-traumatic stress from listening to it, and there may be other kids in the house—"

Valérie put her hand on his arm. He shook it off. She pressed on. "Lou. Did Mina ever say she wanted to leave her home?"

"No." His face was flaming. "But if it's because there's nowhere to go, that's not acceptable."

"Lou, you just did your exams."

"Yes."

"You know the rules. We can't do anything unless she wants to press charges. Does she want to press charges."

His voice was strangled. "No."

"Well, then."

He stood up and knocked the chair over. "Well, I don't know what kind of health care system you run here, but there's nowhere for women to go. And there's a lot of it going on. One of the dépanneurs said that yesterday, he had to do an STD screen on an entire family because a two-year-old had gonorrhea. Two years old! That's disgusting!"

"Lou, sit down."

"Sorry. I have to go back to see my patient and tell her we have nothing to offer her."

"Lou—"

He slammed the door.

* * *

He was still pacing the apartment, hours later, when his phone rang. "Oh. Hi, Alicia." He twirled the phone cord around his finger.

"Well, who died?" Her cheery voice rang in his ear. Had she always been this loud? This insensitive?

"No one."

"Aw, come on. You've got the Darth Vader death voice going on."

"No one died. I think."

"Is something wrong?"

He shrugged. "I saw a pregnant patient today. Her boy-friend beats her."

"That's horrible!"

"I know."

"So, what did you do?"

"I went to see Dr. Charbonneau."

"And?"

"She basically told me to fuck myself until the woman presses charges."

Alicia sighed. "Shit. That sucks." After a minute, she said, "Evan called."

"Yeah?"

"Yeah, he's all excited about our baby. It's cute."

"That's good."

After a minute of silence, Alicia said, "Are you feeling okay?"

"Sure."

Pause. "Is it something else?"

He flared. "Why, is this not enough?"

"No." Pause again. "Just, I don't know, you see a lot of sad stuff. I don't know why this bugs you so much. Like that old guy who came in with no liver—"

"Alicia," he said tightly, "I'm going to hang up now."

"What? Lou—"

He slammed the phone down. Jesus. No one else was going to help him. He had to help Mina. Just had to.

He was pacing around his apartment when the doorbell rang. He'd already had some little kids come by, trying to sell him trinkets for $25. He stepped out of his apartment and opened the landing door.

It was Mina, with a new black eye.

Her hand flew to cover it, but she caught herself. She swallowed hard. Her hand fluttered to her side.

"Hi," he said softly. "Come on in."

She pressed her lips together. "I shouldn't be here."

"Come in," he repeated. He looked behind her. "Did you bring Elisipi?"

She shook her head. Her eyes were on the floor. "She's at a friend's."

He stood aside. Avoiding his gaze, she slipped inside. He took her jacket and hung it up while she took off her shoes. She was wearing the same white socks, which touched him. She hovered in the doorway.

"Come on in. Sit down."

She hesitated. "I fell," she said, jutting out her chin.

"Okay. I'm sorry to hear that. Do you want some ice for your eye?" He crossed to the refrigerator and tossed some ice cubes in a Co-op bag.

"It's okay."

"No, it's not." He pressed the ice bag in her hand. Finally, her fingers closed around it, and she allowed him to lead her toward the olive couch, but she remained standing.

"I'm sorry." Her knuckles were white from clutching the bag.

"For what? I'm happy for your company." He strode back over to the kitchen. "Can I get you a drink?"

She stiffened. He pretended not to notice, went on, "I have water—brought home from the hospital, since they say it's not safe to drink it here—and milk. Well, I have Fruité too, but it's awful. I wouldn't recommend it."

Finally, she sat down. He brought her a glass of water with ice in it. "If you want anything else, I'll bring it."

Her eyes filled with tears. She abruptly turned away.

He set the glass on the coffee table. "Do you want me to call the police?"

"No!" She jerked to a standing position.

"Okay. Okay! I won't. I promise, Mina."

She turned to look at him. Her left eye was puffy and mottled purple, but she still looked beautiful. "I promise," he repeated.

Slowly, she sat back down again.

He crouched down beside the chesterfield. "I guess you don't want to go the hospital, either."

She shook her head.

"So . . . what do you want me to do?"

She shrugged.

"Do you want to stay here?"

Slowly, she nodded at the floor.

"Okay." He stood up. "Can I get you dinner? I was going to boil up some pasta and pour some store sauce on it. Is that okay with you?"

Her voice was almost inaudible, but he could read her lips. "Thank you."

"You're welcome."

* * *

"Whaaaaaaaaaaaaaaaat?"

Lou grimaced and held the receiver away from his ear. He could still hear Alicia's voice: "Are you CRAZY? Or are you just pulling my leg."

"I'm serious," he said into the mouthpiece, quickly moving the receiver away again.

"I can't believe it, Lou, what has gotten INTO you? I thought you were just getting some experience for locums, but now you're telling me you have some strange woman in your house—"

"She didn't have anywhere else to go."

"Oh. Oh, don't tell me that. I am not stupid, Lou. I remember you telling me—didn't Dr. Charbonneau say that it's a community and they take care of each other? They adopt each other's children. Do NOT give me this bullshit that she had nowhere to go—"

"Alicia."

"—My God, it's only your first week. Did your brain get frozen or something? Taking in a woman—"

"She's not—"

"Oh, don't give me that. I can hear it in your voice. She is your PATIENT. You are LIVING with her. I don't know how many rules that breaks. You could lose your license!"

"Alicia, I haven't—"

"And what about ME? What about your BABY? Does that matter to you, you dumb fuck?"

"Alicia—"

She hung up on him. He held the receiver, listening to its dial tone blare, feeling the warm plastic under his palm.

A shadow fell across the doorway. A small shadow.

Lou hung up the phone, crouched, and held out his arms. "It's okay, Elisipi."

Elisipi tore across the room. "Oof," he said good-naturedly, as she bounced off his belly. He wrapped her in his arms and closed his eyes.

* * *

Lou waited until after dinner and the dishes to broach the subject. Mina stiffened immediately. He tried to explain it again. "It just looks bad because I'm a doctor. You shouldn't be living with me. It looks even worse because I'm a male doctor. Now, uh, you and I know that nothing would happen, but it could be very serious. Maybe you could live with Dr. Charbonneau—"

Mina shook her head.

"Or one of the other doctors—"

Vigorous head-shake.

"Or a nurse or social worker."

She stood up and beckoned to Elisipi. "We're going home."

"No, Mina. It's not that you're not welcome here. Maybe I can get Nick to—"

Mina grabbed the stuffed rabbit and handed it to her daughter. Mina hauled Elisipi by one hand as she ripped open the closet door and grabbed her backpack.

"Now, wait a minute."

She twisted the doorknob.

"Mina. Come on!" He ran across the room, but she had already run out. By the time he grabbed his keys and jacket and boots, she and Elisipi were long gone.

* * *

Elisipi's teacher is mad again.

"No, Elisipi. I told you to draw a picture of your family. This is just a picture of flowers again. I told you to pay attention yesterday. Didn't I?"

Elisipi ducks her head.

"Look at me when I'm talking to you. Didn't I?"

Elisipi glances up at her, then down again.

"That's better. Now, go to your desk and draw me a nice picture of your family." The teacher tosses the flower drawing at the bin. The paper floats in the air, drifts, and settles on the edge of the bin. Bye-bye poppies. Bye-bye . . .

Elisipi darts forward and seizes the drawing. She runs back to her desk. Her heart pounds. The teacher's voice follows her, heavy with disappointment. "Oh, Elisipi."

Elisipi doesn't hear her. Her hands are clenched tight around the paper edges. She sits down and, still clutching the paper, places it on the desk and pushes her nose against it until the world is all red and green and yellow marmalade.

Elisipi is safe again. As safe as she will get until the rituals work on the man. Her grandmother will help her get the words just right. Then, Elisipi will get away from the Qalupalik.

Elisipi will be safe forever.

* * *

Nick lounged against the doorway. "Are you finally done?"

"Yeah." Lou rinsed the soap off his hands. "I had to count out the pills for the last patient."

Nick checked his watch. "Wanna do something after supper?"

"Like what?" Lou shouldered his backpack.

"Karate class. The head social worker is a black belt."

Lou hesitated. "Next time. Let me know if you see any good dogs on the way."

Nick held his thumb and index finger up and pretended to fire a gun. "Will do."

After supper, Lou walked up the covered ramp to his house. He opened the unlocked outer door to the building's hallway.

Mina spun around to look at him. Elisipi bounced up and down and giggled.

Somehow, he'd known they'd come back.

"Hi, cupcake." He ruffled the girl's hair. She made a muffled sound of protest. He unlocked the inner building door with his other hand and pushed it open for Mina. "Welcome home."

This time, when he let her into the apartment, Mina hung up her own jacket. She licked her lips. "Thank you. Lou."

It was the first time she'd said his name. It slipped out of her mouth with a low-pitched dip. He smiled at her. Despite everything, it felt right.

Elisipi pitched herself on the floor and grappled with the remote control.

"Let me help you with that, hon." He glanced at Mina first. "Is she allowed to watch TV?"

She smiled slightly. "Always."

"Well, there's not much choice here." He hit the power button. "Playoffs on English CBC; or the playoffs on French CBC."

Mina laughed. Elisipi tried to swipe the remote control.

He dangled it in front of her face. "What do you say, honey?"

Elisipi tried to grab it again.

Whoops. Maybe she didn't know the magic word, especially in English. He held the remote just out of reach. "Can you say 'please', Elisipi?"

Elisipi jumped in the air. He held it higher. "Come on, honey. Say please."

Elisipi jumped one more time, then burst into tears.

Mina picked her up and cuddled her face against her blouse. Mina's mouth was set. "She doesn't talk."

"Not even in Inuit? I mean, I just thought she was shy . . ."

Mina shrugged. Lou felt like the world's biggest heel. Still, it was weird: a five-year-old who didn't talk. But Mina's lips were pressed together into a line as thin as a toothpick, and he knew she wouldn't answer any more questions.

He gestured toward the dining room table. "Can I interest you ladies in dinner?"

Mina wrinkled her nose. She rocked her daughter for another minute, then set her down. Lou held out the remote. Elisipi grabbed it and belly-flopped on the floor, in front of the TV.

Mina sat on the chesterfield. "How are you?"

He stood beside her. "I'm okay. I was worried about you. Both of you," he added.

"Why don't you sit down?"

He hesitated. "I don't want to make you uncomfortable."

She arched her back against the couch. Her breasts were well-defined under an embroidered white blouse. He looked away.

She said, "I'm not uncomfortable."

He studied her toes. She was wearing black stockings under a long, silky black skirt. No white cotton socks today. When he thought his blush was under control, he risked a glance at her face. She looked innocent.

He kept standing. "So . . . where did you go?"

She shrugged. "Around."

"And were you, uh, okay?"

She shrugged again. Her black eye had faded, and she seemed to be wearing green eyeshadow to disguise it. She patted the couch beside her.

He glanced at Elisipi. She was rubbing the floor with both hands, to no purpose that he could see.

Mina smiled knowingly at him.

He sat down.

"How's your wife," she murmured.

"Uh. Not too good. She's, uh, still mad at me. She'll get over it," he said. It sounded hollow to his own ears.

"That's too bad," said Mina. "If I had a man like you, I wouldn't let him go."

He swallowed hard. "Thanks." He pretended to watch the hockey game. The Canadiens scored. "Uh, good game," he said.

She raised her eyebrows. By now, he knew that that meant yes in Inuit. It reminded him of Alicia, though.

Alicia, of the sarcastic eyebrows. Her wide brown eyes. The delicate skin on the inside of her wrists. The way she cried out and shut her eyes when she came. His wife.

He stood up. "I have to call her."

Lou hurried to the bedroom. He fumbled for his wallet, yanking out the calling card. He snapped on the bedside light and started picking out the numbers. 1-8-0-0 . . .

Mina cleared her throat.

He looked up.

In the warm yellow light of the lamp, her skin was a golden brown. She was slowly, deliberately, unbuttoning her blouse. She had already exposed a tender V of skin at her neck.

The receiver clattered out of his suddenly nerveless fingers.

She paused. Then her slender fingers undid the buttons at her breasts and continued downward. When the last one was unfastened, her blouse parted of its own accord around her proudly rounded abdomen.

He could hardly breathe. He advanced on her. A thousand choices were screaming in his ears. Her eyes were black and perfectly composed. She was watching him.

He reached behind her and closed the door.

The latch clicked.

She slid off the blouse. With the barest whisper, it slithered to the floor.

The curve of her collar bones. Her breasts, surprisingly luscious, with delicate brown nipples. But most of all, he was drawn to the smooth, fine skin of her proudly pregnant abdomen. God help him, he reached out to touch her skin, not as a physician, but as a lover.

And she said, "Promise me, you'll take Elisipi back with you."

"What?" His hand jerked back.

Her face was perfectly composed. Her black eyes held his as she enunciated clearly. "Promise me that when you leave, you'll take Elisipi with you."

Dear Jesus. "You don't know what you're saying."

"I know what I'm saying. You can have—me—" She gestured dismissively at herself. "But promise to take Elisipi."

He scooped her blouse from the floor and handed it to her, his head averted. She took it from him, but held it in front of her with no move to get dressed. "Please, Lou."

"No!" He didn't mean to yell. Elisipi might come in, and there were neighbours. "Are you crazy? Why would you give away your daughter?"

"Because I have to." Her voice was calm, but her hands tightened into fists. "I know what I'm doing."

"No, you don't. You'll regret it for the rest of your life."

Her gaze was level. "I don't care. It's for her."

"How? How can it be in any five-year-old's best interest to lose her mother?"

She wrinkled her nose. "You wouldn't understand."

"Try me."

She sat down heavily on the bed. "I can't protect her here."

"From who?" He struggled to keep his voice low. "You have to tell me who."

She sighed. "Dr. Bruce."

He gasped. He couldn't help it.

"I know you don't believe me."

"It's not that I don't, it's just . . ." He struggled for a minute. It would be easy to report Dr. Bruce to the disciplinary college. Lou could do it himself. "I mean, even if it is him, why do you have to move her out of here? Dr. Bruce doesn't have to be her doctor. She could see Dr. Charbonneau. Or the nurses."

She shivered, clutching the blouse against her. "It's my uncle, too."

He didn't ask. Couldn't ask for the details. He couldn't bear them. Not now.

He tried to take another tack. "Why don't you both come back with me? Do you have any money?"

She laughed shortly.

"Mina. I don't know how to tell you this. But I don't have any money, either."

She stiffened. She shoved her arm through a sleeve, almost ripping the fabric.

"Wait. Slow down. It's not that I don't want to. But I don't have much savings, and the way it's looking with my wife, I'll have to split it with her if she leaves. Even if I get a line of credit, it'll take time."

She was buttoning up so fast that she missed a few. The material gaped at her breasts and belly, and it hung askew. She threw open the door, and then she did a funny thing: stamped her feet, first left, then right.

Elisipi looked up.

Lou stared at them. "Oh, my God," he said. He'd only seen that call to attention in one other circumstance.

Elisipi was deaf.

* * *

The next day, armed with written permission from Mina, although no one else seemed to care, Lou studied Elisipi's medical records.

Elisipi would need a formal assessment by an audiologist to measure the extent of her hearing loss, but of course the next audiologist wasn't scheduled to come for three months. She already had a long waiting list, and there were no promises that she'd reach Elisipi, at number 49, on this visit. Or the next.

Then there would be another wait to fit her for hearing aids. God knew what quality of hearing aids she'd get up here.

Was there a speech language pathologist in the region? Probably not, and certainly not one who could dedicate herself to one little girl in Puvirnituq. Elisipi needed daily coaching and periodic re-testing to see if those hearing aids worked.

If they failed, Elisipi could be a candidate for cochlear implants. But it would take years to untangle this process, and even if they proved she needed them, there were no guarantees. One little boy outside of Montreal was refused a cochlear implant, partly because doctors in Quebec City said he was too old, at the age of nine, and partly because he could already speak through sign language. His family ended up raising $68,000 for the procedure in Vermont.

Out in the real world, Lou's world, as long as you had money and influence, there were options beyond cochlear implants.

A 15-year-old got North America's first bone-anchored hearing aid at the Montreal Children's Hospital.

A three-year-old who was born without auditory nerves flew to Los Angeles for stem cell therapy at the University of Southern California.

Lou didn't have money. But as a newly minted M.D. with a cause, he'd have influence. He'd start off with case reports and make presentations to wealthy bleeding hearts. He'd glad hand politicians and wrangle audiologists up to PUV if he had get his pilot's license and to fly them in himself.

But first, he'd bring one little girl to Montreal for the testing and care that she needed.

One little girl who'd need the protection of her mother.

* * *

The children are running. Elisipi is running, too. Her mouth is wide open, and she is ululating.

She can hear herself yelling, thanks to Dr. Lou.

Elisipi is chasing her friend Jason. But she is also chasing the autumn air, the baby blue sky, the smell of dead leaves, the speed of her own feet in bright red sneakers.

Mama is happy. She got a job, and she said it pays so good.

Soon, Elisipi will be in class. School is bad sometimes. Not as bad as she thought the Qalupalik would be—no one has green skin, and only Dr. Lou's wife has too-big teeth—but pretty bad.

Kids make fun of her hearing aid.

Kids try to sneak it off her earlobe before she feels it.

Kids yell at her, then pretend it's because she's deaf.

Kids trip her and call her squaw and Eskimo.

And it is too hot, most of the time.

But for now, Elisipi is chasing her own self, screaming through the playground, and it is enough.

ASHES TO ASHES

by Shane Simmons, 10,000 words

Ashes to Ashes *is a dark mystery/thriller about a stylish death-obsessed couple who are willed the cremated remains of a complete stranger and seek to discover why.*

Shane Simmons is an award-winning screenwriter and graphic novelist whose work has appeared in international film festivals, museums and lectures about design and structure. His art has been discussed in multiple books and academic journals about sequential storytelling, and his short stories have been printed in critically praised anthologies of history, crime and horror. He lives in Montreal with his wife and too many cats. Visit him at eyestrainproductions.com, or follow him on his Amazon author page, Facebook and Twitter @Shane_Eyestrain.

The groundskeeper threw the last few shovelfuls of dirt onto plot eight, row thirty-nine. There was no marker at the head of the grave. The man inside the simple box six feet underfoot was an unknown, listed as "John Doe." He was one of many in the vast family Doe that consumed much space and little thought in the pauper's cemetery. Each was duly accounted for on the detailed chart which mapped out the contents of every plot in every row—just in case it ever mattered. It never did.

There was no priest or holy man to administer the last rites. That was done weekly, en masse, back at the morgue before the accumulated collection of floaters, drug O.D.s, and frozen transients—unclaimed all—were put to rest in holes hollowed out by the long-tooth arm of a municipal backhoe. Total cost per client: fifty-three dollars, charged to the city's taxpayers. It was fifty-three dollars more than the government had spent on any of them when they were alive, and most of it went to pay the groundskeeper's hourly wage for filling in the holes in a neat and orderly fashion so their occupants, in death at least, would never again be an eyesore.

Besides the groundskeeper, no one ever attended the simple ceremony that saw the plain pine boxes lowered into the pre-dug pits and covered over quickly and quietly. A pair of exceptions had recently sprung up, however.

They were a young couple, urban, successful, and thirty. They came to a pauper's burial once every week or two, stood silent vigil over one of the graves as it was filled, and left a single red rose each. They both wore black, for style rather than grief, as though they planned to hit a few trendy clubs once they roared off in their dark European sports car parked down by the gate.

It was on their fifth visit to yet another anonymous grave that the groundskeeper had to ask, "You knew him?"

"Can any of us really know someone?" said the man solemnly.

"It's hard, I'll give you that," agreed the groundskeeper. "Especially when it's some heroin junkie no one bothered to claim."

"Someone's son," said the woman.

"Maybe someone's father," said the man.

"I'm sure the family would have appreciated us being here."

"I'm sure *he* would have appreciated it."

The groundskeeper couldn't quite place the tone of the couple's eulogy. He just knew it made his skin crawl. A few pats with the flat of his shovel settled the earth, and he was off on his break a moment later without pursuing further conversation.

The couple climbed back into their sleek two-seater and consulted the page of obituaries that lay folded on the dashboard. The day's highlights were all circled in red.

"That cleansed the palate," said the man. "I like these little no-name ceremonies. They lack the circus atmosphere of the priest and the family and the crying, but it's nice for a quiet change."

The woman took an inventory of their dozen fresh roses. They were now less four.

"If we wait around an hour, we can catch those two homeless people they picked out of a dumpster," suggested the man.

"No," she answered. "Let's go where the action is."

* * *

The funeral parlour was filled with unfamiliar faces, strangers all, including the guest of honour in the box. The couple stepped into the room and was greeted by an elderly lady hovering over a memorial album, fishing for signatures. She offered her hand, which was eagerly accepted by the woman.

"Thank you," said the old lady, "I'm glad you could make it."

The man took a pen in hand and signed the album for himself and his wife, saying, "We wouldn't have missed it for the world."

The couple's faces didn't ring any bells with the old lady. Awkwardly, she asked, "I'm sorry, I didn't know all of Edie's friends. You are . . . ?"

The woman, still holding her hand gently, consolingly, told her, "Mr. and Mrs. Ashley Carter. And you?"

"Please, call me Louise. Ah . . ."

The old lady waited for a first name from the woman.

"Ashley," was the response.

"I'm sorry, you're both named . . . ?"

"Ashley. Ashley Carter."

"That's quite unusual."

"Well, I thought I'd adopt my husband's name since I already had half of it. It makes co-signing things so much easier."

"It's very romantic," said the old lady, unsure.

"We're very close," Mrs. Carter said as her husband took her arm and led her down the aisle to the casket.

The coffin was open as the Carters had guessed it would be. They tried to restrain their nervous anticipation as they waited impatiently in line for those seeking to pay their final respects to disperse. The queue moved at a fairly brisk pace as each person filtered past the coffin in turn, but the Carters brought traffic to a grinding halt as they lingered over the body and examined the handiwork of the funeral directors at length.

"She looked quite young," said Mr. Carter as he laid eyes on the dead woman for the first time.

"Cancer's an ageless disease," said Mrs. Carter.

"They say she was sick a long time."

"Not a bad job, puffing her up again for show."

"Makeup job's a bit pedestrian."

"I wonder if the wig was her choice or theirs."

"I would have gone with a more summery dress."

"I wish they opened the bottom half too," said Mrs. Carter, lamenting her favourite pet peeve, "I want to see her shoes."

* * *

The Carters were the very last to leave the parlour. Even the body of Ms. Edie Whoever was gone, packed into the back of a hearse for a final spin that would deliver her to the crematorium. There, the embalmer's fine work would be burned to cinders, and the bones of the deceased would be pulverized into tiny shards. Once it was all over, and Edie was safely in her urn, there would be hardly enough left of her to pot a plant.

The Carters soaked up the post-funeral ambiance, enjoying the calm silence after the storm of tears. The recorded organ music had been shut off until the next body and batch of mourners arrived.

Mrs. Carter absently checked her watch, then hissed, annoyed, "Dammit, we missed the Farkas do."

"Yes, but we're still in time for the will reading," said her husband.

"I don't know, Ashley. Will readings don't play as well for me without the eulogy and a bunch of loved ones pretending to sob before the loot is divvied up. It's like skipping dinner and going straight for dessert."

"What about your sweet tooth?"

Mrs. Carter didn't take long to give in.

"All right. We'll make an appearance. But we want to leave in time for that suicide at one."

* * *

The Carters sat together on a bench at the back of the lawyer's office. Fewer people than they had anticipated had shown up for the will reading, so they wanted to be near the door in case a hasty exit was called for. No one had questioned their presence so far, but it remained a possibility. A quick route out always helped minimize embarrassment in the event of unwelcome questions or an unexpected confrontation.

The lawyer was well into the reading, droning the details of Mr. Andrew Farkas's final wishes in as unemotional a tone as he could muster. The few friends and relations present each nodded in turn as their names were matched with a modest amount of estate plunder specified by the dead man. If anyone was happy or displeased with their inheritance, it was impossible to tell.

The reading continued in an orderly fashion and the Carters began to fidget in their seat, bored by the lack of high drama. The only one there who offered any visible signs of emotion was a woman in her mid-forties who maintained a brave front even as a stream of tears ran down her cheeks at a steady pace. Her head tilted up slightly when her name was finally mentioned.

"To my daughter, Elaine," read the lawyer, "I leave all proceeds from the sale of the house and its contents. This is subject to the condition that all these items are put on the block and liquidated immediately upon my death."

Elaine let out a long, sad sigh that broke into quivering convulsions towards the end. It was drama to be sure, but the offering was too little too late for the Carters. Mrs. Carter leaned over to her husband and suggested, "Let's go."

"All right," he whispered, "It seems to be wrapping up. Let's make a discreet exit."

The Carters rose slowly and shuffled silently to the door. Everyone else in the room, with the exception of the lawyer at his desk, had their backs to the couple and didn't notice them leaving. Then, the lawyer read the words, "To my dear friends, Mr. and Mrs. Ashley Carter . . ."

The whole room turned in their seats to look at the Carters. Mr. and Mrs. Carter froze in place, uncertain whether they should start apologizing or fleeing. Before they could make a firm decision one way or the other, the lawyer continued.

"To them I entrust my mortal remains. I have always found you to be a couple of exceptional taste, and believe no one is better suited to arrange for their disposal in a tasteful manner."

With this final legal decree from the dearly departed, the lawyer reached into a desk drawer and retrieved a simple plain cardboard box, fresh from the crematorium. As he placed it on the edge of his desk, the room fell silent enough to hear the soft rustling of ash inside the box. There lay the last of

Andrew Farkas, waiting for the Carters to step forward and claim him.

The number of tears running down Elaine's face doubled.

* * *

The Carters's condominium was clean, modern, and manageably mortgaged. The walls were white and antiseptic, the furniture black and sparse. What personal possessions had been left on open display were precisely arranged. Most were objects d'art from a kaleidoscope of world cultures, carefully selected so as not to draw undue attention from casual visitors. Yet, each and every one pertained in some way to burial rituals and funereal practices lost and forgotten by all but the most specialized anthropologists. On the rare occasions when someone made a comment or asked which gallery they found a particular piece in, the Carters would simply exchange the smile of a couple who shared a private joke.

Today, Mr. Carter added Andrew Farkas's simple box of ashes to the collection, giving it a place of honour in the centre of the mantle that overlooked their living room and dining area.

Mrs. Carter was in the bathroom, filling the tub with the cold water tap on full. She called to her husband over the sound of splashing.

"I think it was a lovely gesture just the same."

Her husband answered from the other room, "I can't argue that. But the man was a total stranger. I mean, don't you find it odd? We never knew he existed until we read his name in the morning's obituaries."

Mrs. Carter had a champagne bucket of ice on hand, minus the champagne. Once the tub was full, she shut off the water and dumped the contents of the bucket into her bath.

"It's obvious he knew us somehow," she said.

"But from where? We don't know any old people. None living at least."

Mrs. Carter hung her robe on a peg behind the bathroom door, tucked her hair under a shower cap, and stepped into the tub. She took a deep breath as the frigid water touched her toes, but routine had prepared her for the shock. She relaxed for a moment as she stood shin-deep, then lowered herself into the water.

"He must have been keeping an eye on us somehow—from a distance—to know so much," said Mrs. Carter.

She took another deep breath and laid down in the tub, letting the iced water flow over her. She shifted to one side, making sure no ice cubes were trapped under her back, then settled to the bottom, leaving only enough of her face above the waterline to breathe.

"He knew our names," said Mr. Carter, "That's all."

"He knew we would be at the will reading. Even before we did. And he knew we had impeccable taste."

"He didn't say 'impeccable,' he said 'exceptional.' That doesn't necessarily mean good."

After only a few minutes, Mrs. Carter was out of the tub again, towelling herself off. Removing the shower cap, she began to pad her body down with baby powder from head to toe, turning her skin white.

Mr. Carter paced around the living room idly. He stopped to sprinkle a few flakes of tropical fish food into the twenty-gallon tank that stood against a blank white wall. The fish didn't touch it. They were all dead, floating at the water's surface, or twirling around amongst the plastic plants at the bottom, caught in the filter's swirling current. After a few minutes, the flakes soaked up enough water to begin their slow Autumn-leaf drift to the bottom where they would remain untouched. Mr. Carter noted his tetras were looking a touch threadbare. Soon he would return to the pet shop for some fresher specimens that had expired on the way to market. Even the rarest and most colourful fish in the sea could be had at a huge discount once their lifelong swim had come to an end.

Mr. Carter found their beauty easier to appreciate once they were stiff and still.

There hadn't been another word from his wife for ten minutes now. Impatient, Mr. Carter called out, "You ready?"

There was no response.

Mr. Carter walked into the bedroom and found his wife lying stalk still on their plush bed, her hands clasped over her chest. Mrs. Carter wore a period dress that was white, lacy and virginal. Two Victorian pennies, double the size of their modern counterparts, rested on her closed eyelids, and her body was perfectly framed by several dozen red roses spread atop the sheets. The tableau was shrouded by a thin veil of white silk strung over the high framework of the bed, allowing only a ghostly view inside.

Pulling aside the drapes, Mr. Carter gently sat down on the edge of the bed. His fingers brushed his wife's pale cold flesh sensuously, but provoked no reaction. Reaching for a small mirror on the end table, Mr. Carter held it under his wife's nose and waited for nearly a full minute. It never fogged.

The illusion complete, Mr. Carter began to unfasten the elaborate clasps on his wife's dress and remove his own clothing.

* * *

The next day, Mr. Carter came up from the condo's lobby with the morning's mail. He leafed through it: bill, bill, bill, funeral director's trade journal, bill.

The postman had made his rounds an hour earlier, which meant it was about time for the couriers to start arriving. The Carters' building had no less than eight lawyers, seven accountants and six senior blue-chip executives all living under the same roof, so overnight packages came daily by the dozen. It was unusual, but not unheard of, for the Carters to have a surprise package arrive from a friend, relative or business associate at this time of day. The knock on the door by a young man in a smart red uniform announced that this would be one of those days.

Mr. Carter signed for the package—a simple square box that was neither very heavy nor very light. He looked for a return address, but the street and house number meant nothing to him. The name was another matter, however.

"Who's that from?" asked Mrs. Carter as she came out of the bedroom sporting the day's new all-black ensemble.

"Him," was the answer she got.

"Who?"

"Him," repeated Mr. Carter, this time nodding towards the box of cremains on the mantle.

Mr. Carter tore off the strip of packing tape that fastened the box-top flaps together. Inside, amongst the Styrofoam chips, was an urn. Tastefully painted, with smooth sloping edges, the urn was a flawlessly fired porcelain receptacle standing a little over a foot tall. Mr. Carter held it up and looked at it skeptically. It clashed with the ultra modern flat where everything was either black or white with straight edges and sharp corners.

"Not quite what I would have chosen for my final resting place," he concluded.

"They're not *your* ashes," said Mrs. Carter. "Besides, I think it suits him."

"How do you know it suits him? We don't know a thing about the man."

Mr. Carter went to fetch Andrew Farkas's cremains from the mantle as Mrs. Carter wiped down the urn with a dish towel in the kitchen.

"On the contrary," she said, "I think we're learning more about him by the minute."

"Hold it steady," said Mr. Carter as he removed the lid of the urn and began to carefully shake the contents of the cardboard box into their new home.

Grey ash and tiny fragments of bone that hadn't been incinerated by the intense heat of the crematorium oven poured into the urn with the sound of sifting sand. Halfway through the transfer, a metallic clink against the porcelain caught the Carters's attention.

"What was that?"

"Something that wasn't a part of Mr. Farkas," concluded Mrs. Carter.

The couple looked into the urn, but could see nothing in the collection of grey soot that used to be Andrew Farkas.

Mr. Carter opened a drawer of cutlery under the kitchen counter and produced a pair of hand-crafted chopsticks usually reserved for the arrival of Asian takeout. He reached into the urn and began fishing around in the ashes. Striking something solid, he carefully took hold of it with the tips of his chopsticks and pulled it free. Blowing the dust off, Mr. Carter dropped a plain ring into his wife's hand. Another few moments of searching through the cremains produced the ring's twin.

The Carters examined the simple bands. They weren't gold, but some duller more durable element.

"They look like wedding bands," concluded Mrs. Carter.

"How'd they get in there?"

The Carters both knew that all jewellery was routinely removed from bodies before cremation. Had Mr. Farkas been wearing them, they would have certainly been noted by the funeral home, marked down on an inventory, and returned to the family after the service.

Mrs. Carter ran through the possible explanations, but only one seemed feasible.

"He swallowed them," she said. "Before he died. In the hospital."

"Why would he do that?"

Mrs. Carter shrugged, "Hospitals are full of thieves. Especially during visiting hours. No one could get their hands on them this way."

"They must have meant a lot to him," said Mr. Carter, taking them both in hand and looking closely at their inner edges for any markings. He found what he was looking for, worn by age and heat and encrusted with ash, but still legible. There were two inscriptions, one in each ring—a short series of numerals.

Mr. Carter read the first to his wife, "One, four, comma."

This was followed by, "Eight, seven, three."

"It's hardly a declaration of undying love," he decided.

Mrs. Carter took one of the bands and slipped it onto her husband's ring finger.

"I thought we didn't do jewellery," he said.

Nevertheless, Mr. Carter followed his wife's lead and placed the other on her finger.

"These are too charmingly macabre not to wear. I let you get away with skipping the whole engagement ring routine, so you can indulge me now."

"The price is right," smiled Mr. Carter.

"I want to know a great deal more about Mr. Farkas. How about you?"

"Where do we start?"

"Where better than the end?"

* * *

A few phone calls was all it took to determine which hospital Andrew Farkas had expired in. Claiming to represent a major insurance company franchise was usually enough to guarantee the full cooperation of the receptionists at any medical facility. They were only too willing to transfer the Carters to the appropriate department, and these departments were, in turn, pleased to offer up whatever information the Carters wanted once they realized they weren't going to be badgered with the usual series of questions insurance companies were dreaded for.

It turned out the Carters were regulars at Andrew Farkas's hospital of choice, and had been going there since their third

date—a magical, perfect evening of multiple code blues cul-
minating in a genuine flatline that was pronounced within
earshot of the young couple. A short car ride later and they
were riding the elevator down to the damp concrete corridors
of the sub-basement. Loud bustling emergency rooms or tense,
dramatic surgical theatres held little fascination for them—
the basement was where the real action in any hospital was.
No one questioned the Carters as they made their way to the
end of the hall—there wasn't a soul between the elevator and
the solid metal door to stop them. What few staff ever came
down here weren't paid enough to question the presence of
a well-dressed couple who looked like they knew where they
were going.

Three sharp knocks on the door echoed through the corridors and fell only on deaf ears. After a lengthy wait, a series
a locks and latches were heard being worked, and at last the
steel-plated barrier swung in, opening a narrow crack that let
some of the cold air on the other side whistle out.

Calling the scruffy man who looked through the gap a
coroner would be generous to an extreme. He was an attendant—part janitor, part petty bureaucrat, in charge of light
cleaning duties and the shuffling of much paperwork. He
resided over his one-room empire with an unquestioned
authority that can only come with the security of a seniority
job, and the knowledge that there was not one other person
in the entire hospital with an eye on his unenvied position.

The man said nothing, though he instantly recognized the
Carters. Mr. Carter produced a fresh pack of cigarettes with
a modest wad of twenties stuffed down one side and held it
out for the man. The man accepted it greedily, paused long
enough to inhale the pleasing scent of money and tobacco
mixed, and then opened the door the rest of the way.

"Ten minutes," the man announced, telling the Carters
how much privacy they had bought. He then left the pair

alone together in the vast hospital morgue, shutting the door behind him as he took his legislated coffee break outside.

The Carters enjoyed the nervous thrill of anticipation they always felt when they stepped into an uncomfortably low room temperature. It was chilly enough to keep the recent arrivals fresh as they waited to be redirected to the appropriate funeral home, medical examiner, or teaching hospital, but the thermostat stopped just short of allowing the live guests to see their own breath.

"What have they got for us today?" wondered Mrs. Carter aloud as she strolled down the wall of body drawers like a window shopper at Christmastime.

Mr. Carter snatched a clipboard that hung on a nail and read the latest, "Couple car wrecks. A floater."

Mrs. Carter stopped at a newly occupied drawer and Mr. Carter compared its number to the clipboard list.

"That's a Jane Doe. The verdict isn't in."

Grasping the handle with both hands, Mrs. Carter gave the drawer a sharp pull, opening it as far as it would go. She unzipped the body bag inside and stared down into the dead face of a young woman who had never made it out of her teens. Probably a runaway, almost certainly a prostitute, her skin was grey and clammy. The autopsy scars up and across her chest had been artlessly stitched back together in a rough manner that enticed Mrs. Carter. She ran her finger along the assembly-line cut-and-paste job some indifferent civil servant had made as required by law. The impersonal desecration to determine a cause of death no one cared to hear sent shivers through Mrs. Carter.

"Nice," she said. "I bet he couldn't keep his hands off this one."

Mr. Carter rifled through an "out" box on the lone desk at the head of the room and pulled one of the files.

"Farkas, Andrew," he said, holding it up.

As Mrs. Carter caressed the dead woman's stitchwork, Mr. Carter scanned the file for highlights.

"He was here all right. Died just a few days ago. The body was claimed almost immediately."

"Cause of death?" asked Mrs. Carter, cutting to the chase.

"Admitted after complaining of diarrhea, severe stomach cramps. Pronounced dead six hours later."

"Sounds like the flu."

Mr. Carter looked at an additional test result clipped to the bulk to the paperwork.

"Sounds like a lot of things. They didn't narrow it down until this morning."

"What's so special about this morning?"

"The blood tests came back. Someone was paying attention and ordered a toxicology."

"And?"

"Positive for arsenic."

"An oldie but a goodie. I don't suppose the police have been tipped off."

Mr. Carter returned the file to its box and began to unbutton his shirt.

"I'm sure they'll want the body back for a full autopsy."

"That may be difficult," Mrs. Carter smirked.

Reluctantly she drew herself away from the body in the drawer—more beautiful in death than it ever could have been in life—and zipped up the bag again.

As Mr. Carter dropped his pants, his wife checked the clock on the wall.

"How are we for time?" she asked.

"Better make this quick."

"I won't be long."

Mrs. Carter shoved the body drawer back in place. By the time she turned around, Mr. Carter was lying naked and still on one of the empty stainless steel gurneys.

Mrs. Carter approached the slab. She took a blank toe tag from a box full of them and snapped the elastic string around her husband's big toe. He didn't flinch.

Mrs. Carter pulled up her dress and climbed onto the gurney to mount her husband. In short order, she was riding him hard, the toe tag jiggling with each thrust. Her passion built steadily, but she remained distracted, talking through their concocted scene.

"It's obvious he was in the funeral club—one of the other casket chasers we always see lined up to pay their last respects to people they've never met. I've been picturing their faces all day, trying to guess which one might have been him."

Mrs. Carter ran over her mental list of these silent acquaintances she and her husband had seen at dozens of other funerals. Some they'd even become familiar enough with to exchange a look of recognition, but never a verbal greeting of any kind. That was simply not done in this anti-social circle of enthusiasts.

"There's the young woman in the old hat, the old woman with the orthopedic shoes, and the lady who's missing a joint of one of her fingers. Obviously not any of them. The men I'm not as clear on. There's that young guy who looks like he's about ready to be fitted for a box himself. There's the one who goes just to hit on widows. And the man who's probably a funeral director himself and wants to check out the competition."

There was no response from her husband, but Mrs. Carter didn't expect one while he was in character. Suddenly, she had a brainstorm.

"Ah, yes! There *was* an old man. I nearly forgot, it's been so long. He liked outdoor, graveside services. He got around on a cane, but he was always alone. We haven't seen him since the weather turned cold."

Mr. Carter spoke, but kept his eyes shut.

"I remember."

"Shut up," she told him, "You're dead."

* * *

Returning to his station at the end of his break, the attendant flicked the ash off the end of his two-thirds smoked cigarette and pocketed it for later. Opening the door to the morgue, he found the Carters buttoning up their final articles of clothing. Mr. Carter offered the man a polite nod as he pulled on a sock.

"Call us if you get anything really messy," Mrs. Carter told him as she slipped out into the corridor.

"I have something else you might be interested in."

The Carters stopped in the hall, interrupting their discreet departure.

"Something messy?" inquired Mr. Carter eagerly.

"Only the handwriting," said the man and pulled an inter-office envelope he had rolled up in the pocket of his lab coat.

On the back, at the end of a long list of staff names that had been written and scratched out over the course of the envelope's life, was the name "Ashley Carter" etched in uneven print.

"What is it?" said Mrs. Carter.

The attendant explained, "It bounced around the hospital all day yesterday until it came through here. I was the only one who recognized the name, so I held onto it. Interested?"

The couple stared at the large brown envelope and silently came to the same conclusion without needing to consult with each other.

"How much?" asked Mr. Carter, and started counting his cash-on-hand.

"A hundred," said the attendant, but quickly thought better of it when he saw how eager the Carters were to cough up a finder's fee.

". . . and fifty," he added.

Mr. Carter paused for a moment, annoyed with himself for having walked straight into another fifty dollars-worth of extortion. His wife stood next to him, dying in anticipation of getting her hands on the contents of the envelope. She was more than willing to pay double or triple the asking price to find what new message had been left for them by the late Andrew Farkas. Still, Mr. Carter hated being played for a sucker, even if his wife had no appreciation for the art of negotiation. He stared down the attendant, telling him with his eyes, "Don't push it."

The money and envelope were exchanged. As the man closed the heavy door behind the Carters, he broke into a pro-tracted smoker's cough that didn't speak well for a prognosis.

"See you soon," suggested Mr. Carter ominously through the narrowing gap, and flashed the attendant a smile that gave him chills and made him latch the door as soon as it was shut.

* * *

A green space behind the hospital had been meticulously designed with paths and bushes and trees for convalescing patients to enjoy as soon as they were up and about, or before they were forced to settle indoors as a permanent fixture of a death bed. Nurses wheeled the less mobile around so they could smell the flowers and hear the birds sing. Benches had been spaced along the path for family visits in a fresh-air environ-ment, away from the smorgasbord of germs and viruses that floated around the hospital halls, waiting to rack up some fresh customers for the ear-nose-and-throat men inside. It was on one of these benches that the Carters sat to open their mail—a single sheet of gift-shop stationery covered with handwriting.

Mr. Carter looked over his wife's shoulder, and together they read the correspondence which ran, "If you've received this letter, I know I've chosen wisely. You remind me so much of my Emma and I when we were your age and newly married. We were the only ones who could understand each others' fascination with the state of death and the act of dying. You're wearing the rings, aren't you? I knew you'd appreciate them as we did when we obtained them from a private collector who claimed they'd been on the fingers of Tsar Nicholas and his wife when they were executed by the Bolsheviks. The tale is doubtless apocryphal, but I know you'll understand why we chose them as our wedding bands. Forgive me for dwelling on the past. It's a terrible habit I've been trying to break myself of. Perhaps you can help me."

The writing trailed off at the end of the letter abruptly, perhaps prematurely.

"That's it?" asked Mr. Carter, disappointed with the vagueness the note closed on.

Mrs. Carter flipped the page over and confirmed, "That's it."

"A man—a total stranger—at the end of his life. And he spends his last moments writing us a letter," pondered Mr. Carter, trying to understand the significance.

"It's sweet," concluded Mrs. Carter, "Cryptic but sweet. I wish we could send him a get-well card."

Down the path, a geriatric patient strolled along in his hospital gown and slippers, using an I.V. pole as a walker. Halting in mid-step, he silently began a slow-motion collapse to the gravel base underfoot. In quick succession, the nurses and interns in the green space saw the man go down and rushed over to assist. One of them began artificial respiration on the unconscious patient while another ran for a doctor. The rest gathered around to observe and offer their concerned stares, but the efforts to revive the elderly gentleman didn't look promising.

The Carters, watching serenely from a short distance away, held hands.

* * *

That night, after a romantic dinner in their condominium, the Carters sat down on the couch to enjoy some wine and a slide show. The wine was red, and so were most of the slides. The light reflecting off the screen bathed the darkened room with a rosy glow.

Mr. Carter operated the projector with his wife cuddled next to him. Between slides he would use his free hand to stroke their black and white cat, Mittens, who never purred no matter how much affection was lavished on him. Mittens had been stuffed and mounted for three years now, ever since the Carters found him lying by the curb, fresh from a fatal encounter with a Buick. The physical damage to Mittens had been minor, so the Carters adopted him and kept him in their freezer for a week until they could get down to the taxidermist. Their expressed desire to immortalize their beloved kitty wasn't questioned, even though the Carters had never met Mittens before he used up the last of his nine lives. Since then, Mittens had assumed his new permanent position, curled into a ball as though he were just sleeping. When not sitting in the Carters's laps like a plush toy, Mittens was mostly used as a novelty throw cushion.

Despite the entertainment value of the Bordeaux and projected pictures, Mrs. Carter was distracted.

"We can't just let it go at that," she said.

Mr. Carter didn't care for what his wife was suggesting.

"If we get another letter, fine. But I'm not comfortable dipping into the man's family history. Especially when it was probably someone in that family who bumped him off."

"He called us his dear friends in the will. No one's going to be suspicious if we politely ask a few innocent questions."

"Details like what sort of exit wounds he and his wife got off on?"

"Wouldn't you like to compare notes?"

"If anyone knows about their fetish, I'm sure it's a dirty little family secret."

"Perhaps we can find someone who's open about it. Maybe they'll talk if we let on we already know. Think of the possibilities. They may have been into all sorts of things we haven't even thought of yet. Things that could spice it up for us."

"Bored?" asked Mr. Carter.

"Maybe a little jaded. I'd like to go further towards the edge."

Mr. Carter advanced to the next slide and the room lit up with a dark red tint much harsher than the others had offered.

"Nasty!" cooed Mrs. Carter.

"I thought you'd like this one," said Mr. Carter. "Aluminium smelter accident. The guy fell into the rolling machine. He was alive up until the moment they cut him out. It seems the roll of metal encasing him was the only thing holding him together."

"Worker's comp must have paid off like the lottery," Mrs. Carter noted pragmatically.

"Actually no. He was a non-union scab."

"Well then," she said, "I guess he had it coming."

* * *

The Carters pulled up alongside the curb in front of the late Andrew Farkas's home. It was a large, stately house that flirted with the title of "mansion" without stepping over that line of opulent pretentiousness. Dating back to the roaring twenties, the house might have included a servant's door had it been built just ten years earlier. As it was, it only had the one front entrance, but it was a double door which made the movers' job easier.

The place was bustling with activity as half-a-dozen men in overalls came and went in singles and pairs, carting furniture and possessions big and small down the path to a waiting van. The truck was a twenty-five footer and nearly full. Judging from the volume of boxes still pouring out of the residence, the movers would have to make another trip, perhaps two, before the place was emptied for the new owners.

A "For Sale" sign hammered into the front lawn had a "Sold" sticker plastered boldly across it. The sign served no other function than being a real estate agent's bragging rights. The property had sold before it ever officially made it to market. Priced low for its size and location, it was recognized for the bargain it was by the second couple to be offered a sneak preview by a well-connected agent. A bid was made for ten thousand dollars above the asking price and was accepted by the family lawyers before any rival bids had an opportunity to cross their desk. The paperwork was already underway and the entire transaction would be settled before the junk mail began to clog the letter slot. The new owners weren't moving in. The sole occupants of the house for the next three months would be a small army of painters and handymen assigned to spruce the place up, add some colour and modernize the fixtures. The property was expected to be back on the market and turned around for a six-figure profit before the year was up.

"I don't think anyone's home," said Mr. Carter as he stepped out of the car and assessed the line of movers who were making the house increasing barren and uninhabitable.

"All the better," said Mrs. Carter. "We can go through his private papers."

"If anything's left."

No one questioned the Carters as they made their way up the path, shuffling out of the way of two movers who were excavating the third couch of the day from the property. Stepping inside, they could see four large chambers branching off from a grand hall. Nothing was where it should be, with furniture and boxes collected into islands of disarray in the middle of each room. Slowly but inevitably, the daunting task of taking it all away was accomplished a piece at a time. As the isles of personal possessions eroded, so did the character of the house.

Elaine stood in the centre of the hall, her back to the Carters, watching her father's life being disassembled and sold off. Mrs. Carter recognized her immediately, even without seeing her face. Her expensive designer shoes were a dead give-away, even if they weren't a precise match with Mrs. Carter's own taste in fashionable footwear.

Mrs. Carter turned on her social smile and strode up to Elaine, beaming, "Elaine! Wonderful to see you again. How are you holding up?"

Elaine turned around. The tears on her cheeks were nearly dry, but had been plentiful enough to erode a pair of matching river beds through her makeup. Her eyes were red and irritated from a long nostalgic cry.

"Oh. It's you," said Elaine simply, not trying to hide her indifference that bordered on displeasure at seeing the Carters again.

Elaine mopped away some residual moisture from the corner of her eye with the back of her hand and made a brave effort to improve her manners.

"Pardon me," she said, "I'm a sentimentalist. It breaks my heart to see all these old memories sold to any dealer who will have them. But it's what Daddy wanted."

"We understand he wasn't big on remembering the past," said Mr. Carter.

Elaine nodded, "Since mother died. Everything he owned reminded him of her, but he couldn't part with any of it. Not until he joined her."

"They were very close, weren't they?" stated Mrs. Carter.

"Oh yes. They shared everything—had all the same interests."

"Interests?" said Mrs. Carter, fishing.

"Oh, you know. Gardening. Travel. They liked to bowl together."

That wasn't what the Carters wanted to hear, but Elaine said it so honestly, it was instantly apparent she didn't know anything about her parents' secret life.

"He scattered her ashes on his last trip to Egypt," explained Elaine. "Of course, I don't expect you to arrange for something so exotic for Daddy."

"We have a nice spot with a view in mind," assured Mr. Carter.

"He must have thought a great deal of you—both of you," said Elaine as she eyed the Carters, perhaps hoping to discover some quality in them—any quality—that might have left a positive impression with her father. She came up empty.

Mrs. Carter probed further, "We were wondering if your father had maybe left a letter or a note with you. For us?"

"A letter?" said Elaine, taking a mental inventory of what was left in the house. "No, nothing like that. There's still a box or two of old tax returns, receipts, a few bills. Nothing very interesting."

"Could we have a look?" asked Mr. Carter.

Elaine stared at the couple for a long moment, her suspicion growing, before she finally, reluctantly, invited them upstairs.

The room Elaine led them to had nearly been emptied, but enough furniture was left to identify it as a study. There were a few boxes stacked high, and paper littered the floor. An antique secretary, sitting in the middle of the room, had its drawers pulled out and piled next to it. Their contents appeared intact.

The Carters split up, picking through the dregs of a man's life like a couple of hounds sniffing out contraband. Mrs. Carter dove head first into the boxes, digging deep in a search that lacked any pattern other than wanton greed. Mr. Carter took to upturning the secretary drawers one by one, scattering their contents across the floor. Elaine stood back, watching the intrusion with increasing discomfort.

Mr. Carter was down to rifling through the secretary's numerous cubby holes, pulling the tiny drawers out one by one in quick succession. They were all empty, but the last of them had a small envelope taped to its underside. "A. Carter" was hand printed on the front.

Mrs. Carter abandoned the boxes of paper refuse as soon as she saw that her husband had found something. He handed the envelope to her and watched closely as she opened the flap and poured the contents out into her hand. It was a single key.

"What's this for?" Mrs. Carter asked Elaine.

"I don't know," said Elaine, looking at the simple unmarked key. "I've never seen it before."

"Is there something left in the house it would fit?" Mrs. Carter asked hopefully.

"My parents didn't keep things under lock and key. I can't imagine what it might be for, unless . . ."

"Yes?" asked Mrs. Carter when Elaine trailed off.

"My parents kept a safe deposit box for years. I don't know where, or what was in it. But it must have been important to them because they had the number inscribed on . . ."

Elaine trailed off again as her eyes fell on Mrs. Carter's left hand, focusing on her ring finger. She glanced at Mr. Carter's hand and found its twin.

Fresh tears started to trickle down Elaine's face.

"He gave you the rings?" she said, her voice shaking with emotion. "And now he wants you to have what's in the box too?"

Elaine was wavering between grief and anger. Anger was starting to win out.

"Who are you people?" she demanded. "I never saw you before in my life and now you're inheriting everything in the world that was important to my father. The lawyers won't even let me keep the family photo albums!"

"I'm sure your father knew what was best," Mrs. Carter tried to assure her.

"What's in the safe deposit box? What else won't he let me have?"

"We honestly don't know," said Mr. Carter.

"Give me the rings!" Elaine demanded furiously.

"What? No!" cried Mrs. Carter, but Elaine was already upon her, clawing at her hand, gripping her wrist, trying to pull the ring free. The struggle quickly grew violent, and when Mr. Carter tried to separate the women, Elaine lashed out at him as well.

Elaine, sobbing uncontrollably, finally managed to wrench the ring away from Mrs. Carter. Mrs. Carter responded by tackling Elaine, throwing her arms over her shoulders and attempting an improvised choke hold. Elaine bucked hard, nearly shrugging Mrs. Carter off. Looking to her husband for help, Mrs. Carter worked her arms around Elaine's neck and pulled her head back sharply. Mr. Carter took advantage of the tempting target and grabbed the largest of the secretary drawers. He brought the drawer down on the back of Elaine's head with enough force to splinter it. All the joints in her body went limp in a split second and she collapsed like a rag doll stuffed with lead.

The ring leapt free of Elaine's hand as she hit the floor, rolling across the ceramic tiles and stopping abruptly as Mrs. Carter stomped her foot down in its path. Only after she bent to retrieve the ring and slip it safely back on her finger did she turn to check on Elaine and her husband.

Mr. Carter sat down heavily on the floor, staring at Elaine where she lay. Mrs. Carter flipped Elaine over on her back, and observed her closely. She put a couple of fingers on the side of her neck, feeling for a pulse. Blood trickled freely from a gash in the back of her head, pooling on the floor. The rate of blood loss might have been a concern if the crushing blow hadn't already propelled bone fragments into soft brain tissue. Elaine's eyes were fixed on two slightly different points in the room, and she wasn't breathing. Her leg spasmed, twitching once in an unnatural way that suggested more than simple unconsciousness, and then settled at an angle that would have been uncomfortable had Elaine still been alive.

Mr. Carter looked at his handiwork, astonished.

"I've never killed anything before," he said, and then added after much reflection, "I think I liked it."

The Carters sat together in the barren room for a long while, watching the body cool while they caught their breath.

* * *

It took the Carters another few minutes to compose themselves. At last they emerged from the study with clothes straightened and heart rates back to a reasonable pace. As they shut the door behind them, one of the movers approached.

"There's nothing left in there," Mr. Carter said, warding off the man. "Try that room down the hall."

The mover did as he was told and the Carters hit the stairs, walking briskly, but keeping their pace slow enough so as not to attract attention. They passed other busy crewmen on the way, but none of them gave the couple a second look. Apparently the sounds of murder had not penetrated the thick oak of the study door.

"You think we're going to get into trouble over this?" wondered Mr. Carter aloud.

"No one here knows who we are."

"That's true. But just in case, I think we should swing by the bank right now while we have the chance. Before anyone asks us any questions."

"Sounds good. But which bank?"

"That's a five-digit number on our rings. I only know one bank with that many safe deposit boxes."

Arriving at the bottom of the stairs, the Carters froze. Through the yawning front door they could see another car parked behind their own. Two burly men dressed in plain suits and ties were coming up the path. Their profession was obvious to the Carters long before they arrived in front of them and flashed their badges and accompanying identification.

"We're here to see an Elaine Farkas," said one of the police detectives.

"Oh?" said Mr. Carter in a somewhat failed attempt to sound casual.

Over the banister, up the stairs, the Carters could see one of the movers making a room-by-room sweep of the building, opening and shutting doors, checking for remaining pieces of furniture bound for the truck outside. He was only a couple of doors away from discovering Elaine's body.

"We'd like to talk to her about her father's death," the detective elaborated.

"Tragic, untimely," said Mrs. Carter, momentarily locking eyes with her husband. They exchanged a look of panic so subtle, it took a connection on a deeply intimate level to recognize it.

"I think she stepped out for a moment," Mr. Carter offered.

The mover was just opening the door to the study, seconds away from exposing the scene of the crime to the whole household. Mrs. Carter interrupted him by shouting, "Excuse me!"

The mover paused in the doorway, "Yes?"

"Have you seen Miss Farkas recently?"

"She was downstairs five, ten minutes ago. Maybe she went out back."

"Which way is that?" asked Mr. Carter.

The mover leaned over the upstairs banister and pointed, "Through that door, down the hall, and out by the kitchen."

"Could you show us, sir?" said the detective.

The mover shut the study door again and came downstairs to show the policemen the way out back. The detectives thanked the Carters for their assistance and let the mover lead the way. As the trio disappeared into the heart of the house, the Carters seized the opportunity to leave. As soon as the police were gone they broke into a frantic trot that became a flat-out run once they were safely outside. The Carters leapt into their car and peeled away the instant the engine roared to life.

* * *

The bank was a cathedral built to the glory of old money. Everything in sight was either marble or mahogany, with a ceiling mosaic highlighted in gold leaf arching so far above the floor, it was impossible to appreciate the finer details without a good pair of binoculars or some very tall scaffolding. This was not a corner branch for people to withdraw a convenient twenty dollars to see them through the weekend. Clients who came here had serious business in mind for serious sums of cash.

The Carters only had to wait in the queue a few moments before a teller was free to assist them. Mr. Carter placed the key on the counter in front of the wicket and stated, "I'd like to check on the contents of my safe deposit box. Number one four eight seven three."

"Yes sir," said the teller. "Your name?"

"Andrew Farkas."

It took only a few more lies and one loosely forged signature for the Carters to get themselves escorted into the vault. They sat down at a long table that was set out for customer convenience while their teller scanned the thousands of armoured boxes, searching for the correct number. Scaling a footstool, he retrieved the Farkas deposit box from high on one wall and then carried it to the table where he placed it in front of the Carters.

"Ring for me when you're done," instructed the teller who then gave the Carters their privacy, leaving the vault and shutting the thick air-tight door behind him. The Carters were alone, with only the hum of the air vents breaking the deathly silence. Together they stared at the box on the table. No words passed between them.

Mr. Carter pushed the key into the lock—a perfect fit. He gave it a quarter turn to the right and the latch released, allowing the top to pop open. Swinging the lid back on its hinges, he took a look inside. Sitting on top of several personal journals was a letter addressed to Mr. and Mrs. Ashley Carter.

Mrs. Carter was into the journals like a shot, pouring through them like a speed reader, trying to absorb as much as possible in a rush of images. She couldn't contain her enthusiasm enough to focus on specific content or context—there would be time enough for that later—but her first impressions were promising, thrilling, titillating. From what she could gather as the pages flipped by, here were a series of recollections and experiences, a scrapbook of necrophilic delight, detailing the factual, the anecdotal, and the intimate from a lifetime of personal research.

Mr. Carter concerned himself with the letter first, wanting to be more methodical and restrained in his approach to this great bounty that had arrived on their doorstep. For him, stretching out the anticipation just a few minutes longer would make the final reward all the sweeter. He opened the note and read it aloud.

"The obsession we share has led you here as I expected it would. As you look through the years of notes and reminiscences Emma and I accumulated in our time together, you'll understand why I couldn't entrust them to anyone but a like-minded couple. Allow me to share this legacy with you: you must let the past die. I believe that absolutely, but I couldn't bring myself to destroy these mementos of our happy marriage in my lifetime—a lifetime I plan to end myself, tonight."

Past the journals, near the back of the deep deposit box, Mrs. Carter spotted a small collection of trinkets and souvenirs, all of it dead flesh. None stood out so much as the one large oval centre piece that dominated the collection. It was a human head—distinctly feminine—mummified by time and the dry climate of the vault. Mrs. Carter looked into the concave sockets of the skull, deep into the dusty eyes that hadn't lost their character even as they dried out and collapsed in on themselves.

Mr. Carter stopped reading.

"This would be Mrs. Farkas," he ventured.

"I guess the good bits never made it to Egypt."

As Mrs. Carter stared at the dead woman's remains, fascinated, Mr. Carter read the rest of the letter.

"For obvious reasons, I can't face the prospect of them falling into anyone else's hands, especially my daughter's. She knows nothing of our special interests, and that's the way I wish it to remain. To assure that, I had to arrange for the contents of this box to be burned. That task falls to you, with my thanks. As you have done me a service, so shall I do one for you. I leave you this gift which I know you will appreciate. It is the fondest thing which all couples of our particular bent might wish for—what my wife and I were denied—to die together."

Mrs. Carter was just lifting the dried head out of the box for a closer look when her husband came to the end of the letter. The ominous conclusion inspired quick nervous glances between the couple, and then a closer inspection of the box's contents. Mrs. Farkas's head had been sitting upon a small incendiary device—two sticks of dynamite wired to a digital timer that was hooked, in turn, to the armoured box's hinges. The clock had been activated and was running down the last five seconds to double zeroes.

The Carters spent three of those final five seconds staring blankly at the bomb that was about to go off in their faces, then at the vault door, shut and locked tight. Husband and wife fumbled for each other's hand, holding on tight when they found a firm grip.

Mrs. Carter beamed at her husband, radiant, "How romantic!"

Mr. Carter returned a wavering smile. It always took him a little longer to come to grips with a new stage in their relationship—a deeper intimacy, or a greater commitment. Two seconds hardly seemed enough.

A bright flash and a loud bang moments later resolved any lingering concerns he may have had.

THE MALTESE CHICKEN

by Allen Appel, 15,000 words

The Maltese Chicken is one of a trio of novellas that feature chickens. These stories came about when, while looking for something interesting to write about, I decided to give myself a challenge by picking a subject that was particularly uninteresting: Chickens. Those readers who find this story amusing and/or intriguing, might enjoy The Christmas Chicken and Flock as well. These novellas and all of my books can be easily found on Amazon.

Allen Appel is the author of more than a dozen fiction and non-fiction books. He is known primarily for his series that relates the adventures of a time-traveling history professor as he ricochets through the past from the Russian Revolution, through World War Two and the Civil War. The author lives in a small town in North Carolina where he spends his time writing fiction, reviewing books for Publisher's Weekly and chasing squirrels out of his garden.

The wind coming down the streets of my subdivision was hot, dirty and unrelenting. It picked up grit from the dried-out lawns and alleys and sandblasted the windows and the cheap siding of my one bedroom rental. It made my dog, Max, so jumpy he followed me from room to room, whining like a nervous three-day-old pup. So, the next morning, when he was barking at the front door, I figured it was just more of the same. I opened the door to show him the world was still out there in all its cheap glory, sand, heat and wind be damned, and he bolted onto the porch. I was ready to give him a whack when I saw what had got him all worked up. There, on the corner of the porch, was a big, black chicken. Off to the side, standing on the steps, were two kids from the neighborhood, little guys, I knew them, six and seven years old. We all held that frozen pose for a minute or two—dog, man, kids and chicken—until I picked up a broom that was leaning nearby, intending to chase the fowl off my property, if for no other reason than to calm Max down. But I stopped. There was something wrong with the chicken. He squatted in the corner, his feathers puffed up, his eyes a dull, filmy black. I glanced over, and the kids were watching me like I was about to hurt something, maybe them. I put the broom back.

Chickens in urban neighborhoods are not particularly unusual. There was a fad for them a few years ago, and it had grown, once local governments declared them legal. The kids must have brought the bird. I was known in the neighborhood as the grownup who could doctor a bird or a lizard or a snake or any sort of unusual animal. I had cages and fish tanks and sometimes they were full of exotic creatures though at the moment they weren't. I let it be known that I was an importer, but I was really a smuggler. When you read in the newspaper about a guy caught with 35 exotic parrots stuffed into tube socks or with a few snakes in his briefcase coming through customs, that would be me, though I never used those methods because I'm smarter than that. Not that I'm a criminal mastermind. The thing is, the U. S. Fish and Wildlife department has a grand total of two, yes, I repeat, two agents guarding the entire Texas/Mexican border. The profits for smuggling illegal animals run about the same as with the standard drug trade, so you do the math. Who's the mastermind now?

Maybe I am. Maybe I'm not.

"He a chicken, Dr. Fish," one of the kids said. The kids called me Dr. Fish because I could cure the goldfish they won at the carnival or even the tropicals that their drug dealer dads kept in giant home aquariums. My name is Raphael, Rafe for short, but I kind of liked going by the nom de plume, Dr. Fish. The kid who spoke was Lamont, and the little one next to him was his brother Chevaleer. They lived a couple of houses up the street. We're in a subdivision in Virginia outside Washington DC, a cheap neighborhood with folks of color and of no color who filled the blue collar ranks of workers who rode the bus or train into DC every day and took care of white folks. I'm a white folk myself, but I'm closer to my neighbors than I am to those that live in town.

"Lamont," I said, "What do you know about this chicken?"

"His name Jack. Momma say she find him on the side of the road. Say he lost and he sick. Told me and Chevaleer to bring him to Dr. Fish. Says you'll make the chicken better. He get better, then we get to keep him."

Their mom, Shameeka, known as Meeka, works in town for some embassy, I'm not sure which one. She and I talk on the sidewalk. She looks just like a Jamaican lady I saw on a poster years ago, rising up out of an impossibly blue sea, wearing an impossibly wet T-shirt. I've never forgotten that poster. Meeka's got a good heart; she loves her boys and watches them pretty close. She's always rescuing animals around the neighborhood and from her friend's homes when she thinks they aren't being taken care of properly.

"Tell your mom I'll see what I can do for the chicken."

"Then, we get to keep him? Me and Chevy. We make Jack our dog."

"Sure, Lamont. I'll bet a chicken would make an excellent dog."

Lamont nodded and gathered up his younger brother who had spent his time staring at me with big, round, brown eyes and sucking on his thumb. The two of them headed down the steps, crossed the dried-up front yard and walked up the sidewalk towards home. They lived in a run-down version of my house with a bunch of broken toys in the front lawn. On the weekends, Meeka's boyfriend Dominique, known as Dom, and his pals used to sit in the driveway in lawn chairs and drink beer and listen to rap music that blared from a beat-up boom box that sat on a stump nearby. These get-togethers have pretty much ended; who wants to sit in a lawn chair and endure a face-full of blown dirt? Crap gets into the beer and the snacks.

The chicken hadn't moved from where it was squatting. Now, its eyes were closed. I know a lot about birds in general, and I could see this one was in trouble. But I thought I could nurse him back to health, and then Lamont and Chevaleer would have themselves a pet.

I opened the garage door and began sorting through the piles of cages I keep there. I found what is called a hospital cage, which is about two by three feet with a solid top and bottom. It has several infrared heat lamps which are used to keep a sick bird's temperature up. There's not a hell of a lot you can do for a sick bird, but I was pretty confident I could fix whatever was ailing this chicken.

I set up the cage, put in a plate of seed and a water-feeder that I had loaded with antibiotics. I fetched the chicken off the porch and put him in the cage and was admiring my work when an old Buick Riviera rolled up and stopped in front of my house. The car announced itself through a punctured muffler. Those old Rivieras can be beautiful cars when they're in good shape. This one wasn't. Cream, rust and primer were the piebald colors. The side doors were dented, the mirror on the driver's side was lashed on with a bungee cord and the tailpipe was dragging. The door popped open and out came a hillbilly-type guy with long greasy hair pulled back in a ponytail. He was wearing a wife-beater shirt that looked like it had several day's worth of lunches stained down the front, blue jeans and Doc Martin boots. He stood for a few moments on the sidewalk, looking at me. I didn't have a very good feeling about whatever it was that he wanted.

He walked up the driveway, looked into the garage at the chicken then back at me.

"That's my chicken," he said.

Funny how you can take an instant dislike to someone.

The hillbilly, I'll just call him Cletus, put his hands together in front of his oversize belt buckle and flexed his jailhouse muscles and gave me a smile that wasn't really a smile. His voice was whiskey and cigarette rough. "You got a problem with that?" he added.

See, here's the thing. Maybe it *was* his chicken. Maybe he had all the right in the world to load it up and head on out to whatever trailer park or tarpaper shack or heavily guarded, conspiracy-nut compound he lived in and go about his business, whatever that might be, surely illegal. Now, I know I'm profiling here, and that's against the rules in our democratic society, but this guy looked like the worst kind of backwoods hick, the kind of human who'd beat the shit out of you for looking sideways at his fourteen-year-old pregnant wife, who had the IQ of a tree stump and the moral turpitude of a swamp rat. Every intelligent brain cell in my head was screaming for me to just nod, shut my pie hole and go back into my house and forget the stupid chicken. But, and this has been a problem my whole adult life, I just can not abide people who don't make the smallest effort to follow even the sketchiest rules of civilization, one of which says you should act pleasant if you're asking someone for something.

"You got any proof this is your chicken?" I asked. I turned so I was facing him.

"Proof?" he sneered. "You mean, like, what? Like a photo ID with his picture and my address on it? A library card in his name? What the fuck, man, it's a *chicken*."

I knew that, of course. He had a point. But the second thing about me, and I understand this is a serious flaw, is that I am stubborn to a fault. To a major fault. This guy looked like the worst sort of cruel, dumb, criminal, lying, cheating, scum-sucking, throw-back, bad news, chicken abusing, no 'count excuse for a human being. Have I made it clear how I felt about the guy?

"I'm sorry," I said, sounding prissy to even myself, "unless you can come up with some sort of proof that this chicken belongs to you, I'm going to keep him here. The chicken is sick, he can't be moved." I pulled down the garage door, turned and made it a few feet towards the house when I heard him grunt and launch himself at me. I spun to the side and pulled the .32 caliber SIG Sauer that I usually carry with me tucked into my waistband, covered by my standard issue Hawaiian shirt. I jammed the business end of the pistol into his forehead, right where his unibrow crossed over his nose. He froze like he'd had guns jammed in his face before and was aware of what would happen if I pulled the trigger. I dragged the gun down his cheek and dug it in hard enough to push his head to the side. That was going to leave a mark.

"Get back in your beater and get the fuck out of here," I said. "This is not your chicken. Even if it *was* your chicken, it's now *my* chicken, just because you piss me off. The next time I see you on my property, I'll blow out both your kneecaps, and you'll be riding a skateboard with wooden blocks taped to the backs of your hands."

He backed up, not liking it but being unable to argue with the gun. I was about as big as he was, and while I hadn't spent a couple of years working out in a prison exercise yard, I look reasonably fit, especially with the SIG in my hand. He threw me a sullen look and climbed into the Buick. He opened his mouth and started to give me some shit just to save face. I pointed the gun at his head.

"I know what you're going to say. 'This ain't over yet, I'd better watch my back, and I ain't seen the last of you.' Unless you can come up with a better line than any of those, start up your machine and get the hell out of here." Which he did. Got the hell out of here.

I watched the Riviera haul ass down the street and turn the corner, swaying on spavined springs, oil smoking from the dragging muffler that hadn't muffled anything in at least several years. I went inside and got myself a beer. I sat at the kitchen table, sipped the beer and scratched Max the dog behind the ears, letting the build up of adrenaline seep out of my system. The day was heating up, the way they do every day. I was beginning to sweat.

"What's the matter with me, Max? It's a damn chicken, for Christ's sake." The dog just looked at me the way he always does when the words 'ball' or 'dinner' aren't involved. Which is to say, basically uninterested, with a small, indefatigable margin of hope.

One thing I knew was that Cletus was going to come back, and he was probably going to bring some friends with him. I didn't know why he wanted that damn chicken, but he did. I could either hand the bird over, or I was going to have to fort up. And I needed some reinforcements. Fortunately, I had some. Reinforcements. His name is Daniel.

Daniel Riboux, who returned about a year or so ago from serving in Iraq and Afghanistan, is a US Navy SEAL. Or was. SEAL Team Six, the same guys who took out Osama, though that was more than a few years ago now. We went to grade school, middle school, and high school together. After high school, we went our separate ways, me to college as a Biology major, Daniel to MIT in Engineering though he's never practiced that trade. I began my long drift into a life of minor crime, or at least to my mind it was minor. My biology training has been a big help in keeping my animals alive as they made their sometimes torturous way into the land of the free from whatever jungle, forest, or ocean they had previously inhabited.

Daniel was always interested in the military, so after graduating he made it into SEAL training, rose through the ranks, participated in hundreds of missions and would have gone on to a lifetime of it if the vehicle he was riding in hadn't hit an EID in Kandahar. Both of his legs were blown off right above the knee. Which ended his career, but didn't stop him from being the toughest motherfucker on the block. This block or any other. He spends most of his time in a wheelchair and while you'd think that would have slowed him down, it hasn't. Before the bomb went off, Daniel was hell personified; now he's hell on wheels. And his warrior personality hasn't changed. He once told me that while in rehab he learned that when someone is injured in a catastrophic manner, the same traits that drove him before the injury remained unchanged afterward, except they were magnified. The weak became weaker, the strong became stronger. Like I said, hell on wheels.

I gave him a call and he promised to come over later in the afternoon. I figured I could hold out until he arrived.

I snagged my Macbook Air laptop, tossed my empty, retrieved another beer from the fridge, went to the front porch and sat down on the glider.

A few minutes surfing brought me to a chicken fancier's website. There was a lot of information on identifying various breeds and tips on how to care for them. My years in the bird smuggling business has taught me that people will value and collect pretty much anything when it comes to animals, and chickens were no exception. Scrolling through the pictures of show chickens brought me to the individual that was now squatting forlornly in a cage in my garage. He was tall, for a chicken, all black with a red comb and his legs were slate grey. There were some others that approached this description, but the grey legs set him apart. He was a Maltese Chicken. I thought about the play on words with the Bogart film and decided to skip the obvious jokes.

The Maltese was a rare bird, confined to a couple of hundred examples left on the Island of Malta and pretty much nowhere else, as far as I could tell. I have to admit that my general knowledge of Malta was singularly lacking, so I looked it up as well. Situated in the Mediterranean it had a long and fairly interesting history, but there was nothing there I could see that led this chicken from a backyard hencoop on an island thousands of miles away to my front porch. I was pondering this unlikely journey when a shiny black Lexus with tinted windows pulled up in front of my house. I was certainly popular today.

No dragging muffler this time, though I did feel a pang of, let's just go ahead and call it fear, thinking that Cletus was back in a better automobile and this time he most certainly would be armed. And of course I had left my gun inside, not far, but a hundred miles away if anyone was really out to get me. So sue me, you try walking around all day with a SIG stuffed down your waistband. It chafes. I was half out of the glider, balancing the Macbook in my left hand when the driver's-side door opened and out stepped the best looking woman that had been seen in my seedy neighborhood in a long time. She was right up there with the Jamaican lady on the poster.

She had thick, curly black hair and a pretty face. She was wearing a pair of jeans and a tight top, both of which told me one very important thing: there was no way she was concealing a weapon, other than the natural guns that God had given her. Sorry, that just slipped out.

She walked up to the porch and bathed me with a full-on smile that made me feel stupid. I'm not sure why that was, but it was so.

"Maria Galea." She held out her hand.

"Raphael Holt. Rafe for short." We shook hands.

"I believe," she said, without preamble, "you have my chicken." When she said it, it sounded vaguely erotic.

I studied her for several long minutes. "Maybe," I said. "Could you describe this chicken?"

She laughed. Her lips were red, bright red, and they matched her shirt. Do women do that? Match their lipstick to their clothing, or vice versa when they get ready to meet the world? I could think of no male equivalent.

"My chicken is black with a red comb and he has grey legs," she said.

Well, she nailed it. I was standing there, stupidly, holding my laptop computer as if it were a tray of hors d'oeuvres that I was offering to her.

Just then Daniel rolled up in his Hummer. It's all black with blacked out windows and heavily armored. I always referred to it as the Deathstar. Her eyes followed mine to the Hummer.

"Company?" she asked.

"A friend of mine." I knew I had a few minutes while Daniel got himself situated. "What makes you think I have a chicken that belongs to you?"

"My associate, Randall, was by here earlier today. His job was to retrieve the lost chicken. He seems to have rubbed you the wrong way, which doesn't surprise me, as he rubs most civilized people the wrong way."

Randall must have been Cletus.

"Is Randall around six feet tall, wears his hair in a greasy ponytail and has big muscles probably acquired in prison? And he talks like a hick?"

"That would be Randall." She crossed her arms over her chest. I tried not to look interested. She had an accent, one that I couldn't place.

I forged ahead. "Forgive me if I'm stepping out of bounds here, but what on earth does that troglodyte have to do with a lovely person like yourself?"

She laughed. This was the second time she had done so and the sound was enough to bring strong men to their knees. I glanced over at Daniel; he was out of the Hummer and into his chair, sitting beside the car. I held up a hand to keep him where he was for a minute.

"Randall needs to learn some manners, some people skills," I said. "I don't have a hell of a lot of interest in chickens, and I have no idea why this one ended up on my front porch, but I would like to know why Cletus, that's Randall, and why *you*, care so much about *him*. The chicken."

She was still smiling at me, which was good. Have I mentioned how red her lips were? I believe I did. The same red, I now realized, as the chicken's comb. Surely, she wasn't accessorizing herself to match the chicken.

"I am Maltese," she said. "From Malta. When I was growing up, we had chickens scratching around the back yard, up in the hills, around the island. They were good layers, and very good eating when they outlived their productive years. I have lived here in Virginia for ten years, I've done well in business, and I have recently brought my mother here from our home in Malta. She's old, my father is dead. She hates it here. But I cannot send her back, she cannot take care of herself. So, I asked my brother, who still lives there, to send me a few chickens, which he has been doing for several years. Did you know it is legal to keep chickens in your backyard these days?"

I did know that. But I didn't say anything.

"Well, it is. This one, a rooster, got out of the coop and somehow ended up on your porch. My eighty-two-year-old mother is worried about him. I'd like to bring him back to her. I would be happy to give you a reward for finding him. A substantial reward."

She turned on that blazing smile again. I wanted to believe her, oh how I wanted to believe. But my bullshit detector was going off at about five alarms.

"I'll tell you what," I said, "the chicken is sick. Why don't I keep him for a few days until he's feeling better. I'll ask around the neighborhood, see if anyone else has lost a Maltese chicken. If no one else claims him, I'll turn him over."

Uh, oh, there goes that beautiful smile. Gone. When she spoke, it was through gritted teeth.

"I'll tell *you* what, Mr. Holt, why don't you just bring me my goddamn chicken and get your nose out of some business that doesn't have anything to do with you. You *know* it's my chicken. And I need him *now*. I don't care if he has Bubonic fucking Plague."

Yeah, it probably was her chicken, but now she was the one that was rubbing me the wrong way. Especially since she stopped smiling and started cursing. I glanced over at Daniel who was was rolling up the walk. "Like I said, Miss Galea, let's give it a few days. If you take that chicken away it's going to die."

"I told you, I don't have a few days."

"Oh, yeah, I forgot, your aging mom misses the symbol of her old home place. As much as I hate to bring pain to old ladies, I still think I'll give it a few days while the chicken gets better and I figure things out."

She gave me a hard look then transferred it to Daniel who was waiting at the bottom of the ramp I had installed so he could easily maneuver up to the porch. He gave her a broad, white-toothed smile that seemed to piss her off even more. She flounced down the steps and out to her car. After she had driven off, Daniel rolled up the ramp.

"The beautiful lady has left in a huff," he said.

"The beautiful lady is angry at me. I seem to be in possession of her chicken."

"The beautiful lady has a name—Maria Galea," Daniel said. "I ran her plates while I was getting the Bot out of the truck.

Daniel's extremely high tech wheelchair, known as an iBot, was made by the guy who invented the Segway. The chairs are no longer manufactured, the $28,000.00 asking price turned out to be too steep for a commercial venture, though Daniel says there are still a few kicking around for sale on the Internet. His has been modified many times and can do some incredible things. For starters he didn't need to use the ramp, the chair can maneuver up stairs, but he likes to use arm power except when he's got his hands full. With guns, usually.

The last year back from Afghanistan, in the chair, has left Daniel with massive upper body strength. He was in great shape before the injury; he's in far better shape now. His only problem is that he has no legs from above the knees down. Not that he sees that as a problem. He always says when the bad guys see him coming, either in the chair or on his stumps, they get more than a little antsy. He's coming at them at balls level, which tends to make even the toughest guys nervous. Especially when he has a combat knife clenched between his teeth.

"You want to explain the chicken thing to me?" he asked. So, I did. Then, I took him out and showed him the chicken, which still looked like an ordinary chicken that was having a bad feather day. I explained that the chicken was sick and his name was Jack.

"It's not a rare breed?" he asked, "Like some of those parrots that mysteriously end up in your garage?"

"It's an unusual bird, and there aren't that many of them left back on Malta, but it's not rare enough to bring out Cletus to threaten me and then the beautiful lady to try to buy me off. As near as I can tell, it's pretty much just a chicken."

"And you're not going to hand it over, which is what anyone who was normal would do."

It wasn't really a question. Daniel knew me well enough to answer that one on his own. He sighed. "Of course you're not. That would be far too easy."

"What I want to know is why they want the bird. So, I guess if we find out how badly they do want it, then we'll know at least something."

"*We.*" He shook his head. "*We'll* know something." He shook his head again. "Because we're pretty sure they'll be coming back, probably tonight."

"Sounds like it. The beautiful Maria didn't seem to want to wait and work out a deal. Hey, if you don't think you can handle some backwoods hillbilly and a beautiful woman in tight bluejeans, just climb back in the Deathstar, and I'll do it myself."

He didn't bother to raise to the bait; we both knew I was blowing smoke.

"OK, they'll wait until dark, then Cletus and his boys, I think we can trust that he'll bring some help with him, will try to sneak up on us, incapacitate us in some way and make off with the bird." He looked around the porch. "There's not much we can do to make this place into something more defensible. Just how far are you willing to go to keep the bird?"

"Far? We'll, I think we should keep things as quiet as we can. I don't particularly want to involve the cops. We both know the further I stay away from the law, the better."

"Don't worry, we're not going to be asking the cops to help us. What I want to know is, are you willing to kill someone if it comes to that? It's a question I always ask my clients." That gave me pause. I wasn't really thinking that far ahead.

"No, not unless they're trying to kill me."

"OK."

"But if you want to seriously bend Cletus, I don't really care."

"Good. Bend, but do not break. I can do that."

* * *

Daniel nudged me awake at 2:00 AM. I was dozing on the couch; he was keeping watch. The house was dark and a thin sliver of moonlight came through the curtains on the front bay window. He handed me a set of night vision goggles and

I slipped them on. He was bright green through the goggles and he gestured to the window.

Without disturbing the curtains I leaned close and looked through the crack where both sides almost met. There was a panel truck sitting at the curb in front of the house. The writing on the side of the truck said: *Mt. Nebo Christ Church.* Beneath that it said, *All Praise His Name.* That made me feel a lot better. The bad guys seemed to have the Lord on their side. While I watched, the front door of the van popped open and a figure stepped out. He was joined by other pale green ghosts who exited the back of the truck. I counted four, but there may have been others on the far side of the vehicle.

We had a plan, or at least the outline of a plan. Daniel was dressed in black SWAT-type gear. He was in his chair but was wearing what he called his "war stumps," heavy plastic covers for the ends of his legs, I had seen him run on these on several occasions and he was damn near as fast as I was with two regular legs. He was armed with a silenced Walther 22, loaded with subsonic rounds which made the weapon as quiet as any gun can be. It's a small calibre, but he can actually hit pretty much whatever he aims at so it works well in situations where stealth is required.

I had a Taser, being deemed unfit for regular weaponry. I will admit, I'm not that good a shot, especially if we are shooting to wound rather than kill. We figured they, or at least some of them, would come straight in through the front door and we would deal with those guys first and whomever else was around after that. The figures moved up the walk to the house. I glanced at Daniel and his grin was wide and white with shades of green through the goggles. Daniel really digs this sort of thing. He rolled away to be behind the door when it opened.

There was a scratching sound while someone outside jimmied the cheap lock on my front door. This was not the first time I had wished I had installed something a bit more substantial. I held my breath as the door swung silently open.

The first guy got just inside when Daniel took him down so fast it surprised even me, and I knew it was coming. The second guy was through, and I zapped him with the taser, and he went down as well, his head hitting the floor with a thunk. Daniel rolled the first guy out of the way and had him trussed with a plastic handcuff that zipped into place. My guy was rattling around on the floor like he'd been electrocuted, which he had. Then, he slumped into unconsciousness. There was a period of silence while we waited for the next wave to come through. I could hear heavy breathing and realized it was coming from me.

The door slammed all the way open and a figure dove into the room firing a silenced automatic weapon which tore through my couch and blasted out the front window with a crash of broken glass. So much for not waking the neighbors. Couch stuffing burst into the air like small bomb blasts. I scrambled away from the couch and rolled to the far side of the room, essentially defenseless. I heard a couple of small pops from Daniel's vicinity and the automatic weapon fell silent. I counted three down and knew there was at least one more.

He must have come around the house and through the back door.

The light in the living room snapped on and all of a sudden the night vision goggles became a serious liability as the overhead light blew out our vision. We both jerked off the goggles and Daniel had his Walther pointed at the fourth man, who turned out to be my friend Cletus, who was pointing an AK-47 at my head. We all stayed frozen in place for a long moment.

"You shoot me, crip, and I'm going to go down sprayin' lead in the direction of Mr. Smart Ass over there," Cletus said to Daniel. That would be me, Mr. Smart Ass, I figured.

If Cletus was nervous or intimidated, he didn't sound like it. For my part, I was glad I didn't have to come up with any quips to show how cool under fire I was.

Daniel had once explained to me that what Cletus said was not necessarily the truth. Daniel could hit the greaser in the kill zone—one inch above the nose and one inch down from the hairline—and the shock would shut down Cletus's nervous system before he could pull the trigger.

Daniel glanced at me. I knew he was asking if I wanted him to prove his point. And I have to admit, I was pretty much leaning in favor of waxing Cletus, who certainly had no compunctions about doing the same to me. Then, the odds got a little longer.

She came through the door as silent as the proverbial cat, dressed all in black, carrying some other version of a silenced handgun, which was pointed at Daniel's head.

"It looks like things have gotten a little out of hand, here, Randall," she said to Cletus.

"It's not my fault these shitbirds don't know when they're licked."

It looked like some strange child's game to me: Maria shoots Daniel, Daniel shoots Cletus, Cletus shoots me, and around and around the mulberry bush we go.

"No," I said. "Everybody cool it. You can have the chicken."

It damned near killed me to say so, but it didn't kill me nearly as much as it would have if one of them started firing.

It's a chicken! I had to keep reminding myself, *It's just a damned chicken!*

* * *

I opened the garage door and stood there, waiting. The overhead fluorescent light flickered on. Maria and Cletus were standing beside me. "There he is," I said. "Go ahead and take him." I was damned if I was going to carry the cage out to the van for them.

Maria turned to Cletus. "Randall, check him out," she said. "Make sure he's ours."

"All of a sudden you're not sure?" I said, pissed off even more than when there were bullets flying in my direction.

Randall, Cletus, whatever you want to call him, went to the cage, opened the door and took the chicken out. Whatever bad I could say about Cletus, I had to admit he knew how to handle the bird. I could see he had done this many times before. He had one big hand across the bird's chest, the other on his back. He held the bird up and stared it in the eye. The chicken still looked plenty sick. Cletus put him back in the cage.

"Yeah, he's ours." He picked up the cage and went to the van without another word.

"Keep the heat on him," I called after him. "And leave the antibiotic water in there. Otherwise he'll die for sure. And by the way, his name is Jack."

Maria looked at me like I was crazy. "Yeah, right," she said, walking to the van. She had no more interest in me.

Once he had the chicken loaded up, Cletus dragged out the wounded: the guy who Daniel shot was hit in the arm and leg, which is just where Daniel wanted to hit him. The fellow I Tasered came back to consciousness and while he was seriously pissed off at me, he climbed into the van with his wounded amigo and the guy Daniel had trussed up with the handcuffs, which we considerately removed. Maria took the passenger seat, which must have been where she was when they pulled up. They drove off, leaving Daniel and me standing on my porch in the dark, watching the taillights recede into the night. I waited for the sounds of sirens or the gathering of curious neighbors who had heard my front window blowing out, but neither came. In my neighborhood one tended to not call the cops for little things like automatic gunfire.

"And what have we learned?" Daniel asked. He had put all the weapons and gear into the Deathstar.

"Well, we learned that they seemed to be willing to kill to get the chicken back. Which means that Jack is extremely valuable for some reason that is not obvious. Other than that, I learned that next time I'm going to have at least a back-up Taser or some other weapon that delivers more than a one-at-a-time punch."

"And we haven't learned, as the lovely Maria suggested, that we keep our noses out of other people's business?"

I had been thinking about that. It was obviously good advice, words that I had used myself in the past for individuals who were a little too interested in my own particular business.

"OK, it makes sense. Particularly since we're not even in possession of the chicken anymore. Let me check out one little detail, then I'll let it go."

Daniel nodded. "One little detail. OK, I'm out of here," he said. "They're not coming back, at least not tonight, they got what they wanted."

I watched him roll down the ramp. I wasn't sure, but it seemed to me he was moving with a little less élan than he usually showed. Maybe he was tired. It was four AM and he'd had a long night shooting people and wrestling them to the ground. Yeah, maybe that was it. Probably didn't have anything to do with the fact that the bad guys had just relieved us of our chicken. I went to bed.

* * *

I waited till ten in the morning before I left the house. Folks in my neighborhood aren't what you'd call early risers. Most of the business that they ran or were employed in operated at night when decent citizens were tucked into their cozy beds. I spent an hour or so putting a large sheet of plywood where my front window used to be.

When I walked up to Meeka's house, Lamont was nowhere to be seen, and Chevaleer was sitting in the dirt fooling with the remains of a Hot Wheels tricycle. There wasn't a blade of grass in his yard or anyone else's. It hadn't rained here in five years. "Is your mom home?" I asked. It was Saturday so I thought she might not be at work.

"She inside," the little boy answered. He was trying to get an orange plastic wheel back on an axle, but it wasn't going to work. The rest of the trike was in at least fourteen pieces. It looked as if someone had dropped a full beer keg on it and then run over it with a car. I nodded and headed toward the porch.

"She beat up," Chevy said. I stopped.

"Dom say he gonna kill someone."

That didn't sound good.

* * *

Meeka was in bed, wrapped up like a mummy. I don't know if she'd seen a doctor; if she had, I expect he would have immediately sent her to a hospital. Thank God no one sent for Dr. Fish to fix her up.

Dom paced back and forth behind me as I stood by the bed and looked down at Meeka. Her eyes were open, but I'm not sure she was in the room with us. Dom had probably given her something to relieve the pain, or at least I hoped to God he had. Every inch of exposed flesh I could see was bruised.

"Lamont said it was some white guy," Dom said. Dom, Meeka's live-in boyfriend, was a good-looking man, light coffee-colored with a goatee, tall and well spoken. I don't think he was originally from around here. "Guy with muscles and one of those old hippy pony tails. Lamont said he came in the house, asked Meeka some questions and then started beating on her. Eventually, she must have told him what he wanted because he didn't kill her. I came home and found her on the floor; she's been pretty confused since then. The only thing I could understand was something about a chicken, but I think she's too out of it to make sense."

Cletus. Had to be. But what led him to Meeka? And to me?

The chicken, of course. That goddamned chicken.

I leaned down into Meeka's angle of vision. "Meeka, did that chicken that ended up on my porch come from the embassy?" I asked. She was staring at some point beyond where I stood, but just for an instant her eyes flickered over me.

"I've got her too doped up to answer any questions," Dom said.

Maybe so, but I was pretty sure she looked back and gave just the tiniest nod of her bandaged head. Then, she shut her eyes.

* * *

Dom told me that Meeka worked at an embassy in Washington that represented some island. I asked if it just happened to be an island called Malta? Yes, indeed. He seemed surprised that I knew what Malta was. I don't think Dom has a very high opinion of white people's intelligence.

"If she comes around, send one of the kids to get me," I said. Meeka knew a lot more about the chicken than any of us, but she wasn't going to be talking much anytime soon. I went back home.

Daniel was sitting in his wheelchair on my porch.

"Get that detail taken care of, did you?" he asked.

"Sort of. I would have, only Cletus got there first." I filled him in on Meeka and how she'd been beaten. And been unable to answer the questions I had for her.

"So, she works for the embassy, and you figure she got the chicken from them? Brought it out here, saw it was sick and had the kids put it on your porch. Then Cletus, who also works for the embassy, went to her house, got her to tell him what she had done with the chicken and drove here to pick up the bird."

I nodded. "But when I didn't hand him over, he called Maria and she came out to try a more subtle method of persuasion."

"And when that didn't work they came out with the troops and got what they wanted."

"Right. But why" What was so valuable about the bird? It gnawed at me, I could feel it right on the edge of my consciousness, something about birds, chickens . . ."

"So, are we going to let this go?" Daniel asked. "Because if you want to move ahead, I think I've got the next step figured out." He smiled at me with a grin that I can only describe as satisfied with the expectation of violence and revenge.

"No, I'm not going to let it go. It sticks in my craw, especially since Meeka got beaten up. What's the next step?"

"Well, last night while you were getting the bird out of the garage, I put a tracker on the van. They're about five hours away in West Virginia. Or at least the van is."

"And I assume we're loaded up and ready to go?"

"The Deathstar awaits."

"OK, let me get my SIG. I'm not going in with a Taser on this one. I've got a theory that might explain what's going on, but I'm going to need to see the bird again."

"So, let's go get it," Daniel said.

* * *

We drove through rural Virginia and into West Virginia. The last five years of drought has changed the landscape radically. All the farmers are gone, the crops burned down to nothing but dirt that blows away, just like in dust bowl days. Vast fields of wind farms have sprung up, supplying the east with plenty of energy, even though the fields of soy, potatoes and tobacco are gone. It's a bleak landscape, one that people are beginning to see as normal. Meanwhile, the cities grow with the displaced. Not that anyone is doing much about it. Nero fiddles, the earth burns, life goes on pretty much the way it always has.

We drove past a vast orchard, or former orchard, the trees now black and leafless, etched against the bright blue cloudless sky.

"I Google-earthed Cletus' place," Daniel said.

Daniel has the military version of Google Earth, not the fuzzy edition available to the general public. He can read license plates with his. God only knows where or how he acquired it. He passed me a half dozen print-out pictures from his computer. I shuffled through them while he talked.

"It's a compound centered around a small church. Looks like there's an electric fence of some sort, but that's about it for defensive measures. Compound is kind of an overblown word; it's not very big: the church, a farmhouse and a bunch of outbuildings."

"Anything that looks like a chicken coop to you?"

"It all looks like a chicken coop, at least from above. As far as we know, he could have Jack in the house living the good life."

"None of them gives a shit about Jack. I'll bet he's stuffed him in one of these little shacks." I pointed at a couple of ramshackle, one-room buildings. Daniel nodded.

"If none of them gives a shit about the chicken, why are they willing to kill for it?"

"They haven't killed anybody for it, yet. At least as far as we know. But I take your point. Why? Actually, I think I have an idea. We'll know later tonight if I'm right."

We stopped once for coffee and again at a small convenience store to pick up some items I needed before arriving in the general vicinity of the compound. We turned off the main highway, then off the local road onto an unused dirt track that looked like an old logging trail, two overgrown ruts that curled up the backside of a heavily-wooded mountain. The Deathstar took it in stride, crunching over brush and small trees without slowing. We crested the top of the hill, and Daniel switched off the ignition. Holding a penlight between his teeth, he stretched out a Forest-Service map.

"This is us," he said, pointing to a spot on the map. "And this is them." He put his finger about an inch from where we sat. "Let's take a look."

We climbed out of the truck and slipped on the NVGs. There were enough stars, plus a nearly full moon, to make the landscape around us look like it was high noon. Daniel had padded stumps on that were designed so he could creep around quietly. I didn't think it was possible to get the wheelchair where we were going.

Down in a valley was the farmhouse compound. We had studied the Google Earth photos, and I told Daniel which of the two outbuildings I thought might house the chicken. Or chickens, for all I knew.

The plan was simple. We creep down to the fence around the place; Daniel breeches the fence, goes in, and retrieves the chicken. Then, he brings it back to me, so I test out my theory, and we know if I'm Sherlock Holmes or not.

We crept down the hill, though mostly Daniel crept; I stumbled, fell down and generally made a fair amount of noise. It didn't seem to matter, as the fence was three hundred yards from the cluster of buildings. We stopped at the bottom of the hill while Daniel studied the electric fence.

"Think you'll have any problems?" I whispered to him. He gave me a look of scorn.

"This probably keeps out the deer, but it's not going to slow down Batman." He fished around in his backpack and pulled out a pair of wire cutters and a length of wire with hobby-store alligator clips at either end.

"Pretty low tech, Batman," I said.

"Whatever gets the job done," he said, attaching the alligator clips to the wire at the top of the fence where it was electrified. He cut the barbed wire and the electrical wire between the clips and pushed it apart so he could maneuver through. We waited a minute, but there was no movement from the direction of the compound. Daniel nodded to me and went through the breach.

I watched him as he moved away. In the goggles, he was a large, greenish-white form that ambled forward. He told me that he was far less visible in any circumstance than a man on two intact legs. People are programed to look for a face, and when a face doesn't appear at the approximate height it should be they tend to not see a human form as they normally would. Of course it doesn't make him invisible, but it's a contradiction that can give him added seconds of surprise. He was quickly out of sight from where I was sitting.

I leaned back against a tree stump and took off my goggles. Even if I had noticed something troubling, there was no way I could have let Daniel know. I asked about a communications set-up, but he said silence was all-important in a retrieval mission. He was probably right. What was I going to do if I saw something suspicious? Shoot it? Jump up and run to the rescue? No, Daniel was better off alone with his fabulous skills.

I looked up at the night sky, which arced in full blazing glory over me. No clouds, no wind, nothing stirring in the underbrush. I began to hear a voice, faintly, that came through the night. Someone was speaking in cadenced tones. I could catch only a few words and fragments that floated in the night air.

"Jesus Christ . . . blood of the lamb . . . sinners . . ."

I remembered the overhead pictures of the compound, with the weatherbeaten, once-white wooden church in the center. Somebody was preaching a sermon. This was probably good; hopefully everyone in the area would be in church.

It really was a beautiful night. In no time at all I was fast asleep.

* * *

I'm not sure what woke me, but I sat up, confused for a moment. I put on the NVGs and scrambled to my feet. Twenty feet away, dragging itself toward me, was a squat monster with a lolling fanged head. Gore dripped from the monster's mouth, white greenish flecks of drool. I was seeing what I was seeing, and knowing at the same time that I couldn't be seeing what I was seeing.

"Give me a goddamned hand!" Daniel whispered, hoarsely.

I could hardly see his face, which he'd blacked-out with makeup earlier. His eyes bloomed wide beside the drooling monster-head. I pushed through the cut wires. As I came up to him he dropped a huge dog, which appeared dead, off his shoulders. It made a significant, but muffled thump as it hit the ground.

"Spanish Mastiff. Big fucker. Drag him through the fence. We're going to have to hide the body."

I picked up a front paw and hauled. The dog slid forward about six inches and stopped. Talk about dead weight.

"Jesus," I whispered, "he must weigh 200 pounds."

"I'd say 250," Daniel said, turning back to me. "OK, you take the chicken, I'll handle the dog."

I hadn't noticed, but tucked into the crook of his left arm, was the chicken. I had coached him on the way to approach and carry the bird: tuck the head under a wing and hold the wing tight. A bird will stay quiet like that, especially at night. I took Jack, who seemed hot but quiet. It probably helped that he was still sick.

Daniel picked up the dog and slung it over his shoulders in a fireman's carry. Loaded down that way, he still moved a lot quieter than I did, and I was only carrying a five-pound chicken.

We made it to the truck at the top of the hill. Daniel opened up the back and removed a shovel and dragged the dog into the woods. I found the bag of stuff I bought at the convenience store earlier and put Jack down in the back of the truck. He seemed to shudder, but remained relatively upright, head still tucked beneath his wing.

I pulled a container of plain yogurt, a small bottle of cod liver oil and a large plastic medicine syringe out of the paper bag and put them on the floor of the back area of the Hummer, next to the chicken. I gently picked up Jack and pressed my fingers into his chest area, underneath his feathers. I immediately knew that I was on the right track.

There was a large, heavy mass beneath the skin.

Here's some basic bird biology. Birds, and chickens, eat a lot of different kinds of things. Depending on the species, they can eat seeds, bugs, small mammals, lizards, just about anything they can catch and cram down their gullets. Rather than the food going down the neck and dumping into the stomach, the food goes through a pouch called a craw and from there through the gizzard. In the craw is grit, literally small rocks, ranging in size from a grain of sand up to a small pebble, depending on the size of the bird. The rocks grind up the food and the gizzard continues the grinding process until the food is mashed up enough to be handled by the regular digestive enzymes in the stomach. Sometimes the crop gets jammed up, food catches there and spoils and the bird gets sick and can die. But in my guise as Doctor Bird, I can fix the problem.

I found a tin camping-cup in Daniel's supplies and made a mixture of yogurt and oil, sucking up a syringe-full. Gently pulling Jack's head from beneath his wing, I squeezed open his beak and forced the solution down his throat, repeating the procedure three times. I massaged the neck and the chest area. I set him down and rinsed out the cup with water from a bottle.

After waiting what might have been the appropriate time, about two minutes, who knows? I picked Jack up by the feet and hung him over the cup, head down, and began reverse massaging the crop from the bottom of his chest into the neck. In the starlight, I could see his beak crane open and he began emitting chicken gagging sounds. And then, music to my ears.

Clink!

I kept it up for another three or four minutes, with more clinks as pebbles and grit accumulated in the tin cup. When

I could feel nothing more in his neck and crop, I tilted him upright and set him down. I swear he looked better than he had since the first time I had seen him. He was purged and pissed off, but better for it.

The tin cup was half full of a gooey, stinking mess. I swished water in, stirring and carefully sieved out the water between my fingers until most of the goo and the finer grit was gone.

"What the hell are you doing?" Daniel asked coming up behind me. "I could have used some help burying that monster." I waited for a minute while my heart stopped stuttering.

"This is probably a stupid question, but why did you kill him?" I asked. "The dog."

"It was either that or be eaten alive. He came at me as I was going into the chicken coop. Before he charges, I checked out the church where your pal Cletus was giving the sermon. Real fire and brimstone stuff. There were around ten or so parishioners, some of whom were armed. Other then that, not a soul was on the grounds. Obviously, they felt that Tyrannosaurus Rex there would protect the place. I didn't want to kill him, but he gave me no choice. Now, what's in the cup?"

"Got a penlight?" I asked. I could feel tension in my gut. I was either right or I was wrong, and I was going to find out in about 30 seconds. Daniel pulled a small mag light from a pocket and handed it to me. I switched it on and looked into the cup.

I expected to see what I saw, I *wanted* to see what I saw, but it still caught my breath. There was a quarter cup of cut diamonds, big ones, the size of fresh peas, sparkling away despite the chicken goo that still clung to them. I handed the cup and light to Daniel. I believe I heard him inhale when he saw what was in there. We were both silent for a long minute.

"Jesus," he said. "What do you suppose these babies are worth?"

I've mentioned my job description: animal smuggler.

Sometimes, folks like to pay in currency other than good old American greenbacks, so I've seen my share of gold and gems.

"There's twelve of them. I'm no expert, but I'd guess between three quarters of a million and a million dollars. That's real value, not what you're going to get because you'd have to sell these off the books. But there are plenty of diamond dealers who are willing to bend the rules."

"How'd you know they were in there?"

"I didn't, but I knew something probably was. Earlier, I said the whole thing was sticking in my craw, a common phrase that triggered a connection. I've handled other birds sick with the same problem and fixed them the same way, though the result has never been as spectacular."

Daniel handed me the cup and loaded the shovel into the back of the truck, careful not to hit the bird.

"OK, let's get out of here," he said. "We can talk about the various ramifications when we get home." I put a hand on his shoulder.

"We'll go. But first, there's one more thing we need to to."

He looked at me with a puzzled expression.

"First you have to take Jack back."

* * *

He argued for a few minutes, but I won him over with my logic.

"They're not going to kill Jack. They must have done this before, maybe they use the same bird for multiple operations. Maybe they were going to ship him on to someone else to get the diamonds out after he got well. Maybe our Jack has a particular gift in his ability to swallow a significant amount of grit, in this case diamonds, into his craw. The point is, yes, sometime in the future they're going to figure out they've been screwed when they realize the diamonds are gone. The longer we can stretch the time before they figure it out, the better prepared we'll be if they come after us again. And they probably will. But right now, they need to see the bird sitting there in the coop just like he was before."

Daniel couldn't really come up with a good argument, aside from the fact that if it was dangerous to go in once, it was doubly so to do so twice. Maybe he was looking for another go-round with a monster dog, just to keep his skill set sharp. We headed back down the hill. I waited while he went through the wire again, carrying poor, long suffering Jack with head tucked back under his wing. This time I didn't fall asleep. This time I was dreaming, eyes wide open, about what I was going to do with my share of a million dollars.

* * *

Daniel and I were at the house installing some self defense measures when my cell rang. I put down a roll of wire and a hammer and answered.

"OK, Shitbird, I want my property back." He didn't need to say who was calling, the voice was unmistakable. So much for gaining some extra time before they found out what we had done.

"Ah, Cletus, I have no idea what you are talking about."

There was a moment of silence while Cletus figured out who Cletus was. Across the room Daniel heard and stopped wiring a flash-bang grenade to the back of the door. I nodded to him. I put Cletus on speakerphone.

"No more tricks. You've got my property. I want it back. And there's others who want it back, too."

"Cletus, the next time Daniel's got you in his sights, I'm going to let him shoot you. I'm about tired of your bull-shit. Who you got backing you up this time? The beautiful Maria? Who the hell is she anyway. Catwoman?" Cletus gave a snort of laughter.

"She ain't no kitty-cat. You got to worry about her, they's quite a group behind Maria. That was her chicken, I'm just the facilitator. You ain't afraid of me, fine, but her people gonna eat you alive."

"This is all very interesting, but if you don't have more than vague threats about who pulls Maria's beautiful strings, I'm going to say so long, we'll just see what you've got later."

"Maybe you just ought to listen a minute longer. Got a boy here, says his name is Chevalier. What the hell kind of name is that anyway? You know his momma, Meeka, bitch that stole my chicken in the first place. Here's the deal, Shitbird, you head on out here this evening, say around eight o'clock, and we'll make a trade. Young Chevy here for my property. Don't be late. I might have a few doubts about killin' a kid, even a colored kid, but Maria's people don't give a shit. I don't give them what you stole from me, they're gonna kill everyone in sight. Including this little kid." He hung up. There was a dial tone. Which told me he was calling from a landline, but nothing else. I looked at Daniel.

"I assume you know who Chevaleer is?" he asked. "And what kind of name is that anyway?"

"Yeah, I know Chevaleer. I'll be back in a few minutes."

I ran the two blocks to Meeka's place. Lamont was sitting on the steps. The hundred or so pieces of Chevy's Hotwheels trike were still scattered around the yard.

"Where's your brother?" I said, out of breath.

"Ain't seen him."

I banged on the door and pushed it open. Dominique was sitting at the kitchen table talking on his cell phone. He held up his hand to stop me, finished his conversation and put his phone on the table.

"You seen Chevy?" he asked, before I could ask him.

"No. But I think I know where he is. And it's not good. How's Meeka?"

"She's better. Strong girl. But now you're gonna have to be straight with me. I need to know what the hell is going on."

So, I told him. All of it. He just sat and listened, didn't interrupt.

"You think they're telling the truth about the trade?" he asked.

"Maybe. Though I'm troubled by Cletus saying there are other interests involved. Do I think they'll hurt Chevy if I don't give them what they want? I don't think it matters, because I'm going to have to give them the diamonds anyway. I can't take a chance."

He nodded. "If we leave now, can we make it by eight?" he asked.

"Yes. But you're not involved. My guy and I will go. We're the ones they want."

"It's Meeka's chicken, isn't it? At least she's the one who started it all by taking the chicken. She's right in the middle and took a bad beating to prove it. That means it's my business. Besides, like you said, none of that matters. They've got Chevy."

I nodded. "Talk to Meeka, get the whole story. Again, you don't have to go. My guy can handle them. He's the expert."

Dominique laughed. "I did two tours with the Marines in Afghanistan. Since then, I've dealt with my share of trouble. I'm not worried about a bunch of crackers. You go on. I'll talk to Meeka. You tell your guy to get his shit together. I'll be over in half an hour. I want to get some of my boys out here to watch Meeka and Lamont while we're gone."

So, we had a new soldier in the unit. Fine by me. "Ask Meeka who Maria is. From the embassy."

* * *

Dominique was at my place in the promised half an hour. I told Daniel we had a new recruit who probably had some skills. Daniel was fine with that as we were heading into what he described as a shitstorm, and we were undermanned.

"I can't say I think that what Meeka did was cool," Dominique said. He told us to call him Dom. "You know how she is, right?" he said to me. "She can't stand to see any of God's creatures harmed or in danger of harm. Evidently, this chicken thing had happened before." We were sitting around the kitchen table. Daniel had the Deathstar loaded with whatever tools he needed. I nodded to keep Dom talking. We had another half an hour before we headed out.

"Cletus, as you call him, works as some sort of support person for the embassy. He does various chores, arranges for supplies, oversees maintenance and provides personnel for any kind of physical labor that needs to be done. He's one of those guys who has a huge number of keys attached to his belt. All of which sounds like bullshit to me; why bring a guy like that in from West Virginia when there's plenty of labor available in DC? Anyway, the chicken. There are a ton of regulations concerning bringing animals into the US from foreign countries."

"I know all about that," I said. Most of the rules say you can't import them for *any* reason, not without a long quarantine period. It's a hell of a lot easier, and probably cheaper, to let me smuggle them in.

"But if an embassy is concerned, there are almost no regulations at all," he continued. "They would bring these chickens in, one at a time, every four or five months or so. They were supposed to be for indigenous food, but Meeka said the chickens would come in with other supplies from Malta, Randall would take charge of them and they would never be seen again. So, this one came in . . ."

"His name is Jack," I said.

Dom frowned at me.

"Don't look at me like that," I said. "Lamont and Chevy named him."

"OK, the chicken comes in, and Meeka says he looks real sick. Randall was supposed to pick him up, but he got hung up—traffic on the beltway, he had to preach a sermon, I don't know. Anyway, the chicken is there looking sick, no one is going to take care of it, so Meeka, the female St. Francis of Assisi, just scoops him up and brings him home. Maybe she was going to take him back the next day, maybe not, it's hard to tell, especially since Randall beat her so badly she can still hardly speak. By the way, just so everyone is clear on this, Randall's ass is mine. No one lays a hand on my women or kids and lives. Understand?" I looked at Daniel and we both shrugged. Randall/Cletus had moved into entirely new territory once he beat up Meeka and kidnapped Chevy. My conscience was clear no matter what happened.

"Meeka gets the chicken home," Dom continued, "and he looks like he's going to die at any moment. The next day, in the morning, she has Chevy and Lamont bring him to your house because you're another soft touch when it comes to saving poor little animals." He gave me a look I couldn't decipher, halfway between admiration for my supposed spiritual qualities and disgust with my ridiculous sympathies.

"Then, the shit hit the various fans and we end up here."

"You really want to go along on this?" Daniel asked. "I have a feeling this time people are going to die."

"Hell, yes," Dom said, standing. He was dressed all in black, wearing a leather jacket. He opened the jacket and on one side was a Tec-9 semi-automatic weapon and on the other a Glock, both in specially-sewn holsters that didn't show on the outside.

"Fine, " Daniel said, looking at me. "Here's the way I think it should go. We travel down in two cars, Dom and I will be in the Deathstar, you'll be in your own car. You go in the main entrance, which should be no problem because you've been summoned. If you were to come walking up the road, they'd know someone came with you and dropped you off. Dom and I will put the truck up on the hill behind the compound where we were last night. We'll go through the same breach we made then.

"You tell Cletus that you have the diamonds, in fact you should take them. Show him the stones, get him to bring in Chevy, then we'll bust in and snatch the kid. You take the kid and get the hell out."

"Do I hand over the diamonds?" I asked.

"It's mox nix to me, I'm there to get the kid out. There's probably going to be some shooting no matter what happens, so it's your job to protect the kid. After you get him, forget your car and go straight to the breach. We'll meet up at the Deathstar. Your car is copasetic, right? Wipe it down before you take off from here and wear gloves on the drive down. Again, we can't go together; you have to drive in like you're alone."

Daniel was asking if my car was clean. Years ago he showed up with a car that he suggested I buy. All the parts that contain VIN numbers had been swapped out so there was no way to trace it that way. Through various other ploys he'd made the car generally invisible as far as the government was concerned. I thought he was being over-cautious at the time, but now I could see how it might save my ass. I certainly didn't want anything to tie me to whatever was going to happen tonight.

"We need to go," Daniel said.

"One more thing," I said. "Dom, what did she say about that Maria woman."

"Oh, yes, Maria. She's the ambassador's wife. They've been at the embassy for a year. They replaced an old guy that everyone loved, who had been in the residence for 25 years. The local staff don't like her. Everyone thinks there's something funny going on, but no one knows what."

"Looks like it's got something to do with smuggling diamonds inside of chickens," I said.

Daniel stood up. So did Dom. I followed suit. "Let's do this," Daniel said. He had that same twisted smile that I had seen before in similar situations. I looked at Dom. He was smiling as well. For a brief moment it occurred to me that

I was in the company of homicidal maniacs. But you know, once something like this gets moving, there's no time, or inclination, to back out.

Whatever.

Time to roll.

* * *

The only thing I was going to miss if I had to leave my elderly, non-traceable Honda behind was my XM radio. I had signed up for the service with a fake name and a credit card under the same fake name. Over the five hour drive back to West Virginia I listened to a *Live From the Met* broadcast of Puccini's *Madame Butterfly*, which never fails to wring tears from me at the end and a program devoted to Johnny Cash after he became really old and started doing Nine Inch Nails covers and the like. I suppose I should have been taking stock of my life or something, after all there was a high probability that there was going to be a significant amount of lead zinging around pretty soon, and I was going to be in the middle of it, but I've never been very good at that sort of thing. Thinking about myself bores me. So I listened to Johnny Cash sing *Hurt* and hoped some of the lyrics didn't apply to me before the night was over.

I was right on time. I assumed Daniel and Dom were somewhere behind me. Daniel said he would call if there were any problems. He had given me a throwaway cell to see if it was actually on. It was. I knew this was just my nerves acting up.

I found the turn-off to the compound, thought about calling Daniel for a little reassurance then decided to hell with that, no one wants to look like a pussy in front of guys like Daniel and Dom.

As I slowly drove up the gravel road and neared the house, a fellow with a shotgun stepped out of the shadows and held up his left hand. His right hand leveled a shotgun at my face through the side window. I turned down the radio. He didn't look like an opera lover.

"Who the fuck are you?" the guy asked. A guard, obviously. He was tall and rough-looking in the way that was pretty much the standard with these hill thugs: long brownish-blond hair tied back, sleeveless T-shirt and pale dirty blue jeans with holes that weren't part of the original design. Then I realized he was the fellow I had tasered the night before. He didn't seem to recognize me. Either he was stupid or electrocution has a bad effect on short term memory.

"I'm a guest of Randall's," I said "I believe he's expecting me."

The guard nodded. "He said you were a smart-mouth asshole. He's right. Go on up to the house and wait on the front porch." As I drove off I could see him talking into a walkie-talkie.

It looked like every light was on in the farmhouse. I climbed out of the car and walked up a set of rickety wooden steps onto a wrap-around porch that held a couple of broken-down sofas and a rusty glider.

Another guard stepped around the corner of the porch. He was carrying an AK-47. You can't go anywhere in the world without seeing one of those things. He motioned with the AK that I was to assume the position. I leaned my hands against the side of the house and he frisked me. I had given Daniel my SIG to bring along as I knew they'd never let me in if I was carrying. The guard wasn't very good at the frisk, but he found my cell phone and got to my side pocket where I was carrying the bag of diamonds. I grabbed his wrist and held it. "Those are for Randall. I'll hand it over when I get the kid." I could see the thought process work his way through his head: fight on the porch? Kill me? Leave the next step to his boss? He opted for the last choice, but decided he needed to save a little face.

He dropped the cell phone on the porch and crushed it under his boot. "Hey," I said, "That's an iPhone. They're never going to replace that now."

He didn't bother to acknowledge my wit. He nodded at the door so I opened it and went in. He closed it behind me, and I heard the lock click. Cletus was standing in the middle of the room. He was the first person I'd come across that wasn't pointing a weapon at me, though I'm sure he had one close to hand.

"Hello, Preacher Man, I said. "I believe you have my friend Chevaleer. It's getting late, and his mom says it's time to bring him home."

"Fuck her. I'm surprised she can say anything at all after I taught her a lesson 'bout stealing from me. I guess now I'm gonna have to teach you the same lesson."

"We'll get to the subject of your beating up a woman in a minute; I want to see Chevy." Another thug with a gun had slipped in behind me. I turned and saw this one was a woman. She had red hair that was braided and a hard-knock face that would frighten squirrels down out of trees. So far, she was the meanest-looking one of the bunch. Then, two more guys came in from the back, both carrying shotguns. One of them had Chevy by the arm. The little boy looked like he had been crying, but right now his lower lip was stuck out in defiance.

"You come take me home, Dr. Fish?" he asked. He looked up at the goon beside him and jerked his arm out of the man's grasp. The guy looked like he was going to smack him.

"Hold on, Big Man," I said to Chevy. "We'll be out of here in a minute."

"Yeah," Cletus said. "First of all your friend's gonna hand over my property, then you'll be on your way. Both of you."

Somehow this didn't sound very comforting. Randall was smirking. He held out his hand to me. "Give 'em up, asshole."

"Watch your mouth in front of the kid," I said.

"Oh, please. Just give me the diamonds, or I'll kill him— then you, and then I'll go back and kill his bitch mom."

I heard a light thump and then a whirring noise from outside. No one else seemed to notice. I took this as my cue.

I pulled the bag out of my pocket and threw it in Cletus's face. That was the moment I had scripted in my mind for Daniel to come to the rescue. Instead, the bag hit Cletus in the face, burst open and the marbles I had put in it clattered to the ground and began rolling around. There was a stunned minute where we all stood their with our mouth's hanging open. I felt my skin go cold with fear.

"All right, motherf . . ." which is as far as Cletus got when the front door exploded into the room.

Daniel was standing upright in a device that I had never seen before. There were treads in a triangular formation like a mini tank on the sides, a kind of low battering-ram, metal shield in front that protected his body from stump-level to waist. Daniel was driving the machine with his left hand and shooting a small automatic weapon with his right. The two goons with Chevy went down, hit by gunfire and the woman behind me got tangled up in the machine and went down, her weapon firing wildly into the ceiling. I grabbed Chevy and pulled him to the side as Cletus dug a gun out of his belt at the small of his back. At which point, Dom appeared in a doorway behind Cletus, pushing a guy whose face was covered with blood. Dom shot Cletus in both legs from behind and and the greaser collapsed to the floor like he'd been cut off at the knees, and maybe he had. Daniel unstrapped himself from his machine and jumped to the ground on his war stumps. At that moment, the woman guard got to her feet and brought her gun to bear. As she was pointing the weapon toward him, Daniel hit her with a couple of Israeli Krav Maga moves to the face and throat and she went down hard.

"Get Chevy out of here," Dom growled at me. I gathered the kid up and hightailed it through the hole where the door once was.

The air outside on the porch was clear and fresh compared to the stink of gun smoke that hazed the rooms inside. "Those my marbles, Dr. Fish?" Chevy asked. My heart was beating so hard I could barely breath. I pulled him down the steps to the bare earth yard. There was shouting going on in the front room of the house. "Yeah, Chevy, I picked them up at your house. I'll buy you some more." I bent down and felt the small bulge low in my sock where I had hidden the real diamonds. There was another shot from the house and someone started to scream. I felt like every nerve in my body was buzzing. I held Chevy's hand and attempted to appear calm. No adult would have been fooled by my act.

"Where Jack?" Chevy asked. "He my dog."

Damn. The chicken. "I'll buy you a new chicken," I said, squeezing his hand. "Maybe I'll buy you a real dog." Chevy pulled his hand out of mine.

"Jack real," he said. He started to cry. "Jack a real chicken."

I looked around. The night was quiet. Sort of. At least there weren't any new thugs charging into the fray. "OK, Chevy, sit right here." I gently pushed him down on the bottom step. I took the steps two at a time and ducked into the front room. Daniel was putting zip ties on the people who were scattered around on the floor, some of whom were moaning. Dom was kneeling over Cletus. Dom had his gun pushed into the the man's head and he was talking in low tones. There was blood everywhere, but none of our guys seemed to be hurt. Daniel looked up at me with a frown.

"I've got to go get the chicken. Chevy is worried about him." I held up a hand to stop the inevitable. "I know, it's crazy, but the kid has already suffered enough. It'll only take me a minute. I saw which of the two sheds he was in when you retrieved him last night."

One of the things about Daniel is, he's able to recalibrate plans without any handwringing or argument. He handed me his miniature mag light and my SIG. "While you're out there, take a peek in the other shed. I removed the lock before we came in here. And hurry. Tell Chevy not to move off the porch. Dom will take care of him."

I nodded, took the light and my gun and went outside to tell Chevy to stay put. As I moved away from the house, I saw Dom come out and sit down on the step beside Chevy and put his arm around him.

The two sheds were fifty yards away. There was enough light from the moon so I didn't have to use the flashlight. I trotted up to the first shed and saw that, as Daniel said, the hefty lock on the door was unlocked and hanging from the hasp. I pulled the door open and flashed the light inside.

I was stunned. The shed was built of weathered barn wood and from the outside looked like it was storage room for old broken farm machinery. My light played over shelf after shelf of meticulously arranged, gleaming modern weaponry, from hand-held missiles to racks of machine guns to boxes of grenades and other explosives. I didn't have more than a minute to look it over, but I knew that the value was easily in the millions. All of a sudden the Reverend Cletus and his dirt-ball minions took on a far more ominous aspect than just a bunch of everyday hillbilly diamond smugglers. I clicked off the light and shut the door.

I moved up to the next shed as quietly as I could. Daniel didn't say if Jack was in residence by himself or if there was a coop full of chickens perched inside, waiting for me to wake them up so they could begin flapping around and squawking. I didn't know if there was a need for quiet now that the bad guys seemed to be down and under control, but it seemed the wiser course of action. Between handling the light and the door, I tucked the gun in at my waist. I opened the door and let my eyes adjust to the dark interior. I flashed the light for a half-second. There was Jack, still in his hospital cage on a shelf. The rest of the building seemed empty, other than a large pile of grain sacks to one side. I stepped quietly to Jack's cage. I could make him out in the dim light. His head was tucked under his wing. I reached out and gently gathered him up.

"What the fuck you think you're doing?" a voice said to my left. As I turned I could see the outline of a man with a gun step out from behind the pile of sacks.

Without thinking, I flung Jack straight at the man's face. Jack's head popped free and his claws were straight out when he hit the face in front of him. His wings beat at the man and he pecked with his beak as he hung on with his claws.

The man screamed and tore at the chicken, ripping himself free. I picked up a shovel that was leaning against the wall and slammed it into the man's head. He dropped to the dirty floor and lay still as Jack thrashed around. I bent down and picked up Jack, folding his wings closed and stroking his head. He pecked me a few times, but I had so much adrenaline coursing through my bloodstream I barely felt it. Something moved at the door; I pulled out the SIG and turned.

"It's me," Daniel said, stepping inside on his stumps. "Give me the light."

I tucked the chicken into the crook of my arm and handed him the mag. He turned it on and knelt by the man on the floor. After running the light over the guy, he stood up.

"That one won't be coming around for a long while. If ever. But let's make sure." He slipped a zip tie over the man's hands and ankles. "Give me the shovel," he said. I picked it up off the floor and handed it to him. He wiped the handle clean with a piece of cloth he was carrying. He flashed the light around the interior of the shed. "Let's get out of here."

We collected Dom and Chevy from the steps. "Leave your car," Daniel said. "I don't want to take any chances by splitting up at this point. It's clean, right?"

"Yes, Mother."

We walked across the field that led to our entry point of the night before. I say we walked, but Daniel rode in his chair, which he called The Tank, which wasn't really a chair because he was strapped in standing up, rather than sitting. The Tank rolled almost silently on its tracks, navigating the rougher areas of terrain without any problems. None of us spoke. Dom was carrying Chevy, who seemed to be asleep.

We went through the gap in the fence, and Daniel collected his wires. He had found the alarm box in the farmhouse and smashed it. We followed the Tank as it lumbered up the hill through the underbrush to the Deathstar where Daniel loaded everything in and we took off.

The ride back to Washington was quiet. Chevy slept the entire way. As did the chicken.

* * *

Daniel had a fresh pot of coffee going when I stumbled out of bed later that morning. He had been busy taking down the defensive devices we put in place the day before. I sat down at the white metal table in the kitchen and poured a cup of the coffee. "What do you think?" I asked. Daniel looked far more together than I felt. But then Daniel always looked far more together than most of the males on the planet.

"I believe we've got those guys off our ass. The stash of weapons ties them into some far larger organization, at least on the supply end. My gut tells me that they were just middlemen. The real heavies are on either of the other ends of the spectrum, suppliers and buyers. And I don't think either of them are going to be gunning for us. We stole middleman money, the basic product is still there. Speaking of which, what were you trying with the marble thing? Where are the diamonds?"

I blew on my coffee and took a swallow. I could feel it seeping into the pores of my body.

"I had the diamonds with me as a last resort. I would have handed them over if I had to. You were a little slow on your entrance, pal. A few seconds earlier and it wouldn't have been a problem."

"A few seconds later and you would have been waxed by Cletus. I'd say I got there in time. The guard on the porch was a little sharper than his pals. I took out the guy under the tree who stopped you on the way in, but the porch guy put up a pretty good fight. I think he's probably dead, though I was trying to keep the body count as low as possible. Back to my original question: Where are the diamonds?"

I took another long gulp of coffee and went to the refrigerator. I pulled the velvet bag from the ice maker and put it on the table.

"Every thug keeps his stash in the freezer," Daniel said. "Or in the tank of the toilet. It's the first place the cops and criminals look."

"OK, so I'm an amateur. You think we'll be able to keep our hands on the diamonds or are we going to have to turn them over to some authority?"

He shrugged. "That depends, Rafe. I've got some feelers out, we should know more in a day or so."

I didn't question him. Daniel has a lot of contacts. I don't know who he works for, but I know his client list goes far beyond rich guys setting up security arrangements.

"If we get to keep them, what are we going to do?" he asked.

"There are twelve of them. I figure we split them three ways: You, me and Meeka. Four apiece."

He nodded. "Sounds fair. Dom was an equal participant in the rough stuff; Meeka started the whole thing by stealing the chicken. They deserve them."

"I don't think she thought she was stealing anything, she just saw Jack as another of God's unfortunate creatures that needed to be rescued."

"I agree," Daniel said, pushing back from the table. He was in his chair.

"By the way, that was a pretty impressive machine you were riding around in last night."

He gave me a big smile. "Yeah, that was the first time I took that one operational." He turned the chair around and rolled to the front door. "Gotta go. Keep your eyes open. I think we're cool, but you never know."

* * *

Two days later, I was on the front porch with Max trying to keep my eyes open, but I was having trouble. Every sound woke me up at night, so I still hadn't caught up on my sleep. Max wasn't even bothering to stay awake. He was laying on the floor beside me dreaming of tennis balls and dinner.

The day was warm, just like all the days, and I was nursing a beer. Chevy and Lamont had been by earlier bringing Jack, who they had on a string as a leash. The chicken looked good for a bird who had been through what he had been through. I'll always carry fond memories of ol' Jack flying into the last thug's face and clawing and pecking at his eyes. The boys said their mom was better and wanted me to come by for dinner in a few days.

That's when the big Chevy Tahoe with the black tinted windows pulled up. I felt my gut clench.

Like Daniel said, you never know.

The driver's door popped open and a big guy in a suit climbed out. He wasn't smiling, but he also wasn't shooting at me, which I took as a good sign. I stood as he walked up to the house. He reached into his breast pocket and pulled out a badge wallet and flashed it at me.

"Agent Will Anderson," he said, "Homeland Security."

"OK," I answered.

"Daniel Riboux said you wouldn't mind if I asked you a few questions. Actually, it's more like I'll be giving you some answers. All right if I sit down?" I nodded that it was, so we both got comfy and agreed to call each other Will and Rafe. Max woke up long enough to give Agent Anderson the once over, but he didn't seem to find anything disturbing to worry about. He put his head down and went back to sleep.

I wasn't sure if I had broken any Homeland Security rules in the last few years, but in my business you never know. Besides, cops are cops, no matter which particular organization they belong to.

"I thought you might like an update on your situation of the other night."

"And what situation might that be, Agent Anderson?" Even though we had agreed to the use of first names, I was having trouble letting go of the formalities.

He laughed. "Mr. Holt, Daniel said you might be a little reticent about talking to me. You want to call him and ask about my bona fides?"

That sounded like a good idea, so I did. Daniel said Anderson was a good guy and he trusted him. If that's good enough for Daniel, it's good enough for me.

"OK," I said, putting my phone in my pocket. "You mean the situation where a bunch of grits in West Virginia seem to be arming themselves for Armageddon and decided to kidnap a little boy. Not that I would know anything about such a situation."

"That would be the one. Except I don't think the guns were meant for them, they were just the felonious middle men."

"That's what Daniel thought."

"Daniel was correct. We've been working on the edges of this case for six months now. We knew something was not right at the Embassy of Malta after the old Ambassador was suddenly replaced by a new government on the island. Malta is independent, but the proximity and economic ties to Italy always makes Mafia involvement in their affairs a possibility. We've been seeing international crime organizations, particularly the Russians, becoming involved in the weapons trade. Our intel was that a fairly large transaction was taking place through the island, but we didn't know where the shipments were being sent and stored or how money was being transferred for the transactions. Then, Daniel called late last night and said he had made an interesting find that we should take a look at. Which we did. And found the guns, and a bunch of bad guys nicely tied up waiting for us to take them into custody. That was a good job you fellows did. The United States Government is in your debt."

How often does an ordinary citizen ever hear those words? It almost gave me a warm fuzzy feeling. But not quite.

"What shape were these bad guys in? Not that I know anything specifically about what you're referring to."

"There were six individuals there, though evidence point to more than that living on the property. One was dead and the rest were wounded, some more seriously than others. They have all been taken into custody and are being treated. After they recover somewhat, they'll be transferred to facilities where we can interview them. For all intents and purposes, their present operation has been dismantled, and we hope to learn more about the suppliers and the eventual customers for the weapons."

"And the Maltese ambassador and his wife?" I briefly pictured the beautiful Maria.

"They have been quietly withdrawn and returned to Malta. I'm not sure what their fates will be."

At that point I was surprised to see my car pull up behind Anderson's SUV. A guy wearing a suit just like Anderson's got out and climbed into the SUV. Anderson pulled a car key out of his pocket and handed it to me. "We had a couple of copies made."

I took the key.

"Do you have any other questions for me?" he asked, politely.

Oh yes, I thought, many many questions, none of which I am going to ask. How about the diamonds, Will? And was the dead guy you found carrying the impression of a shovel on his head?

"Are we going to be reading about this case in the news-papers, Agent Anderson?" He flashed me a brief smile.

"No, I doubt that you will. Cases like this tend to move through the system kind of slowly. The guys, and one woman, we found at the farm will be dealt with by Homeland Security rather than by Justice. I don't think you or anyone else will ever hear anything from or about them. You don't have to worry about that." He stood up and walked to the steps. Then, he turned and put his hand in his pocket. He pulled out a bag and tossed it to me.

"There's your marbles," he said. "You did a good job cleaning up the car. If we had employed a few of our more advanced resources we would have traced it to you, but there was no point in that. The marbles made it easy. Your fingerprints are all over them. You might remember that in the future."

"Remember to always clean my marbles?"

"Something like that. More like, it's always the little things that catch you up. Not that you would need to be careful about fingerprints any time in the future, right?" He gave me a smile that was considerably colder than the others had been.

A gave him the same smile back. "No, I can't think of any reason why I would have to worry about that." He nodded and walked down the steps. I watched him climb into the blacked-out SUV and drive away.

I picked up my beer, but it tasted like warm spit. I put the bag of marbles on the table, thinking I might take them over to Chevy later after I cleaned off the fingerprint powder residue. I rocked in my glider and watched the hot sun disappear behind the few dry, dying, dusty trees that still lined the block.

Later, I went inside and made a few calls. It turned out that a friend of a friend who knew a guy knew a guy who would definitely be interested in the diamonds. I made an appointment for tomorrow.

I felt pretty good. Everything seemed to have turned out OK. Still, I wasn't sure I would be sleeping any better. Like Daniel says, you just never know.

* * *

Three days later, the diamonds had been converted into cash and the proceeds distributed. They were worth even more than I thought, and we each ended up with a half million dollars. Who knew there could be so much money in chickens?

That night I got a call from a guy named Gregor, a Russian expatriate I had worked with in Brazil a few years ago. He had a tale to tell. It seems that a native in the Curacao region of Bahia had put out the word that he had trapped a Spix's Macaw. Gregor said the native was willing to sell the bird to the highest bidder. In my world, this is like getting a call saying some grit down in Arkansas had captured an Ivory Billed Woodpecker and was putting it up for auction. The Spix is supposed to be extinct in the wild, but a bunch of wealthy Arabs in Qatar have a breeding program that is in desperate need of any new wild-caught birds. There's a couple of problems, chief among them is that catching one in the wild is highly illegal, something close to committing treason against the Brazilian government. And we all know what the penalty is for treason. Gregor asked if I wanted to join him in an expedition to Curacao to see if the bird actually existed or was the hallucination of a fevered, drug-addled indian.

Good question, Gregor. On the one hand, I didn't really need the money at the moment. On the other, we're talking getting enough loot out of this job to make my four diamonds look like, well, chicken feed.

I hung up and spent fifteen minutes on my laptop finding an excellent air fare to Brazil. All I needed to do was pack, load up the car and drive Max over to Dom and Meeka's to take care of while I was away. I figured Chevy and Lamont could handle two dogs for a couple of weeks, even if one of them was a chicken.

Jesus, it's a funny world we live in, isn't it?

IRON MANIMAL

by Harry Seitz, 21,000 words

A catastrophic train wreck gives a circus troupe and their tiger baffling new powers. Stranded and confused, they must find new ways to cope with the world and each other. Is a person who can read minds actually being led and controlled by the thoughts of others? And if power comes through physical and emotional trauma, what happens to a newly powerful person or entity who still thinks and feels like a victim? Alcoholism and the death of American rail are also explored.

Harry Seitz currently lives in Woodside, Queens, and works as a legal financial proofreader. For more information, visit Harry Seitz page: https://www.amazon.com/H.-Seitz/e/B01N29E7VS/ ref=dp_byline_cont_book_1

Iron Manimal by Harry Seitz was originally published by Amazon Digital Services LLC (June 2016).

C1 A CIRCUS TRAIN

Circuses used to get a parade when they pulled into town. Our parade was the transfer of the animals from the train to the truck. We led with Roger, our 500lb Bengal tiger. His fur was matted, his eyes were bloodshot, and he was slumped down panting against the bars of his cage. A few of the kids in the small crowd of spectators asked what was wrong with him. Their parents told them not to worry, that he was just tired from his long trip. His real problem was that he belonged in a jungle.

Next were Rob and Rhonda, the last of our Indian elephants. Rob and Rhonda were both nearing fifty years old and showed every day of those fifty years and then some. Rhonda was blind in her left eye and had a habit of turning her head back and forth while she walked to try and keep everything in her limited field of vision. Some of the kids pointed at her and yelled at the others to look at the dancing elephant, but to the rest of us it looked like she had Parkinson's disease. Rob gave the impression that he was baffled at how he could still be alive and wasn't at all happy about it. He looked like someone who had been struck by lightning fourteen times, like he was both dreading and hoping for the likely death of number fifteen.

Roger, Rob, and Rhonda were our headliners. By the time we got to our sickly looking llamas and Shetland ponies, the disappointed crowd had begun to disperse.

After supervising the transfer of the animals, I went back to inspect the train. From a layman's perspective, the locomotive looked dated but functional. From there, the train was a hodgepodge of shipping containers, animal enclosures, and Amtrak passenger cars from the 70s, 80s, and 90s. As conductor and chief engineer, I wasn't proud of The Crying Ghost per say, but I was proud of the fact that I had managed to keep the train in some state of working order for as long as I had. She wasn't pretty, but almost everything worked most of the time. The only problem I found was with Roger's meat cooler. It wasn't running as cold as it should and this, combined with his appearance, was enough to warrant a call to the local veterinarian. Roger's death would rightfully enrage animal rights groups across the country, and that would be the first and last national coverage we ever got—the final nail in our coffin. Even if we survived it, Roger was our biggest draw by far. A circus with one tiger is pitiful enough. A circus with no tigers is just a sleazy petting zoo.

After my walk through, I joined Leon Harvey the Fifth in the parking lot. Supposedly, naming all the firstborn males Leon was a way to maintain brand recognition and ego at the same time, but for the last few Leons, I suspect it was just cheaper than repainting the train. Like me, he was waiting for a lift from The Other Crying Ghost. We were usually the last two to go, along with whatever junk the others might have forgotten. While I inspected the train, Leon walked around the neighborhood putting up posters and striking up conversations with the locals.

Leon was nearly impossible to dislike, and not just because of the aura of failure that surrounded him and the circus and circus people and animals in general. The charisma and magnetism of the ringmasters of days past still clung to him. Maybe the idea of being a ringmaster, of being surrounded by chaos and still somehow able to maintain the illusion of control, still held an antiquated sort of romantic appeal not only to others, but to Leon himself. More than simply a person, he was a part of an institution in which he truly believed and this insanity, the insanity of the true believer, drew people toward him.

"Mr. Scott," said Leon, "I do believe our luck is beginning to turn. Breathe in that fresh autumn air, this is a prime time for the circus. Circus season. And I do believe this is still a circus town."

My name isn't Mr. Scott. Someone, maybe Leon, started calling me Scotty as a reference to the chief engineer on Star Trek and it stuck. I doubt anyone aside from Leon knows my real name.

"I appreciate your optimism, but exactly how much would our luck need to turn in order to be in the black? I need axle grease, a vet, a new cooler for Roger."

"What's wrong with Roger?"

"And I need to eat. We all need to eat. Roger is a wild animal; he isn't supposed to spend days and weeks at a time rattling around on an ancient train."

Leon slumped and exhaled deeply.

"I know we've been having difficulties lately—"

"We've been losing money for at least the last ten years."

"—but this last stretch of shows will get us through the winter, and come spring, we already have shows lined up in the Southeast; they love us in the Southeast, and I almost forgot."

Leon pulled an envelope from his pocket and handed it to me. There was $5,000.00 inside.

"Your pay minus room and board for the last three months, and here." He opened his wallet and fished out another $1,000.00. "This should cover the initial fees for a veterinarian and a new cooler, axle grease and what have you."

"Leon, where the hell did you get this money?"

Leon flashed a false look of injured pride.

"Well, Mr. Scott, I may be a bit slow with the bookkeeping, but as I've been trying to impress upon you, we are a turning a small but consistent profit."

"Like hell."

"Well, there's also the emergency fund, passed down from the Leon Harvey's of more remunerative times."

"You're lying to my face. Whatever shady business you're trying to pull, don't you realize that it's already too late? That you're basically flushing this money down the toilet? All you're doing is delaying the inevitable."

"Well of course I'm delaying the inevitable! Dying and losing are inevitable. I am delaying the inevitable, and I plan to go on delaying the inevitable because we're not through yet! Love and dreams, we give up on these things first and always too early, and flushing them down the toilet is what turns them, and life, into shit."

C2 THE DUGGAN BROTHERS

The Other Crying Ghost pulled into the lot and honked at us as the Duggan brothers waved and flipped us off from the cab. She was an old, rusty mack truck with flaking red paint, bad suspension, and fancy chrome rims. She summed up our priorities, bad style, and no substance.

Leon gazed off into the distance. He knew I wouldn't continue this argument in front of the others. We all knew the reality of our situation on some level, except for maybe Leon. There was no point in rubbing it in.

"That was a beautiful speech, Leon. But I still want to know where the hell the money came from."

Leon sighed sadly for a second, then stretched and straightened himself as he let out an exaggerated yawn.

"It's been a long and lonely road, for all of us. Once we get back to camp and eat and relax, I'll tell you all about it in no uncertain terms."

My left eye began to twitch.

Leon and I squeezed into the cab behind the Duggan brothers. We were all at least six feet tall, and we were surrounded by the accumulated fast food wrappers and containers of the last nine months of the Duggan brothers' diet. Dan and Dave Duggan were both smoking real cigarettes, Marlboro Reds, instead of the more usual roll-your-owns. There were also two relatively new, mostly eaten, buckets of KFC between their feet. Apparently, I wasn't the only one who got paid.

"It looked like you two were having a deep conversation," said Dave, "please don't stop on our account."

"What's the matter, Leon? Scotty blowing smoke up your ass again?" asked Dan.

"We all know how Scotty loves blowing things," said Dave.

"Actually, Leon and I were discussing firing one of you. Isn't that right, Leon?"

Leon kept staring listlessly out the window.

"That's right," he replied a beat too late, "it's bad for morale having two of you around."

"What the fuck are you talking about?" asked Dan. "Dave and I only see you cocksuckers a few days out of every month."

"We've been with you for years, and I don't even know everybody's name yet," said Dave.

"That's another reason we want one of you out. We're afraid one of you might be mentally retarded. Maybe even both of you."

"Which one?" asked Dan.

"Obviously you," Dave answered.

These conversations quickly grew tiresome for me. They were more Leon's forte, and he was seemingly preoccupied with the dull and nearly featureless landscape passing by outside his window.

"Didn't you two idiots grow up around here?"

"We grew up in Latham you asshole. Two towns over," said Dave. "You think we grew up in some bleak field along the side of a highway?"

I scoffed. "Maybe."

C3 LULU THE BEE-EARDED LADY

It was dusk when we finally arrived at our campground. The main tent and most of the booths and personal tents had already been set up. The Duggans dropped me off at the edge of camp so I could check in with the others. My first stop was at Lulu's, our fortuneteller and bee-earded lady. For my money, Lulu was one of the most beautiful women I'd ever seen. It made perfect sense that she spent 90% of her time covered in bees. She was just finishing up her beekeeping duties when I arrived.

"Just give me a second."

She put down her smoker and took off her mask.

"Are you going to dinner tonight? I'm not going to dinner. I'm going to eat pancakes with honey."

It was a loose tradition for all of us to eat together our first night in, but only Leon and The Flying Sweeney Sisters, whose families had been with the circus for generations, stuck to this tradition consistently.

"Maybe I'll put in an appearance. It is free food."

Lulu winked at me. "I can't eat with those perverts."

"What about this pervert?"

Lulu rolled her eyes and waved me into her tent. We sat down opposite each other, her crystal ball between us on her small, purple covered table. She popped up suddenly and returned promptly with two ready-made plates of pancakes covered in honey.

"I knew you'd be stopping by. The crystal ball told me."

"The crystal ball have any stock tips? Career advice?"

She looked down into the ball and then up into my eyes slowly.

"Trial and tribulation have brought you here, and there is worse yet to come. At this place, at this moment, you feel you are the sum of all of your mistakes and regrets. But remember, always remember, that your fate is your own. Move with your fate, not against it, and someday, you will be free."

Lulu delivered these lines with the eerie conviction of her trade.

"Are you hitting on me?"

"Maybe." She winked at me. "Eat your pancakes."

She gazed back into the crystal ball and passed her hands over it as she rolled her eyes back into her head until only the whites were visible.

"Well that's attractive."

"It's supposed to be." She winked again with her eyes still rolled back.

"And that is really attractive."

She laughed, cut a big piece of pancake, and stuffed it into her mouth.

"Please roll your eyes back down."

"Why don't you just roll your eyes up?" she said as she chewed. "It's easy once you get used to it. It just takes practice and dedication. Mental instability helps, too."

"Lulu."

She rolled her eyes back down, smiled at me sadly, and swallowed. "Fine, you big baby."

She started to hum as she ate, and her bees began to accumulate on her face. In seconds she had a full beard of bees.

"You should do that in your act."

"What act?" She held my gaze a few seconds before giggling. "You're a funny guy, Scotty."

C4 A STRONGMAN

When I had finished with Lulu, I stopped at Hector's booth. He was our resident strongman/fat man, but he was never really fat enough to replace our last fat man and had lost too much weight to pull it off even with padding. People want to see naked rolls of flesh when they see the fat man, and in contemporary America 1,000lb men and women aren't novelties anymore anyway. I found Hector sitting in his cage, staring out toward the line of trees ringing our camp.

"Why are you sitting in the cage?"

"Louis died in this cage."

Louis was our last fat man. Staggering before a show, he had gripped onto the cage for support and fallen in, or more accurately, pulled the cage down around himself. Hector, the Duggans, and I had had to haul him into his tent before the crowds showed up. Cause of death was a heart attack.

"I know Louis died in there. I was there."

Hector stood up and stretched; he was nearly seven feet tall and at least 400lbs.

"You bring my scrap pile?"

"The Duggans will bring it by later."

At every small town, we stopped at the local Salvation Army to buy kiddie bicycles, aluminum ironing boards and other assorted junk for Hector to bend into pretzels or maul in front of the spectators.

"I could do with some scrap right now."

"Christ Hector, what the hell is it?"

"Don't mind me. Maybe it's the weather here, the dead trees. Every now and then, I can't help wondering what went wrong, why life seems to work out for some people and not for others. Maybe the further down you go, the more you can see it, how senseless it all is. I know in some ways I should be grateful, or angry, or miserable, but lately I feel something close to nothing." Hector sat back down. "I think Louis might have had the right idea."

If he hadn't already known, I would've told Hector that we all feel that way sometimes. Maybe I should have told him anyway.

"What do you think about all of us getting paid?" I asked.

Hector let out a long sigh.

"Leon is shady, you worry too much, and me? Today, next week, next year, what's the difference? I don't see the point in giving a shit."

I was about to say something, but Hector cut me off.

"You have the Duggans bring me my scrap. I'll save some for the show, don't you worry."

C5 GARBAGEMAN MIKE

On the way to the animal enclosures I ran into Mike, our head garbageman and would be conductor. The rules of the rails are that there should be at least two people aboard who can drive in case one of you keels over in transit. The railroads argue that information technology systems have made a second man redundant, and they're the ones who usually check the trains and enforce, or don't enforce, the rules.

Much like the small children of yesteryear, Mike was fascinated by trains. He had been a conductor, just as we all had been something else before whatever personal catastrophes had brought us here. So sometimes, under my supervision, I let him conduct the train through the relatively straight, flat, and lonely stretches that make up most of America.

"Still hauling shit, Garbageman Mike?"

"You know it. You still lingering around Lulu? Making a general menace of yourself? And how is young Roger doing?"

Mike always seemed to know what everyone was up to. It made sense in a way. The one thing all of us have in common is garbage.

"I was going to ask you about Roger, anything funny come out of his asshole lately?"

"Unless you think tiger shit is funny, no."

"What's going on with Hector?"

"Nothing funny came out of his asshole either, glum bastard." Mike pulled a pint of brand name bourbon from his back pocket and took a long pull. He handed it to me, and I did the same.

"You know what I realized lately?" asked Mike. "Everywhere I've ever been, everything I've ever done, I've fucked it up. I'd move to a new place, try something new, tell myself it'd be different this time, and fuck that up, too."

"You're just realizing that now? Christ."

"Hear me out. What I realized is that I'm cursed. Don't laugh at me, I'm not an idiot, I'm not going to hand you some horseshit about all of us carrying our problems with us. It's true, but everybody knows that. I take responsibility, I know I have to change, I wanna change more than anything in the world, but you know what I realized?"

"I barely know what you're talking about."

"I realized that I don't really wanna change at all. And not because I love myself or even like myself. But if I did change, I'd just wanna change back. And you know exactly what I'm talking about."

"Yeah. You're afraid of change."

"Of course I'm afraid of change! But I'm afraid of life, too. We all are. But the same goes for all of us. None of us really wants to change."

We shared a final drink.

"I'll see you around, Garbageman Mike."

"You give my finest regards to Phil and Roger."

C6 BEAST TRAINER PHIL AND ROGER THE TIGER

It's creepy to be alone around caged animals. They pay more attention to you, they ask you with their eyes to please be let out, and a part of you wants to do it. But another more rational part of the mind is terrified of this freedom, particularly in regard to carnivores like Roger. I have no idea if it's true, and I'd never try it out of anything other than necessity, but I read somewhere that if a large cat is about to attack you, you can hold it in thrall by gazing into its eyes. Unfortunately, the cat might as well be holding you in thrall, too, while one of its brothers or sisters creeps up behind you. Even if there is some truth in this, I doubt it applies to solitary hunters like tigers.

"Scotty?"

"Christ, you scared the crap out of me. Where were you?"

"I was just washing up. What were you doing staring at Roger?"

"Nothing. Just checking on him. Saying hello."

"Right." Phil smiled and gave me a look like he knew I was up to something. "Anyway, I got your text about calling a local vet, but I don't think it's necessary. He was just a bit dehydrated."

"The cooler worried me that maybe his meat had gone bad."

"The standards set for that cooler are for humans. If he was hungry enough, Roger could eat 100lbs of rancid meat, nap for a few days, and eat another 100lbs of rancid meat. A tiger's stomach is basically a toxic garbage disposal."

Roger was looking terrifyingly healthy. The water and the few hours of fresh air had puffed him up. His fur was immaculate. He sat on his haunches like a giant house cat, staring at us. I wondered what he'd look like in his jungle environment, if he would continue to grow stronger and stronger the closer he came to his natural element.

"Do you ever think about setting him free?"

"I don't think Roger would function well in the wild. He's spent too much time away from other tigers. He has his instincts, but he's never been taught how to hunt properly and worse than that, he's never been properly socialized. Imagine being snatched away from humans during your formative years, never learning how you're supposed to communicate or act."

"It isn't that hard to imagine."

"Then, imagine being caged, whipped, and put on display, forced to perform in front of hundreds of people, the last place a tiger or any cat wants to be."

"Let's not be overly dramatic. It's more like dozens of people."

Phil gave me a searching look.

"Roger is relatively well off here. I take good care of him, no one abuses him."

"Except for Leon."

"Leon may seem harsh with Roger, but it's the only way. Roger would be more uncomfortable if Leon wasn't as firm, and Leon would be dead."

Phil appeared to reflect for a moment.

"What is it?"

"It's probably nothing. You know how people say their cat loves them or their dog is depressed? Researchers, vets, zookeepers, basically anyone who has to deal with animals professionally, is taught never to anthropomorphize, that animals are not people. Treat them like people and you're liable to get hurt or worse. But this isn't to say that nothing is going on inside."

As he said this, Phil's eyes moved to Roger. Roger blinked his implacable yellow eyes once before yawning and stretching. His massive muscles rippled beneath his fur. He started licking his asshole.

"Anyway," said Phil, "you coming to dinner?"

I nodded, and we headed off toward Leon's quarters.

The walk to Leon and the performers' area passed through the grounds crew's area, which was already a minefield of dog turds and empty beer bottles. These people kept the entire circus clean, they cleaned up after the performers, the animals, the crowds. Maybe by the time they got home, they were fed up with cleaning. You clean things all the time, it takes hours a day almost every day of your life if it's your job, and when you wake up the next morning all of it is even worse than it was to begin with. Our grounds crew had learned the secret. There is no point in cleaning or fixing anything, at least not while anything alive is anywhere near it just waiting to turn it into garbage. Or maybe they were just a bunch of lazy, drunken slobs.

A warm yellow light emanated from Leon's tent. I could hear laughter and general merriment and was hesitant to enter, but the prospect of free food won out. Leon was at the head of the table telling stories and making jokes. He seemed to have recovered from whatever had been occupying him earlier. Surrounding him were The Flying Sweeney Sisters, three ripe blondes just exiting their youth. Their parents had been with us up until around ten years ago. They had decided to retire off to some rural hamlet in Minnesota. Their faces had grown old, but their bodies were still well muscled and taut from years of aerial acrobatics. Six months after they retired, the Flying Sweeney Sisters returned to us without them. Whatever happened, only Leon knew for sure.

Leon was in the middle of a story when we arrived.

"My hand to the heavens, the gentleman was half fish and half man, and the crowds loved him. But one day, he refused to come out of his tank and perform. My father spoke with him. Giles, or The Fish Man as we called him, I know it isn't very original but capturing the public's imagination was more important in those days, being direct."

Leon paused to sip from an old prop goblet.

"Anyway, my father asked Giles what was troubling him, and Giles told him that he had had a disturbing dream. You see, because of Giles' physiology, he was unable to be with a woman. I have no doubt that he had dreamed of women previously, our women performers tend to be extremely beautiful, especially in the main tent. In any case, in this dream, he was able to see inside the women during their conjugal relations and all he could see were fish, endless schools of fish swimming within their loins. Ah, Scotty, Phil, please come join us."

"Finish the story!" said Sue Sweeney.

"Yeah, finish!" said Sarah and Samantha Sweeney.

Leon waved his hands in an appeasing fashion.

"The story will be continued at the farewell dinner."

The Flying Sweeney Sisters flashed dirty looks at Phil and I and pouted. We sat down off toward the foot of the table in our customary seats. We left the other seats open so if Lulu, Hector, the Duggans, or Garbageman Mike straggled in, they would know that they were always welcome, that their places had not been taken. Leon warmed everyone up and dinner proceeded pleasantly. Something passed between Leon and I. His eyes told me he didn't want to talk about it, and mine told him I didn't want to hear it. What would be the point?

The Sweeney sisters left after about an hour, Phil and I left an hour or two after that. No one else showed up.

* * *

Our upstate run proceeded relatively uneventfully for the next couple of weeks. As we had little to do compared with the others, Phil and I spent most of our time getting drunk together behind my tent. Despite his never ending ordeal of dealing with garbage, Garbageman Mike managed to join us almost every night.

C7 THE FAREWELL DINNER

"As he watched, the schools of fish began to notice him and swarm around him. In a flash, he realized that they were his children, and that they had come to devour him. He woke up saddened, because he knew that he could never have children. He would never know the pleasure of being devoured for a greater purpose."

Leon finished with a strange smile as he looked off at nothing. The dopey Sweeney sisters gawked at him in amazed admiration. The Duggans exchanged a conspiratorial glance. They had a theory that the Sweeney sisters had murdered their parents to be with Leon and the circus, and this story seemed to confirm this to them. Honestly, the idea didn't seem too far-fetched.

Phil leaned over to me and whispered, "The Fish Man should have dreamed about women with better personal hygiene."

I answered that a woman with good personal hygiene is an impossible dream for any man in the circus. Samantha Sweeney overheard me and shot me a look of pure hatred. I took a big pull of wine from a prop goblet. Samantha Sweeney and her idiot sisters were seven year old girls trapped in thirty some odd year old bodies. Samantha Sweeney might kill someone for any stupid reason.

Lulu sat slightly apart from the rest of us.

"I have excellent personal hygiene."

"You're a rotten snob!" said Samantha Sweeney.

"Go fuck a bee you whore!" said Sarah Sweeney. The sisters giggled and smiled at each other like this was the most clever insult in the history of the world.

"Yeah," said Sue Sweeney, "go fuck a bee. Maybe it'll shake the bug out of your ass."

The Duggans laughed. Lulu already seemed preoccupied with something else. Maybe she was a bit of a snob. Leon was strangely out of it. Normally he would have intervened and smoothed everything out, but lately he didn't seem to care about the circus or us or anything. This was as disconcerting to all of us as any of our petty grievances and worsened them.

We had had an okay run in upstate New York. Leon should have been spewing optimism. His crazy fish story should have had a happier ending or moral, or at least a comprehensible one.

"Sarah, what the hell are you feeding under the table?" asked Phil.

Sarah Sweeney set her face in a scowl and looked down at the table defiantly.

"For the love of God, Leon. Leon! I've told you a hundred times, you can't let those girls play with Jim. Jim is not a toy."

Jim was an old Capuchin monkey. He was nominally still a part of our small zoo but was treated more like a pet at this point.

"Why are you yelling at him! Why don't you talk to me? Do you think I'm too stupid to understand?" asked Sarah.

"Well it appears that way, doesn't it? Doesn't it? Honestly, I don't know why I bother speaking to any of you, but I'll say it again."

"Yeah yeah yeah, a monkey is not a toy, blah blah blah," said Sarah.

"That monkey will cause a disaster someday! Maybe not today, maybe not tomorrow, but one day, one of you won't tie his leash well enough or lock his cage properly, and then it'll be anarchy!"

The Sweeney sisters started laughing uncontrollably, as did the Duggans, Lulu, myself, even Leon. Jim popped up from under the table and perched on Sarah Sweeney's shoulder. He wasn't wearing his leash. Phil's face turned bright red.

"And I'm the idiot," he muttered before swallowing hard. "Jim is old and cute and friendly as monkeys go, but you know the expression 'monkey see, monkey do?' Well it's true, and when it comes to the animal enclosures, old Jim probably knows just as much as I do."

There was another eruption of laughter.

"Don't you think you're being a bit paranoid?" I asked.

"You know what? Fuck all of you."

Phil drained his prop goblet and stomped out of the tent. He wolf whistled from outside and Jim scampered off behind him. In a second we were all laughing again, except for Lulu. She looked at me and moved her chair closer to mine.

"It's funny when Phil gets angry, especially about Jim, but I think I understand."

"What I don't understand is why Phil doesn't just buy a decent lock."

"A lock those skanks couldn't pick wouldn't fit on Jim's cage."

Sue Sweeney overheard this and another fracas followed. I saw Garbageman Mike peek in and hurry away and wished I had whatever it took to do the same. When dinner finally ended I lingered. I knew I would regret asking but also sensed that it was unavoidable at this point.

"Mind if we have a chat, Leon? Leon?"

"Of course. Follow me, I think we'll be more comfortable in my personal chambers."

Leon had a well-stocked bar and cigars. His tent was filled with old posters, pictures and chairs, the pictures and chairs of former circus members long dead and gone. There were also second hand Tesla coils, small hand cranked generators, antennaed horror movie props, and old televisions from the 50's and 60's. He'd always intended to reincorporate them into an act but admitted it was more of a hobby at this point.

Leon fixed us two large whiskey drinks and cut us cigars. He took a long pull from his drink.

"You're in love with Lulu. You should do something about it."

I laughed in his face.

"I'm too old to be in love with anybody. And what I do or don't do is none of your goddamn business as long as I drive the train from point A to point B."

Leon chuckled.

"You're too close to see it, everyone else does, except for maybe Lulu. It's like me and this damn circus, I love it too much to see it clearly, or to accept what I see. I'm not a fool, Scotty. I'm not completely blind, although sometimes I wish I was. I wish I had that kind of conviction, but in the end, I'd rather be a liar who can see than some blind asshole telling the truth about being blind."

Leon took a big puff of his cigar, and I couldn't help laughing at him.

"Don't laugh at me, don't give me that look. I'm not being politically incorrect and even if I am, blind people know the truth. They know that they're a bunch of annoying assholes with their stupid canes, glasses, and neutered dogs. They've got bigger problems to worry about, namely, being blind, and the sad truth is that we are all blind. Figuratively, at least."

I was reminded of a conversation I'd had with Lulu. She didn't particularly like anyone, but had told me that Leon was especially creepy if you paid attention to him. The longer you spoke with him, the more he spoke with your voice and ideas until it became hard to tell the difference, whether the ideas were coming from him or from you.

"Leon, I wanted to tell you to forget about the money. I don't care. I don't know, and I don't want to know. And thank you for not implicating me."

Leon laughed sadly.

"The last thing I would ever want to do is to implicate anyone or expose anyone to harm, but in this case, with you and I, I'm afraid there's no longer a choice. Whatever you decide, I'll abide by, and I apologize for putting you in this situation, I didn't think it would be necessary."

"Leon, just spill it."

Leon stared sadly into his drink before gulping it down.

"The circus is a lie now. It's a sham. We're a garbage truck, or train. We're being paid to haul garbage. The Duggans were going to handle it but there's too much, it has to go on the train. I'm sorry, Scotty."

"What kind of garbage?"

"I've been assured that it isn't dangerous, but I honestly don't know, and it's safe to assume that if this was safe or legal they, whoever they are, wouldn't have had to hire us to haul it."

"Leon, you asshole. You've already paid everyone. It's already too late and you know it. You aren't asking me, you're telling me."

Leon fixed himself another drink.

"You might be alright out in the world. You might never conduct a train again, but you would find a job, maybe as a mechanic, maybe even with the railroads again. The world forgets faster than you realize. The same goes for Phil. He will never be a licensed veterinarian again, but he would find work. The Duggans, Mike, all of you would survive. But Lulu, the Sweeneys, Hector, and the grounds crew? The world might forget, but it will never forgive them. And even if it did, they wouldn't make it. How the hell could they take care of themselves?"

"Lulu could be a fortuneteller in the city, I see lots of those places, they somehow function."

"Those places are all literally fronts for whorehouses."

"Well, that takes care of the Sweeney sisters."

"You're too rough on those girls. They've had difficult lives. You can't even begin to imagine"

I finished my drink and fixed myself another large one.

"One thing Leon. If you could've snuck this crap on the train, would you have told me about it? Would you have told anyone?"

Leon slugged down his drink.

"Honestly, it's impossible to say. Either way, it would've been a rotten thing to do."

I thought to myself that it is a rotten thing, and you're doing it. You tried it one rotten way, and now you're trying it another. Probably both depending on who he could get away without telling. I wondered how many other rotten, twisted things were inside Leon. He could see the nobility in telling me and the Duggans, in letting us "choose" to take the risk. He could also see the nobility in keeping us in the dark in order to protect us, in carrying the burden alone. What he either couldn't or wouldn't see was that he hadn't actually done either. In reality, he had done the rotten opposite of both. Or maybe, now that he knew it was happening for sure, he just didn't care.

C8 CLOWNING AROUND

The "garbage" Leon had stuck us with came in ugly forty gallon industrial strength yellow barrels, and they were unbelievably heavy. The Duggans and I had dragged Strongman Hector into it just to see if he could lift one.

"That had to weigh close to 800 pounds, and there's not much in there. And whatever it is, it's liquid. Most of the barrel is just casing, you'd be able to tell if you could lift one alone."

Hector looked happier than he had in a long time. Some might say it feels good to be the biggest and strongest, and that's probably true in some cases, but I think Hector just needed to be dragged out of his cage.

"It kind of reminds me of your mom," said Dave.

"Yeah," said Dan. "A lot of fucking grief for a giant fucking whore."

"I could break both of you in half," said Hector.

The Duggans looked at each other and snickered.

"Well, you've already broken at least one person in half. Your mother. When you were born. You giant fucking monster," said Dave.

Hector picked up Dave by the scruff of his neck like a kitten. Dan attacked his knees, but he might as well have been attacking cement columns. Hector started laughing and dropped Dave. He looked at me.

"What the hell is inside? Shouldn't we at least try to find out?"

There were 300 barrels. That's around 240,000 pounds, or roughly 120 tons, of whatever the hell this crap was in addition to all our other junk. The Crying Ghost might be The Crippled Ghost if she managed to haul herself through this trip. She was a relatively light train at around 600 tons fully loaded, and she hadn't been asked to carry much more than that in several decades. Compared to what I was used to, she would run heavy, slow in general and fast coming out of rising inclines. I double checked the brakes and suspension on each of the cars and asked everyone to abandon as much useless garbage as they could. It's never easy to get people to abandon junk, but it's actually harder the more crap you have to cram on board. People see 300 enormous barrels and don't see how dumping an old television or a few boxes of books or knickknacks could possibly help.

Leon's contractors had already paid off the Albany-Rensselaer station. A flatbed car had been loaded and hitched right behind the locomotive. The original plan had been for Leon, The Duggans, and I to drive that one car and leave the rest of the train parked in Albany while we ran our little errand. The first problem with this plan was that Leon either didn't know or wouldn't tell us where the hell we were going. There wasn't enough money to leave most of the train in the yard and the others at the campground indefinitely, and winter was coming. The second problem was that the flatbed car was rated for a maximum of 140 tons fully loaded. Combined with her own weight of 30 tons, our payload would put her around 10 tons over, and she was old, rusty, and generally dilapidated. Just enough maintenance and repair had been applied to get her through her last inspection. She fit right in with the rest of The Crying Ghost, too much so for comfort.

Whoever had loaded her had known this and left 20 tons worth of barrels, or 50 barrels, in the loading area. These would obviously have to be loaded into some of our other cars. When I explained the situation to Leon and the others, they got flustered with me. I made a point of looking at Leon when I told them that this situation had nothing to do with me, that it was actually just a simple law of physics. If you can't fit all of your contraband in one place, some of it will have to go in another, regardless of the personal inconvenience.

Aside from not caring what was in the barrels, most of the others would have rather risked their lives, or at least the lives of Leon, the Duggans, and I, than take their junk off the train and wait while we moved the fucking barrels. At least a dozen times, after at least a dozen circular arguments, another damn grounds crew yokel would repeat that we should just overload the flatbed car and take our chances. Getting rid of their garbage was just too much to ask. And they definitely weren't going to wait around for us in the goddamn woods while we sped away with most of the train and with it, honestly, any good reason to ever return. In the end it was decided that it would just be stupider and easier to bring everyone along.

The Duggans and I finally got them to part with a few tons of their garbage by telling them we'd put it into storage. We dumped all of it into the Mohawk River. The Duggans said they knew a spot where no one would care, that in general no one would care, and if I cared so much about being arrested or the environment, why was I illegally hauling over 100 tons of toxic waste to god knows where? Of course it was toxic waste, what else could it be? Then, we put the truck into a long term parking garage and realized that there was no reason to dump all of that garbage into the river, it would've been easier to just store it on the truck.

The only direct resistance to Leon and his barrels came from the Sweeney sisters. They were scared shitless of the barrels.

"Those barrels don't look safe. They're too yellow. They look too hard to break," said Samantha.

"And what if they do break?" asked Sue.

"And if most of them are out here, away from where people sit, I don't want one next to me!" said Sarah.

"Ladies, I assure you you're being silly," said Leon. "If you'd just listen to yourselves you'd see. What does it matter what's inside the barrels or where the barrels are if they're impossible to break anyway?"

"That's not what we're saying at all!" said Sarah.

"If it doesn't matter where they are I say leave them here!" said Samantha.

Sue was about to say something but Leon moved his hands in a placating gesture.

"Okay, okay ladies," said Leon. The sisters looked relieved.

"What we can do is leave you here and come back and pick you up once we're done. Happy?"

The sisters looked horrified. Leon was right about one thing. They would never make it out in the world on their own, and they knew it. Maybe because they knew it. They looked to me for help. I think they were as surprised as I was.

"Christ. These barrels are not indestructible. Nothing is. But they are tough. The Duggans and I tried to break one open with an ax and we couldn't do it."

"You did what?" asked Leon.

"We even shot it with Mike's .22 and that barely left a scratch."

Leon looked aghast. He was about to interrupt me again but I continued.

"We're worried about what's inside, too. Anyone who has to ride with them on a train, or be anywhere near them, has a right to be," I stared hard at Leon. "But Leon is right in one way. If anything happens to the train catastrophic enough to break those barrels, whatever's inside will be the least of our worries."

Leon hardly looked satisfied and the Sweeney sisters looked more resigned than relieved, but I had bigger things to worry about.

Yet another aspect of this fiasco that disturbed me was our destination, which of course Leon had waited until the last possible second to tell me. We were heading into what's referred to as a dead zone. When enough towns on a railroad line either die or switch to cars and trucks, that line is no longer profitable and shuts down. Typically, the other towns on the line that still relied on the railroad die, and this ultimately kills the nearby towns that switched to cars and trucks. The line is still physically there, in some cases for tens of years, but it is no longer serviced, and in many cases, there is no longer any civilization around it to serve.

There are several good reasons why it's highly illegal to drive a train full of passengers, mystery cargo, and at least one endangered animal on track that has been closed and left to rust for years. Leon feigned ignorance when he told me where we were supposed to go, but when I raised concerns about the switches still working and the switch operators going along with the route or even if they could, or if I might have to stop the train and make the switches manually, he told me not to worry, that he had been assured that it had all been taken care of, just like the flatbed car and the barrels. I was ready to murder him, and he must have sensed this because he pressed a few thousand dollars into my hand, thanked me for putting up with everyone, and left me to puzzle over what I had gotten myself into.

C9 Shop Talk

Trains are front loaded because of momentum. A heavy caboose will try to crush you or make you jump the rails every time you brake, so we loaded as many of the barrels as we could into the shipping containers toward the front. This is where we packed the generators, propane tanks, and tents that were usually crammed on board The Other Flying Ghost. After our final show of the year, The Other Flying Ghost was always put into a long term parking garage and the tents always came with the train. No one could give me a good explanation why. Even Leon admitted he couldn't figure it out, but that's the way his father had done it and his father must have had some good reason we just weren't seeing, some reason that would jump up and bite us the moment we decided to change. Honestly, I agreed with him.

The rest of the barrels were loaded into the Sweeney's car, which had the misfortune of being located toward the front. Phil brought out Rob and Rhonda to help us with the barrels but the stationmaster stopped us almost immediately. Those elephants could have heart attacks and die and then what would we do?

"I think I'm about to have a heart attack," said Dan.

Work was relatively easy in the shipping containers. They were built to transport cargo. The Sweeney's passenger car had to be torn apart in order to properly secure the barrels. Sensing the uproar this would cause, Leon had taken them out for ice cream and a movie.

We carefully unloaded their crap first. We'd all been

through their car before but it was always mildly unnerving. There were several old doll houses and Barbie play sets and piles of coloring books and crayons that were clearly still in regular use.

"It's a damn shame," said Garbageman Mike.

"What is?" asked Dan.

"The Sweeney sisters. I think it's part of the reason it's so easy to get mad at them. By all accounts, all three of them are lovely girls, extremely attractive. But you hear them talk and you see this shit and you can't even try. You'd feel like a child molester."

"I know what you mean," said Phil.

"I've fucked them," said Dan.

"Me too," said Dave. "Are you guys fucking nuts? They're acrobats. Are you saying they don't deserve a ride just because they're stupid? The human race would go extinct."

"Best ride of my life," said Dan.

"Which one?" asked Phil.

"I have trouble telling them apart," said Dan.

"I like Sue best," said Dave. "She's a real whore's whore."

We worked for a while in silence.

"Hey Scotty," said Dave. "What about Lulu?"

"What about her?"

"Crazy is usually good in bed, and she's about the kookiest chick I've ever met."

"I wouldn't know about that."

"You're shitting me. Really? Didn't you tell me I should try her honey?"

"Her honey from her bees you idiot." I was starting to feel depressed. Happy that apparently no one else, especially the Duggans, had been with her, but depressed nonetheless.

"She's not going to wait forever," said Dan.

"Look around at the alternatives," said Garbageman Mike. "She just might."

C10 RAGTAG PILEUP

A few hours later, we finally had the train loaded and rolling. It was one of those crisp, cloudless afternoons that can give even the dreariest rural hamlets the appearance of having a charming character. Bleak houses looked rustic, inbred cats and dogs looked feral and natural, and the chill in the air kept them and the few people we saw moving and out of trouble. Time passed easily. By nightfall we were in the dead zone and the first two switches went off without a hitch.

Trains are considered to be fail safe, as opposed to space shuttles and jetliners. If the space shuttle fails in transit between the earth and the sky, there's no way for it to fail safely. Trains have the advantage of already being on the ground. If something fails, you usually just grind to a halt. This is particularly true of the brake lines. The brakes are held open by air pressure while the train is moving. If the brake lines fail, they depressurize and lock, stopping the train. This is usually the example that engineers point to when explaining that trains are fail safe.

I've read multiple times over the years that probably around 90% of car accidents, industrial accidents, plane crashes, train wrecks, etc, are due to human error, and that it usually takes multiple errors, six to eight, to take out an airplane. Through painful experience, people have learned that we're all idiots in certain tragic fundamental ways. It's all too easy for any of us to get distracted and flip an errant switch or stick a plug into the wrong outlet and blow up a house or a factory. Because of this, several layers of protection have been put into place. Plugs and outlets for different devices have different shapes, dangerous machines and appliances are covered in bright warnings, potentially lethal switches and buttons are protected by locks or put under glass. Still, despite all of these protections, disasters still occur. There is a Swiss cheese theory, it posits that each of our seemingly solid layers of protection is actually riddled with holes. When enough holes in enough layers of protection align, disaster strikes.

We were starting up the first incline I was worried about when there was a sharp lurch, and the train exploded. My guess is that the last of the locomotive's wheels had crushed down a section of rail that was no longer adequately supported due to washout. Bending this part of the rail down jackknifed the back end up into the flatbed car, continuing a chain reaction that led to the explosion of the propane tanks in the next car and the subsequent decimation of the train.

At the time, I felt a split second of blinding heat as my ears were overloaded with the roar of explosion. My last thought before I lost consciousness was that at least I wouldn't have to unload those fucking barrels.

C11 A NEW ACT

Sometimes when you get knocked out you can get knocked back in; I'm pretty sure that's what happened to me once whatever was left of the train finally crashed and crumbled to a halt. I had pissed and shat myself and was sweating profusely. It was extremely hot, but I was still too stunned to feel any pain. When I remembered myself, I was shocked that I was still alive, awake again, with at least a few more problems to deal with before I died.

I couldn't see out of my left eye. I tried to rub it, but my left arm was stuck in the remainder of some ruined console. I tried to dislodge it and my forearm broke off just below the elbow. I was strangely calm about this, I expected death at any moment. I wasn't altogether aware of my surroundings but surmised that other cars and trees must have piled up close to the locomotive, the sounds, shadows, and heat of a large fire had forced themselves into my consciousness, there just isn't enough wood or plastic in a locomotive to burn like that. There was enough fuel left inside of her to blow whatever was left of me to smithereens, but that was highly unlikely. Locomotives are built with exactly the opposite intention. So I would probably asphyxiate or be roasted alive.

I pawed at my left eye with my right hand and felt a pen sized metallic cylinder protruding from it. So it's true, eyes don't have pain receptors, and that explains why the old eye isn't working. These questions resolved, I started staggering toward the ladder that led to the emergency exit, or hatch, on the roof. My right ankle was dislocated, but even with just one good leg and one good arm I could probably haul myself up. I touched the ladder and it was hot but bearable. Did I really want to climb out of here? Did I really want to go on living with one eye and one arm and god only knows whatever other damage to my brain and other organs, to start all over again as a mutilated cripple and criminal? Even with the relative security of my last job, back when I had all my limbs and eyeballs, I hadn't been too happy. I was actually kind of miserable. How the hell did I expect to function now? I spent a long time at the bottom of that ladder, too long. The choice was taken from me, which I guess is a choice in a way.

A change in the light and shadows brought me out of myself. I looked out one of the windows but my view was obscured by smoke and the competing colors of the fire. A pulsating white light grew in frequency and intensity, like a strengthening heartbeat, until it reached some critical mass and blazed into life like a newborn star. I was certain my remaining eye had been blinded, all I could see was white quickly fading into red and black. I felt a creeping death begin at my toes. It wasn't the escape or relief I had imagined, the pain was overwhelming and it had me trapped. It pushed me to lurch away from the light. I fell and dragged myself away on my belly. I felt it overtake me and pass through my calves and thighs and into my torso. When it reached my heart I was sure I was dead. I didn't have time to revisit my past or say my goodbyes or renounce or endorse whatever. I felt my heart being torn from life into death and my consciousness fled to hide in some other darkness.

C12 Freak Show

I woke up with a start. I had been dreaming. In the dream, I could see and feel them: Lulu, Leon, Phil, Garbageman Mike and the others, even some of the grounds crew. Lulu and Leon were clearer and brighter than the others, but behind and above them all was a malevolent pain and rage, the power of it throbbed behind my eyes. Instinctively, I pushed it away and blocked it out. I did the same to the others.

I checked for my wallet, cell phone, and keys. It was an automatic reaction to waking up confused in a strange, dark place. I should have thrown the wallet, phone, and keys into the gutter twenty years ago. I stood up and started fumbling for a light switch when it all came back to me. I laughed because there was nothing else I could do. Maybe my soul didn't have the sense to leave my body. Maybe I would live forever in darkness and confusion and other torments I couldn't yet even begin to imagine. As long as you're alive, there is no bottom, and already something new seemed off.

I grabbed at my left hand and felt it. It was there, whole and solid. I rubbed my left eye. Whatever had plunged into it was gone. I couldn't feel any blood or damage. I realized the same was true of my ankle, it seemed to be working fine. I won't deny it, mixed with my confusion was some genuine happiness. I knew that it was fleeting, that my appreciation of being whole again would last all of ten seconds. I was still blind and trapped.

In a fit of dying optimism, I pulled my phone from my pocket and touched the screen. The light was blinding. That's three times, chief engineer Scott, three times that you've blinded yourself in the last five minutes you've been conscious. I tilted the screen away from myself and shaded my eyes. The light from the phone was much brighter than it should have been. My vision had a definite blue-gray tinge to it, like looking through a pair of high resolution night vision goggles. I noticed the windows were covered by a layer of ash, enough to block out any moonlight. I felt that it was night because the air had that dewy night taste to it and it was cold inside the locomotive, which was puzzling because it would have taken days for all that metal and the surrounding rubble to cool off, even if the fire had been extinguished the second I passed out.

According to the phone, it was still the same day we left Albany. It wasn't even 11 p.m. yet. I looked back at the ash and felt a sudden, dizzying hunger. The ash made me hungry, but what I really craved was charcoal, wood, or diesel fuel. And how had my phone survived? I'd gone through at least three or four similar phones in the past couple years-I'd sat on one, dropped another one that must have landed funny, and the last one just gave up. Still, it wasn't uncommon for random, relatively fragile, objects to survive man level industrial disasters, the whole oak and the willow thing. Still, I hardly thought of my phone as bending like a willow. Maybe I was just losing my mind. Another pang of hunger jolted me and a voice in my head told me to get the hell out of the locomotive and eat now, coal, wood, mud, anything, or I would die. I'd already tried dying once and I didn't like it, so I climbed out of the damn hatch and started eating.

Even with the canopy of conifers and cloud cover the light of the waning crescent moon was almost unbearable to me at first. From the roof of the train, I could see a dark gray circle of death about 50 feet in diameter. An edge of that circle overlapped the locomotive at right about the spot I had passed out. Nothing was alive within that circle. The blades of grass, small trees and shrubs were all still whole, but even with my limited vision I could see that all of the color and life had been washed out of them. When I looked at that circle, the voice in my head told me "no nutritional value" so I climbed down and walked into the woods, away from the pile up of wrecked cars and incinerated trees, and started eating fresh pine cones by the handful. Once I had gorged myself, my thoughts turned to Lulu. My eyes pulled toward the hills in the distance, toward Lulu, and I started running.

As I ran, I could feel my body contorting, I picked up speed and noticed I was running on all fours, that my hands were no longer hands but massive clawed paws. A part of me was very skeptical about my apparent willingness to take all of this for granted as being real. I imagine this is how it feels to dream. The part of your mind that balks at the dream is easily pushed aside because while you're dreaming the dream is reality. There can be no question when the answer is so obvious. Question the dream or anything loudly enough and it all falls apart.

I spotted a friendly, pulsating glow just over the hills in a small valley below. As I got closer it resembled a galaxy. There were innumerable points of light punctuating the soft illumination they gave to all around them as they moved together in orbit around their brilliant heart. As I got closer still I could see that the stars were actually millions and millions of bees. Lulu was standing at their center radiating light and power. She was waiting for me. I slowed as I approached her and felt myself turning back into a man. Her light was too much for my eyes to look at so I looked down toward the ground and noticed I was naked except for my belt and pants pockets and a few other stray rags.

My clothes must have already been shredded by the calamities of the day. Turning into a giant fucking wolf had been the last straw. For the first time, I noticed my naked arms and legs. My right foot up to the knee and my left arm up to the elbow were robotic, they were made of iron and stainless steel and other metals and composites I recognized from the locomotive. I knew without knowing that the same was true of most of my skeleton, that my internal organs, including my heart and parts of my brain, had been repaired in a similar fashion. I shaded my eyes and looked at Lulu. She winked at me. It was probably the only thing that kept me from fainting. On top of everything else I was famished.

"So what have you been up to, Mr. Scott?"

"You mean before I turned into a giant fucking wolf and then back into a naked man, or cyborg? Between that and the train exploding?"

"Yeah."

"Well, it's a long story. The part that stands out right now is eating pine cones. I must have ate about ten pounds of pine cones less than an hour ago. I'm starving. I think I'd better go eat some more pine cones or a chunk of wood. Anything. Excuse me, I'll be back."

"Oh Scotty. Oh no. Are you insane now?"

"I don't know. Maybe."

She had seen me change from a wolf into a man. What did she think was so crazy? The pine cones?

"It isn't the pine cones, Scotty, and I understand that you're hungry. Maybe you'll be better once you've eaten. No, don't go off into the woods, I have honey. The honey will do you good."

And why the hell was she talking to me like I was a god-damn child? So what if I was acting funny or talking funny? Get blown half to hell, knocked unconscious twice, stabbed in the eye, even without all the rest and spread over time any one of those things might make a guy a bit loopy.

Lulu laughed.

"You're right Mr. Scott. And you're still you, at least where it counts."

"Wait a second. Are you reading my fucking mind?"

"Either that or I'm insane now, too."

"You were always insane, you crazy bitch." I figured I might as well say it out loud if that crazy bitch could read my mind anyway.

Lulu rolled her eyes and waved for me to follow her. Within her constellations of semi-mechanical glowing bees was a hive the size of a small, two story house. Luna led me around the curving outer wall to a small entrance; we fit through easily enough but it would have been difficult to find without her. A passage curved with the outer wall as we circled inward, it throbbed with a soft yellow pulse. Th e light of her bees glowed through the thin walls and illuminated her inner chamber. Or perhaps it was the light of the larvae still in repose.

"Come eat your honey. I think I have some sunglasses for you in my purse. And stop searching for me. You've found me, get it? Block me out like you did before and I won't be able to read your mind. And keep the others blocked out, too."

"I don't care if you can read my mind."

"Sure you do. And maybe I'm sick of reading it. Pervert."

Lulu's honey restored my strength, but it also made me hungrier as I ate. Once I had finished, I bombarded Lulu with all the obvious questions. Eating had become a serious business for me, all the mysteries and fortunes of the earth and everyone on it could go to hell while I was eating. The light of her bees glowed through the thin walls and illumi-nated her inner chamber. Or perhaps it was the light of the larvae still in repose.

"Scotty, you have to get a grip on yourself. And you have to close your thoughts. You are driving me crazy. Rule num-ber one, we talk. All this mind reading is overwhelming for me, especially in your case, so please, stop and listen to me. Listen to me."

Lulu took a deep breath. I was about to start asking ques-tions again with my mouth, but Lulu shushed me with her hands.

"I don't know what's going on either. I have some ideas, but it's important for me to talk with you first and find out exactly what happened to you. I don't want you to be influ-enced by what I think until I hear what you think. Okay?"

I nodded my head.

"I can tell you want to ask a question. You don't have to be a mind reader. One question."

"Don't you already know what happened to me, what I was thinking while it happened, how I remember it, everything?"

"Yes and no. There are limits for me, limits of distance, sight, touch. The closer someone is, the better I can read them. The more I read a person, the better I can read that person. Strong thoughts and emotions are easier to read. So yes, I know some of your thoughts and feelings and I know that whatever you went through, it must have been excruciating. But I don't know exactly what happened to you, no. And that was at least four questions."

"So you don't really know anything."

"Scotty, tell me what happened. Spill it."

I waited for a moment. I wondered if she could just grab me and drag it out of me, I was almost sure that she could. I wanted to see if she would.

"We've known each other for almost ten years, Scotty. We've always been friends. It isn't difficult for me to guess what you're thinking from that look on your face."

I had a flash. If I was close enough, if anyone was close enough, she couldn't shut them out. I wondered what would happen if I grabbed her.

"I know this is the least trustworthy thing to say, but we have to trust each other and be honest with each other. You're at a very dangerous point right now. You didn't have time to mentally recover from your injuries, and now you're more powerful than ever but you still feel weak and victimized. Traumatized. You're searching for enemies because you want revenge. I can't help you in that way, Scotty. I'm not your enemy and I don't want to be."

Lulu held her hand out to me. I looked into her eyes. They were no longer brown. They were a dead metallic gray. Or maybe that was due to my new vision. Maybe that was the way I'd see the entire world for the rest of my life. Whatever I thought I knew about her, she was far more powerful than I was. I knew that in my bones, like a rat cornered by a cat. Maybe she could just take what she wanted and destroy me, or maybe she needed me around to use for something. I was sick of myself for not trusting people, and then going ahead and trusting them anyway-for never learning a goddamn thing. I couldn't go on this way. I'd rather go back to being a blind asshole. I'd rather die.

"Whatever happened, it seems to have changed you for the better."

"It hasn't, Scotty. But I have to pretend."

People may think that they want to connect with someone, to know all their secrets, but when it comes right down to it, they don't. Leon knew some of our secrets, and he could tolerate us. Those secrets were at least bad enough to get us all fired and shunned from society and stuck roaming around with a circus, but he had known them from the start. But Lulu, poor Lulu. Turning into a wolf is confusing to say the least, but it's nothing compared to the constant onslaught of garbage and madness that must assault her every time anyone comes near her. No one can take that kind of forced intimacy, not for long. And here she was with her hand out asking for more, the crazy bitch. What she might see in me, I couldn't care less. I was already finished anyway. I had been for a long time. The train wreck was just an exclamation point. But Leon was right. I did love Lulu, or at least I did now, and I had no intention of sullying it or her with the madness I would doubtless see whirling within her skull.

"Scotty. It'll be okay."

She batted her gray eyes at me and I took her hand. I brought her back with me through all the tribulations of my last few hours. Her sympathy for me was tinged with disgust at my ambivalence towards life, my fear, selfishness, and pettiness. All of my negative contradictions, all for nothing.

Afterward, she shared her view of the situation from outside the train. I was given to understand that she had sent several swarms of bees to monitor the wreck and search the general area; she could see through them but not read through them. She brought me to Roger. Roger was half crushed and pinned by a section of rail car suspension. Several of the broken bars from his cage had impaled his torso and his jaw was shattered. His entire body was severely burned and his hind legs were mangled. He was little more than a trapped open wound, and already flies and rats were gnawing away at him, eating him alive.

Roger roared plaintively once but had clearly resigned himself to his fate. Looking at him, trying to see life from his perspective, I saw an existence full of pain and confusion almost utterly bereft of any joy. He had been bullied and alienated his entire life and now, to end like this, it was just too much. Beneath his resignation I saw bitterness, miserable bewilderment, and rage.

A heavy mist gravitated toward him, engulfing him and scattering the rats and the flies. As Roger breathed it in, vigor returned to his body. The suspension pinning him began to lose substance and shrink. His jaw and upper body were quickly repaired, but it was already too late for him. The life flickered out of his eyes and his head slumped.

The mist within him and surrounding him formed tendrils that stretched outward from his eyes, mouth, and the pores of his paws. It glowed a pulsating white that grew in intensity as the tendrils continued to extend and branch off. As the light pulsed forward and contracted, all of the color and life was drained from whatever it touched. It crept toward the locomotive, then blazed into supernova and overlapped it.

My heart began to palpitate. Half of it had been touched and ruined and the other half warped and contorted to pick up the slack. To me, this explained the essence of my transformation, of my ability to transform. It was rooted within my heart.

The light and all of its energy returned to Roger in a flash. The vacuum it left in its wake put out the several large fires surrounding the locomotive. Lulu's eyes, the eyes of her bees, quickly readjusted, and I could see Roger resurrected. He was now the size of a minivan and made almost entirely out of stainless steel and iron. He inspected the surrounding area and found elephant Rhonda, who was crippled but still alive and nearly repaired. Roger looked down at her and let out a deep growl. His eyes were the same dead metallic gray as Lulu's. He roared and tore her head off with one paw swipe and then devoured her in much the same way as I had devoured the pine cones. From tusks to tail, he ate all of her. He looked up at the moon and roared at it with crazed malice, stretched, squatted, and exploded upward into the sky.

Lulu's swarm pursued him, he must have jumped over a mile, and they had almost caught up with him when he leaped again. After some more bumbling around in the dark they found him, and Roger was ready for them. He let out an earsplitting roar as he again sucked the life from all around him. Lulu's vision crackled and fizzed into darkness.

Lulu released my hand and we were back in her luminescent chamber. It was difficult not to feel safe and warm in there, but I managed.

C13 KING POLE

"You can't block us out, Lulu. And if Roger gets too close to you he'll either kill you or drive you completely crazy. I know you want him to be stopped, for his sake, your sake, the sake of living things in general. I felt that much from you."

"Go on." said Lulu.

"You want me and Leon to stop him. You think we're all responsible, but that maybe Leon and I are the only ones who maybe have a shot."

"But?"

"You would've had a better shot at getting me to go along with this if you hadn't shown me that. As far as I'm concerned, it's live and let live anyway. Roger doesn't seem to want to have anything to do with us. He's doing the smart thing, getting the hell away, and maybe he'll calm down in a few decades. Frankly, I empathize with him. What we should do now is start moving in the opposite direction as quickly as possible. I can move pretty fast, and I bet you and your bees can move even faster, so grab your purse and your bees and let's get the hell out of here."

"Scotty, it isn't that simple."

People have been telling me that bullshit my entire life, they even had me telling it to myself. Actually, everything is exactly that simple. You want to quit your job or divorce your wife or move to Zimbabwe, you go ahead and do it. Other people do it every day.

"Okay Scotty. Maybe. But there are still a few things we should figure out first."

"We've figured out enough and we can deal with the rest on the way."

"The way to where? Do you honestly think we'd be safe anywhere if Roger decided to come for us? You felt us when you first woke up, as we all felt you. We can protect ourselves while we're awake and sleep seems to protect us naturally, but in those in between moments, between sleep and being awake, we're exposed. So, what's the rush? Especially for someone as indifferent toward life as you are."

"I may be indifferent toward life, but I'm still a physical coward. But I get it. There's no point in running."

"Dammit Scotty, of course there's a point in running!"

She was trying, in her own mixed up way, to tell me that there was more to life than just avoiding pain.

"You, Roger, Leon, you're all dead. All of you died in the train wreck. And since I felt you all when I woke up, I must have been the last to be repaired. But I didn't die."

Lulu was looking away. She was still upset with me but I could tell that she was listening.

"You and the bees, me and the pine cones, my cravings for wood, diesel, coal, that makes sense in a way. I came back in a locomotive and that's what locomotives eat. Anything that burns. I know it's not a perfect fit, I don't know enough about you, but immediate environment seems to play a role. Roger, fuck if I can understand that, the mechanics of it, but you and Leon are probably doing something similar in a more controlled fashion, at least in your case."

"Anything else? Even if it seems obvious, I want to hear it from you before I say anything."

Lulu was mad at herself now, for getting upset.

"Right now everyone is worried about staying hidden. If I wanted to find someone, we'd both have to take a chance and reveal ourselves to each other. Roger doesn't bother blocking anyone. He's too preoccupied with his rage and power. Which is why we instinctively try to push him out of our thoughts. It hurts me when I don't. I'm guessing this is true of the others and especially you. That we all have at least this much in common."

I started to shake. I was hungry again and exhausted.

"You lie down, and I'll bring you more honey to eat while I scrounge around for some wood. Do you prefer pine cones? Okay, pine cones it is."

C14 A TROUPE OF TWO?

In the coming week, despite our relative detachment from life outside the hive, we managed to figure out a few things. Most of the grounds crew were permanently dead in the traditional sense. They had been riding on the roof despite my many warnings over the years. They said they did it to smoke, but they also ignored my warnings not to smoke inside the train. A cool crisp day on the roof was preferable to riding in the filth and stench of the quarters they were too lazy to ever clean. When disaster struck they were flung in all directions. Inertia had not brought them close enough to the rest of the train, or more importantly, to whatever had leaked out of those barrels.

The few that had made it far enough were basically zombies. Whatever was in the barrels had gotten to them first, and while it had been programmed or endowed with some knowledge and instruction, it still needed practice, some real practical experience. The first to survive it were like clockwork compared to the circuitry of those of us to follow. The complexity of their simplicity was maladaptive. Most of their resources were devoted to self-maintenance, toward moving and staying alive. A smart phone is infinitely more complicated than a Turing thinking machine but much easier for people to use and interact with, especially if they have no idea of how either works.

They were a pitiful, unlucky lot before and they were again now. Hands might be little more than hooks or pincers, one leg might be made of steel while another was made of rotting wood. They clicked and lurched around the wreck, frequently pausing to scoop up handfuls of dirt and leaves to cram into their ruined mouths. Occasionally, they would find what they considered to be a salvageable piece of tent or furniture or junk and put it into a pile in the woods. They had garbage piles at seemingly random spots all over the forest. Several of the barrels were unbroken and laying in plain sight, maybe the majority of them had survived the wreck and were still buried beneath the rubble, but as in their former lives, the grounds crew appeared to want nothing to do with them.

On the morning of the second day after the crash, they were gone. Lulu sent her bees far and wide, but there was no sign of them or any of the others. We guessed that they felt the same way as we did, that they needed time to collect themselves and try to figure out what was going on. We were all too afraid of ourselves and each other to let our guards down, so we were all stuck in relative ignorance and inertia.

"Okay," said Lulu, "let's go through it again, but this time, I want you to disagree with me. Agreement is getting us nowhere. I don't trust this, Scotty. There's something we're not seeing and you're not fooling me, I can tell it's bothering you, too."

"No, it isn't."

"Very funny."

"No, it isn't. Maybe I'm bothered by this carousel of madness you have us on. Of course we're missing something, but we should stick to what we can actually see. What's in the barrels, where it came from, how it works, we don't have enough information and it's out of our depth anyway."

"Agreed. And you don't have to sugarcoat it."

"So, where do you want to start this time?"

"The barrels. The zombies are not interested in the barrels. And you don't have to be snippy."

"Maybe I do and yes they are, but why? They literally can't chew and walk at the same time."

I missed Phil and Garbageman Mike. Sometimes you need a third or fourth mind to fill in the gaps, or at least come up with anything new.

"It's Leon." I said. "It has to be him. All he cares about is his damn circus. He's controlling those poor saps just like he always has, selling them some load of bull about rebuilding. They don't know how to do anything else. He doesn't know how to do anything else except run his damn show. His plan is the same as it was from the start. He wants to sell the barrels or get them to whoever he was supposed to deliver them to."

"If he is controlling them, then why aren't they taking any of the barrels?"

"They are taking the barrels, we're just too stupid to see it."

"Explain it to me."

"I'm too stupid to see it."

And that was exactly the point. It was how Leon and his shady family had survived through the centuries, by duping people. By making fools of us. By robbing you blind right in front of you.

It hit me.

"They're digging them up and hiding them in pieces of tent."

Lulu looked up at the ceiling of the hive and exhaled.

"Leon's testing whatever's inside the barrels. He doesn't need a lot to run tests."

This was all disturbingly plausible but that was all. They could be sneaking barrels out that might be for Leon who might be testing them. But Lulu was already angry and probably rightfully so. Whatever was going on stank to hell.

"That clever bastard. He must have noticed my bees, all those piles of trash he has scattered, the pieces of tent. I know we still need confirmation but this feels like Leon. A bunch of cheap parlor tricks from a second rate carnival barker."

"Who was our boss."

"Shut up, Scotty."

I shut my mouth and tried to shut my brain, but it was becoming harder and harder to block Lulu the more time I spent with her. She told me she wasn't really reading me, that her previous knowledge of my mind just made it easier for her to read my expressions as any person might, but she agreed that it didn't really make a difference. Either way, her accuracy was uncanny whether I was blocking her or not.

When we touched there was no way to block her, and I could read her to a certain extent as well. So far we had respected each others' boundaries, but I didn't really have a choice. There was no way I could take anything from her that she didn't want to give.

My theory was that Lulu and Leon had died relatively bloodlessly and painlessly in comparison to Roger. Aside from her eyes, a new paleness to her skin, and the artificial warmth of her touch, Lulu looked and felt as she had in life. At night, she could probably pass as a normal, living person.

Death had given all three of them an extra boost, but Roger most of all, perhaps due to the extent of the repair he required. Or maybe because he was a tiger, because he was just that much bigger and more powerful to begin with. And again, order had something to do with it. For once, being last should have worked out for me, but as far as I could tell I was little more than an advanced model of the grounds crew. Lulu confirmed my impression that my light in her mind was average at best, that I was nothing compared to her, Leon, or especially Roger. Death appeared to be the crucial ingredient, and Lulu wasn't ready to tell me how she had died. I was curious, but I didn't press the issue. What was more important now was to figure out what she could do. Regular people plant stupid ideas into each others' heads all the time, powerful, insidiously influential ideas. How much of a leap is it, from reading minds to controlling them outright?

I had no intention of facing Roger or Leon, but if it became unavoidable, I wanted us to be as prepared as possible.

"I was wondering, Scotty. You haven't turned into a wolf or anything since the night you arrived. Can you control it? And if you can turn into a wolf, maybe you can turn into other things, too, or alter yourself in other ways, don't you think?"

She winked at me and it was even creepier than when she used to wink with her eyes rolled back. Either we were on the same page or she could read me now despite herself and my efforts to block her. It's difficult to trust or know what's going on when you don't know the extent of a person's power over you. Maybe she didn't know either.

"Reading minds is a funny thing, Scotty. Who's really in charge? Who's leading who? I can't help but be dragged along with your thoughts. After a while it becomes difficult to tell, whose thoughts are whose."

"Or if you're reading my mind or feeding it. I trust you Lulu. I don't think you'd do something like that if you could help it, and I don't think you're doing it now. For whatever it's worth, I still feel like myself."

Lulu was silent for a moment. Maybe she was double checking, to make sure her thoughts were her own.

"I know you want to know, and it's been selfish of me not to tell you. So I will. But afterward, I need you to leave for a few days."

"I understand. And honestly, I need some time, too."

She told me, and I left.

C15 ANIMAL TAMER PHIL AND GARBAGEMAN MIKE REBORN

After a few days of wandering around aimlessly in the woods, I came to a small stream by an abandoned cabin. I sat down to drink and nibble on some branches when I heard the door creak open.

"Scotty? Nice outfit."

Phil was referring to the tunic Lulu had made for me out of some bedding her bees had salvaged from the wreck. That and the ridiculous sunglasses she had lent me.

"Where have you been? I've been trying to call you all week."

I felt for my phone and realized I'd left it at Lulu's.

"Phone must have died. How is your phone still working? And why didn't you just . . ." I tapped the side of my right temple. "And where did you get the clothes?"

Phil was wearing winter clothing, most of it looked like hunting gear. I hadn't noticed how cold it was outside. As long as I kept eating, I didn't get cold anymore.

"Mike ran into town for me. And I guess I was paranoid. About giving away our location."

"The nearest town must be at least thirty miles from here." Phil looked off into the woods.

"Come inside. It's probably nothing but better safe than sorry."

There was food inside the cabin, clothing, solar batteries, and whiskey. Phil was preoccupied with his phone.

"I'm glad you're here Scotty. Mike and I have been driving each other crazy."

I knew the feeling. Too confused and afraid to really trust anyone but too confused and afraid to be alone, and when you finally do trust someone to a degree, one or both of you has had enough. People tend to trust others in similar states of futility. Eventually you realize you can't really help each other. That you might actually be hurting each other.

"We can't figure out why no one has come for us. There's been nothing about us in the news."

"That's pretty par for the course for us, don't you think?"

"You know what I mean. The train explodes, the barrels don't get delivered. There's money involved."

Phil must have noticed me eying the whiskey.

"You're right. There'll be plenty of time to drive you nuts later."

"You might be a bit late for that."

Phil uncapped a bottle and handed it to me, then started fumbling around in a brown paper bag.

"Here, take these." He tossed me a couple of cold McDonald's hamburgers. "What have you and Lulu been up to?"

"How did you know I was with Lulu?"

Phil tapped his right temple. "There are other ways aside from phones or weird telepathy or whatever it is."

I realized that Phil was already loaded.

He tapped his temple some more and looked into my eyes. "Watch this."

BILL ADLER JR. AND SARAH DOEBEREINER

He closed his eyes and put on an exaggerated expression of concentration. Jim dropped down from a rafter and held out his little hand for me to shake.

"Meet the little guy responsible for the destruction of the train. Shake his hand. Good monkey. I warned you idiots."

"What? How?"

Phil laughed.

"I'm just kidding. I have no idea what the fuck happened. Neither does Jim."

"Was Jim changed too?" I took a big slug. Even with someone you're familiar with, it's hard to be comfortable when one of you is much drunker than the other.

"Jim escaped unscathed. He's the same little idiot he's always been. Wait a second, just wait! Watch this. Look out the window."

I looked out the window and saw a moose staring in. He looked to his left and bolted and was replaced by a large black bear as Phil laughed.

"I'm like Aquaman now. Except on land. And vindictive. And drunk."

He waved at me to pass him the bottle and took a big pull.

"The one thing I've learned from talking to them, is that animals really are kind of stupid. Smarter than we think, but stupid. There's always a vague warning about something, so I hide in here."

He took another pull and passed the bottle back.

"But there have been a few specific warnings, Mr. Wolfman. Nice hand and foot by the way. Do you have a cigarette?"

"I didn't know you smoked."

"I quit twenty years ago, and how could you have a cigarette in that sheet or muumuu or whatever the hell it is you're wearing? Wait a second."

He grabbed his phone and called Garbageman Mike.

"No, I need you to go back and get cigarettes. What? No, you're misunderstanding me, I need you to get cigarettes.

What?" He fumbled around in the same brown paper bag and removed a pack of Camels. "Yeah, I found them. Sorry. And thank you. You gonna be back soon? What? I can't understand you. We'll talk when you get back, okay? What? Okay, bye. Goodbye." He looked at me. "Shit. Do you have a lighter? How could you? Wait a second."

He started to reach for his phone again.

"Maybe check the bag first?"

"Oh yeah. Here we go. Horrible phone reception out here." He lit a cigarette. It seemed to calm him down and sober him up a little bit.

"What happened to Mike?"

"He just ran into town. Oh, you mean with the barrels. Or whatever was inside the barrels. He's kind of like the Flash now, except much much slower. He's more like a decent horse. Or actually another animal. What's an animal that can run pretty well but can't really carry much? A non-pack animal?"

"An ostrich?"

"That's perfect. An ostrich. He turned into a fucking ostrich. And speak of the devil."

Phil passed out. The door creaked open and I smiled up at Garbageman Mike. He looked down at Phil.

"Poor bastard has been this way ever since the accident. Believe it or not, he's actually worse sober. What have you been up to? How's Lulu? What brings you out to our humble abode?"

"Just lucky I guess."

"Huh. Lady trouble. I figured it might be something like that."

He gave me a frank look. I wondered how much he knew about Lulu. He chuckled.

"I always knew we were the sanest of the bunch."

"We're screwed."

"Maybe. Pass it here."

Garbageman Mike took a long pull.

"I've been trying to tell Phil all week. Maybe you'll listen. We've all been a bunch of paranoid, dithering idiots. You know who isn't an idiot?"

"Leon."

"That's right. You may not know this, but his pappy started him out, all the Leon Harveys start out, at the bottom. As kids they're with the grounds crew. They train with the acrobats. They get a little older, they work with the fortune tellers, game vendors and other hucksters. Then they start barking, learning how to reel 'em in. Leon acts like a buffoon because it works for him. You've got to show people something or they start to wonder about you, thinking you're crazy. A buffoon like Leon, it's hard to take someone seriously when you think they're an idiot, especially when we're all idiots ourselves. It's hard to imagine another way of life."

Garbageman Mike took another pull and passed me the bottle.

"Leon would start getting his shit together before he even knew what he was doing and from what I hear, he already has. It isn't Roger or each other or the authorities we should be worrying about, it's Leon."

"I think I can manage to worry about all of it."

"No point worrying about Roger. Nothing we can do about that."

"But I don't see the point in worrying about any of it."

Garbageman Mike gave me another frank look.

"Pardon my French, but it's time to yank your head out of the honey pot. We can't hide in the goddamn woods forever. Sooner or later, we're all gonna wanna return to the world, and one way or another, it's gonna be through Leon."

I was about to open my mouth, but Garbageman Mike waved me down.

"Maybe you think you can stay in the woods forever. Maybe you can. I agree with you, fuck the world. But I want back in. And if you wanna be with Lulu, and I know you do, you're gonna have to at least pretend to be a little socially conscious. So what do you say?"

Phil let out a loud fart in his sleep. I passed the bottle back to Garbageman Mike and gave him a frank look.

"I've got some time to kill. And I guess I'd like a better idea of what the hell's going on."

"Now you're talking."

C16 ELECTRO ZORKO

According to Mike, Leon and his zombies had lugged their junk seven miles to the terminus of a dirt road that led to an access road that led to a small highway on the edge of nowhere. They'd camped on the dirt road just past where they'd exited the forest proper. Technically, they were still in the forest, just about everything in this part of the country was in forest. Leon sent the Duggans off with plane fare to collect The Only Remaining Crying Ghost. They were back within 24 hours. The next afternoon, Leon had a little carnival going just outside the town of Coldwater, the only town anywhere near us. Within four days of the wreck, Leon was back in business. He had the grounds crew, the Duggans, Hector, and poor heartbroken Rob, who was still alive maybe indefinitely.

He was calling himself Electro Zorko and pitched his act as a phantasmagorium of spectral electrical delights. Hector was again caged. Rob was giving elephant rides at $5 a pop.

Zorko was costumed as a sort of disco gypsy clown. He was pulling double duty as Zorko the fortuneteller and Zorko the Mighty Magician. He wore bright yellow and purple robes and a big red Ronald McDonald afro. He looked so utterly ridiculous that no one noticed his deathly pallor or lifeless gray eyes. He told the townspeople he'd decided to overwinter in Coldwater and figured he might as well try out a few new acts.

Why would anyone overwinter this far north in some rundown hicktown? Why, because the finest people in the world live here, that's why! Like a vampire, Leon went out at night to cavort with the locals in the town's lone bar. He could pass for human at night, and he was virtually unrecognizable from the bozo Zorko. Ever the showman, he wore a casual but respectable suit and had himself primped to perfection. Just as the female attention was beginning to arouse the jealousy of the more unstable elements in the bar, in trotted the Sweeney sisters like trained seals. Why yes, of course they're with the show, we're just waiting for some equipment they need from back east. These girls are like family to me, like daughters. The local women would continue to swoon while the men exchanged glances knowingly. Acrobatics, that's their specialty, isn't it ladies? Come by tomorrow, the day after at the latest, as long as those boys back east can get their act together.

Garbageman Mike had run into the Duggans during one of his trips into town. They were playing poker in the bar with some of the locals when he spotted them. He was going to ignore them, let them run whatever scam they were pulling, but Dave gave him a look. He and Dan were up a couple hundred bucks. Time to leave.

"Dave, Dan, what the hell are you doing? You were supposed to be at work half an hour ago."

"Well boys, time to earn some money," said Dave as he took the cash from the table.

Dan was wearing large sunglasses and a goofy baseball cap. Most of his brains had been blown out during the train wreck. He was alive but empty. Somehow Dave was animating him. It didn't make much of a difference according to Garbageman Mike.

Dave had given him the gist of it. Leon was definitely powerful, but he kept his powers hidden. He still had a lot of money left and was actually turning a profit. The train blowing up was the best thing that had ever happened to him, he should have sold the train and scaled down the show years ago. Sure, he seemed shady but what else is new? Leon didn't want to push anyone into anything, he was waiting for us to come to him whenever we felt ready. This experience has been traumatic for all of us, of course we were all free to do whatever we liked, to take as much time as we needed, or to even quit if so inclined to start anew. But at least stop in to say goodbye and collect your wages.

"So what do you think?" asked Garbageman Mike.

"We should stop in and say goodbye. Collect our wages."

So, we went. Getting into town was an ordeal. We could have just called the Duggans for a ride now that we were coming into town to see them anyway, but we were still wary of Leon and each other and curious about our powers. Garbageman Mike and I stripped down and packed our clothing into his backpack.

"Just like everything else, I had to learn the hard way. The first time, I didn't even notice my clothes were gone until I was almost in town," said Garbageman Mike.

"I had a similar experience."

Garbageman Mike was a lot faster than me, even after I'd turned into a wolf, but like me, he had to stop to eat and refuel frequently.

"Can you turn into anything else aside from a wolf?"

"I don't know."

"Why don't you give it a shot? See if you can change into a hawk, something more efficient for travel."

It had never even occurred to me that I might be able to fly. I started running and flapping my arms, I felt my hands and arms expand and take hold of the air. I was flying, and it took a lot less effort than running. Garbageman Mike could barely keep up with me. I heard him yelling at me to land as we approached the access road. I couldn't hide the joy I was feeling.

"That was beautiful Scotty, but maybe don't try that around other people. A hawk the size of a hang glider is bound to make some folks suspicious."

I had somehow known that I couldn't shrink or grow, that I had to conserve mass, but it's easy to forget about the details in a situation like this. What person hasn't dreamed of flying, of really flying like a bird? What did I need the world or other people for? I was finally free. I could happily spend the rest of my life exploring jungles and forests. I could hide away with Lulu forever.

"I know that look. I'd be thinking the same thing if I could turn into a bird and just flap the hell out of here. You could go to the ocean, turn into a dolphin, maybe even learn to speak dolphin, especially with Phil helping."

But if it wasn't for Garbageman Mike, maybe I never would've tried to fly at all.

"You seem to have a lot better ideas than I do." Honestly, I'd had no ideas in regard to my abilities. Turning into a wolf had been automatic, instinctive.

"I've known you awhile. Long enough to know that having better ideas than you isn't much of a stretch. You have a good mind, but you like to keep it tucked up your ass most of the time. And it's usually easier for an outside observer, to see the forest through the trees or whatnot."

Garbageman Mike looked a bit disappointed or envious.

"All I can do is run in circles faster than I used to, it's made it easier to shoplift and commute, but not much else."

I laughed at him.

"You could join the NFL or play baseball, return punts or be a pinch runner."

"At forty-three that'd be a bit suspicious."

"The Braves had a forty some odd year old pinch runner back in the mid-90s. Shit, what do they care how old you are? They'll pay you the league minimum, peanuts to them, if you can do the job."

"What's the league minimum nowadays?"

"I'm not sure. For MLB, I think it's around 300 grand a year."

"You're shitting me. Goddamn, that's actually not a bad idea."

We walked in silence for a while. It was good to talk with Garbageman Mike again, to someone who couldn't read my mind, but something about the undercurrent of our small talk was getting to us.

"I wonder what bright ideas Leon has," said Garbageman Mike.

I was thinking the same.

Dusk was closing in, so we decided to wait on the access road until dark. Town was still a good 30 miles away and neither of us wanted to walk it like regular people. For two large, middle aged men, one wearing a tunic, hitchhiking didn't seem like a good bet either.

* * *

We got to town an hour or so after dark. Garbageman Mike had me wait on the outskirts while he found me more acceptable clothes. I recognized most of them as belonging to Hector. I looked like a goddamn clown, and the shoes were the worst part of the deal. I couldn't get three steps without stumbling or losing one. Thankfully, it was a short walk to Zorko's, and we managed to slip in without attracting too much attention from the locals.

Leon had his Tesla coils blazing as he brought the grounds crew back from the dead. Of course the locals knew that the grounds crew had never really been dead, but the claw hands and the wooden legs were creepy and clever, and the lightning leaping out of those coils sure looked dangerous.

Still, good old Zorko appeared to be completely in control. It was all just an act, everyone knew that, and look at that Zorko go! The crowd broke into laughter as "Everybody Dance Now!" blared from the loudspeakers and Zorko and his zombies began to dance. Garbageman Mike hadn't been exaggerating. Zorko looked like Ronald McDonald's sleazy, colorblind, maybe epileptic uncle. Zorko hopped and grooved himself into position between the two largest Tesla coils. He continued to shake and shimmy as electricity danced across his body. He raised his hands to the roof. Something was coming, but before it could, the coils and the disco lights faded as the music slowed into silence. The crowd began to murmur in confusion.

"I apologize ladies and gentlemen. It appears I overtaxed the circuits. But I believe I have a solution."

Zorko drew in a deep breath and brought his hands together. A bright ball of lightning began to grow within them and push them apart. He closed his eyes and lightning leapt from his fingers to the coils, lights, and speakers, bringing them roaring back to electrical life. The music was louder than ever, the coils looked on the verge of explosion, and gyrating in the middle of it all was Electro Zorko the Mighty Magician, the man with lightning in his hands. The crowd screamed with glee and danced along with him. If anything like this had happened outside of a phantasmagorium they would have been terrified. Garbageman Mike and I were terrified.

The song ended and the houselights came on as the coils settled into stasis.

"I hope you all enjoyed the show, and to see you all at the bar later this evening."

Zorko saw us in the crowd and waved us over. He brought us back to his personal chambers. A few smashed chairs, posters, and pieces of old photographs had been salvaged from the wreck. Old pictures of Roger, Lulu, and Leon had been added to his gallery of the dead. Just off to the side, hovering between life and death, was a recent picture of Dan Duggan in his sunglasses and oversized baseball cap, smiling dully back from oblivion. Zorko brought us drinks and cigars and tapped at an old picture close to the center.

"Giles the Fish Man."

The poor bastard really was half fish and half man. He looked aghast at having his picture taken. He was small and misshapen, his arms were short and stubby, his head of hair looked like an old beaver pelt, and he had enormous dark buck teeth. His eyes were oversized, you could see the sad self-awareness in those eyes beseeching to you from back across the gulf of mortality to please, for the love of god, at least take down the fucking picture. I didn't like the pictures of Lulu, Roger, Leon, or Dan either. Maybe all nostalgia is bizarrely mean spirited and cruel. Zorko's eyes moved to the picture of Lulu.

"Poor Lulu. She was aloof, but never really crazy. At least not until now."

"I wish I could say the same about you."

Zorko looked into my eyes and chuckled.

"Leon, if you're about to make an argument for your sanity, it'd help if you at least took off the fucking wig." said Garbageman Mike. He slugged down his drink. Zorko took off the wig and moved to refill our glasses. He returned to his snuff collage and tapped on Giles' picture again.

"Do you want to know what my father said to get him back on his fins? He told Giles to start swimming again, or he'd beat him to death.

"Giles was already an old fish by the time I was around. I loved him dearly, but once my father found out about our friendship, he bludgeoned Giles with the back of his bullwhip and told me never to go near him again. He told me about Giles' dream, that part of the story was true, but my father's interpretation of it was just the opposite. According to him, Giles was weeping because he would never know the vengeance of poisoning his own children. This is what all parents do to their children, it can't be helped. Parents and people in general transmit through infliction all of their crippling doubts and fears. Giles embraced this truth, at least on an unconscious

level. He was too isolated from humanity to avoid seeing it
or to know to withhold it. And it is a perverted irony, being
stuck in the water and never getting your dick wet."

Leon took a large sip from his charred prop goblet and
tapped at the picture of his father.

"Our children came to us poisoned and now, they have
become powerful. Still, I'm not worried about them, or us,
or you. We belong with the show more than ever now, and
most of us have the sense or instinct to know it."

"You think you can just go on, back to business as usual?"

"Maybe a bit better than usual. You were right about the
old act, Scotty. Everyplace we showed up, people were surprised
to see that something like that could still exist, and that was
about the extent of their interest. But this new act, it's really
something to see."

"What about the train, Zorko? What about the barrels?"

Leon refilled my glass.

"Stop trying to drag everyone down to your version of
reality for once. Trains, barrels, all that balderdash. Haven't
you learned that nobody wants to hear it? No one will miss
that 100 year old jalopy. That jalopy tried to murder all of
us, and the way I see it that lets us off the hook. You want
your barrels, you're upset we didn't deliver? Well I'm sorry,
our fucking train exploded. If they want the barrels or the
government wants the barrels or whoever wants the barrels, I'll tell them where they can look, and this is assuming
they even think we're still alive. Regardless, we're out of the
loop. We're a bunch of ignorant, worthless afterthoughts,
just like you're always trying to tell us. So, appreciate that
fact for once."

I had the feeling I was being duped, but was too stupid
and tired to try to fight it or stop it. It's difficult to fight
when someone is showing you step by step how to convince
yourself of what you want to believe, that basically, you won't
have to face the consequences of your actions. I looked at

Garbageman Mike. He nodded at me to go on. For all their twists and turns, conversations with Zorko were predictable in their way.

"Zorko, what the hell do you want?"

"Call me Leon, Scotty. And there is one thing."

Leon gestured toward a flat screen television and it flashed into life. He chose the internet option and navigated to YouTube.

"As you've probably already gathered, I have been granted certain abilities which allow me to manipulate electricity or electromagnetism or what have you."

"You're like a living, breathing remote control."

Leon had his videos cued up but paused.

"My power, as impressive as it is, is quite lacking in some ways. It would be nothing compared to the ability to read or control minds, for example, without the entire infrastructure of the modern world to bolster it."

He looked into my eyes. "Lulu feels responsible for Roger, she thinks we all are."

He looked at Garbageman Mike. "No, you're misunderstanding me. I need you to go back into town and get cigarettes."

"Oh fuck," said Garbageman Mike.

If we ever wanted to plot against Leon or keep anything private we'd have to communicate by carrier pigeon. He knew everything, or at least he wanted us to think he did.

"You're looking at me that way because you feel violated. You want revenge. I'm not your enemy Scotty, and I don't want to be. I don't think you'd like it if I tried to help you in that way."

"Like you're helping me now?"

I knew I was overmatched, but I was angry. I could feel my left hand turning into a mace.

"Now come on boys, this isn't helping anyone," said Garbageman Mike. "I don't give a shit about the eavesdropping.

If you think my gibberish is interesting, go ahead and listen. Just enough with the theatrics."

Leon played us some conspiracy clips on YouTube. Mysterious orbs of light leave circles of death, demented hinterland shut-in claims bomb shelter blasted by giant mechanical cat, mass moose and bear migration baffles local hunting authorities, mellifluous metallic wailing reported throughout region.

"To use the parlance of the conspiracy minded, Roger is the lynchpin of it all. Once Roger decides to pull his antics in a more heavily populated area, which he eventually will, there will be investigations that will undoubtedly lead to all of us and uncover the entire sordid mess. The train, the barrels, all of your prior interactions with the legal justice system, everything will come to light. There will be no hiding for any of us, not for long. I want my circus, you want whatever it is you want, we have to contain Roger."

If I helped, Leon would know it was for Lulu, and I didn't want him knowing anything about me or who I cared about or even if I cared about anyone. But if I ran off to hide in some jungle, I would lose Lulu. She would see that Leon had appeared to want to do the right thing, for whatever vile reason I couldn't even bring myself to think about, and that I had basically said fuck you, fuck the world and fuck everything. If the definition of love is going out and fighting a tiger for someone, maybe I've never really loved anyone.

"What are you planning, Leon? And when?" asked Garbageman Mike.

"Three days from now, after dusk. Where the sink factory used to be. Come around noon tomorrow, and I'll walk you through it."

"We'll be there." said Garbageman Mike.

Leon looked at me.

"I'll be there."

We went to the bar to drink but we were too paranoid. Cell phones and cameras are literally everywhere. We ended up hiding Garbageman Mike's phone in a birdhouse and heading out to his stash on the edge of the forest.

"If it was any closer to the cabin, Phil would have one of his animal friends find it and drink himself to death."

Garbageman Mike uncapped a bottle of whiskey and took a long pull, then passed it to me.

"Are we really going to do this?" I asked.

"Leon is slippery, but he's got a point. We just might be in the clear, but if Roger acts up, starts killing innocent people, someone's gonna come calling for us."

Garbageman Mike looked off into the forest.

"There's something you should know about Lulu if you don't already. Pass it here."

He took a long pull from the bottle. I had a pretty good idea of what he was going to say, but nodded at him to continue.

"Lulu came back after Leon and I and most of the others. When she did, it was different. We sensed her, but we were also forced to sense each other, all the pain, anger, confusion. Lulu started blocking us out, as is par for the course, but as she did, well, she wasn't exactly blocking as much as she was killing. What happened to Dan Duggan, the same thing happened to half the grounds crew. Their brains were blown out before they knew what hit them. Lulu must've figured it out quickly enough, she cut it out and took off, her and her bees, deep into the woods. I'm not blaming her, she just did what we all did naturally, there's no way she could've known. At least, not until it was already too late."

He took another long pull and passed the bottle to me. Lulu had told me a similar story. It was the reason she had wanted me to leave. Her mind could only take so much before it defended itself, and she didn't trust her ability to control it. She had taken my post-traumatic stress and my awareness of it. It was locked within her, partitioned somewhere in her brain, just waiting to either rupture or be dispelled into another mind or minds. I explained all of this to Garbageman Mike.

"So you understand, why Lulu can't help us."

"That's where you've got it backwards." said Garbageman Mike. "I have a pretty good idea of what Leon's up to. But the way I see it, we can't really help them. All they really need is Leon, Phil and Lulu."

"I don't like it, and I know Leon's not going to like it."

"Like it, hell. What is there to like?"

"So what does Lulu do afterward, if she can even take it?"

"That's something we're going to have to leave up to her."

C17 STEREOTYPIC MOVEMENT

The next day was crisp and sunny. We woke up just after dawn and headed to the remains of the sink factory a few miles outside of Coldwater. It had burned down years ago, all that was left now was a dozen or so acres of concrete foundation and several crumbling concrete pillars.

"Not much alive for Roger to eat." said Garbageman Mike.

"Except for us."

A large opening had been made over a subbasement and covered with a tarp. Piles of rubble were propped up on a ramp. A push from Hector would fill in the subbasement and trap Roger, at least in theory.

"That isn't going work. Roger is going to hop right out of there."

"Won't hurt to have a way to slow him down."

We still had a few hours to kill, so we sat down on a comfortable slab of rubble and had a wake me up with acorns for breakfast. I took a pull and passed the bottle.

"This plan seems a bit light to me from what I can see."

"I'm sure Leon has something up his sleeve." Garbageman

Mike chuckled. "Hell, I'd bet he'd charge admission to see it if he could, and people'd pay."

The Only Remaining Crying Ghost pulled up a little before noon. Leon came over to talk with us as Hector, Dave, Dan and a few of the grounds crew unloaded the truck. Among the items they removed was a large railgun. Leon could see that Garbageman Mike and I recognized what it was.

"You've already seen the tiger pit as well no doubt. Just precautionary measures I assure you. The basic plan is to lead Roger here and have Phil explain the situation to him, that he can either rejoin the circus if he wishes to or run off and live and be free, as long as he's discreet."

"That sounds like a pretty complicated explanation," said Garbageman Mike.

"You don't give Roger enough credit," said Leon.

"Complicated for Phil," said Garbageman Mike. "His nerves are completely shot, and they'll be even more so with Roger around."

"And let's not forget that Roger is a bottomless cauldron of rage. Have you actually seen him Leon, what he's like now? I have, and he doesn't look too inclined to listen to reason."

"I agree with Scotty," said Garbageman Mike. "We need Lulu in on this, if she can calm him down maybe Phil can tell him a simple message like 'hide' or 'stay away from humanity.'"

"Absolutely not. As far as I'm concerned Lulu is just as dangerous as Roger, and the last thing we need is another unstable element. I believe that I can still control Roger to a degree, but not if I have to worry about Lulu as well. There's only so much I can do."

"You believe you can control Roger? Only so much you can do? Leon, you're dreaming if you think you can control Roger now, and you've already led us from one disaster into another. You've done more than enough."

"So you want Lulu involved, is that what you're saying?"

He had me stumped. I didn't want her anywhere near this.

"I'm saying this plan is crap. That's all I'm saying. And I don't see what you need us for."

"I need you here in case things go south. Maybe all together, we can overpower Roger."

I started laughing. Leon pushed on.

"Or at least distract him, force a kind of truce."

"So, you're deliberately bringing us into harm's way. You know the plan is lousy, you know it's probably going to blow up in your face, and you want us here to get shit on when it does. This is the barrels all over again. This is actually even worse. At least you didn't think the train was going to blow up. Did you?"

"Are you done Scotty? I acknowledge I helped to create this situation."

"Helped?"

"We all did, and now we have to deal with it."

"To do that, we need Lulu," said Garbageman Mike.

"No." said Leon and I.

I turned from Garbageman Mike back to Leon.

"While we're at it, what the hell are you doing with the barrels you dragged out of the woods?"

"I don't know what you're talking about."

"You lying piece of shit. You rotten, shifty, son of a bitch."

"Not now, Scotty," said Garbageman Mike.

"I didn't want you to have to worry about that," said Leon.

"I knew it! You devious cocksucker. And what's your angle on Roger? You want to stick him back in a cage like Hector, have him jumping through hoops again? You're insane, Leon."

Leon took a deep breath and slumped down, caricaturing his idea of defeat.

"My intentions toward Roger are as stated. As far as the barrels, I just wanted to better understand what had happened to us, how it all works, but in the end I was too wary to experiment. Suppose I inadvertently created some kind of super flea or rat? I'm not completely blind, Scotty. I don't have a death wish."

Nothing about Leon sat well with me. Every time he spoke I felt like I was being dragged further into his machinations. I was about to lay into him some more when Garbageman Mike interrupted.

"First things first. No point in worrying about any of this if Roger kills us all anyway, or if he doesn't bother to show up. How you got that figured?"

My head started to throb. Leon and Garbageman Mike rubbed at their temples as well. There was a metallic shriek and a loud crash as Roger landed on the truck and flattened it. All of the people still inside were crushed. Hector, the Duggans, and the rest scattered as Roger tore the truck apart. He looked like he was tearing into the belly of an antelope. He paused to look around frantically, as if guarding his carcass against scavengers, and spotted us. His eyes locked in on me and I felt Leon and Garbageman Mike quickly back away. He pounced and I froze, I was dead for sure, but Leon pushed me out of the way with a magnetic pulse and stunned Roger with lightning bolts.

Roger raised a paw to swipe at Leon. Leon tried to deflect it with another magnetic pulse, but Roger was far too massive and Leon was sent tumbling. He had avoided the actual blow, but not most of the force behind it. Roger moved in for the kill. I grabbed his tail with my left hand and tugged it as hard as I could. Roger spun before I had a chance to let go and threw me on my ass. Leon jolted him again from behind as he approached me but Roger ignored him. Roger was done playing with us. Garbageman Mike lined up to try and grab me but I waved him off. There was no way he would make it. Roger's presence at this range made all of us slow and woozy. My ears buzzed as Roger loomed over me, and I was separated from him by a wall of bees.

He glowed and pulsed with light, the intensity increased quickly, then leveled off and subsided. I was nearly blind again, but I could make out Lulu's silhouette against his glow. She was kneeling down in front of him, holding one of his huge paws in her hands.

Through Lulu, we were all connected. I felt Roger's yearning, Leon's discipline, Garbageman Mike's stoicism, Phil's terrorized confusion. I understood the anarchy of animal thoughts, the frustration of always having to attend to others, the thanklessness of trying to protect others from the world and themselves.

Roger bounded away. Bees swirled in the vortex of his wake.

Lulu's eyes glowed a deep red as she rose to her feet. My heart pounded in my skull as blood dripped from my nose. I looked to Garbageman Mike and Leon as we collapsed to our hands and knees. Blood leaked from every orifice. Lulu intended to destroy herself and all of us with her, and we accepted it. Roger's rage had poisoned her, just as we had poisoned him. She lowered her face into her hands and sobbed as her millions of bees scattered and exploded all around us. As the last of them popped out of existence, Lulu glowed brightly for an instant, then disappeared.

C18 ALL OUT AND OVER, ALL OUT, ALL OVER

After a long and crippling walk, we finally made it back into Coldwater. We had tried to hitchhike, but there weren't too many people in Coldwater, and even less driving back from an abandoned sink factory. Still, even as beat as we looked, I would bet that if a single car had passed us, it would have picked us up. Small towns are accommodating in that way.

Leon, Garbageman Mike and I headed straight to the bar and sat down in front of the taps. We had already recovered from our injuries but were still haggard and disheveled. Leon told the locals that we had had some problems with a new trick and car trouble to boot. He still managed to sound charming and engaged. Garbageman Mike and I were on autopilot.

"You don't know that she's gone," said Leon.

"A part of me hopes that she is."

"You don't mean that. I didn't give her enough credit, and neither are you. I admit that I was skeptical, but she came through when it counted."

"Pulled our fat out of the fire is what she did," said Garbageman Mike.

I wondered if she was really gone, what had changed her mind.

"I know that look," said Garbageman Mike.

"I know it, too," said Leon. "You can't always worry about 'why?' or 'what if?' We're alive. All is well." Leon raised a glass. "To Lulu."

We clinked glasses.

C19 AFTERSHOW

I returned to Lulu's hive later that night. It was cold, dark, and deserted. I found my cell phone in her chamber and collected it. I couldn't stay there. It had become another one of those places, another empty memory. All of the things that a person goes through in life, all of the things a person loses. We're either too late or too blind, too afraid of ourselves and each other. And I was still afraid of her. As much as I wanted her back, a part of me was relieved that she was gone, and not only because of her power and instability, but because I knew deep down that I would have fucked it up in the end anyway. Some of us are born knowing that, and it ruins us. But that doesn't make it any less true.

I turned into a giant bat and flapped over to Phil's cabin. He looked perplexed.

"God, am I happy to see you. This place is magical in some ways, every time I wake up I seem to have enough booze and food and cigarettes around, but fuck! I had an ordeal earlier, maybe the worst fucking nightmare of my life. Lulu was forcing me to talk to Roger, she kept screaming at me to be more forceful, but I was too afraid of Roger. I started to wonder who I was more afraid of, then what the hell difference it made. You don't know what it's like, being stuck between two maniacs."

Phil paused for a second before grabbing a bottle and taking an enormous pull.

"Fuck it. Dream or reality, what the hell does it matter? If I can't tell the difference, to hell with it."

"You'll know when you're hungover."

Phil cleared up for a second.

"I don't get hungover anymore, and it's beginning to worry me. Not enough to change of course, but nonetheless. Nonetheless."

He took another enormous pull and passed me the bottle.

"Do you think you could talk with dolphins?"

"Fuck no! I mean probably, but why the hell would I want to?"

"Maybe their thoughts will be more organized than these woodland creatures. Maybe it'll be easier for you to cope."

Phil eyed me suspiciously.

"You thinking about turning into a dolphin? Well why the hell not? Maybe. At least it'll be a change of pace from slowly losing my mind out here in the middle of the fucking wilderness."

We stayed up until dawn. When I finally fell asleep, I didn't automatically block out the others, and they left themselves open as well. We dreamed together of the hiss of air released by the brake lines as a train settles into town, of parades led by marching bands down wide tree lined streets, the mighty circuses of old behind them. We dreamed of buckets of fried chicken, of endless rivers of whiskey and silence, of old locomotives well-oiled and repaired. We were carried off to a new, southward wilderness of long grasses and scrub brush, where we dreamed of river and jungle, of tigers, children, and freedom.

THE WORLD BEYOND

by Jennifer Porter, 23,000 Words

The World Beyond takes place in the year 2068, long after the Collapse when the weather wreaked havoc on our world and existence and unleashed epidemics. Amanda Butler is 104 years old and lives on her farm on the outskirts of Detroit where she is one of the only people for hundreds of miles to raise cats and dogs solely for pets. Nearby is Quarantine Center #554. Eva and Iron, two young children, have lived their entire lives at the center and are aching to live in the world beyond. They escape the center and show up at Amanda's farm. While Moses, Amanda's adopted grandson, struggles with forgiving his grandmother enough that he can return home and take over the farm. There is always a calm after a storm, and eventually, we get on with living.

Jennifer Porter lives near East Lansing, Michigan. Her writing has appeared in such literary journals such as Fifth Wednesday Journal, Old Northwest Review, The Dos Passos Review, Apeiron Review, *and* drafthorse. *She is a graduate of the Bennington Writing Seminars and the co-founding prose editor at* The Tishman Review. *Follow her on Twitter: @ Journeybooks.*

Eight-year-old Eva and five-year-old Iron were walking the inner perimeter of the fence at Quarantine Center #554. Eva wore her cotton shift, now stained yellow from bleach, over last-year's faded-black ragged leggings. Her fine, black hair had been bobbed without consideration for her beauty, as if someone had drawn a crooked line across her forehead and chopped at the bangs with dull shears. Iron was so thin his pants drooped around his waist, exposing a frayed elastic waistband on dingy underpants. They kept their eyes along the ground, where the rusty fence met the soil. Some places seemed to have deteriorated enough to dig under. It was the year 2068, and Eva and Iron knew there was something outside the perimeter—a whole other world. A world they could not even begin to imagine.

* * *

Center #554 was one of hundreds of mammoth, concrete structures erected during the outbreak of contagious diseases that followed the record-breaking natural catastrophes of the 2020s that wiped out most of the American infrastructure. The five-storey building with its prison-like narrow, rectangular windows was surrounded by steel fencing topped with razor-sharp barbed wire, but the windows were designed more to keep the weather out than to keep the patients inside. The patients were too ill during the first decades to even fathom an escape. At its peak, the well-regulated center housed three thousand people, along with two hundred staff members. There were even teachers to school the children. A teacher hadn't set foot inside the center since 2055.

The less fortunate ill had been shipped to the centers after either turning themselves in or having been rounded up, as if they were cattle with mad-cow disease. With the electrical grid largely disabled, hospitals with compromised staff had been unable to stop the spread of diseases not seen in decades or never before seen, simply because they couldn't treat their patients. Pharmaceutical manufacturing plants had been destroyed or were unable to produce without power, supplies ran dry, and people died by the thousands.

Eva and Iron had spent their entire lives at Center #554. They weren't sister and brother, but their mothers both came to the center with a contagious illness. Eva's father died before she was born. Iron's mother was sent to the center while pregnant and died shortly after giving birth to Iron, just as Eva's mother had. Eva took a special interest in the brown baby and took him on as her own. His mother had named him Ryan, but Eva never could say 'Ryan', only 'Iron,' and the name stuck.

Center #554 sat due north of Detroit, out in what was once rural-burbia, where farms existed alongside upscale, sub-urban development. Lacking in self-sufficiency, most people had fled the outlying areas, and of course, all areas devastated by tornadoes, floods, blizzards, hailstorms, and wildfires. The survivors congregated in what became known as 'urbanized locales': pockets inside a former city where utilities and services were brought back on a limited scale.

The staff thought it was cute to see the Korean girl hover over the Potawatomi boy, so they let Eva and Iron be. The children had been tagged as diseased due to their mothers' conditions when enrolled and would remain at the center, unless they ran away.

"We need something to dig with," said Iron, squinting with scheming at Eva.

"Spoons would work," she said. "We'll have to steal them."

The children ran inside, with an eagerness for lunch they'd never had before.

* * *

No one missed Eva and Iron while they were outside digging under the fence with spoons, unless they were absent from roll call at the start of a meal. The center now housed a couple hundred, mostly lifelong, patients, along with eighteen staff members. Eva and Iron were the last of the young children. Everyone resided on the first floor, though each floor had its own dining, nursing, and activities area. The children's days were marked only by mealtimes and bedtime—leaving long stretches of free time in which they roamed: the main floor with its vacant lobby, dusty reception center, and abandoned library, the first floor (where they slept) with its countless empty rooms, and the fenced yard. Often, they pestered old-timer George, with the funny accent, for stories about life on the outside, but more and more, the stories had only caused them to feel unsettled.

The children missed roll call not long after they had dug a small depression beneath the fence. They came skidding into the dining room—their knees caked in soil, their hair wind-blown, their eyes wild with freedom.

Nurse Carrie, in her thin, worn scrubs, charged over as the children got in the end of the queue. The other patients silently waited for a tray of colorless slop the center referred to as a meal. If old-timer George had been there, he would've let the children cut in front of him, but lately, George wasn't showing up for meals. He was coughing all the time now and that made it difficult to shuffle around. He was nice to the children and told them things about the world beyond that made them want to go there, like how ocean waves sounded when they crashed ashore or that there wasn't nothin' better tastin' than his daddy's rack of barbecued ribs. Nurse Carrie always reminded the children that George was on his end days, and this made them sad.

The other patients largely ignored the children or were annoyed by their presence, and the children avoided them. Many of the patients raised in the center suffered attachment disorders. Nurse Carrie had seen to it that Eva and Iron could form an attachment, as she'd done through the years with other patients she developed a unique fondness for. It wasn't easy putting herself out like that: two of her special patients had run away last summer.

Nurse Carrie, a middle-aged, plump woman with stringy, gunmetal-gray hair, loved all of "her children" though not in a selfless, unconditional, altruistic way. She'd been unable to have children of her own and had run away from an abusive father to join the nursing corps right out of high school. From there, she'd jumped at the chance to work and live at the center. Though she liked to think otherwise, she knew very little of life outside the center. Her anxiety over its possible future-closing often got the best of her. Her pasty white hand was hot with rage as she gripped a handful of dirt-encrusted spoons, shoving them in the children's faces. "Look what I found hidden beneath someone's mattress! Stolen property!"

"But we were just borrowing," Eva said. She wore a steely look that always gave Iron the courage to be dishonest.

"Borrowing spoons? What are you doing with the spoons? Why are they so dirty?"

"Making mud pies," Iron said, his dark-brown eyes carefully cast down. He didn't have it in him like Eva did and was afraid his dishonesty would show.

Nurse Carrie drew her neck back. "I don't believe you."

"It's true," Eva said. "We were playing behind the gardener's shed." The children had not been behind the gardener's shed, but they didn't want Nurse Carrie to find the escape hole.

"How do I know you're not trying to run away?" asked their nurse, narrowing her eyes.

"Oh, we'd never do that. Would we, Iron?"

He shook his head with great dramatic emphasis, his dirty, dark-chocolate-colored hair slapping against his temples. "We'd never try to run away."

"We love it here," Eva said, using all of her will to make her face match her words. "It's our home, right, Iron?"

He nodded.

Nurse Carrie regarded them with deep suspicion then relaxed her death grip on the spoons. Her fingers had flat, red, spoon imprints. "I'm going to have to confiscate these, you know. And banish you to your room without supper."

The tears welled up in Iron's eyes. "Okay." Now, his stomach was going to complain instead of letting him sleep.

Nurse Carrie's voice softened. "Go along now, the both of you, to your room. You're not to play outside anymore. You're not to steal spoons. You're not ever to leave. Do you understand me? It's for your own good. The world beyond is no place for children."

"Yes, Nurse Carrie," the children responded in unison. They ran off to the room they shared together. It didn't matter to Eva that they'd missed their supper, what mattered was how to steal more spoons.

* * *

After nearly a month of digging in the rear southwest corner where the fast-growing pine trees on the other side cast permanent shadows, the children had created a shallow hole beneath the fence. Iron could squeeze under, flat on his stomach, though only with much pushing of his rear by Eva and not without a degree of discomfort. After making it through, he hopped up, turned toward Eva, and smiled from ear to ear.

"Ha! Ha! I'm out, and you're not!" he said. He turned away from her, toward the woods. "Look it, Eva, trees." He began stepping toward the trees. The trees had crusty, crinkly bark that he wanted to touch.

"You stop it right this second, Iron," Eva hissed.

But Iron didn't listen. The wind was whispering to him as it touched him gently, giving him small shivers that reminded him of his mother he could not picture in his mind. Though he felt she was always there with him like the hair on his body or the nails on his toes and fingers.

"Where are you going?" Eva shouted.

"I want to go in the woods," he said. He continued to take small steps forward. The woodland floor was dappled in golden light and Iron wanted to feel the dapples upon his skin and the amber shed pine needles beneath his feet. He bent over and slipped out of his ill-fitting fallen-apart shoes.

"Iron, no! You can't go in there."

"Why not, Eva?"

"It's dangerous."

"I don't think so," he said, distracted by the pleasant and compelling idea of walking among the trees. The woods didn't seem dangerous at all.

"Iron! Stop! There could be a bear. Or a wolf!"

The children had learned about dangerous woodland animals from Nurse Carrie. The nurse said after the Collapse the animals migrated, living in places the people left.

Eva's chest began to constrict, and her blood rushed haphazardly through her as if it could not locate her heart. She gripped the chainlink as Iron began weaving between the gray trunks, the wind shifting the branches heavy with pine needles. She wanted to scream at him to return but it was like someone was shoving a thick scarf down her throat. She shook her head to fight it off.

When she could no longer see Iron, Eva's mind swirled into a black panic. She felt as though the disconnection between herself and Iron—that she'd never experienced before—was going to kill her. As if someone were skinning her alive.

Eva's shrieking slammed into Iron with such force that he stumbled forward and landed on his knees. He covered his ears, but her distress sliced through him.

He raced back to the fence. Eva lay face-up on the ground, her legs and arms thrashing, her head careening, her cheeks smacking against the hardened graveled dirt. He scrambled beneath the fence as quickly as possible, a broken link of the chain latching onto his pants and tearing the fabric. He crawled over to her, crying her name over and over. Eva went still.

"Eva! Wake up," he said into her ear. He shook her shoulder. She didn't move.

"Eva, please! I'm sorry. Please don't be dead." He took a corner of his shirt and wiped the white foamy drool from her chin, begging her to return. Her face fell to the other side, as if she could not bear his presence.

He rested his head against her chest then pressed against her, anxious to hear a heartbeat. Eva's heart was going very slowly, the space between beats frighteningly long, but if he closed his eyes and quieted his thoughts, he could discern an uptake whenever he stroked her arm, or her scratched cheek, or her hair.

Iron spread out against Eva, stretching his toes to her calves, and eliminating the space between the front of his body and the side of hers as he did often during the long nights when his stomach complained, when the bad dreams woke him, or when his heart ached for a mother he couldn't picture. He wrapped one arm over her stomach and slipped the other arm beneath her neck, and he buried his face into her shoulder. When the wind rustled through the trees on the other side of the fence, he took hold of it and passed it along to Eva, gently exhaling over her face and wishing her back.

"Come back, Eva," he whispered.

Eva took a sudden and dramatic intake of air, her head turning toward the sky. She brought in her outstretched arms and returned Iron's hug, her fingertips clumsily caressing his back. They lay still together, listening to the wind move through the trees.

"You almost killed me," she said. "You left me, and I almost died."

"I'm sorry."

"Why did you do that to me, Iron?"

"I don't know."

"You can't leave me."

He nodded, his snotty nose brushing up and down against her arm.

"Say it out loud. I will never leave you, Eva. Never. Ever. Say it." She turned and grabbed his mouth with one hand, squeezing the water out of his eyes. "Say it."

"I will never leave you, Eva."

"Never. Ever."

"Never. Ever."

"Okay, then." She pushed him off then got up. "You nearly killed me, Iron."

"Sorry," he said, looking up at her. The sunlight behind her black hair like a white-hot starburst.

* * *

As soon as the hole was big enough for both children to squeeze under the fence, they began venturing farther and farther away. They came back dirty with the earth and amber pine needles in their hair. Nurse Carrie would yell at them about playing outside then force them into the shower. She was far too busy changing adult diapers and dispensing meds to watch the children that closely. Six nurses took care of two hundred patients—Nurse Carrie on day shift. Nurse Carrie was in charge of the children. Her children, she reminded the other staff.

She started following them around whenever possible; sometimes neglecting her duties, and sometimes the children couldn't get away from her long enough to go outside. Nurse Carrie wasn't sleeping well, thinking about the children escaping into the world beyond. No one else would love them like she did. They were damaged children, institutionalized children, and their survival was dependent on the center remaining open. This was their home. She was their nurse.

Eva couldn't take the chance of keeping the spoons in their room; she and Iron buried them out in the yard, marking the spot with a small mound of gray gravel.

"You know what happens to the people who try to run away," Nurse Carrie said. She had come into their room for tuck-in and had caught Iron slithering back out from beneath his metal cot. Outside their sliver of a window high up on the wall, the stars twinkled against the night sky.

Iron plopped down next to Eva on her cot, shaking his head until she punched him in the arm. "Yes, Nurse Carrie," Eva said. "We know all about that."

"You know it would just do me in if you two children tried to run away. I say tried because no one, and I mean no one, has ever managed to run away." The nurse kneeled beside Iron's cot then leaned forward, resting her weight on her hands. She stuck her head beneath the cot. "We always catch them and bring them back. It's important that those infected be contained." She stretched her arm beneath the cot then snatched it back, a dirty pillowcase sack in her hand. She stared at the sack. "I'm very fond of both of you. You know that, don't you? I feel as if you could be my own children." She turned and looked at them with eyes of the palest blue.

Nurse Carrie lost all her colors long ago, thought Eva. She loved her nurse in the way water and sunshine causes plants to grow, or so George explained. The plants can't do nothin' 'bout what it is they need to stay alive, he'd said.

Eva nodded her head enthusiastically and with a feigned spirit of innocence while Iron kept his eyes on the cold yellowed linoleum floor. The children had heard rumors that last summer the teenagers Lauren and Meaghan escaped. The girls weren't seen at the center after that one night, so they must have gone somewhere. Somewhere was better than always in here.

Nurse Carrie began undoing the knot that kept the sack closed. "I just couldn't handle it if something terrible happened to my little orphans." She dumped the sack's contents onto the floor and began sorting through them, pushing them into little piles. Pebbles. Feathers. Leaves. Sticks. "It would break my heart. It always breaks my heart when my special patients just up and leave. You don't want to break your Nurse Carrie's heart, do you?"

Eva shook her head and jammed her elbow in Iron's side so that he would also.

"You understand what I'm saying to you? Eva? Iron?" She stood up, staring down at Iron's collection.

Eva nodded enthusiastically. Iron stared at his pebbles, feathers, leaves, and sticks: his treasures. Each thing conjured up the image of where he'd found it in the woods. He didn't like it that Nurse Carrie touched his treasures, contaminating them.

"If we caught you children running away we'd have to punish you. We'd have to make sure you learned a lesson. Why would you want to put yourselves through something as painful as that?" She bent over and picked up the pebbles, the feathers, the leaves, and the sticks, dropping them into the sack then she walked over to Iron. As she handed him the sack, she said, "I'm the only person who cares about you children. Outside the center, no one will care about you. No one will tell you bedtime stories and tuck you in. No one will let you draw, Eva, or keep things from the outside, Iron. No one will let you make mud pies behind the gardener's shed. Don't you ever forget it."

* * *

Five years ago, the government stopped sending people to the Quarantine Centers. The epidemics had "officially" cooled off. The centers had always been expensive to operate to any decent standard, and the general population had gotten well enough to begin questioning the ethics of the policy. The government had also refined its ability to control the weather to a degree and lessen the extremes and the severity of the weather-spawned catastrophes, with a better handle on mitigating the traumatic effects of climate change. More and more of what was left of the habitable areas of the country was brought back on the power grid and infrastructure re-construction was reaching a fifty-year high.

* * *

Back in 2047, Amanda Butler was eighty-three years old and living in an ancient foursquare that sat atop a gentle grassy hill where she'd survived it all. Not far from Quarantine Center #554, though the Butler family had been living on their spot of land long before any centers were built. She'd awoken feeling light-headed and slightly sick to her stomach, but needed to feed and water her animals. She'd been living alone for the past year, since the last of her bloodline had died.

Winter had come early, as it was prone to doing, and Amanda tromped through the brittle snow to the cattery that sat behind the farmhouse. She raised cats and dogs and either sold them or bartered them to the Fortunates to enhance her survival. The Fortunates had ready access to lampante oil, medical supplies, books, fabric, yarn, paper, batteries, black tea, whatever Amanda needed, and were willing to swap those items for the rare and unusual gift of a pet for themselves or their children.

As she opened the cattery door, she thought she heard someone hush someone else and her heart quickened, so she raised her shotgun in her right hand and grasped the barrel with her left then stepped inside the outbuilding, greeted by a loud chorus of meowing. The door sprung closed behind her. Soon, her cats were rubbing against the sides of her legs, and she couldn't tell if she was just tired or if the room was spinning. It took longer than usual for her eyes to adjust to the dim interior, and while she waited, she soon realized she heard soft child-like whimpering. Someone was in the cattery. There was a muffled cough and Amanda whipped around to see but lost her footing. As she fell to the ground, she saw an African-American boy and an African-American man crouched in the darkest corner of the cattery—her cats swarming all over them, desperate for affection.

She fell forward onto her chest and was relieved that the shotgun was not blasted, but the pain of landing upon the weapon caused her to cry out.

The man rushed to her side. His skin was as dark as the night sky and he asked Amanda if she were all right.

"Are you here for the animals?" she managed to hiss. "They're not food. Pets are not food."

"No, we don't want your cats."

Amanda heard the boy cry louder.

"What do you want then?" She tried to move, but could not because of the pain. Her two house dogs barked outside the cattery door, always protective, and started the kennel inhabitants into a frenzy of barking and howling.

The man just looked at her. Then, the boy shouted, "He's sick! My daddy's sick, and they tried to round him up and take him to the center."

Amanda rolled onto her back and laid the shotgun by her side. The man leaned down. "Don't get any closer I can still shoot you."

He rose up, his palms out. "Don't shoot. I'm just trying to keep my boy outta the centers. He's not sick. I don't want him growin' up there. Stuck there with no future."

"Oh," said Amanda. She wasn't sure if she should believe him. She turned and looked at the stocky school-aged boy. He reminded her of her grandson Lucian, the way his eyes let in anyone, anyone at all, to the innermost reaches of his soul. "You're not ill?" she asked the boy.

"No, I'm not."

"How old are you?"

"Ten."

She turned toward the father. He probably was going to kill her and take over her farm. Feed her cats and dogs to his boy.

He reached his hand out, "Here, let me help you."

So this was the end for her. Well, she was glad for it. Sick and tired of her sorrowful heart bleeding all over her life. "There's lots of food stored up, you won't ever need to eat the cats and dogs. People come a long way out here to trade for one. You've got to take good care of them, though. Socialize them to be affectionate and obedient to people."

"You make it sound like you gonna be dead real soon," the father said. He took his hand back. The disappointment on his face hardened over to disgust.

"I might as well be," she said. She rolled over onto her side and tried to sit up. The pain knocked her back. "What's your name?"

"Thomas. And this here's my boy, Moses. We're from Detroit."

"My father lived in Detroit. Until the '67 riots. Then, he got us the hell out." She vomited and was unable to keep the cats away. Thomas bent down and softly made her some breathing space. The cats already liked him, a surprising but good sign. She looked up at him. "I'm sorry I said that. I don't feel well. I'm a very old woman."

"That's alright," he said.

"No, it's not really." She couldn't draw in her breath as deeply as she wanted. "I think I broke a couple of ribs." She forced herself to sit up. "Ran all the way out here, did you? What is that, about sixty miles?"

"Just about," Thomas said. "I'd do anything for my son."

"I know the feeling," she said. She had no other choice but to trust them. Not only was she ill, she was injured. "Moses, there's a bucket of food and a bucket of water for the cats outside the door. Your dad's going to help me to the house while you take care of the cats, okay? Then, you come inside too. Bring my shotgun with you." She looked Thomas in the eye. "Deal?"

He wiped the sweat from his hairline with his shirtsleeve and nodded. "Done and done."

"I've got medicine and Moses will have to help me wrap my ribs. He'll have to take care of the animals the way I say to. Think you can do that?" she asked the boy.

He nodded.

"Can you read and write?" she asked.

Moses nodded. "My Daddy taught me."

"Good," she said. "Let's do this thing, Thomas, before I pass out for good."

* * *

Thomas died within a year. It didn't matter what remedies Amanda told Moses to give him or compresses she had Moses apply. She crawled out of bed and oversaw the trade of two of her best puppies for a batch of antibiotics that didn't do a damn thing for him. She was thankful to be too ill to sit bedside with the boy as his father left this world and went on to another. The boy sunk into a deep depression, doing his chores as if he were an automaton, hardly eating. Amanda could hear his sobs from where he slept on the couch at night all the way to her upstairs bedroom.

She got tired of yelling at him from the top of the stairs to get his lazy butt off the couch and go do this or go do that and stop moping around when we all had to die sometime anyway. A broken heart doesn't mean broken feet, she'd say. His grief made her unbearably irritated.

She'd had to send the boy down the road to her neighbor's for assistance in removing the corpse, resentfully enduring the neighbor's heated questioning on Amanda's wisdom in allowing blacks to live in the house with her, especially as sick as one was. She reminded Justin of the many times she'd seen his family through with gifts of food and medicine, and never once had she turned him into the authorities, though she could have. Easily and without blinking an eye. He considered her respectfully, but at night, she lay awake and worried.

She'd silently refused to allow Thomas to be buried by her grandchildren beneath the oak tree with the tire swing and the self-loathing also kept her awake. She'd manipulated Moses into selecting a spot past the vegetable garden but not too close to the creek, where Thomas could listen to the bird-song and bullfrogs. At times, she was grateful for Thomas's death as it had forced her to get out of bed and get back to her animals. Moses had a lot to learn about being a breeder, but her dogs and cats couldn't get enough of him and he was good with them.

What was she going to do with boy? Justin had asked, and she had to consider this also. She could use the help and while his company at times annoyed her (he asked too many questions), at times he also delighted her with his optimism and his intelligence, and she found herself beginning to like him. He listened well and responded appropriately and after the moping ended, he was a hard worker just as her children and grandchildren had been. Amanda had always loved children and having one of them around again made the days feel busy and light.

* * *

The dogs started barking long before the military vehicle could be seen coming down the dirt road in a cloud of dust. Amanda wasn't expecting anyone, and she had a sneaking suspicion that Justin hadn't been able to let things be. The reward would be very hard to pass up for a struggling young family. She ran out of the kitchen, leaving the sterilized canning jars hot and ready to be filled with bubbling applesauce, and into the back yard, where the maples glowed yellow and orange. The bitter wind cut right through her brittle bones and she wished she'd grabbed her coat. Moses was just making his way out of the kennel, where he spent large chunks of time playing with the puppies and dogs. He was a dog person, he kept announcing to Amanda. Though he liked cats alright, he guessed. The kennel dogs were barking so loud the boy covered his ears with his hands.

He couldn't hear her shouting, but when he looked up and saw her, he rushed to her.

"We've got to get you inside," she said. "Hurry. They're coming." She watched his young strong body run quickly to the door and disappear inside the house. If only she had his energy, she thought, her ankle bones popping and clicking in her feeble attempt at running.

He stood waiting for her in the kitchen. "Don't cry," she said. "It'll distract me."

He nodded, pressing his hands hard against his eyes.

She ran into the front parlor and poked her head out from behind the curtains. A rusty Humvee was making its way up her dirt driveway, taking the bumps and holes hard. The CDC had purchased old throw-offs from the military at bargain-discount rates. She turned toward the boy.

"Follow me," she said. She grabbed his hand when he got close enough and dragged him down the hallway to her library. Moses liked the library (he was an avid reader) and especially enjoyed it when Amanda read to him.

They'd had a thoughtful conversation about Huckleberry Finn and how much and how little some things had changed. The boy had asked Amanda: if they all woke up one day the same skin color, wouldn't everyone be the same then? She'd gone into a ramble about cultural differences, but the boy was too wise for her inadequate deflection. She'd taken a deep breath and said, "I was raised up in a different America than the one you're living in now. Some things are better, we seem more color blind, having to work so hard to survive, but some things still seem pretty rotten." Was *she* color blind, yet? She had watched the boy as he lay on the floor, playing with one of the indoor cats and felt secretly guilty that her heart was not more open to him.

The steel door to the Cloak Room, as she called it—where the Butlers hid people from the authorities—was behind a section of wooden book shelves that she opened by leaning against a middle shelf with both of her hands and releasing quickly. Her husband had designed and built the secret room long ago. The room had once been a downstairs half-bath off the kitchen.

Her mind was so frantic with the sounds of the Humvee getting closer that she couldn't remember the code for the keypad of the door's lock. She kept punching four keys in a row only for them to turn red and deny her entry.

"Are they gonna take me? I don't want to go to the center. I like it here with you," said Moses. His voice cracked as he spoke.

"Be quiet," she said. "I can't remember the damn code."

"Do you have it written down somewhere? I can look." He started touching things in a random, scattered pattern. "Maybe here?" He kept speaking as she tried to recall the four-digit code. She worried maybe the batteries were dead and it wouldn't matter what she entered. The boy kept telling her that he liked her. He liked the dogs. The cats. The farm. He wanted to live there with her and take care of her and the animals.

"Goddammit, Moses. Get over here," she said and when he came close enough she brusquely grabbed him by the arm. The Humvee's engine cut off. "Stand here and punch in the numbers when I say them."

He held his pointer finger out straight and tight, aimed at the keypad. "Okay, go." Truck doors slammed shut outside.

She took a deep breath and closed her mind to everything, just made it a big blank space of quiet darkness. She put her hand gently over Moses's mouth as he started to speak again then closed her eyes.

"Four . . . seven . . . six . . . zero!"

The keypad chimed and the lock clicked and Moses opened the door.

He stood there, fascinated with the little room. "Hurry," she said, pushing him in, "There's a cot and a toilet. I'll let you out as soon as I can."

He turned to her. "Promise?"

"Yes."

Tears welled up in his eyes and she knew he didn't quite believe her.

Her two inside dogs were barking at the front door. "If it takes me awhile to get back to you, there's supplies. You can live in here for a couple of weeks. There's also another way to get out, if I never come back. The directions are inside a little notebook inside a manila envelope marked 'In Emergency.'"

He looked around. There were no windows, but there was order. The cot was made, a nightstand beside it with a lantern, stacked boxes lined against the walls, water jugs. Some books on the shelves. Extra bedding beneath the cot. A toilet and small sink.

"See that red metal box there under the cot?" The doorbell rang and her dogs went crazy.

"Yeah."

She had to speak louder. "The envelope's in there."

He turned to her. "Don't forget me."

"I won't. I wouldn't do that, Moses. If I don't come back it's because they took me. Please, go sit down. Be very quiet. You can turn on the lantern, but remember to just sit there and be quiet and still." There was a pounding now on the front door. "You can read a book. Okay?" If she didn't answer it soon, they'd bust in.

He nodded. She shut the door and the lock buzzed as it set in place.

* * *

Moses rolled over, the back of his nightshirt soaked in sweat. He drew his arms down from around his head and rested them straight out, expecting her to be there. He felt around for Shammi without opening his eyes then knew she was gone. It was always the same bad dream. He was in the Cloak Room and Grandma never came back. The food in the boxes was

349

black and moldy and maggots crawled everywhere. The water came out of the sink thick and brown with chunks of rust. He always woke up at the part when he opened the envelope, and there wasn't a notebook inside.

He opened his eyes, the sunlight filtering through the slatted metal blinds diffused by the overcast sky. He'd been living in the same cramped apartment in the urbanized locale since he'd left the farm. It was his 31st birthday. He wondered if his memory played tricks on him or if it had taken Grandma Mandy longer to let him out of the Cloak Room than it should have. But then, he knew it had. He should stop fooling himself and accept it. She'd let him stay in there, knowing he was frightened. After she'd shut the door the room was pitch black, and he'd had to crawl around to find the cot. He'd found the lantern but without being able to see it, couldn't figure out how to turn it on. But who was he to complain? So he'd sat in the dark, all alone, until sometime the next day. She hadn't turned him in.

He was in a comfortable bed, the intoxicating smell of his lover on his sheets, making a way for himself as a joiner, especially well-known for his furniture. He believed the future was wide-open. More and more he'd been thinking and talking about having a family, being a father, being invested in the creation and nurturance of life, maybe even getting back to the farm. Grandma wanted him to come back, raise a family there.

Some days, he thought he was ready, but other days, the old anger rose up within him and he couldn't bring himself to give Grandma what she wanted. When he had wanted her to love him, she'd kept her distance. Sometimes, he had great disdain for the boy he'd been—how needy, begging for love from an old, white woman.

There was a curled note on Shammi's pillow. He picked it up, then sat up to read it. Shammi hadn't been taught to read and write as a child and Moses had spent many nights after long days of hard work patiently teaching her. She'd been a reluctant learner in the earliest most difficult phases, but after she could read basic signs and labels, she attended the lessons with more enthusiasm. In her child-like scrawl, she'd written with a pencil that while thankful for all he'd done for her, only a crazy-person would bring children into this world.

"I guess I'm crazy then," he said aloud. He *was* crazy, expecting to find a woman that also wanted to settle down, get married, do things the way they used to. Some of the people his age *were* acting old-school, now that more of the country was back on the grid.

"The government ain't some kinda God that can just take over the weather and end global warming with a snap of the fingers," Shammi had said. She'd said it during a terrible spring blizzard, and it felt like what she said was true, but he wanted to believe otherwise.

He wanted to be the kind of father his father had been. They'd been as close as a father and son can get, and Moses missed his dad every day. What a crappy birthday, he thought, then got out of bed to go to work.

* * *

Amanda spent her afternoons rocking on the porch, pushing off with her toes in a maple rocking chair Moses had made for her 100th birthday. She was tired of surviving the inconsistent winters and turbulent summers even though the weather *had* calmed considerably. Her bones ached from another low pressure system moving in, and she wished it would go ahead and storm already. She'd been sixty years old back when it all went to hell in a handbag. She'd known it was coming, and she'd prepared her family, but she hadn't expected to live so damn long. She had the constitution of an iron horse, as her grandmother would've said.

Amanda stopped rocking because she thought she saw a couple of children peek out from the tree line at the bottom of the slope of the hill her house sat on, but then she had imagined seeing children before only to be deeply disappointed. After the delusion, she'd spend days wallowing in grief and aching to hold a child. Moses called them baby mirages, and with a tight jaw, endured the mirage aftermath which consisted of pointed questions about his lady friends and marriage prospects and the fact that at his age he should become a father soon. "If only it were that simple, Grandma," he always said then sighed.

Amanda shaded her eyes as if that could've helped her see any better that far off in the distance and peered intently as she was certain two children came out from behind the trees and were now standing in the meadow. They must've escaped from the nearby center. Moses had said the authorities weren't going after the center fugitives. Things had gotten that much better, but Amanda wasn't sure to believe that or not. She could kill two birds with one stone though, if those really were children she saw. She could hold a child in her arms again and she just might finally catch a fatal disease. Something she'd been hoping would happen for twenty-two years. Her dogs, Wrangler and Sugar Bear, barked and got up from where they'd been sleeping on the porch near her feet, and this gave Amanda hope.

* * *

Eva and Iron stood at the edge of the waving field of new green and looked up at the weather-beaten gray slanting house. They'd been staying outside later and later and travelling farther and farther away from the center, and on this day, the children realized that at the end of the woods there was a field and a hill and a house, and what was that?

"A really, really, old woman," said Eva, though she'd never seen one that old, only heard the staff talk.

"Let's go see." Iron raced into the field and began running up the hill. This frightened Eva, and she shouted for him to stop. How could there be a woman that old? What had she done to survive? Some people had eaten other people back during the darkest of days. That's what Nurse Carrie said.

Iron refused to listen to bossy Eva. He saw the old, white woman, she stood hunched over at the edge of the porch with her hand making shade on her face, and he could hear a series of continuous but strange animal sounds. Iron saw movement through the meadow and knew something was headed right toward him, but he didn't care. Something had happened to Iron since playing in the woods, finding small creatures and fascinating plants—a shift in his sense of security, and now he felt safer outside of the center than in it. He knew this hadn't happened for Eva yet, but he hoped it would. He laughed aloud at the thought of seeing the old woman and what was coming through the grasses, something new and wonderful and alive, but the sound of his laughter still surprised him. He abruptly stopped but couldn't stop grinning.

Then, two dogs were leaping on him. They knocked him down and licked his face. "Sugar Bear! Wrangler!" the old woman shouted, but Iron didn't want them to go. He had never seen a dog. Well, except in tattered, old books at the center. The dogs smelled delicious. They were so soft, and their tongues were warm and comforting, but Eva was shouting now, in great distress, and because he loved her more fiercely than anything or anyone else, he hopped right up and waved his hand at her. "Dogs, Eva! Come see the dogs." He bent over and tried to hug them, but they couldn't stop moving around him, sniffing his butt and licking his hands. Iron's laughter rose up from the field and spread out over the earth and when it reached Amanda's ears, her mind clicked like the shutter of a camera trying to capture the exquisite sound. It *was* a child, and she smiled.

Eva raced to Iron, her mind imagining the scary, bad things Nurse Carrie had told her the diseased and starving dogs had done to the people after the Collapse. Nurse Carrie had never seen a dog, but her mother ate them like everyone else—just trying to survive, not because she'd wanted to. They ate the cats too. There weren't any cats anymore, or she was told. Eva was glad she'd never eaten a cat or a dog after seeing them in a moldy picture book. In the book, a little white girl held a kitten, and the kitten looked snuggly with its soft pink nose and long white whiskers. Even the insides of its ears were pink. In the picture, the girl had a very wide smile, and Eva hoped someday she'd know what it felt like on the inside to smile so wide. A large stain of black mold was on the girl's polka dot dress, right over her heart, and Eva thought she too had this black stain covering her heart, keeping the mother she never knew inside. The only thing that ever made her feel better was Iron.

When Eva reached Iron and the dogs, she was shocked at the sight of them rolling around on the ground. She saw the color of love bursting out, as if there were soap bubbles being popped above their heads. She wanted the patchy, brown dog and mottled, black dog to lick her too, but she was scared. So she stood there, slightly bent over, reaching her hands out as far as she could stretch her malnourished arms so that when the dogs circled around Iron with their fiercely wagging tails sometimes a tail or a back or an ear brushed against her fingertips. They *were* very soft; she had never felt anything like it. The field grasses tickled her legs, reaching up and under her loose cotton shift and the meadow rustled and whispered. Eva wondered if maybe she and Iron had died and gone to Heaven, so she stood straight up to search for her mother.

* * *

The girl hadn't been properly fed and held her body tense with apprehension. Amanda approached slowly, so as not to frighten her away. But the dogs had smelled their master. They lifted their noses and bounded over to Amanda. Then, everything stopped: the playing, the laughing, the motion of life. The snotty-nosed boy popped up then hid behind the girl. He was far too thin.

Amanda was exhausted from the stillness and the quiet, and when it came again so abruptly she resented it. She had forgotten how to speak to children. "What are you children doing here," she said, but that wasn't what she wanted to say at all. She shook her head and cleared her throat and tried to remember what children were like. What are they made of? Snails, she remembered, and puppy dog tails, and sugar and spices. "Don't be afraid of the dogs," she said this time, "they won't hurt you," but her voice still sawed through the air, and she could see the ripples race along the children's bare skin. The children shivered as if Amanda were the Ice Queen. She didn't want to be the same with these two children as she had been with the other child of color dropped into her life years ago.

The boy poked his head out from behind the girl and said in the most quiet of whispers, "Are those your dogs?"

Amanda nodded and remembered to smile. Her dogs sat at her feet, thumping their tails and panting.

"Are you going to eat them?" the girl asked.

Amanda wanted to give the children a hot bath, a decent haircut, some good clothes. And feed them.

"No! People shouldn't eat dogs," she said with too much force. "Are you going to want to eat my dogs?" She was frightened a bit herself now. The children could run back to the center and tattle about the dogs, and then the hungry might show up at her door. That is what used to happen, and Amanda didn't like to think about the past. The past reminded her of the madness of a Salvador Dali painting when what she'd always loved was the world of Mary Cassatt and Degas's ballerinas. She had to remind herself that things had settled down after all these years; Moses said the dangers were nigh-near over—she could stop keeping a loaded shotgun by the front door. But the trauma felt ingrained inside Amanda, locked into her very cells, something she breathed in and out.

Amanda was still the only person for four hundred miles who'd been breeding dogs and cats to keep the species alive. The dogs were a conglomeration of breeds now, and Amanda distinguished them by their ears, floppy or raised, and the length of their fur, short or long. Moses brought visitors from the urbanized locale from time to time. The upper crust, Amanda called them, then pinched her nose and rolled her eyes. The Fortunates, who could trade supplies for a pet.

Her dogs and cats were her only companions.

She was foolish to have approached the children.

"It's okay, we won't tell anyone about your dogs," the girl said, softening in response to Amanda's fear. Only a special person would not have eaten dogs, and Eva thought that maybe the old woman hadn't eaten people either. The old woman had her knobby hand on the head of one of the dogs. She rubbed it back and forth without using her stiff fingers much, stroking the dog's ears. Eva pretended that she could feel the old woman caressing her hair and smoothing it off her forehead. Eva moved her head as if this was really happening. No, it wouldn't bother her to be touched by fingers that look like the gnarled roots of a centuries old tree.

"We've never seen such an old lady!" the boy said as he came out from behind the girl.

"You haven't?" Amanda said. She tried to straighten some, but her back hurt and she'd been out in the field for too long and wanted to go back up to the house. She put her hand against the small of her back as if she could have held herself up this way.

The boy shook his head, his brown hair swinging back and forth. It was chopped as if an inverted bowl was put on his head for a guide. Amanda got a bowl cut once, back in the sixth grade when she asked the hairdresser in the slick black, polyester disco pants for a Dorothy Hamill hairdo. With her big lavender plastic glasses, Amanda had looked ridiculous.

When she'd complained to her mother about the crappy hairdresser, her mother had slapped her.

"You can call me . . ." She began telling the children that her name was Amanda Butler, but it sounded too formal, so she said, "Grandma Mandy." That's what Moses had named her after she let him out of the Cloak Room, as if a term of endearment could cement and forge a bond she hadn't known she needed until it was too late. Her ever-growing list of regrets followed her like a cloud of locusts.

She was willing on this day though to risk everything: the dogs, the cats, even Moses's sorrow.

* * *

The old, white woman had short, stark-white hair that shimmered in the sunlight. Her translucent skin hung in folds on the underside of her arms. Eva could see blue lines on the grandma; there wasn't much between the outside of the woman and her skeleton. She wore a bulky, navy-blue sweater as if it were cold—which it was not—but there were black roiling clouds heading their way and sometimes after a storm the air was much cooler. There had been times out in the woods when the children cowered beneath the bushes and waited for the thunder showers to pass. The air after always gave Eva exquisite shivers.

"It's going to storm soon, children. Would you like to come in the house?" the grandma said. Eva scrunched up her face in concentration, wondering if this was a scheme to eat them after all. "I could make you a sandwich," she said.

"Okay," shouted Iron. Eva slapped his arm for his over-enthusiasm. Iron ate everything. Eva had been pulling creepy crawlies and clumps of vegetation out of his mouth all summer.

"Don't tell me what to do, Eva," he said, glowering at her.

And before Eva knew it, Iron and the grandma were walking toward the house, and the dogs were racing ahead, racing back, circling around, and racing ahead again. Iron was laughing at them. He took the hand of the old woman (he was *such* a baby). The grandma stopped and looked down at him and the love burst out again in pinks and blues and warm yellows. Eva wanted the colors to shower down upon her also so she ran up, without thinking, and took the old woman's other hand. She thought maybe the hand didn't have the right number of fingers but was too nervous to check. Then, the old woman swung the children's hands back and forth. Eva was surprised at how strong the Grandma Mandy was for being so near to death. The old woman's softness skipped up Eva's arm and deliciously drifted across her shoulder. Iron bounded up the porch steps, but Eva stayed put and the old woman smiled at her, too. She *was* very hungry and even if she were to be thrown into a big black kettle with boiling water, she could finally say that she'd seen a dog and a really old woman and the old woman had held her hand.

Grandma Mandy's house smelled good. When Iron hopped inside, he stopped and took it all in. There were dried bunches of plants hanging from the ceiling and glass jars gleamed on shelves in the kitchen. In some of the jars were hard-boiled eggs, long thick green vegetables of some sort, and possibly jam. He could not even guess at what was inside the other jars, other than that it was food. He licked his lips at the thought of strawberry jam. He'd had strawberry jam twice in his life and couldn't remember the first time, only Eva could. Out of the corner of his eye, he saw a flash of orange, a creature of some sort. It frightened him and he stiffened. Grandma Mandy shuffled in behind him and gently placed a hand on the top of his head. He began crying from the fright.

"Don't cry!" she said as if he'd done something wrong and the crying worsened.

"Now, now," she pulled him closer, wrapping her arm around his shoulders. He was embarrassed to be such a big baby and furiously scrubbed at the tears. "There's nothing here that's going to hurt you. Look at me," she said and he looked up at her. "What's your name?"

"Iron."

"Iron? Hmm."

"I saw something run by."

"You did? That's probably just one of my cats. Tigger! Here kitty, kitty." Grandma Mandy made a funny noise through the side of her mouth—chit chit chit. The orange blur was really a cat, and the cat stealthily approached Iron and Grandma Mandy.

"Good kitty," she said and the thing rubbed against her legs with its tail straight up in the air, making a loud meow sound. Then it rubbed against his legs.

"You have a cat?" he asked her, entirely astonished. It was as if he had come to a place of magic.

"I have lots of cats, but they don't all live in the house with me. Just my pets do." Grandma Mandy chit chit chitted again and a couple more cats appeared out of nowhere and that's when Eva howled and climbed up on top of a couch then crouched there. Eva rocked back and forth, clenched together in a tight curl. She cried hysterically in between choking and spitting and this made Iron cry. Grandma Mandy said, "Oh dear." She clapped her hands loudly and the cats scattered. She walked over to Eva with Iron attached at her hip. She smoothed the bangs back off Eva's forehead. "What's your name?"

Eva hiccupped then said, "Eva." Her eyes darted about the room.

The old woman took a small white cloth with blue and yellow flowers embroidered upon its corner out of her sweater pocket and dabbed at the wetness on Eva's face. "Well, Eva, don't you worry about those cats. They would never hurt you. Come down off there and come in the kitchen with me and Iron. I'll fix us some lunch. I bet you're hungry. I know I'm hungry." And just then thunder boomed so Eva hopped down and grasped the old woman's hand. The three of them walked into the kitchen together.

It got dark so suddenly that Grandma Mandy had to strike a match and light a hurricane oil lamp that sat in the middle of a round wooden table and on top of a red checked cloth that was badly stained but smelled freshly washed. Iron liked the hiss the oil lamp made and he stuck his face very close to the glass. Eva shouted at him, "Hot!"

He slumped back in the wooden chair and crossed his arms, sticking his tongue out at Eva.

"You are such a baby," she hissed just like the oil lamp.

"*Me?*" he whispered.

Eva kicked him under the table.

"Ow, you meanie."

Iron was about to kick Eva back and even harder but he felt fur brushing against the bare of his leg, where his too-short pants had lifted to just below his knees. He didn't have on any socks, and his worn-out shoes were a tad too big, so they slipped off all the time, especially when he sat down and kicked his legs back and forth. He wiggled his bare toes then felt the hard edge of the side of a cat's silky face pressing against his toes. He giggled. Grandma Mandy puttered around the kitchen with the jars. She lifted a blackened, steel kettle from the black, iron woodstove, carried it to the sink and poured water into it from a pitcher. The wood crackled as it burned inside the stove.

"Do you children take milk in your tea?"

Eva couldn't answer Grandma Mandy because she was certain there were many, many cats roaming beneath the table. She stayed stock-still so they couldn't chomp off one of her fingers. She was too scared to bring her hands up onto the table. Her neck started to ache. Nurse Carrie said people shouldn't keep cats because cats suffocated babies in their sleep by stealing the breath right out of their mouths. Eva always wanted to ask Nurse Carrie what it was the cats did with the stolen breaths, but Nurse Carrie would've only laughed at her the way she always did when Eva asked questions about things that didn't make sense.

Iron saw the look on Eva's face, the look he knew meant she was scared. Everyone else thought Eva was angry when she scrunched her face like a wrinkled soft potato but her face did opposites. This was something about her that Iron loved. When she was angry her eyebrows rose up into her bangs and her eyes grew round and she pulled her mouth into a little circle. Iron pointed his finger at her and said, "Scaredy cat!"

Normally, this would have made Eva punch him in the arm, but when she didn't, he felt bad, hopped out of his chair, went over to her, and lifted up the tablecloth. The cats were buffing Eva's legs. "It's just Grandma Mandy's cats." He tried to do the chit chit chit sound. The cats stopped. The two cats sitting had fur the colors of autumn. The other cat was smaller, sleeker, black with golden eyes.

"Get away from me!" Eva suddenly shouted then frenetically kicked. The cats rushed out from beneath the table.

* * *

"What's the matter now?" Amanda said with too much edge in her voice and the stillness resumed. Only the sky grumbled and pitched, back and forth. Lightning illuminated the entire house for a moment and it made Amanda think of a faded, now colorless, Polaroid photograph. In the photograph are her three children—two boys and a girl—playing on a swing set. Her sons were ten and eight at the time and her daughter just a toddler with long curly hair swung back away from her face as the camera captured her in the forward movement of a fast-moving rubber baby swing. The older boy was midway down a slide and the younger one hung upside down from the monkey bars. Amanda must have pushed the swing then run in front and taken the picture. She could feel this photograph in her heart and had to set the strawberry jam down and grab onto the counter. She hadn't thought of her children when young in twenty-two years.

"Children, I have to sit down," she said as they watched her hobble to a chair, their eyes wide. She hoped they wouldn't break out crying again, for she was too shook up to speak.

Iron approached her cautiously then stood beside her. He patted her on the upper back while making a shushing sound Amanda knew he hadn't heard very often. He corrupted it by pressing air through his teeth while his mouth was in a shitty grin, as her grandmother would've said. It was more like having someone thump on her but he was so cute that Amanda wanted to hug him fiercely, drink in his exuberance. Instead, she wrapped her arm around his waist to see how close she could draw him in, but he resisted and broke away to chase the cats. Sugar and Wrangler whined at the screen door. She had forgotten to bring them in during all of the hustle and bustle.

"Eva, can you let my dogs in? They don't like storms," she said.

"I'll do it," shouted Iron but this caused Eva to move even quicker off the chair. She blocked the boy's way with her body, her arms lifted to push him back.

"I can do it!" she said, her feet planted until Iron backed away and sat quietly on a chair. Eva had an ardency in her eyes that made Amanda chuckle. "She's a toughie," she said.

"You're not the boss of me, Eva Chen!" Iron thunked his elbows down on the table and pouted, chin in hands.

"I am too! And there's no one else who's ever going to love you like I do. You don't forget that, Iron Begay."

"Oh my," said Grandma Mandy and Eva felt instantly embarrassed. She was sorry she said it. She whipped around and unhooked the eye latch on the wooden screen door, rising on the tips of her toes, and the dogs tumbled in, damp from the pouring rain. The dogs smelled like the earth, and they rubbed wet coldness all over her legs and her cotton shift until the grandma called them.

The grandma said 'oh my' quite often, and it made Eva feel warm on the inside where she'd never felt before like when the North Pole melted and the polar bears drowned, just like Nurse Carrie said happened right before the Collapse. She wondered if she could drown in the 'oh my's' and make her past life extinct. It was possible, she thought, seeing as how this old woman had dogs and cats and strawberry jam and other things that had mostly only existed in Eva's imagination or in the cruddy old books at the center or in George's stories. The slop they served at the center came in three colors—concrete, dirty snow, and diarrhea. But in the old woman's house were many colors.

"Eva, come over here please and help me, would you?" Grandma Mandy said.

The grandma stood at her kitchen counter struggling with a jar. Eva walked over and took the jar. The old woman had only three fingers on her right hand, her pointer finger sheared off at the protruding base knuckle, and the top of her right thumb was missing also. Eva unscrewed the steel rusted ring but had a very hard time breaking the seal on the lid and had to have Iron do it. Before she could take the jar back he had already stuck a finger in it and was sucking the sticky redness off the finger.

"You're so rude!" she said but he only smiled, his eyes closed, owning the jam.

"How come you lost your finger?" Eva said to the old woman.

"Oh, *that* is a terrible story. You don't want to hear it." The grandma spread the jam thickly on large slices of yeasty whole wheat bread. The bread had a thick crust the color of the muddy creek they had found in the woods. Eva asked for the end piece as the crust was her favorite part. The old woman smiled and said that was her favorite also but gave it to Eva. Eva smacked her two slices together and could hardly wait to eat.

"Hold on, we need more color on our plates," Grandma Mandy said. She shuffled over to a wooden crate on the floor, far from the big iron stove, and pulled three bright orange thick carrots out of black crumbly dirt. The carrots had fine white hairs. Sometimes there were mushy pale carrots in the stew at the center and they had no taste just like the mushy potatoes. Since Eva had become excited about the sandwich it seemed that the old woman moved much slower.

The old woman washed the carrots in a bowl of water, wiped them with a towel then sliced off the green top. She put the greens in a bucket, saying that Iron could take them out to the chickens after lunch. She gave each plate a carrot and told Eva to set the plates on the table and sit down.

Much to Iron's surprise, Grandma Mandy set an indigo mug of steaming dark tea by his plate then poured white creamy liquid from a pitcher into the mug. He thought it might have been milk, but he wasn't sure. He didn't want to ask and betray his ignorance. He had heard the older nurses admonish him about crying over spilled milk, but he'd never actually seen milk. Grandma Mandy held the pitcher handle with her two middle fingers and her blunted thumb.

It took forever for her to sit down and Iron had to sit on his hands to make himself wait. Normally, he wouldn't have waited before scarfing everything down but there was something about this old woman that inspired in him a compulsion to care not only about what she thought of him, but to care about her.

"Well, children, shall we?" she said and Iron was struck for the first time with indecision. Should he drink the milky tea? Should he bite the carrot? Should he eat more jam? Eva was already nibbling away at her sandwich and then her carrot, but not touching her mug. He watched her facial expressions. True to her nature, her face seemed grim and determined so he knew she was happy. Grandma Mandy ate with confidence, sipping her mug as if it brought her great satisfaction and the smells of the delicious food overwhelmed Iron.

"Oh my," Grandma Mandy said. "Now what? You children sure cry a lot."

Eva kicked Iron under the table but he couldn't help it.

"I thought you were hungry," said Grandma Mandy.

Iron was hungry but his hands were quite simply stuck under his bottom.

* * *

Amanda wondered what she'd gotten herself into with these disturbed children. She'd had to lock the cats in the den. At the sight of the felines, the little girl gripped Amanda's arm so hard that she feared a bone would break. Every time lightning struck and thunder crashed, the children cried out. Thankfully, the storm passed quickly. Amanda tried to remind herself the children had spent their lives inside an institution much like the old asylums of the past. Institutions not only made to withstand violent weather but to separate man from man.

But the boy wouldn't eat his lunch and looked like he might throw up. It surprised her how much their crying annoyed her more than the osteoarthritis in her hands and knees. The crying went on and on, louder and louder.

Amanda brought the side of her fist down upon the table with enough force to jump several nearby items, rattling the spoon on her saucer, her tea sloshing over the side of the mug. "Enough!" she shouted. "Eat your lunch!"

And much to her surprise, the children bolted out of their chairs and out of her house.

"Oh my," she said. "What have I done?"

* * *

When the children reached the center fence, nearly out of breath, their hearts still racing as if they'd seen a monster, they scrambled alongside it, unable to locate their hole. Finally Eva bent over at the waist, her hands on her knees, drawing in large breaths to steady herself.

"It's not here anymore," said Iron, still hurriedly walking up and down the fence line.

"I know. This is all your fault, Iron Begay."

"We can climb over," he said when he got back to her.

Eva stood and looked at the razor-sharp wire curled like ribbons along the top of the twenty-foot high fence. "Don't be stupid." She leaned against the rusty chainlink and stared at the center. It was the only home she'd ever known. She just wanted to climb onto her cot and go to sleep.

Iron kneeled on the ground and began scooping dirt away from beneath the fence. The compacted soil made his fingers ache.

There was shouting by the main entrance and Nurse Carrie, along with two security guards, came running toward them. Nurse Carrie's heavy chest bounced and made her unbuttoned black cardigan flap open.

"Busted," said Eva. Iron stood up. They grasped each other's hand.

It took Nurse Carrie a minute or two to catch her breath. Her face was red and her cheeks puffed out then flattened then puffed out while her eyes threw beams of rage. "I knew you were getting out."

The children both looked at the ground.

"What made you come back? What did you see out there? I told you it was dangerous. I told you center children should not go beyond."

Eva looked up at her. "Don't be mad! Please, Nurse Carrie, don't be mad. We're sorry. We didn't mean to. Just, just—"

"We were just playing in the woods," said Iron.

"You were running away!" the nurse said.

"No, no, we weren't," said Eva. "We promise," said the children together.

"You were. You were going to break my heart. Is that how you treat your Nurse Carrie? The only one that's ever loved you? The only one that's taken such good care of you all these years."

Eva began crying. "Sorry."

"You know how scared I was when you children were missing at roll call? I looked everywhere for you. Then, then, I had to come out here and find the hole! I knew then, I knew then you were bad, bad children. Why if someone opened you children up and looked inside, all they would see is pure evil. Nothing but pure evil."

Iron was also crying now. He wished he could push Nurse Carrie down and stomp on her face.

"We want to come back inside," said Eva.

"Oh, you do, do you?" the nurse said. "Now, after you've made a fool of me in front of the other staff, you want back in?" She turned toward the guards. "What do you fellows think? Should we let the naughty children back inside where it is safe and warm and there are good things to eat?" The guards chuckled uncomfortably.

She whipped her head back around to the children. The veins throbbed on the sides of her temples and Iron thought she was going to explode. "Well, guess what? You can't come back in here until I say you can. We don't need your kind here. Stay outside and play! See if I care if the wolves and bears drag you away and eat you." She turned and stormed off. The guards seemed confused and the one with wide shoulders looked at the children with sad eyes. "Come on, fellas, the children are playing outside," Nurse Carrie said.

The children watched the nurse and the guards walk back inside the center.

* * *

Eva and Iron sat in the gloaming, their backs resting against the fence. They were near the gate, in case someone came and got them for dinner. It was still as warm as when the sun had been out and the children felt parched. The sun was reluctant to go at this time of the year and stayed way past bedtime. They had hardly spoken to each other in the hours since Nurse Carrie stomped back inside the center.

"Think we missed dinner?" Iron asked. His stomach painfully growled.

Eva shrugged.

"Maybe we should go back to the grandma's house."

"In the dark?"

"There's still some light."

"Not for long." Eva looked at the woods. Wolf and bear shadows roamed amongst the thick black below the treetops. They were waiting for the children.

The lights on the first floor came on but most of the center stayed in the dark. None of the exterior security lighting was turned on anymore.

"Someone's coming," Iron said.

Eva turned. A bulky mass made its way down the center steps and across the yard with a narrow flashlight. The gravel crunched beneath its boots. "A guard," she said.

The guard stood at the gate. "Hey, kids." He was a tall brown man with wide shoulders and a long black ponytail.

The children went over to him. He jangled his keys then unlocked the gate. After the gate opened, Eva and Iron stood there, staring at him. "Come inside," he said. "It's okay. Just don't tell anyone—especially your nurse—that it was me who let you in." He reached out and grabbed Iron by the shoulder and gently pulled him past the gate. Eva followed.

The guard took them into the kitchen down in the basement, which they'd never seen before, and made them sit at a long stainless steel table. The other guard was there, and eight cafeteria workers and kitchen staff, eating and drinking. Some of them ignored the children and some of them smiled. One of the ladies that smiled always gave Eva and Iron extra cookies when she served them. They smiled back.

She wore glasses that were like two tiny black circles over her big eyes.

The guard asked a woman he called Bessie to get the children something to eat. He sat next to them. Bessie had coffee-colored skin and kind dark eyes and Iron wanted to crawl into her lap and be rocked to sleep with her arms wrapped around him. She brought a large steel tray with three plates of food. The guard helped her take the plates off the tray and give them to the children and to himself. He patted Bessie's rear end as she walked away with the empty tray. She playfully chided the guard, calling him Manuel, to just wait till later. She was gonna make sure he got some of that. Manuel puffed up his chest and whistled and called Bessie a sexy thing. The children wondered what that was, a sexy thing, but were too hungry to wonder for long.

What was on their plate was food like the kind of food at Grandma Mandy's house. Food that had color. Long white noodles covered in a red thick sauce and little balls of brown meat. There was a chunk of bread also, that had melted yellow stuff on its top.

It was so delicious Iron couldn't stop saying "yum yum" and he made nearly everyone laugh. Even Eva.

* * *

Moses closed his eyes and listened to the creak of the gray wooden porch swing. The magnolias were in bloom. The warm mid-morning air touched his eyelids, his cheeks, his ear lobes. His adopted grandmother sat next to him on the old swing that hung by two rusted chains. She'd drifted off in her recitation of the unfinished farm tasks to an anecdote about a lichen-clothed snapping turtle that had laid eggs in her pea patch. He compiled a list in his mind of what he was going to tackle during this two-day visit and in what order. He'd start with the screen repair in his old bedroom, even though no one slept there. Moses slept on the couch.

Something had been going on with Moses lately that he couldn't quite put his finger on. Though he suspected it had something to do with the recurring Cloak Room dream. He denied it had anything to do with Shammi leaving him—it wasn't the first time he'd been through a breakup. But, he'd been unusually short-tempered, snapping like Grandma's new turtle friend at everyone in his path. Even at his customers— the Fortunates. He felt settled now though, swinging with Grandma, and the tension rolled off him like hard rain on a steel roof. He knew it was going to wrap a vice around his head when he stepped into the canoe on his journey back to the urbanized locale. He had to walk five miles then canoe another eight then hop onto a train to get back. It took him four hours one way to visit the farm.

When Grandma Mandy stopped laughing about the turtle, Moses thought about asking her again what the darkest of days were like, back before he was born in 2037. He'd heard other accounts and some of it was still going on while he grew up, but it was the decade after the Collapse that everyone knew was the worst. Whenever he'd asked her in the past she'd always said, "Oh, *that* is a terrible story. You don't want to hear that story." But there were things Moses didn't understand about her, and he thought the answers were hidden in her past.

"Guess what I read?" he said. "The government has decided to stop funding the centers. They've stopped enforcing the regulations."

"When they built the centers we thought it was to help people. But it was really just a prison system. The wealthy still had access to healthcare and life's necessities but the rest of us survivors were shit-outta-luck. There was nowhere else to go and then no escape," Grandma Mandy said.

"Well, we've got a decent handle on the weather now. They want to re-build just about everywhere over the next ten years or so. Give us some options. We're all tired of being confined to the urbanized locales. Things are changing."

"It's been a long time coming." Grandma Mandy crossed her arms then looked out at a murder of crows cawing from the nearby treetops.

Moses was a bird-watcher like his grandma. The birds that lived in Michigan had changed since Grandma's youth, and after the Collapse. Some breeds had been unable to cope with the climate change or the strange new maladies; some had gone off to more conducive habitats; there were native breeds that had made a startling comeback; and interlopers that had found the upper Midwest more suitable to their survival. Moses participated every season in the annual bird count, relishing in the solitude and quiet of the land largely reverted back to its pre-Columbian state.

"They're going to re-electrify your neck of the woods soon," he said, his tone upbeat. "The river is deep and easily accessible. Before you know it, Grandma, boatloads of people will be landing on the riverbank, looking to settle here. Raise a family." Moses had been thinking about the possibility of building his furniture and cabinets at the farm rather than in his shop in the urbanized locale. Electricity would bring better ground transportation. People *were* going to move back.

"I hope I'm dead by then," his grandma said.

"Gee, thanks," he said, abruptly rising, making the swing go skelter. He let the screen door slam after him.

"Mose!" she said. "Geez, Moses, I didn't mean it the way it sounds." She shouted, "I'd love for you to come back, you know that. That's what I'm waiting for."

* * *

For weeks, Amanda watched the tree line for the children, staying out on the porch long after the sun set, listening to the cicada hum. The remainder of July passed and the heat and humidity intensified, yet she rocked on her porch, hoping with the extended daylight hours of summer, the children might come out late in the evening. She didn't tell Moses why she was so glum when he visited, hardly speaking, not enthused over the rare copy of Alice Munro's *Selected Stories* he brought.

"You love Alice Munro," he said. He had on a Panama straw hat with a narrow brim and black embossed trim, a loose pale blue cotton short-sleeve shirt and twill buckle-back chinos. He kept his hair cut close and his face clean of facial hair. Amanda thought him extremely handsome.

"I hope you didn't trade too much for it," she said. Her grandson was always being far nicer to her than she deserved. Besides, she wasn't interested in reading the book. She wasn't interested in anything lately and the only reason she'd been getting out of bed was to take care of her animals.

"Don't you worry about that, Grandma. That's my problem."

"What *did* you trade?"

Moses always tried to avoid telling his grandmother what he paid or traded for the things he brought her, but her persistence always broke his resolve. She was and had been obsessed with the cost of everything and he figured this was a direct result of having lived through the worst days. The days of eating the inner bark of pine trees, fried crickets and pillbugs, cattails, chicory, dandelions, and wood sorrel.

He lied and said he didn't trade directly for the book, but that it was thrown in to seal the deal on an oak table. The book had cost him two extra chairs for the dining set. She relaxed back in her rocker then, thinking he'd not gone out of his way for her. She set the book in her lap rather than read a bit of it aloud to him.

"What's the matter?" He noticed that the blue veins on either side of her forehead were throbbing with a particular intensity and this made him a bit nervous.

"Tired."

"But you love to read to me. What's going on with you?"

"I'm 104 years old! That's what's the matter with me!" And then: "It's so quiet here."

"Now, now," he said. "You *could* come stay with me for awhile."

"In the city? You've got to be crazy. What would I do in an *urbanized locale*? An old lady like me. What a foolish idea. What about the cats and dogs? No, I'm staying right here. You can have the whole damn city to yourself. That's what you want, isn't it?"

Moses stood up; it was time to go. Her words had struck him as if she'd banged on his funny bone with a steel rod. He bent down and pushed back the stray hairs on her forehead then kissed her above her wiry white messy eyebrow.

"Don't forget your pickles," she said, "and make sure you wrap them good."

He went into the house to pack the five jars of Grandma Mandy's dill pickles into his backpack. Three of the jars were for him to eat and the other two would be sold for enough money to pay his train fare for a year. Moses hadn't told her, but he'd been thinking seriously about accepting her long-standing offer: move into her house that she was leaving to him anyway and help her carry on. She'd already taught him everything he needed to know to breed the cats and dogs, to grow and can the pickles, to make the strawberry jam, to milk Flannery the cow, and he could build furniture and cabinets in the barn. The electricity was coming back soon. He wished he could find a suitable partner, though. The thought of having Grandma as his only companion made him nervous. He wasn't the same boy she'd known, afraid to say his mind. He wished he could forget about the Cloak Room.

Before he walked down the porch steps he reminded her that next time he'd have to fix the loose clapboard on the side of the house.

"I love you, Mose," she said. "I hope you know that."

He nodded then turned before she could see the doubt in his eyes. She'd left him in the Cloak Room and when she'd let him out, had no patience for his tears. She'd only said 'I love you' to him a handful of times. And only after he'd moved away. Then she loved him, not when he'd needed her to—when he was that scared, tender-hearted boy with a chronic ache in his heart for his parents.

He stopped at the bottom of the porch and turned back toward her. "Grandma?"

"Yeah?"

"Someday, I want you to tell me about what happened after you put me in the Cloak Room."

"What do you mean what happened? You were there."

"No, I mean, what happened when I wasn't there. When I was inside the Cloak Room."

"I told you, I convinced them to leave. Remember, I gave one a kitten and one a puppy."

"I know that. But when, when did you convince them to leave?"

"Oh, right after I fed them some supper." Moses had never heard this before.

"But, Grandma," he said.

"What are you trying to get at, Moses?"

"You didn't let me out until the next day."

"I didn't?"

"No, you didn't."

"Are you sure? That doesn't sound right."

"I'm sure."

She sat there, staring at him, her forehead scrunched. All the wrinkles in her face fell and her eyes darkened. "I think I'd remember if I intentionally left you locked up in the Cloak Room. No, I don't think you're remembering that correctly. That'd be a very cruel thing to do. You were just a boy. A little boy."

Moses started walking down the old driveway.

"That's not something I would've ever done," she said. "Moses? Come back here. You can't bring up that shit and then walk away."

He waved at her without turning his face or body toward her. "Just think about it, that's all I'm asking. When I get back, you can explain it."

"There's nothing to explain," she said. "There's absolutely nothing to explain."

Amanda watched her grandson walk strong and tall down the path, disappearing into the woods. It was five long miles to the river that she hadn't seen in ten years, since she walked him down there to wave good-bye as he paddled away in a neighbor's borrowed canoe. He had to go off and see what he was made of. That was the reason he'd left the farm she told herself. She should have told him then that he was honest and hard-working and smart and the reason she hadn't given up on life when she'd desperately wanted to after her grandson Lucian had been knifed in the stomach and left to die on a city street. Her boy had been left to die as if he were a piece of trash and not the last of her flesh and blood. Oh, how the pain stays within us, and can resurrect memories as crystal clear as if captured on film. Amanda didn't want all those old movies to start up again, she knew already she wouldn't die from a broken heart.

* * *

Iron had been crying to Eva about going to see the old lady every single day. He never got to eat his strawberry jam sandwich! He never got to taste the milky tea! He wanted to play with the dogs! On and on he went in Eva's ears until she punched him good and hard to shut his trap about it and get to sleep. Since they'd been caught, Nurse Carrie had been tracking their whereabouts relentlessly.

Eva lay on her cot that she'd pushed beneath the window. The window was open and the air was still and sticky. Eva tried to stay still also so it didn't feel so hot. She drew pictures that Nurse Carrie wouldn't let her stick onto the white-washed concrete wall of their room.

Those are awful pictures! Nurse Carrie had said then she'd smiled in a way that deeply disturbed Iron. He didn't like Nurse Carrie, never had. He knew the woman liked working Eva into a fearful panic by telling her scary stories. Iron always covered his ears with his hands, even though he could still hear, and hid under the covers during "Story Hour." His cot was against the wall nearest to the door. "Story Hour" had gotten particularly horrifying lately about the world outside the center and had included laments by Nurse Carrie of how much she truly loved the children and that there was absolutely no one else who did or would, ever. She'd crush Eva into her arms, sobbing about the fright they'd given her when they'd run away, begging Eva to promise to stay with her always.

But Iron didn't like Eva's drawings either. They were drawn in black and had lots of scribbled red crayon on them. They were pictures of how Grandma Mandy might have lost her finger:

- A big black snarling dog rips the grandma's finger off with sharp fangs that are so long they curve to the dog's neck.

- A white woman in a nursing uniform hacks the grandma's finger off with a pointed metal hair comb. She has red eyes and jagged flames come out of her mouth.

- Two cats suck the breath out of the old woman then chew her finger off, fighting over the bits of finger. Then more and more cats come, all fighting over the bits of finger then fighting each other then eating each other.

- Grandma Mandy is younger but still a skeleton because she's starving and she eats her own finger and part of her thumb.

And then there were the pictures of the finger and bit of thumb just lying around places, all bloody. On the grandma's porch. On her kitchen table. Inside the sink. Sizzling in an iron skillet on top of the stove. Floating inside a jar.

Iron was glad Nurse Carrie wouldn't let Eva hang the pictures where he'd have to see them all the time, but he knew it was because the nurse would have gotten in trouble if the administrator saw the pictures and asked why Eva thought of such things and Eva told about "Story Hour."

"Why can't we go see the old woman, Eva?" he pleaded.

"'Cuz," she said.

"Cuz why?"

"Cuz I say so, that's why!"

"You're not the boss of me, Eva Chen!"

"Oh, shut up, Iron Begay! I'm busy drawing."

"I'm gonna go see her," he said. "With or without you."

"How ya gonna dig a hole, huh? They took all our spoons."

Nurse Carrie waddled in, sat on Eva's cot and told a story about the nearby urbanized locale, where people were killed for no reason at all. "Why, you could just ask someone for directions to the nearest Food Bank and get your brains blown out with a shotgun," she said. Then, she told the children that the center would be closing and no one knew what would happen to those who lived there but, rest assured, the government wasn't going to support them any longer. Eva and Iron were nothing but a burden on the decent, hard-working, law-abiding taxpayer, she said. Then she kissed Eva on the forehead and tried to kiss Iron but he thrashed enough beneath his blanket for her to miss.

Nurse Carrie switched off the lamp on the one metal nightstand and Iron's friend darkness covered him. Sometimes, he knew that he missed his mother but since he'd never known her, the missing had no image or smell or touch associated with it, it was only a longing. Like his insides were empty and he needed to fill them up, but with what, he was unsure. He couldn't explain this to Eva when she got mad when he ate everything, but those were the only times the longing went away. That and when he sucked his thumb. And when the old woman had held his hand.

* * *

It was too hot to do anything, so Amanda fed her animals breakfast then she lay back down in bed. She had all of the windows open, but there was no breeze, just the buzzing sound of hordes of insects and the occasional crowing of the rooster. Wrangler curled up in a ball, his back pressed against her, and Sugar Bear slept with her chin resting on Amanda's feet. All four cats were strewn across the bed. She should have gone out and checked her garden for ripe tomatoes and ready zucchini but she didn't care. She wished she could die from depression as if the inertia of it could pull her down into the earth and be done with her.

She was angry thinking about what might have happened to Moses in the Cloak Room. Had she done that to him? Every once in awhile she'd get a fleeting image of collapsing into bed after the CDC Humvee had driven off, and there'd been silence. The boy would not have been silent, she told herself. Where had he been? Sleeping on the couch, exhausted probably, from the ordeal. But this didn't bring her relief from the anxiety that he thought she'd left him in there. What kind of person would do that to a boy?

She was angry that she'd let the center children stir up her insides and even angrier that she'd been dreaming about Lucian again. If she hadn't taught Lucian to read he would've been content to stay on the farm. But no, he'd read so many books he thought he could change the world.

And when he'd left, she'd thought he could also.

She'd had to go into the city herself and claim his body and hire men to help her bring her strawberry-blond wiry boy home and bury him, out underneath his favorite oak tree, where the tire swing still hung. Wrapped in a puce colored section of canvas and tied with twine, she'd made the men wait to cover him over with dirt while she read a Dickinson poem that she felt acutely apt for the occasion and which had always been one of her favorites:

> On this wondrous sea,
> Sailing silently,
> Knowest thou the shore
> Ho! pilot, ho!
> Where no breakers roar,
> Where the storm is o'er?
>
> In the silent west
> Many sails at rest,
> Their anchors fast;
> Thither I pilot thee, —
> Land, ho! Eternity!
> Ashore at last!

And of course, thinking on Lucian, reminded Amanda of her daughter, his mother, and the typhoid that had taken her despite Amanda's best efforts.

Amanda could recount a list of tragedies:

The 2024 Tornado Outbreak took Amanda's oldest son and his family. F-5's rampaged across miles and miles of the Midwest—cyclonic monsters destroying everything in their paths.

Her husband and other son succumbed to MERS in 2035. Streptococcus pneumoniae killed two of that son's children in early 2038, leaving Amanda with two orphaned grandchildren—Lucian and Rosalie. And then Rosalie had been swept away in a flash flood while she and Lucian were fly fishing in the river. Lucian was fifteen then and Rosalie but twenty-five. It was a miracle Lucian had been able to pull himself out of the raging current.

Amanda and Lucian found her downriver at the spot where her arm was caught against a downed River oak, and they carried her home on a travois. Amanda combed Rosalie's long brown hair, getting the flotsam and jetsam out of it. Lucian picked daisies and Grandma Mandy chained the flowers together then crowned her beautiful granddaughter's head.

Rosalie was buried under the oak tree that now also sheltered Lucian and was the place that Moses was instructed to put Amanda when the blessed day arrived.

Oh, when that blessed day arrives, Amanda sang in her heart, as if singing an old church hymn.

* * *

Amanda thought if she went inside the Cloak Room her memory would be stirred and this whole bad deal of what she'd done or didn't do to Moses could be put behind her. Had she repressed the memory to cast herself in a better light? She had a sneaking suspicion that she had. She *had been* especially hard on him the eight years he lived with her, but could not fathom why at this juncture. In her heart, she loved him as if he were her own. But she knew she'd gotten to the stage in her life when her childhood came through crystal clear, while the recent past not so clear. The people moving in those recollections hazy silhouettes.

She leaned against the bookshelf to pop open the secret door, and noticed a childish carving in the wood of the shelf—formerly hidden beneath a book. It was the code for the door. She imagined Moses with his pocket knife meticulously picking away until the numbers were clear. She punched the code in and the door creaked open.

No one had been inside the room for twenty-one years. She propped the steel door open with a pile of heavy books then sneezed forcefully into her handkerchief. Dust swirled in the air as she walked into the room. She bent over and switched on the LED lamp on the nightstand. Cobwebs hung from the ceiling and Amanda thought of Miss Havisham's wedding cake room and how cruel the jilted old woman had been to Pip. Amanda had never wanted to be cruel to anyone. Her knees began to give out, her eyes watered, and she plunked down on the cot, releasing spoofs of mold spores and dust particles. She sneezed again, violently.

She thought about why it was that God had made her so resilient during times of crisis when she felt the opposite at the core of her being. When the aftermath of being the tough one and the one who cared for everyone else consisted of assorted ailments—such as headaches, insomnia, debilitating depression, back aches, but never anything that would kill her. Her life was just going on and on when she'd been done with it long ago. Twenty-two years ago to be precise and this thought triggered the long buried unpleasantness. She'd had to once again rise above it all, be the better person, and care for yet another person. A child this time. An orphaned black boy from Detroit that the Lord set inside her cattery one day, expecting Amanda to never be cruel, to be some kind of super woman, that crazy Proverbs 31 woman. She shook her head. The Lord was unrealistic, to say the least. He'd asked the wrong woman, once again.

Amanda fell over on her side, her feet still on the floor. Her arm hung over the cot and her fingers hit against cold steel. She reached for the handle of the red metal box and when she had it, she pulled the box from beneath the cot. She sat up then brought the box into her lap. She fingered the clasp for a long time. She'd gone to bed after having convinced the CDC that the boy had fled days ago to where she didn't know, plying their goodwill with one of her kittens and one of her puppies, feeding their greedy faces with her best jam, her fresh bread, her fresh eggs. It had exhausted her and Moses was a chatterbox. Always yappin' his trap. She hadn't the energy to interact with him, explain what had happened. She'd meant to take just a nap (or so she told herself now) and had awakened in the morning, startled, knowing she'd forgotten something.

She opened the red metal box and removed the manila envelope with the emergency instructions, setting it next to her. Inside the box were the certificates of her life and her ancestors' lives. Marriage. Birth. Death. Photos of her grandparents, her parents, her brother, her husband, their children, their grandchildren. On and on and on. All of them gone. They'd all left her.

She'd never wanted to love anyone again after Lucian died. It was too much to ask of her to love one more person, only for that person to be taken from her. Yet, Moses hung on. Moses had thrived under her care though she resented his presence. He'd been a delightful boy, a quick learner, affectionate, and optimistic. He'd given her far more than she'd ever given him.

Moses had taught her how to love someone not your own.

He was the reason Amanda was still alive.

* * *

Iron wanted to go see Grandma Mandy, and no one was going to stop him. He'd been digging with a large chunk of gravel and with his sticks until they broke. He thought the hole was big enough. Nurse Carrie had slacked off after several months, bored with the tracking. Eva had stood by, angrily watching but refusing to help dig.

He thought he might just move in with the grandma, so he filled his pillowcase with five pairs of underwear, a shirt, the beaded bracelet his mother had been wearing when she died, and his bird feather collection. He'd buried the pebbles and leaves in the yard as a way of saying good-bye to the center. He had brown feathers, white feathers, one red feather, two blue and white feathers that had black stripes. His favorite feather was the length of Nurse Carrie's finger and he'd found it beneath a flowering crabapple tree. He thought the bird had been murdered there. The feather was half black and half white, but its tip was a white circle. He sat and ran his finger along the feather, smoothing its edges.

Eva barged in their room and yelled, "What are you doing?"

Iron had thought it would take her a long time in the bathroom as it usually did this time every day. He jammed the feather in his pillowcase and hid his sack behind his back.

"Nothing. What's it to you, Eva Chen?"

"Let me see!" She stood there with her feet spread apart and her hands curled into fists.

"Stop telling me what to do."

Eva burst upon him, attempting to grab the pillowcase and shouting about what he had in there. When she finally gained possession of the sack and looked in, she said, "You're running away!"

"What's it to you?"

"You're not going anywhere, Iron Begay!"

"Give me back my bag." He held his hand out, curling and uncurling it.

"No," she shouted and hid the sack behind her back.

"I said give it to me." Iron stood so close to her their belly buttons shifted against each other as he grasped for the sack and she blocked him with her shoulders. "Eva!" He pushed hard against her. She tumbled onto her bottom on the cold linoleum floor. She landed with enough force to not only thump loudly but also to leak a single tear out of her left eye.

"Here! You can have the stupid bag." She threw it across the room, and it slid under his cot. "You haven't got anything in there besides those dumb feathers anyway. What are you gonna do, Iron, go be a big baby and live with that weird old white woman?"

"They're closing the center, Eva!"

"So? Who said that was really gonna happen?"

"You're just afraid. You're afraid of the cats. You're the big baby!" He knelt down and shimmied under the cot, retrieving his pillowcase sack. "You're not my mother."

"And you're not my brother. You know what? You're nothin' to me. I just felt sorry for you—that's all. All this time, that's all it was. So go on! Get out. Go eat jam. I don't need you. I don't need anyone." She plopped down on her cot, her fists smashed into the mattress, and looked at her drawings on the wall. She tried to whistle but she wasn't any good at it.

One time Iron had found a baby bird that had fallen from its nest. He scooped the wrinkled pink naked thing up—it had closed bulging eyes the color of bruises—and watched it struggle in the palm of his hand. Its dirty yellow beak was still soft. Iron slowly put the nestling into his mouth. He held it there, its angled wings pushing against the sides of his cheeks. He wondered what it would taste like. He had once bitten into a many-legged long bug that tasted sharp and bitter and spat it out. All at once though, it seemed like the woods began speaking to him: the trees, the squirrels, the birds, even the mosquitoes. They were voicing their disapproval. He bent over, opened his mouth and allowed the nestling to fall softly into his cupped hands. Sorry, he said then gently deposited the bird into its nest.

Iron stood and crept toward the door. He put his hand on the handle, turned to Eva and said, "Why don't you come with me?"

"To that stinky grandma's house? Where the cats are gonna suck out your breath? I don't think so!"

"Fine then, good-bye." He slipped through the door then raced down the long antiseptic hallway before he could change his mind about leaving Eva.

* * *

Eva sat and listened to Iron's footsteps as he pounded down the hallway. She'd known he needed to go back to Grandma Mandy: it'd been only a matter of time. She tried to think about other things, like what she should draw next. But the farther Iron got, the more she could feel it. It was something that happened to her whenever Iron was not beside her. It churned her stomach sour and wobbled her knees. She felt like breaking her crayons into little bits but then she wouldn't have any crayons for a long time. Maybe not until Christmas when the generous religious people dropped off gifts—like crayons and socks and one orange each.

She walked to Iron's cot and punched his pillow. The pillow was mottled with amber stains and had little stuffing; she picked it up and smacked it against the wall while she yelled that she didn't care. But she could picture Iron crawling beneath the fence then running down the path through the woods and she couldn't take it. They were strung together by an invisible force that kept her from going to a very bad and dark place in her mind and the string was stretching to its breaking point. She took her gruesome drawings down off the wall, rolled them into a tight cylinder and tied the roll with a blue hair ribbon. She grabbed her pillowcase and punched the roll into the bottom. She threw her crayons on top, some underwear, her pajamas and her mother's identification tag. Her mother—swollen and feverish and resigned—stared out at her from the tag.

Eva wondered if she should say good-bye to Nurse Carrie, but worried the nurse would catch on and stop her from leaving.

Eva couldn't *be* without Iron.

* * *

"Grandma Mandy," said Moses, shaking his grandmother's shoulder. Never before had he found her asleep in bed when he arrived for a visit and it rattled him.

Amanda was dreaming of the time when she was a child and her father was there. They were driving down a sandy lane through the woods near Ontonagon in their station wagon with the wood grain paneling. Her father had a large flashlight, and he was shining for deer and black bear. She could see her father so clearly and hear him so clearly and it had been such a long time that this was where she wanted to stay but something was pulling her back. One of her children—no . . . one of her grandchildren. Something was wrong; she could hear it in his voice.

Amanda startled awake as she always did and as her father had. "Moses! You scared me. I was sleeping."

"Sorry, Grandma, but it's the middle of the morning."

Amanda scowled, trying to gather her wits.

"I came to fix the leak in the cattery roof."

"Yes, yes, I remember." Amanda slowly sat up then got out of bed. It always took awhile for her body to get moving again.

"Aren't you feeling well?" he asked.

She mumbled and grumbled about people nosing into her business and why couldn't she take a nap whenever she felt like it and who was he to up and decide she couldn't then told him to go on ahead, she'd be down in a few, needed to use the toilet.

Amanda found Moses on top of the cattery roof, on his hands and knees, his hammer in one hand, spare nails in his mouth, his leather tool belt hanging down and clanking as he moved. She stood on the outside of the fenced enclosure and her cats took turns rubbing against the fence where she stood. She asked Moses if he needed help, and he shook his head. Beads of sweat broke free from his hairline, ran down his face, glistening on his neck. It was the heavy weeping days of August.

She felt only slightly guilty that she'd failed to provide the morning dose of proper socialization and physical affection to the eleven cats living in the cattery. She had let all kinds of things go recently and wondered if Moses noticed.

Moses sat back on his boots and looked down at her. He wiped his forehead with a white kerchief he kept in his back pocket. "Why so glum today?"

His concern was sincere but it annoyed her that he'd forgotten about bringing up the Cloak Room, upsetting her with his questions. She was annoyed that the children had never come back. It annoyed her that she was still alive, standing there talking to him. She kicked the fence and the cats scattered.

"You really want to know?" She shaded her eyes with both hands when she looked up. "You might not like it."

"I do," he said, getting back to work.

"I can't do it anymore, Mose."

"What's that?" He hammered in a perfect rhythm. "Take care of the farm? I see a lot of things that need to be taken care of. You've got zucchini in your garden big as a child's leg."

"You noticed."

"Sure did."

Amanda was glad to hear this, wanted to tell him that she wished he'd come home for good. But she knew now that he thought her cruel, possibly heartless. She had been cruel at times, harsh at others, distant mostly. That's why he'd beat it the hell out of there as soon as he turned eighteen.

"I can't do lonely old lady anymore."

He stopped working.

"It's not that I'm afraid. It's just that . . . When I was a young mother all I ever craved were two things—sleep and alone time. Ha. That's what my mother called it when she put us kids in our bedrooms and locked the doors. You need your alone time, she'd say. Anyway. I've had all the alone time I can handle. Know what I mean?"

"I think I do. More than you realize."

"But you can't come back to the farm because I'm a mean, old lady. I locked you in the Cloak Room and left you there for days and days, as if I didn't care. As if I didn't take you in, feed you, protect you—"

He narrowed his eyes. "I never said days and days."

"What did you say, then? Why did you bring it up?"

Moses climbed down off the roof and came to stand in front of her. She was remarkably shorter than he remembered. She seemed about to snap in two. "I said longer than you needed to. You said so yourself that the CDC left after supper, but it was the next day when you let me out. I sat in the dark for a very long time."

"You should've turned on the lamp."

"I couldn't figure out how. I was just a boy. Scared out of my mind."

Amanda took a deep breath and shook her head. "I just don't think I would do that on purpose. That's all I'm saying. Maybe it was an accident. Have you considered that scenario? Maybe you're the one not remembering it correctly."

"I heard the Humvee engine turn back on," he said.

"And?"

"And, you didn't let me out of the room until the next day. At least I think it was the next day. Maybe it was days later. Children have a different sense of time, especially when frightened."

"But wasn't I always good to you?"

"Well,"—Chipmunks were chattering, he'd need to make sure they weren't nesting in the wood pile—"in a way, yes."

"And in another way?"

"It took you a long time to trust me."

"You mean like how you say that I never said 'I love you' when you were little?"

"*Did* you love me when I was little?"

She looked him in the eye. Tears came. "I'm a rotten bitch."

He rolled his eyes. "No one said that."

"But, it's true. The CDC left, and I went upstairs and crawled into bed. I didn't want to deal with the fact that there was a black boy locked up in a room in my house. A boy I would have to raise as one of my own if I let him out. I didn't think I could do it. I wasn't sure if I *should* do it. I lay there and cried. It was pathetic. I'm pathetic."

"A *black* boy?"

"I was ignorant."

"Racist."

"Yes, I guess. I didn't think so until confronted with you and your father, the reality of you and what to do about you."

"Why'd you let me out then?"

"Because I didn't want to be that way. I wanted . . . I wanted . . . to be better than that. To do the right thing."

"I just wanted you to love me," Moses said.

"I do love you."

"Now, now you love me. After I moved away. When I became a grown man and could take care of myself."

"No, that's not true. I didn't love you *only* after you moved away. What happened is that's when I realized how much I love you."

"You're not being truthful, Grandma."

"The truth is I didn't want to love anyone ever again, but you showed up anyway. I didn't want to live anymore, but then I had to because you needed me. I learned to love you best as I could. I came to love you, Moses. I really *did* come to love you. You are my grandson."

She gently brushed his wet cheek with the side of her hand. "I'm sorry I hurt you. I never wanted to hurt you. Here, come here." She took him in her arms and held him close. "I'm sorry you got stuck with me. You deserved better. You were a most wonderful boy."

He let out some heartbroken sobs, and she rubbed his back. The trees rustled and the insects buzzed and the hot afternoon sun beat down upon them.

He lifted his head off her shoulder and looked at her. "I appreciate all you've done for me, Grandma. I really do."

"I want you to come home, Moses."

Just then Sugar and Wrangler began barking and charged toward the house. Soon all the dogs in the kennel were barking. Amanda turned and she and Moses stayed very quiet. Someone was hollering up at the house and when Moses heard breaking glass he took off running while Amanda followed him as fast as she could—like an ancient turtle.

* * *

Eva rounded a corner, and there was Nurse Carrie. Quickly, she thrust her hands behind her back, gripping her sack.

"What's the matter, Eva?" the nurse asked. Her words seemed to echo throughout the hallway, bouncing off the cold white walls.

Eva was breathing hard and she swallowed, trying to push the rumble in her mind down into the soles of her feet. "Oh, nothin'."

"Really," said Nurse Carrie and turned her face slightly, looking over Eva out of the side of her colorless eyes. "What do you have there, behind your back?"

"Nothin'."

"Let me see then," said the nurse and she reached for Eva's arm but Eva dodged, quick and light as a wren. "Now, now, you better show me what you've got in your hands." The nurse lunged again but missed. "Cut that out, Eva Chen!" She began cornering the girl with her bulk, shifting her over against the wall. "That looks like a bag behind your back!"

Nurse Carrie grabbed onto Eva's arm with such fierceness that she dropped the sack. "You're running away!" the nurse said while bending over to retrieve the stuffed pillow case. Eva knew this was her only chance. She slipped beneath the nurse, whisked up the sack, and scrambled. "You bad girl!" Nurse Carrie shouted, trying to right herself. "You know what this means! You and Iron will be separated. I will have that boy transferred to another room. Is that what you want?"

Eva did not want this and took several steps back then charged forward, ramming Nurse Carrie in the rear. She'd never used so much force in her life and the nurse went flying face first onto the floor. The nurse desperately attempted to grab at Eva's feet, but she *was* quick and light and she whizzed by, only turning back briefly to see the nurse struggling to stand. "Go ahead and run away. You'll never make it on your own.

You'll starve to death or get your brains blown out. There's diseases out there and bad, bad people." Eva raced down the hallway, heading for the stairwell exit door. Nurse Carrie kept shouting. "You'll be back, Eva Chen! There's no one out there that's gonna give a rat's ass about you."

Eva slammed through the door and flew down the stairs. She was willing to take the chance, any chance, if it meant being with Iron. Always. And forever.

* * *

Iron couldn't control himself. There was no one in the house other than the grandma's cats and after he petted them, he began tearing through the kitchen. He opened jars of red jam and blue jam and scooped out fingers full, getting the sticky goodness all over his face. He opened jars and shoved his mouth full of salty vegetables and sweet diced fruits and slices of vegetables that made his mouth pucker. He left the jars everywhere, some tipped over and running out. He ripped off chunks of warm bread and stuffed his mouth. He grabbed the pitcher of milk from out of the ice box, lifted it to his face, tipped it back and the milk ran smooth as he poured it into his mouth, much of it flowing down his chin and onto his shirt. The cats lapped at the white puddle on the floor. He grabbed a sharp knife off the counter and hacked at the ice block in the ice box then sucked on the ice chips. He was spitting out grains of rice as he sat on the wood floor with his hand in a large burlap bag when Eva barged in. Iron wasn't surprised to see her.

"Iron Begay! What are you doing?" Eva said.

Eva took in the heaps of destruction in Grandma Mandy's kitchen. "You are in *so* much trouble." And then she saw the cats tiptoeing around: sniffing, licking, thinking of ways to steal Iron's breath. They were creeping closer and closer to Iron, and she knew she had to do something.

Eva yanked a broom out of the pantry and flew at the cats, swishing and smacking the broom this way and that.

She made contact and the cats cried out and skittered away, their claws clicking across the floor, poofs of fur exploding everywhere. Sugar and Wrangler barked at the screen door and the barking hurt Eva's ears. When she couldn't take it anymore she hollered at the top of her lungs, "Shut up! Shut up! Shut up!" Iron was crying like a big baby now, smeared with food. The moldy stain inside Eva swam all over her, fuzzing up her vision and plugging her ears.

A big man charged through the back door and stomped into the kitchen, shouting and shouting. Iron shut right up, scrambling to get up off the gooey wet floor.

"What the hell is going on here?" The man was so angry, his eyeballs bulged. Eva thought then Grandma Mandy had died and this new man lived there.

The man grabbed Iron by the arm, lifted him off the floor and plunked him down on a chair then came for Eva. "No, no, no," she said. She barreled out of the house, flying down the porch steps.

* * *

Eva couldn't run back to the center when the man had Iron and was probably going to eat him. Or feed him to the cats. Or drop him off at the urbanized locale where he would get killed. She stopped abruptly and frantically looked for somewhere to hide. The screen door slammed, and she thought the man was coming for her now. Her heart beat inside her ears. She ran to a structure that looked like a mini-house.

She found a narrow door on the front of the wooden mini-house but couldn't get the latch undone because her hands wouldn't cooperate. She threw her hands to her sides, took a deep breath and forced herself to calmly operate the latch. She pulled a pin out of a hole, flicked up the latch, moved the bar, and the door opened. She stepped inside then pulled the door closed, listening to the latch re-hook. It felt good to be locked inside. There were two small square windows covered with steel wire mesh and the breeze that flowed between them moved her hair. Eva turned and pressed her bum against the wall then slid to the cool concrete floor.

Inside the structure were shelves with quilted pillows and her nose got itchy. Something tickled her nostrils. She swiped at her nose, but nothing was there. It was a strange place with narrow ramps leading up to shelves and a small open door accessed by a longer shelf and another door the same size near the floor. She wondered what would use a door that size. And while she was thinking about this, a cat popped its head through one of the doors.

She kicked out one of her legs and crashed her heel against the floor. "Don't you come in here," she said. The cat didn't listen.

She slipped off her shoe and whipped it at the cat. The shoe thudded against the wall. She had poor aim. She yelled at the cat that was only trying to be friendly. The hullabaloo drew in the other cats. These were cats that loved people as they had been loved. Before Eva knew it, she was surrounded by eleven loud cats, skulking around her, seeking her breath. She flailed at them but they only tried harder to convince her of their good intentions. She was slipping to that very bad, very dark place that would have swallowed her whole if she let it. But this time, she couldn't stop dropping.

* * *

The boy refused to speak or move from the chair, even after Amanda wrapped her arm around his shoulders and pulled him close. Iron wept quietly.

"Where's the girl, Mose?" Moses was on his knees, scooping up messes into the compost bucket.

"How would I know? She ran out."

"You scared her!"

"Scared her? Damn straight. She was whacking at the cats with the broom."

"You didn't have to yell like that."

"She shouldn't have been in here. Neither one of them should be in here," Moses said.

"It's my house. I can have in here whomever I want."

"They were wrecking the place."

"Stop cleaning up," she said. She made Iron blow his nose into her handkerchief.

"Someone's got to. It's a big damn mess. A lot of money gone to waste."

"I know. It's okay. The children will clean it up."

Moses sat back on his heels and looked hard at her. "I take it you know these kids."

Amanda nodded.

"Oh boy, Grandma. What have you gotten yourself into?"

"They're just little children."

"Well, little children don't just show up one day."

"These did."

Moses sighed.

"You did," she said. "You and your father."

"I know. I know. You don't need to remind me. I suppose you're going to keep them, too."

"Me?"

"Not *me*."

"Why not you? They'd be a big help around the farm."

Moses gave her one of his long sideways looks.

Just then they heard shrill screaming. "Eva," said Amanda. "She's out back."

Moses found Eva in the cattery as Grandma Mandy and Iron hobbled along, trying to catch up. Iron liked to hold the grandma's hand that was missing the finger. He thought it made the hand feel better because the old woman smiled when he latched on. He had his mouth full of thumb, but his insides were not as empty as they were before.

Eva was in a catatonic state in the corner, curled into a fetal position, her arms wrapped around her legs. There were four or five cats hanging around her. Her chin covered in foamy drool.

Moses had no idea what to do. "Look at her," he said to Amanda.

"It's okay. She's afraid of cats. Let's get them out into the enclosure. Shoo shoo kitties. Come on now." Moses and Iron helped herd the cats outside. One of them wouldn't leave, a fat silver and white male, so Iron stood in the enclosure yard and practiced the chit chit chit sound. He said, "Here kitty," way up high in his throat like Grandma did and he was pleasantly surprised when the cat finally approached him. He crouched down and rubbed the cat's silky pink ears.

Grandma Mandy leaned down to Eva and caressed her forehead, sweeping back her damp bangs. The girl slowly opened her eyes then was surprised but pleased with the affection. Grandma hummed a bit of a John Denver tune, the one about leaving on a jet plane, then said everything was okay now. Maybe Eva would like to come up to the house for a nice cup of cold milk and a slice of fresh bread, an end piece, and Grandma just made raspberry jam. Had she ever had raspberry jam and when Eva shook her head, Grandma said, "Moses, come pick her up, would you, and we'll get her inside."

"I'm not sure if I've had raspberry jam," said Iron. "Can I have some, too?"

"Of course, you can," she said. "And then you and Eva can clean up your mess."

"Okay," Iron said, his face colored with shame.

"I didn't make that mess," said Eva. "Iron did." She had both arms wrapped around Moses's neck and a glare on her face.

Amanda raised her eyes and gave her a long sideways look, her head tilted.

"Aw right. I'll help. I did make things worse with the broom."

* * *

Eva liked to walk from gruesome picture to gruesome picture, Sugar at her heel. She stood in front of each of her drawings and thought about what it would be like to lose a finger in the manner displayed in the drawing. Grandma Mandy had hung Eva's pictures on one wall in the cozy room with all of the books, where the house cats curled up in miniature beds on shelves in front of the window, soaking in the sunshine. At first, Eva protested because of the cats, and she would only look in the room, staring wistfully at the picture wall. She'd stand outside the doorway while Grandma Mandy read aloud and Iron lay on the floor with his thumb in his mouth on a softly-worn braided rug, his eyes closed, imagining the story in his head. Wrangler curled up beside him. The rug was in all sorts of colors and sometimes Grandma had on a dress or a skirt or a blouse with the same fabric Eva could see bits of in the rug. Eventually, Eva could stand inside the doorway then sit on a chair next to the doorway then sit on the floor with Iron. She wanted to sit in Grandma Mandy's lap but she wasn't a baby anymore.

When Eva had showed her drawings to Grandma, she'd been afraid of rejection.

What do you have there? Grandma had asked about the clutched tube of papers. Eva kept them in a dresser drawer with her new clothes. Sometimes the papers served as a spy glass when she and Iron played in the woods. The center of the roll was crinkled and dirty from Eva's sweaty hand.

Eva unfurled the roll while Iron said loudly that no one would want to see *those* pictures, but Grandma shushed him with one disapproving glance. She let Eva describe and narrate each drawing and instead of being dismissive or patronizing, the old woman listened intently and understood entirely. Grandma's favorite drawing was the one where her finger was sizzling in the frying pan. She thought it was funny and not horrific, and this made Eva almost break into the smile the moldy little polka-dotted girl had in the book at the center.

Grandma hung the pictures in the exact order Eva instructed her and she remarked that it was the finest art work she'd seen in a long time. This made Iron jealous enough to refuse to speak to Eva the rest of that day.

But that night he showed Grandma Mandy his feather collection and Grandma ooh'd and aah'd so much even Eva had to walk over and look too and listen to the names of the birds the feathers may have come from. Grandma gave Iron a very special red metal box with a clasp on it and she let Iron line the inside bottom of the box with some of her fabric scraps. He chose pieces with greens and blues in the patterns. Then he put all of his feathers in the box as if the feathers were made out of glass. Grandma said the box used to hold something very important, but they didn't need that important thing any longer. Now it could hold Iron's important things.

While Eva walked from picture to picture she listened to Grandma Mandy read about the spider that weaved words into her webs to save a pig. Eva cleared her throat in an exaggerated manner, and the grandma stopped and looked at her. "I want to learn to read," Eva said.

"Me too," said Iron.

"You'll run off to the dangerous city then instead of staying here on the farm with me," said Grandma Mandy.

Eva and Iron said at the exact same time, "No, we won't!"

* * *

Moses was surprised that his grandmother wasn't rocking on the front porch when he got there. It was still warm, but the first light frost had come and it was time to put everything up for winter. He needed to pack acorn and butternut squash with hay into wooden crates and carrots into crates of dirt. He needed to carve up pumpkins for stewing and then canning. It was Moses's favorite time of the year—the turning trees and diluted autumnal sunshine. He loved Grandma Mandy's applesauce and eating apple pie for supper every night. He heard voices out by the corn field. It was the children and his grandmother. There was laughter and a lightness in his grandmother's voice that had long been absent. He was going to help his grandma shuck then shell the dried corn and store the corn in burlap bags. Some of the dried corn would be beaten fine into cornmeal and some would feed the chickens and the cow. There was a lot of work to do, and he decided to be glad there was more help this year.

Moses walked in the front door and set down a large trunk. Inside the trunk were his worldly possessions, as Grandma would've said. Some trustworthy men were going to bring his tools in the next couple of days. Moses had closed down his shop and told the Fortunates where to find him in the future. The electricity was set to be back on at the farm before winter set in.

* * *

It had been such a relief to have Moses there. Amanda slept in while her grandson rose before dawn and got the fire going in the woodstove, lit the lanterns, fed the cats, and let the dogs out. It had been a winter like the ones of her youth—pleasant snowfalls, sledding, hot apple cider, lopsided snowmen (Amanda supervising from her rocker on the porch.) Amanda taught the children how to make cut-out sugar cookies on Christmas Eve and even Moses helped decorate, turning his cookies into edible art. He had become more patient with the children, catching himself when he started to shout and removing himself until he had regained his composure.

There was a delay in the re-electrification program. Legislators were fighting over whose district had more priority so a gridlock had set in, much to Moses's dismay. But not to Amanda's. Lately, she'd been plagued by memories and she feared that re-entering a life with electricity would bring back long-forgotten details of her past. The sum total of our lives is held within the sensory impressions our consciousness stores forever; our mind only need turn the spotlight on that section of the stage and all comes rushing back in. Sometimes it was like whacking an already bruised thumb with the hammer yet again, but sometimes, it was like the first days of spring when birdsong erupted, trees bloomed, and the peeper frogs peeped after a long and dark winter.

Amanda was having a hard time staying present with Moses and the children. She drifted off throughout most of Christmas. Moses chopped down a Colorado blue spruce and dragged it inside. He and the children rummaged around in the attic until they found the box of old ornaments—filthy with dust. She sat on the couch and drank in the smell of the tree and could *not* stop remembering her own children when they were little.

Then one morning she couldn't get up. She heard the sizzle of frying eggs and the whistle of the kettle. There was a pressure inside her chest. Eva and Iron were tussling nearby, and she worried about them getting hurt. Moses yelled at them not to kill each other on the dang stairs. Wrangler had not left her side but she couldn't ask him: What was the matter, didn't he need to go out? He had his head on her aching chest and whined softly.

Hundreds of butterflies began fluttering about her—monarchs, swallowtails, whites, coppers, elfins, fritillaries, checkerspots, duskywings, skippers. They landed on her bed then arose in a mass, banging against the ceiling before returning to Amanda. They brushed their wings against her face and up and down her arms and they moved about in her hair. The morning light shimmered across them. She managed to stroke the soft spot between Wrangler's eyes, one last time.

AFTERWORD

Did you enjoy *The Binge-Watching Cure*? If you liked our antidote to television binge-watching, we'd appreciate a review on Amazon, Goodreads or your favorite book review blog. Feel free to mention any particular stories you especially liked. Reader reviews are as important to indie publishers like Claren Books as oxygen is to human beings.

We've enjoyed entertaining you with these stories. We'll be back, so keep your eyes open for the next, genre-specific, *Binge-Watching Cure* books.

Hang out with us on Twitter at @clarenbooks and on Facebook at www.facebook.com/clarenbooks.

ABOUT THE EDITORS

Bill Adler Jr. is the author of numerous books, including *No Time to Say Goodbye*, a time travel love story, *Tell Me a Fairy Tale*, a storytelling guide, and *Outwitting Squirrels*, which the *Wall Street Journal* called "a masterpiece." His ghost story about Japan, *Akiko and Peter: Into Eldritch Island* will be published in 2018.

He's the publisher at Claren Books, www.clarenbooks.com, a fiction publishing company.

Adler grew up in New York City, went to college in New England, lived for two decades in Washington, DC and now makes his home in Tokyo.

He's a licensed pilot and unlicensed writer.

Adler's personal website is www.adlerbooks.com. He tweets from @billadler and can be found on Facebook at www.facebook.com/billadlerjr and Goodreads at www.goodreads.com/billadler.

Sarah Doebereiner is a short story author from central Ohio. A wide range of her horror fiction has appeared in anthologies both locally and abroad. Her romance novella "A Turbulent Affair" was released by Black Opal Books in Jan. of 2016.

Sarah is the general editor at Claren Books. She coordinates efforts across departments for acquisitions, inquiries, and marketing.

BILL ADLER JR. AND SARAH DOEBEREINER

Macabre themes fascinate her because of their tendency to stay with readers long after the book closes, but the joy in short fiction is the opportunity to try out all kinds of genres. You can connect with her via facebook at https://www.facebook.com/sarahadoebereiner or twitter https://twitter.com/SarahDoeberiner.

www.ingramcontent.com/pod-product-compliance
Lightning Source LLC
Chambersburg PA
CBHW071149250626
47159CB00001B/30

* 9 7 8 1 9 4 5 2 5 9 1 2 8 *